PLAYGROUND

PLAYGROUND

A NOVEL

RICHARD POWERS

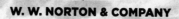

W. W. NORTON & COMPANY
Independent Publishers Since 1923

Copyright © 2024 by Richard Powers

All rights reserved
Printed in the United States of America
First Edition

For information about permission to reproduce selections from this book, write to Permissions, W. W. Norton & Company, Inc., 500 Fifth Avenue, New York, NY 10110

For information about special discounts for bulk purchases, please contact W. W. Norton Special Sales at specialsales@wwnorton.com or 800-233-4830

Manufacturing by Lakeside Book Company
Book design by Barbara M. Bachman
Production manager: Anna Oler

ISBN 978-1-324-08603-1

W. W. Norton & Company, Inc., 500 Fifth Avenue, New York, N.Y. 10110
www.wwnorton.com

W. W. Norton & Company Ltd., 15 Carlisle Street, London W1D 3BS

1 2 3 4 5 6 7 8 9 0

For Peggy Powers Petermann
(1954 –2022),
who gave me a book on coral reefs
when I was ten.

And for RayRay, old friend:
Seven hundred and fifty thousand—
no, make that a million thanks.

PLAYGROUND

Before the earth,

before the moon,
   before the stars,

before the sun,

before the sky,
   even before the sea,

there was only time and Ta'aroa.

———

Ta'aroa made Ta'aroa. Then he made an egg that could house him.

He set the egg spinning in the void. Inside the spinning egg, suspended in that endless vacuum, Ta'aroa huddled, waiting.

With all that endless time and all that eternal waiting, Ta'aroa grew weary inside his egg. So he shook his body and cracked the shell and slid out of his self-made prison.

Outside, everything was muted and still. And Ta'aroa saw that he was alone.

Ta'aroa was an artist, so he played with what he had. His first medium was eggshell. He crunched the shell into countless pieces and let them fall. The pieces of eggshell drifted down to make the foundations of the Earth.

His second medium was tears. He cried in his boredom and his loneliness, and his tears filled up the Earth's oceans and its lakes and all the world's rivers.

His third medium was bone. He used his spine to make islands. Mountain chains appeared wherever his vertebrae rose above his pooled tears.

Creation became a game. From his fingernails and toenails, he made the scales of fish and the shells of turtles. He plucked out his own feathers and turned them into trees and bushes, which he filled with birds. With his own blood, he spread a rainbow across the sky.

Ta'aroa summoned all the other artists. The artists came forward with their baskets full of materials—sand and pebbles, corals and shells, grass and palm fronds and threads spun from the fibers of many plants. And together with Ta'aroa, the artists shaped and sculpted Tāne, the god of forests and peace and beauty and all crafted things.

Then the artists brought the other gods into being—scores of them. Kind ones and cruel ones, lovers and engineers and tricksters. And these gods filled in the rest of the unfolding world with color and line and creatures of all kinds—land, air, and sea.

Tāne decided to decorate the sky. He toyed with the possibilities, dotting the blackness with points of light that spun around the center of the night in great pinwheels. He made the sun and moon, which split time into day and night.

Now that there were days and months, now that the world was sparked with branching and unfolding life, now that the sky was itself a work of art, it was time for Ta'aroa to finish his game. He fashioned and split the world into seven layers, and in the bottommost layer he put people—someone to play with at last.

He watched the people puzzle things out, and it delighted him. The people multiplied and filled the lowest layer like fish fill up a reef. The people found plants and trees and animals and shells and rocks, and with all their discoveries they made new things, just as Ta'aroa had made the world.

Growing in number, human beings felt hemmed in. So when they discovered the portal that led up to the level of the world above theirs—the doorway that Ta'aroa had hidden just for them—they pried it open, passed through, and started spreading out again, one layer higher.

And so people kept on filling and
climbing, filling and climbing.
But each new layer still
belonged to Ta'aroa,
who set all things
moving from
inside his
spinning
egg.

....

It TOOK A DISEASE EATING MY BRAIN to help me remember.

The three of us were walking home from campus one night in December, almost forty years ago. The year that Ina first set foot on a continent. We had seen a student production of The Tempest and she'd sobbed through the whole last act. I couldn't for the life of me figure out why.

Rafi and I escorted her back to her boardinghouse, a dozen blocks from the Quad. Ina wasn't used to square blocks. They disoriented her. She kept getting turned around. Everything distracted her and stopped her in her tracks. A crow. A gray squirrel. The December moon.

We tried to warm her, Rafi and I, one on each side, each almost twice her height. Her first-ever winter. The cold was homicidal. She kept saying, "How can people live in this? How do the animals survive? It's insanity! Pure madness!"

Then she stopped in place on the sidewalk and yanked us both by the elbows. Her red face was round with awe. "Oh, God. Look at that. Look at that!" Neither of us could tell what in the world she was seeing.

Little pellets were dropping through the air and landing on the grass with a faint click. They stuck to the ends of the frozen blades like white, wet flowers. I hadn't even noticed. Nor had Rafi. Chicago boys, raised on the lake effect.

Ina had never seen anything like it. She was watching bits of eggshell fall from the sky to make the Earth.

She stood there on the iron sidewalk, freezing to death, cursing us in joy. "Would you look at that? Look at that! You stupid shits! Why didn't you tell me about snow?"

INA AROITA WENT DOWN TO THE BEACH ON A SATURDAY
morning to look for pretty materials. She took her seven-year-old
Hariti with her. They left Afa and Rafi at the house, playing on
the floor with toy transforming robots. The beach was only a short
walk down from their bungalow near the hamlet of Moumu, on
the shallow rise between the cliffs and the sea on the eastern coast
of the island of Makatea, in the Tuamotu Archipelago in French
Polynesia, as far from any continent as habitable land could get—a
speck of green confetti, as the French called these atolls, lost on an
endless field of blue.

Born in Honolulu to a Hawaiian petty officer first class and
a Tahitian flight attendant, raised on naval bases in Guam and
Samoa, educated at a gigantic university in the American Midwest,
Ina Aroita had worked for years as a maid for a luxury hotel chain
in Papeete, Tahiti, before boating 150 miles over to Makatea to
garden and fish and weave and knit a little and raise two children
and try to remember why she was alive.

Makatea was where Rafi Young caught up with her again at
last. And on that island, the two of them married and raised a
family as well as they could, away from the growing sadness of the
real world.

Four years on Makatea convinced Ina Aroita that she was alive
for the sole purpose of enjoying her moody husband and their two
children, her crab boy Afa and her timid dancer Hariti. She grew
things—yam, taro, breadfruit, chestnut, eggplant, avocado. She
made things—shell sculptures and pandanus baskets and mandala-
painted rocks. Sometimes one of the handful of tourists who sailed
to Makatea to see the fabled ruins or climb the spectacular cliffs
would buy a piece or two.

Ina Aroita built her beachcomber assemblages in her yard, turning the fringe of jungle behind her restored cottage into an open-air
museum for no one. Tendrils of *Homalium* and *Myrsine* grew over
her work and covered it in green, the way the jungle buried the

island's rusted engine parts and remnant railroad from the time of the phosphate mines.

On that Saturday, mother and daughter combed through the stretch between high and low tides, sifting for riches. The treasures were plentiful: clam and crab and snail shells, pretty bits of coral and obsidian polished by the merciless surf. They walked across the salt-sprayed rocks down to where the waves broke. Troves of incredible loot hid everywhere in plain sight.

Hariti found a flat blue stone that sparkled when she wetted it.

"Is it a jewel, Maman?"

"Oh, it's a jewel, all right. Like you!"

The girl decided it was safe to laugh. She stuffed the stone into a mesh bag to bring back up to the house. Later, she and her mother would plan together what to make with all their smooth, speckled, shining things.

While they searched, Ina Aroita told her daughter all about Ta'aroa.

"Can you believe it? He built the world out of shells from his own egg!"

Ina had learned the tale from her own mother, at the soft-serve shack on Waikiki Beach two miles down from Diamond Head, when she was seven years old. And now she taught it to this new and strange seven-year-old artist who badly needed myths of bold enterprise. The world with all its bright and surprising contents was created out of boredom and emptiness. Everything started by holding still and waiting. The perfect story to tell such a dark and anxious child.

Ina was just getting to her favorite part, where Ta'aroa calls up all the artists to help him, when Hariti let loose a bloodcurdling cry. Ina scrambled over the rocks toward her daughter, searching everywhere for the threat. There was always a threat, with Hariti. Her birth parents had died just as she was reaching the age of memory, and she never forgot that the world was forever poised to take everything.

Whatever the threat this time, Ina couldn't see it. Nothing on the length of that beach had the power to harm them. The coast was truly clear, all the way up the curving shore and around the headlands to the ghost settlement of Teopoto at the island's northern tip. And still Ina's excitable girl froze in place, wailing.

The terror lay two steps in front of Hariti's small bare feet. In a shallow pit on the beach lay the corpse of a bird. Its limp wings draped, its legs sprawled, and the beaked head hung helpless to one side: an albatross, dead for a long time. It was not fully grown, for the wings of a full-grown albatross would have stretched twice the height of Ina Aroita. Still, the bird spread over the beach, almost as big as Hariti.

The soft parts had dissolved into a golden outline against the gray sand. The pinnate remains of the rotting wings looked like dried palm fronds. Two great sticks—the creature's humeri—came out of the empty shoulder sockets. The silhouette still struggled to rise and fly away.

A chunk of sternum and the slim brown bands of friable rib enclosed what was left of the bird's abdomen. Inside that chest, immune to decomposing, lay two fistfuls of plastic pieces.

Hariti screamed again and kicked sand at the dead thing. She took a step toward the carcass in disgust, as if to tread on the remains and grind them into the beach. Her mother tugged her back, too hard. But the shock of being yanked back and held tight at last halted the girl's howling.

"What happened to it? Why is that stuff inside?"

She asked in English, a new habit that Ina Aroita was trying to break.

"*Il a mangé un truc qu'il n'aurait pas dû.*" It ate something it shouldn't have.

"Like junk food?"

"Yes."

"Why? Why did it eat junk food, Mom? It's a bird. Birds eat good food."

"It got confused."

Ina's every answer made the world more terrifying. The girl pressed her wet face into her mother's bare thigh.

"It's creepy, Maman. Make it go away."

"It's a creature, Hariti. We should give it a good burial."

That idea took hold of the girl, who loved both rituals and digging in the sand. But as Hariti started to drop handfuls of ground-up coral and shells onto the cadaver, Ina Aroita stopped her again. Ina reached her hand into the chest of the decomposing bird and drew out two bottle caps, a squirt top, the bottom of a black film canister at least fifteen years old, a disposable cigarette lighter, a few meters of tangled-up monofilament line, and a button in the shape of a daisy.

She popped the colored hoard into their mesh bag, alongside the morning's other treasures.

"*Nous pouvons faire quelque chose avec ceux-ci.*" We can make something with these.

But she had no idea what.

They shaped the grave into a mound, round and smooth. Hariti wanted to put a cross at the head, like the graves in the island's two churchyards. So they made a cross out of hibiscus twigs and pushed it into the sand. Then they lined the mound with green snail shells and small yellow pebbles.

"Say a prayer, Maman."

Ina paused over the choice of languages. This confused bird might have come all the way from Antarctica, via Australia or Chile. It had lived its life mostly on the water. Ina said a few words in Tahitian, because French and English didn't seem right and she knew too little of the many strains of Tuamotuan to say anything useful.

Fifteen minutes after their brief service, Ina's daughter was skipping down to the waves again, finding new jewels, as if death by plastic ingestion were just another inscrutable myth, as mysterious as a god huddled up in a spinning egg before the beginning of the world.

....

*I'M SUFFERING FROM WHAT we computer folks call latency.
Retreating into the past, like my mother did in her last years. This
curse doesn't always run in families, but sometimes it does. Who
knows? Maybe my mother had it, too. Maybe the undiagnosed
disease lay behind the accident that killed her.*

*As more recent months and years grow fuzzy, the bedrock
events of my childhood solidify. Closing my eyes, I can see my
first bedroom high up in the crow's nest of our Evanston Castle
in more detail than memory should permit: the student desk cluttered with plastic sharks and rays. The shelf of deep-sea books.
The globe of a fishbowl filled with guppies and swordtails. The
closet piled high with masks and snorkels and dried sea fans and
chunks of coral and fish fossils from the Devonian Period, bought
at the Shedd Aquarium gift shop.*

On the wall above my bed hung a framed article from the Trib
*dated January 1, 1970: "First in Line for the New Decade." I must
have read that thing a thousand times, growing up. The black-
and-white picture showed me, newborn Todd Keane, delivered in
Saint Francis Hospital, Evanston, in the barest fraction of a second after midnight, staring at the camera with infant bafflement,
trying to focus on the great mystery looming up in front of me.*

*Mr. First in Line: My parents called me that for years. It put
some pressure on me when I was small. An only child, I took the
title and the birthright seriously. I bent under the obligation to
become the first person to reach the Future.*

And here I am, successful at last.

MY MOTHER DIDN'T WANT *to wreck her perfect body with child-
birth, but my father needed someone he could play chess with at
home, any time of day or night. I don't know how they settled the
matter. Maybe rock, paper, scissors. Feats of skill. Moot court or
Oxford-style debate. Maybe I was born by a roll of the dice.*

One continuous war game between the two of them dominated my entire childhood. Their tournament was driven as much by lust as by hatred, and each of them took their different superpowers into the fray. My father: the strength of mania. My mother: the cunning of the downtrodden. I was a precocious four-year-old when I realized that my parents were locked in a contest to inflict as much harm on each other as possible without crossing over the line into fatality—just enough pure pain to trigger the excitement that only rage could bring. It was a kind of reciprocal autoerotic strangulation of the soul, and both parties were generous givers and grateful recipients.

My father was a quick man, so quick that he found much of the rest of the world tedious. He worked in the pit at the Chicago Board of Trade, in the age before electronic trading. A warrior of the open-outcry system, he stood in the heart of the octagon as the furious waves of capitalism crashed all around him. Casting a cold eye on others' fears and turning them to a profit, his brain knew no difference between thrill and stress. Keeping his head while others swelled and broke, making and losing insane amounts of money all with little twists of the palm and flicks of the finger (backed up by delirious screaming), had long ago flooded his cortex with so many surging neurotransmitters that he could no longer function without constant low-level threats to his well-being. These my homemaker mother dutifully supplied.

Other doses took the form of a souped-up 450SL convertible, a Cessna Skyhawk that he kept at Midway and liked to take out in rough weather, and a mistress who carried an unregistered Smith & Wesson Model 61 in her Louis Vuitton leather shoulder pochette.

My mother was a closet romantic. When she found out about my father's secret life, she hired a private detective to hunt down a boy who had doted on her at New Trier High School and who went on to play utility infielder in the Cubs' farm system for several years before buying into an AMC dealership in Elk Grove. She was constantly breaking up and furiously reuniting with this *man in semi-public places, all but begging my father to put an end to it. My father rose lovingly to the bait, time and again.*

Don't get me wrong: If being rich meant having feckless parents, I accepted that. I loved being rich. The consolation prizes were many and outstanding. But I hated my father for betraying my mother, and I hated my mother for betraying me. I wasn't old enough yet to know how to pretend that everything would be fine. The secret seemed to be to find some other place to live.

I found that place under Lake Michigan. When my mind raced and the future rushed at me with knives, the only thing that helped was looking out from the castle and seeing myself walking across the bottom of the lake.

All dramas sounded muffled, under the water. I knew this from summers on the Lee Street and Lighthouse Beaches. All friends and foes looked fluid and subdued, crawling through liquid resistance with a languid blue-green cast. On the floor of the lake, there were no people. I couldn't imagine a better place to live.

MY FATHER WRECKED HIS BACK *while skiing with his mistress in Big Sky. He came within millimeters of full paralysis. The pain crippled him, and he needed immediate surgery. My mother took me to Montana to see him as he never was—prostrate and almost benign. They gazed at each other and grabbed hands, fused again by near-disaster. But the minute the ICU nurse stepped out, they were at each other's throats.*

"You told me you were in New York for a convention."

"You're so gullible! Why would a Chicago pit trader go to New York for a convention?"

She whispered, as if I couldn't hear, "You are a piece of sordid shit and I'm divorcing you."

"Too late!" His bright eyes danced with oxycodone. "My lawyers are working on the papers already."

My mother gasped, and her whole body folded. You can't play poker against a pit trader, especially one who doesn't care if he wins or loses. My father just wanted to score one more point.

He reached out with his good arm and embraced her waist. "I love you," he said. "You'll believe anything."

THEY NEVER STOPPED THREATENING *to divorce. One June night when I was five, Mr. First in Line sat at his student desk up on the third floor of the castle turret, cowering from the shouts rising from the kitchen two floors below me. My father's voice was as brisk as a news announcer's. "Bitch! I cannot wait to be free of you." My mother snorted. "Free? You stupid cocksucker. You'll have Toddy. He was your idea." There came more shouting, then nothing at all, then soft screams of animal satisfaction begging for more.*

I looked out at the lake, and as I had learned to do, I proceeded to walk into it. I walked along the bottom of the green and muted mystery, all the way across to Michigan, which I imagined as a land of dunes and beachgrass.

THAT SUMMER, THE ALEWIVES DIED. *All up and down the beaches of the city, hundreds of thousands of fish lay rotting. Belatedly, I realized: When I walked underwater to another state, the lake wasn't empty, as its surface made it seem. It teemed with living things. At first this terrified me. But soon enough, it turned wonderful. The next time I walked across the bottom of the lake to Michigan, it was through shoals of fish, all swimming up to examine me as if I were the most amazing thing.*

SO KEEP THAT MUCH IN MIND: *After the hundreds of hours of video, after the countless interviews, after the two biographies (neither one authorized), after the hundreds of thousands of web pages and documents about me and my company, the millions of emails and texts and phone transcripts, the endless digital bread crumbs of a life lived under surveillance in the public fishbowl, after everything that the data lead you to infer, none of the rest of the puzzle of my life makes any sense without this one piece.*

It's a simple, small thing, but I've never told anyone but you.

When I was young, I could breathe underwater.

INA AND HARITI UNPACKED THEIR RICHES LATER THAT
morning. They lined up their finds by color on the edge of the brick
front walk in the midday sun. Ina plucked out the film canister and
lighter and all the other man-made trinkets from the treasure line
and put them in a bucket, quarantined by the porch.

The man-made pieces were ugly. They had killed a bird. Just
looking at them made Ina sick. But she couldn't throw them away.
Where could she throw them, anyway, where they wouldn't drift
back on the tide to kill something else?

The colored bits of plastic fascinated Afa when he came out
to look. Ina's son was drawn to them more than to the shells and
rocks. He kept fingering the toxic junk, asking, "You found them?
In a *bird*? *Inside* the bird?"

He craved them. He and his father could make them into playing pieces for all kinds of games. He asked several times in quick
succession, *Can I, can I, can I just . . . ?*

"No, *mon ange*. I need them for something."

"For what?"

Ina had no clue. The bits of rubbish sat in the sun, waiting for
her to decide their fate. The expectation oozing from them infuriated her. She wanted to punish them. She pictured a mother albatross, coughing the plastic pieces up her own throat and into the
mouths of her young.

————

THAT NIGHT MĀUI VISITED her dreams. Which Māui—whether
the Hawaiian, the Tahitian, the Māorian, the Samoan, the Ton-
gan, the fire-bringer, the sun-stopper, the magic fishhook maker,
or the wormy rapist of goddesses—she wasn't quite sure. It was
embarrassing. She didn't want to tell the god that she didn't believe
in him and that he really shouldn't be there.

Things grew strange, as they will in dreams. The rules of existence got folded up into the waving fronds of great coconut palms.

Things happened that may have involved sex. Bodies were being pressed down like copra, into their original, oldest selves.

She woke, choking.

She heard her husband say, "It's okay. You're awake." She couldn't see how the one fact followed from the other. Holding each other's shoulders in the dark, both felt the irony without either saying it out loud: by long tradition, it was *her* job to rouse *him* from nightmares.

Rafi longed to know her night fears. But he didn't ask. She loved that about him: he could love, fight his own terrors, and leave her alone to do the same.

His hand drew slow spirals, tattooing her back. "All good?"

All was not good. She didn't want to brave unconsciousness again. But neither did she really want to tell him the nightmare. What would her husband think about the trickster coming to take her in her dreams?

"The gods are bothering me, for some reason."

"Hey. They do that shit sometimes."

She elbowed him in the flank. But his thin and too-findable ribs reminded her of the bird, and the image of her skinny black husband filled up with colorful plastic was worse than the nightmare had been.

He turned away from her and curled up on his side, gone again in minutes. She held on to his shoulders, as if riding a leatherback turtle—a beast longer than her husband was tall—along the thousand miles of the archipelago and far out to open water.

A leatherback, she'd once read, must cry two gallons of water every hour, just to keep its blood less salty than the sea.

....

I'D BARELY STOPPED TEETHING *when my father started me on Chutes and Ladders. He rolled and moved for me, our pieces climbing heavenward or falling back down toward hell at random. Teaching me that game before I was old enough was just one small move in his patient grand strategy. He was training me up for the good stuff. Someday, I would provide a challenge to him in the long and desolate hours when the Board of Trade was closed.*

From Chutes and Ladders we progressed to Sorry!, then Parcheesi, before arriving at our first major landmark: backgammon. Roll two dice and move your people in a great circle, racing home: even a reticent little submarining boy could handle that.

The game was five thousand years old, and my father was thirty-seven. He fancied himself a strong player, and for our first fifty games he wiped the floor with me. He was not generous with pointers; the whole grand plan depended on me learning things for myself, so that one day I would grow up to be as clever as he was, making and losing fortunes in mere days. Leaving me to flounder was his idea of the perfect education.

After an especially stinging defeat, I'd sob my way up to my room at the top of the turret. When my mother stepped in to defend me, my father strengthened her character much as he had just strengthened mine. It's amazing my mother and I kept playing against him. But the truth was, I had begun to see things.

Not hallucinations, yet. Those wouldn't come until decades later. But I did see living, changing patterns all the same. In my mind, the backgammon dice began to resemble a creature built up through time, thin at both ends and fat in the middle, not unlike the Little Prince's drawing of the snake that had eaten an elephant. There was only one way of making a two or a twelve, but six ways to roll a seven. The maker of the world whispered that secret to me, and it changed everything.

From that moment, the board turned into a seething hive,

where the pitfalls and promise of each location rose and fell with each move. The twenty-four points of the circular route began to pulse with plans, like kids jockeying for power on a playground. Whole new ways of shepherding my people to safety called to me. I stopped grabbing at quick payoffs and started making moves that would leave me with the best chance for better moves ahead. And the best moves of all were the ones that made my father's chances worse.

My first win came on a Saturday in July. We were playing on his Flicka 20 sailboat, bobbing with its sail down half a mile northeast of Wilmette Harbor. This was before cell phones, and playing backgammon with his son while sailing, reading, and listening to the Cubs game on the radio was near the upper limit of recreations that my father could cram in at once. When I started bearing off my pieces well before he had all his own pieces in his home board, he set down the book and turned off the radio. But it was too late. All the dice-cursing in the world wasn't enough to catch me.

"Again," he commanded. "Let's go."

This time, with sustained luck and my newfound ability to see the changing patterns that animated the board, I beat the best my father had to offer.

I thought he might lay into me. I was mistaken. "Best of five," he declared. "And if you win, I'll take you to Kroch's and Brentano's and you can get any book in the store."

My father doubled down. He took the next two games. Neither was even close.

In game five, I tumbled from grace into hell as if we were back playing Chutes and Ladders. I wanted that book so badly my hands shook, and I felt the prize slipping away. The patterns dancing across the board turned scattershot. My moves grew as random as the roll of the dice.

I jumped off the side of the sailboat and sank to the bottom of the lake. There, in the murky womb of the opaque water, my friends the fish found me. They took me to a slow place many leagues underneath the bottom of the boat, far beneath hope and

*anxiety, smelling of sand and algae. Then they began to feed me
moves, every one of them perfect.*

*I played my game, move by dictated move, and when the final
blow fell, my father drew back as if slapped. But, appraising his
loss, he beamed.*

*"Bookstore, first thing tomorrow morning. Tomorrow after-
noon I'm going to kick your ass at checkers."*

*He sailed the boat back to the marina, singing sea chanteys. My
fish had gone silent.*

A QUARTER OF THE WORLD SUFFERS FROM INSOMNIA. THAT means twenty or so people on Makatea lay awake the night Ina couldn't sleep. Maybe fewer, on an island like that. The place lies four thousand miles from the nearest survivable continent. That must give a little peace of mind. And no need for a white noise machine: you can hear the surf from almost anywhere.

Call it a dozen sleepless souls waiting for oblivion that wouldn't come. Eighty-two people on an island not half the size of Manhattan, and twelve weren't sleeping.

Ina Aroita tossed for hours, wrestling with the trickster Māui.

The two inseparable fishermen, Puoro and Patrice, who jointly owned a twenty-foot wooden fishing boat, were trying their nighttime luck beyond the island's western shoals.

Wen Lai, the owner of Makatea's only store, stayed up until dawn despite himself, poring over a doorstop-thick tome of science fiction, obsessed with finding out what would happen when the aliens beamed hallucinations directly into the minds of Earthlings.

As on most nights, a few crabbers with underpowered flashlights risked everything searching for *kaveu*—coconut crabs—up on the central plateau. They crossed and recrossed the treacherous limestone pinnacles and pits that ran along the length of the island like a surgical scar. Some of the paths were half the width of the crabbers' flip-flops, and a slip into the jagged pits on either side meant death.

Tamatoa, the Hermit of the ghost town Tahiva on the southern tip of the island, fought unconsciousness. His motto was scrawled on the walls of his hut in red vegetable dye: ALERT OR DEAD! He never slept, or at least he was never around to notice when he did. He certainly never slept at night, because he knew the night to be superior to the day and far more interesting. At night, every stirring of the sea made bursts of blue light.

Makatea's elected mayor and *tāvana*, Didier Turi, lay awake beset with worries. Le Maire had just learned things about the island's future that none of the eighty-one other inhabitants had any idea about yet. That was the price of office, and it turned his restless leg into a full-body aerobic workout.

His wife Roti had moved out to the bed on their back deck, to escape his twitching. That left Didier an expanse of kapok all his own to turn into a solo soccer field of backward passes and hedgehog defense. Out on the deck, Roti slept deeply. She always did better in the remote bed than she did in her own, next to her twitching husband.

A few decades before, three thousand people lived on the island. Three thousand had dropped off to eighty-two in the space of one lifetime. That was like the population of the world that night plunging by morning to what it had been when the Europeans started using the horse collar and the Arabs picked up papermaking from the Chinese. Eighty-two relentless survivors, and twelve couldn't sleep.

———

LYING NEXT TO INA in their mosquito-netted bed, Rafi Young dreamed his fourth-most-common nightmare. The first day of first grade was coming around again, as it had thousands of times in his life. His father, the Chicago firefighter, was going to make him walk to school. His mother thought the bus would be safer. Rafi watched from the top of the stairs as his father hauled off at his mother. *Damn it to hell, woman. This ain't K-Town. My son gotta learn to walk through his own neighborhood.*

Sondra Young bought Rafi a flaming orange cap and coat, so she could watch her boy through the front window of their low-rise Chicago Housing Authority row house near Fifteenth and Ashland and follow him as he walked the four blocks to Joseph Medill Elementary School. Flaming orange: She could spot him the whole way. So could every thug in the entire school.

She only wanted to keep him from harm. But every time Rafi reached the school—and even in late middle age he ran the gauntlet several times a year—the kids of Medill mocked that coat without mercy, spewing hate and scorn at him until he broke down in tears and his name was ruined forever.

Always in the nightmare, he threw the coat and cap in a dumpster behind the building after school, just as he had done in real life decades ago. He sliced his arms in five places with a broken bourbon bottle and went home to tell his mother that some kids stole the coat and beat the living daylights out of him.

The dream never departed much from what had happened that day. Rafi and his sister listening from the upstairs bedroom as their parents' shouts seeped up through the floorboards. His mother and father blaming each other for the disaster. His little sister begging him, *Make them quit, Rahrah. Make them stop.*

He had stopped trying to make them stop a long time before. The dream had decades ago become a routine of passive acquiescence in the face of what would never stop. In the nightmare, as always in real life, his father punched his mother, for her own good. And the dream ended when the punching woke the frightened first-grader up and promoted him once again to instant fatherhood all his own.

———

BUT BACK IN THE DREAM, and beyond it: The next morning, when Rafi's father went on his next twenty-four-hour-shift at Engine 44 Truck 36 Fire Station in East Garfield Park, Sondra Young took Rafi and Little Sondy away in a car to live with a friend on South Morgan until she could get a divorce. And there, Rafi Young learned again and again how he had wrecked his family and ruined their collective futures. The lesson was a simple one, reinforced by a lifetime of continuing education: everything that happened to the Young family afterward—the half century of their shared pain and suffering—all started with one little lie.

The dream had grown rarer over the course of half a century. With a Ph.D. in ed psych, Rafi now worked at Makatea's one-room school, helping, in his spotty French, to teach the island's nine school-age children. He was as happily underemployed as anyone in French Polynesia. His own son's greatest crisis was that his father refused to let him go crabbing on the pinnacles of the old phosphate mines at night. It seemed like a step upward on the ladder of psychic trauma. Despite every lesson life had ever taught him, Rafi Young found himself believing at times that islands could sometimes heal.

But Ina's own nightmare triggered his dream again that night. While his wife held on to his back in the dark, Rafi dreamed through his first day of school as it had always gone. The orange cap and coat. The self-organizing brutality of first-graders. The cut arms. The stupid lie. His sister's pleading. His father's violent self-defense. The wreck of his family, laid at his feet.

This time through, a part of his sleeping brain chuckled a little at the storybook drama of it all.

....

I WANDERED AROUND THE BOOKSTORE *for so long looking for my prize that my father lost it. "All right, already. Pick one and be done with it."*

But that was the problem: How could I pick the right one when it might be any book in the entire store? Thousands of them. Tens of thousands. I started my rounds again, across Chicago's finest chain bookstore's two large floors.

"Five minutes," my father said. "Then I'm picking one for you."

I was in the Nature and Science section of the Young Adult books when my eyes fell on a turquoise spine with shimmering letters that read Clearly It Is Ocean. *I opened the book and was dismayed. The font was smaller and denser than I liked. But the pictures of surreal sea life were incredible, and I wanted them. On the back was a picture of a skinny woman with long red hair and a diving mask pulled up over her radiant face. I had never seen an adult look so fulfilled. One glance at the author and I fell in love as only a ten-year-old can.*

My father scowled at my choice. "Are you sure?"

I was sure.

"Are you sure you're sure?" He waved his hand, taking in all the superior treasures that I was passing up.

I was sure. The author in the photo was sure. All the fish in all the lakes and oceans were sure. Clearly this was the book I was meant to have.

I READ THE BOOK *every day for two weeks. When I finished, I started it again from the beginning. The book sparked endless living experiments inside my head. Every page animated the incalculably large and inexplicably bizarre universe beneath the ocean's surface. Each sentence was a blue-black mystery populated by creatures more fantastic than any role-playing dungeon crawl.*

Thirty thousand kinds of fish. Fish that migrated their faces across to the sides of their bodies as they grew. Fish whose barrel heads were transparent, revealing their brains. Fish that changed from male to female. Fish that grew their own fishing rods out of their heads. Fish that lived inside the bodies of other living creatures.

But the book insisted that even the oddest fish was still my first cousin, compared to the other beings down there. The ocean teemed with primordial life—monsters left behind from evolution's oldest back alleys—ring-shaped, tube-shaped, shapeless, impossible plant-animal mash-ups with no right to exist, beasts so unlikely I wondered if my beloved author invented them.

Evanston was nothing. Chicago was nothing. Illinois and even the U.S. were a joke. There were insanely different ways of being alive, behaviors from another galaxy dreamed up by an alien God. The world was bigger, stranger, richer, and wilder than I had a right to ask for. The trauma of Keane Castle faded. Life on land couldn't hurt me anymore.

Throughout the book were pictures of the tall redheaded author diving, gracing the decks of ships in her wet suit, or cavorting with dolphins and giant manta rays. She'd had more adventures than any superhero, communing with sharks and mapping wrecked battleships on the floor of the Pacific. She was fearless and free, and her dives set off the weirdest cascade of tingles through my ten-year-old body. The pictures of her on her expeditions filled me with a happy distress, the advance warning of sensations I didn't know existed. Reading her, I felt like something unspeakably wonderful was just about to happen to everyone. I loved the gawky explorer more than I loved my own mother, in an inchoate way I couldn't understand. True, deep, embracing first love.

I saved up my dimes and bought another copy of the book. I cut out the pictures and hung them all over my room, reserving the space above my tiny student desk for images of the author. I wanted to read every word she had ever written, and it crushed me to learn that this was her only book. But I had this one. I had the ocean. From then on, there was nothing for me but the endlessly inventive, unfathomable deep.

I checked out every book about the oceans in the school library and the district's bookmobile. I consumed every book with a 551.46 number in the Evanston Public. I checked out books I couldn't yet read, just to run my fingers over the mysterious words. I studied the charts and cross-sections. I quizzed myself on the different kinds of corals and memorized which creatures lived at which depths. I learned the names of a dozen sponges. I mastered the difference between cnidarians and echinoderms, though I couldn't pronounce either word.

I vowed to spend the rest of my life the way my love did. I would give myself to the ocean, that wilderness that made the land seem an afterthought. I would dive in all latitudes and descend to all depths, and in each place I would find whole, new, impossible kinds of life.

WE HAD TO WRITE three paragraphs for Mrs. Haga in fourth grade about what we wanted to be when we grew up. I wrote about everything I would do when the world let me become an oceanographer. I spelled the word wrong but got an A anyway. She circled the grade and wrote, I could learn something from you! The proudest moment of my entire education.

My father called me Water Boy. Like I'd willed myself to become the most pathetic child he could have birthed. I would come to him with the tale of some new, outlandish creature, and he'd just shake his head. "Whose son are you, guy?"

I wanted to know that same thing.

I'M FIFTY-SEVEN YEARS OLD. My net worth puts me in the top five hundredths of the top one percent. I created a platform from

scratch that ended up with a billion devoted users. One of my for-
mer companies is on the verge of announcing a breakthrough that
will rush an unsuspecting humankind into its fourth and perhaps
final act. What more do I have to live for?

The answer is simple: to be buried at sea.

MAKATEA'S CRAGS ROSE STRAIGHT UP FROM THE WAVES. The whole island floated two hundred feet above a narrow beach and the rim of cerulean shallows just beyond. None of the eighty low-slung islands of the Tuamotus remotely resembled it. Only ten such uplifted plinths existed across the entire Pacific, and Makatea was the highest.

It had started out as a flat-topped seamount hidden for an eon beneath the ocean's surface. For fifty million years, tiny sac-like animals in partnership with single-celled dinoflagellate algae fringed the mount, building miles-long underwater cities. The limestone dwellings of these corals accreted on the seamount until they broke at last above the ocean's surface as an atoll.

For fifty million more years, mats of cyanobacteria fed on sunlight in the shallow ponds of this creature-created island. The energy they harvested went into all of life's enterprises. One of these processes involved extracting phosphate from seawater and sequestering it in the layers of the bacteria's own cells. As those cells died, the island's pools filled up with phosphates.

A rash of volcanoes 150 miles to the southwest belched up the islands of Mo'orea and Tahiti. The weight of those sudden land-masses pressed down like a mallet slamming a high striker at a carnival. The seafloor bulged and lifted the fringe atoll of Makatea high into the air.

Hundreds of feet of limestone coral skeletons dissolved in two million years of tropical rain. But the phosphates did not dissolve in water. Instead, they concentrated into dense deposits, veining the shrinking column of island with a substance that human beings would come, in time, to need.

———

MAKATEA'S FATE WAS SET in stone in 1896, a few years after France annexed the island and added it to its growing Pacific empire. That was the year when Sousa wrote "The Stars and

Stripes Forever" for a country that had just committed to separate-but-equal. The year that Daimler built the first gas truck, Röntgen snapped the first X-ray, Puccini premiered *La bohème*, and the soon-to-be Nobel laureate Svante Arrhenius published a paper showing how rising carbon dioxide levels would soon cook the planet's atmosphere.

In that year, a ship called the *Lady M*, sailing under the flag of the Pacific Islands Company, made a brief stop on the atoll of Nauru, twenty-five hundred miles northeast of Sydney. On Nauru the ship's supercargo, a man named Denson, stumbled across a mysterious rock that he mistook for petrified wood. He pocketed the rock with vague plans of carving it into marbles for his children. The game was growing in popularity, and Denson and his children loved playing it.

Instead, Denson's weird rock ended up as a doorstop in the Pacific Islands Company's Sydney office. It sat there for three years, a chunk of Rheingold hidden in full view. One day, Albert Ellis, a prospector who worked for the company, came to Sydney. The doorstop caught his eye, and he sent it to be analyzed. Chunks of phosphate rock had just been found on Baker Island, two thousand miles southwest of Hawaii. Ellis suspected that more magic stone had to be out there, spread across the stray, tiny periods that punctuated the vast blank page of the Pacific.

The analysis came back. Ellis's hunch was right. The strange doorstop contained the substance that now fed the world.

Phosphate went into making all kinds of things: detergents, construction materials, and munitions. But its effect on crops was world-changing. For fertilizer, nothing matched it. With phosphate, food yields everywhere shot straight up. Without it, civilization faced a Malthusian die-off.

The Pacific Islands Company traced its chunk of doorstop back to Nauru. Overnight, the worthless flyspeck turned into precious real estate. Nauru became a cash machine, although the residents saw little of the profit. More phosphate turned up on Banaba, not far away. The hunt for the rock that would feed the world spread south of the equator and thirty-two hundred miles east before it came across a third great lode. There, in the middle of the Pacific, lay Makatea—farther from Nauru than San Diego was from Montreal.

Makatea had reefs, soaring cliffs, and spectacular caves filled with underground springs. It teemed with insects, snails, fish, and birds, including species that existed nowhere else in the world. Fresh water abounded, a rare thing in the Pacific. Its virgin forest crawled with coconut crabs, the largest land invertebrates in the world and a delicacy on par with lobster. But the swath of phosphate running diagonally across the island trumped those other gifts and doomed them all.

Only 250 people lived on the island when the foreign joint venture came ashore in 1911 to take the magic rock. No one on Makatea who turned out to greet the invading *Popa'ā* knew what hit them. The Europeans promised the islanders one franc for every coconut palm destroyed, two francs for every breadfruit tree cut down, and one franc for every thousand kilograms of phosphate hauled away.

Few Makateans wanted to work for the *Popa'ā*. They liked their lives and found this new kind of labor barbaric. The whites had to look elsewhere for their miners. The island swelled with scores of Japanese indentured laborers. Hundreds more arrived from China, Vietnam, and islands throughout the Pacific. In time, the Compagnie Française des Phosphates de l'Océanie hired thousands of miners to excavate an island four miles wide.

Makatea turned into an anthill. The miners used no gear more advanced than picks and shovels. Each man was lowered down into a hole where he spent the rest of the day loading hand-cut phosphate rock into a bucket and breathing the dust into his lungs. Above the pit, a partner hauled up the buckets and dumped them into a wheelbarrow. When the wheelbarrow was filled, the surface man wheeled it across the growing chasms on a network of bouncing planks to a conveyor belt that fed a train whose route grew to half the length of the island. In this way, a third of Makatea became a moonscape of jagged rock pitted with cavities several feet wide and a hundred feet deep.

For decades, the island boomed. Makatea was French Polynesia's only cash cow, and it grew into one of the most developed spots in the colony. It had electricity and plumbing, shops, billiard parlors, a bistro, tennis courts, a soccer field, and even a movie theater. It also had miners succumbing to lung disease and children dying from contaminated water.

The course of civilization is carved in ocean currents. Where sea layers mix, where rains travel or wastelands spread, where great upwellings bring deep, cold, nutrient-rich waters to the energy-bathed surface and fish go mad with fecundity, where soils turn fertile or anemic, where temperatures turn habitable or harsh, where trade routes flourish or fail: all this the global ocean engine determines. The fate of continents is written in water. And sometimes great cities owe their existence to tiny ocean islands. For a while, Makatea fed millions.

When the mines shut overnight in 1966, Makatea crashed. The large imported labor pool moved elsewhere. Many people chased jobs seven hundred miles away in the islands near Moruroa, where the French began their next ambitious Polynesian venture: blowing up atolls with nuclear bombs. The population of the island shrank to a fraction of those who had lived there before the CFPO arrived. The only enterprise left was a jungle set on revenge.

Some people of the Pacific like to say: *Every island is a canoe, and every canoe is an island.* When the phosphate mines closed, Makatea capsized.

———

TO MAKATEANS, LAND—*FENUA*—IS SACRED, the soul's house. But the land of Makatea ended up all over the Pacific Rim, boosting crop yields in several distant countries. Boosted yields meant rising population, and rising population powered all the breakthroughs, inventions, and miraculous discoveries of the next twelve accelerating decades. Humanity's suite of hockey-stick graphs required phosphate rock. Makatea helped *Homo sapiens* subdue the Earth. But in the process, the island was consumed.

Everyone needs to eat, but few people are aware of who sets the table. *Makatea l'Oublié,* a few books call it: Makatea the Forgotten. But that's a misnomer. You can't forget what you never knew.

....

DAY AND NIGHT, *the final pages of* Clearly It Is Ocean *haunted me. I couldn't stop rereading them.*

In the last chapter, the woman I crushed on with all my ten-year-old heart told of a research trip she had made off the coast of Eastern Australia. She stopped one day in the middle of a dive to watch a giant cuttlefish near the mouth of its den. This tentacled mollusk, kin to squid and octopus, was performing a long, wild color-dance for no one.

It flashed complex patterns of every imaginable color, cycling through its designs as if sending a desperate, interplanetary broadcast. It seemed to be struggling to say something, but what? The diver's presence didn't alarm the cuttlefish, nor was the creature responding to anything else nearby. It simply looked out toward the open ocean and went on singing in colors. The signals were long and patterned, varied and unpredictable—a burst of messages that my diver author could not decode.

I wondered if the creature might be praying. But even to an excitable child, that didn't seem like a very scientific hypothesis.

I read and reread the book's mysterious ending, looking for theories that would explain that cuttlefish and reveal its mystery. Everything in me was moved to help my beloved author answer the question that eluded her. So when my father (pretending it came from Santa Claus) got me the year's most astounding new toy for that Christmas, it seemed like part of a very large design.

I'd had my share of fabulous toys over the years: telescopes, microscopes, and chemistry sets. A stunt car that always righted itself after it flipped over and crashed. An electric pegboard and little colored peg lights you could paint with. A blue plastic clock-face of nursery rhyme characters that spoke out loud the rhyme of any figure that you pointed the dial at. All my best and most mysterious toys eventually succumbed to dissection as I tried to discover the source of their power.

The saucer-shaped toy that my parents gave me could do

what no toy in history had ever done. On its top were four large buttons—blue, green, yellow, and red. The device invented sequences of flashing lights and musical pitches, daring me to remember and copy them by pressing the colored buttons in the right order. When I did, the sequences got longer.

It was the creature from Clearly It Is Ocean, *in electronic form. It was the flashing, strobing cuttlefish singing its epic song.*

The connection thrilled me, but it also fanned all my anxious need for explanation. I went to my mother and asked her how the toy worked.

"Maybe there's a tiny genie inside."

She was mocking me, treating my needs with contempt. I wished her at the bottom of the ocean.

I brought the device to my father, who was lying on the floor of his study listening to psychedelic rock on his new high-end stereophonic headphones he'd bought himself for Christmas. His back still tortured him and he still took pills for the pain. I poked at him until he came out from under the pricey earmuffs. Indignant, I pushed the toy into his hands.

"How does it invent the patterns? How does it remember them?"

My father gazed at the toy in a happy stupor. He always had an answer. In all my childhood, I never heard my father say, I don't know.

"Well," he declared, buying time. "Computing. It's complicated."

For weeks, I trained my memory on that machine. I worked my way up to sequences of thirty-two colored lights and pitches, twice what either of my parents could manage. That was enough to beat the game on the highest skill level. But winning produced no answer to what the patterns meant or how the device made them. I had nothing left to do with the toy but autopsy it.

I went at it with a hammer and butterknife chisel. That made my father laugh and my mother tear up. I didn't understand either reaction. People and their emotions puzzled me. They were stupidly complex, and there was no way to break them apart and see what was inside.

*Cracking open my toy produced no answers. All I found in
its guts was a green circuit board. It looked like a little city with
metallic streets. In that city were two rectangular buildings, black,
with eight pairs of silver legs. The buildings could not be opened
or inspected. There was nothing more to take apart. There was no
way to look deeper inside. The toy was dead.*

*I was stymied in my search for understanding until a few
months later when, for my eleventh birthday, my parents gifted
me a hulking black-and-white TV tube hooked up to a fat gray
keyboard and a cassette deck. When I powered it up, nothing happened. In white all-caps letters at the top left of the screen, it read:*

READY >_

"What is it ready for?" my mother asked.

My father looked unimpressed. "Not much, apparently."

*But Mr. First in Line knew. Everything inside my eleven-year-
old brain was flashing: Ready or not, here comes everything.*

WHO KNOWS HOW *a boy's thoughts work? Each hidden message
led to the next. I loved the woman who wanted to know what
the cuttlefish was saying. I had a toy that flashed in similar mysterious patterns. A brand-new present—this so-called* personal
computer—*gave me a way to peer into that toy's secret codes. And
that might help me crack the cuttlefish's wild song. The gray plastic box and keyboard were ready for anything. Clearly, they, too,
were ocean.*

*Half a century later, as the rogue proteins eat my brain and
rob me of my ability to remember, I can hold a five-inch flat black
slab up to my face and ask, "What is the name of that old toy
from the 1970s that created sequences of colored lights for you to
copy?" And the little black monolith, always ready, remembers
everything for me.*

DIDIER TURI HELD HIS CELL TO HIS FACE IN HIS OFFICE IN the Town Hall, next to the open-walled community center. Le Maire listened, punctuating the words of the official on the other end with staccato bursts of, *Oui, bien sûr—Oui, certainement.* All the while he looked at the map on his wall and thought: *Menteur!* Liar!

He did not mean the map itself, although the map did lie. Almost all print maps of the Pacific did, in showing things that, at scale, should have been invisible. Even if the ocean map had been the size of Turi's nine-foot-wide office wall, the twelve-hundred-mile-long chain of a hundred and twenty–some islands and atolls of French Polynesia would have taken up just over one foot, and Didier's tiny island would still be only four-hundredths of an inch across.

But the real liar was the man on the other end of the call, the one who bent the truth in two on behalf of the President of French Polynesia. That title was itself a bit of a lie, given that the so-called *overseas country* over which the so-called President governed was itself a fabrication. The twelve-hundred-mile-long archipelago was not a real country. It was a *collectivity*, ultimately administered by France, a country that hung on to the former colony despite the mounting costs of ownership.

And the so-called President's man was pouring falsehoods into Didier's ear.

"The Council of Ministers believed they had your approval."

"*Bien sûr, bien sûr,*" Makatea's mayor kept saying, which in the local dialect meant *bullshit*. But the mayor of the island that ought to have been invisible on any but a house-sized ocean map had to admire how well the President and all his ministers on Tahiti knew how to play the game.

"Monsieur le President signed the memorandum of understanding with the American consortium several years ago. It has long been on file for anyone to object to. The representative from the Tuamotus expressed her interest. We've received the environmental impact studies for the pilot project. All parties are ready to proceed to the next stage of the joint venture."

But when had anyone announced that Makatea was *the next stage*? Now, apparently. An impact study: When had that been done? "I don't believe that we ever saw any of these American . . . environmental engineers in our lagoon."

"The ministers understood that they had the approval of your representative and of all concerned."

There was nothing safe to say, and the mayor of Makatea said just that.

"Congratulations, Monsieur Le Maire. This is exactly what you and your party have been working to make happen for years. Am I right? Hello?"

Didier had no party. The only thing he'd been working for as mayor was the survival of his eighty-two constituents, including himself.

"I'm sorry," he said. "The signal seems to be breaking up."

"Seriously? Didn't the OPT just put in a new cell tower? Quite a gift, for a few dozen people. I was just saying that you must be very happy. Who knows where this initiative might lead? The pilot program alone is sure to boost the well-being of the entire country."

Certainly. Of course. Except that the *country* this deal promised to boost was itself a work of fiction.

Didier Turi hated politics. In high school, he'd almost failed civics. He never wanted to be *tāvana* of anything. The only thing Didier Turi had ever really wanted to do was start in a World Cup as a striker for Les Bleus. Barring that, he was fine doing home repairs and handyman work on Makatea's old and crumbling buildings. For most of his adult life, doing the latter while daydreaming of the former was all the happiness he needed.

Like everyone else on Makatea, Didier had figured that the previous office holder—the real *Mister Mayor*—would guide the island forever. Jules Amaru had a vision for how to save the island. Jules Amaru could charm and cajole and make peace and call in favors and blast through his days in high gear on half a shot of

kava with a coffee chaser. Jules Amaru managed to outplay the
always-circling Australian entrepreneurs who wanted to come in
and "complete" the abandoned phosphate mining. Jules Amaru
knew how to get Papeete to cough up a budget sufficient to sustain
the island and stave off disaster. For years, Jules Amaru had fought
the island's predators to a draw.

But Jules Amaru died in his sleep of an exploded heart.

Didier Turi, on the other hand, was just a guy who used to kick
a ball around a little bit better than any other Mihiroa guy his age.
A local hero, for leading the vastly outnumbered island to a miraculous fourth-place finish in the once-every-few-years all-Tuamotu
tournament. Someone you'd love to have a drink with while throwing a few rounds of darts in a pub, if the island had had a pub.

Just do it for a year, his friends told him. *You're the only person
on Makatea who doesn't have any enemies.*

It didn't feel like much of a qualification.

You've never held an unpopular position.

He'd never held *any* position. Didier struggled with basic economics. He knew nothing whatsoever about history or sociology. His *gāti*—his clan—was undistinguished. The farthest he'd
ever traveled was Wellington. He wasn't sure where he stood on
the whole development question. He wasn't even a particularly
convincing Catholic.

Exactly, all his self-appointed advisors said. *Man of the people.*

His friends guilted Didier into running on patriotic grounds.
They claimed that if the opposition got in, the Australian entrepreneurs who wanted to reopen the phosphate mines would be running the island within two years. Didier ran. He promised nothing.
His whole campaign sounded diffident and apologetic. He won in
a landslide, forty-nine to nine.

Two years later, he was still on the job and the island was still
above water. It turned out there had been nothing much to fear
about being a good *tāvana*. Nothing until now. Now Didier Turi
was playing way above his league.

Jules Amaru had studied economics in Montpelier. Jules

Amaru could hold his own against the *Popa'ā*. Jules Amaru
would have known how to deal with the Californians and their
nonexistent environmental impact statement. Jules Amaru had
mana—the respect of everyone—major, big-time *mana*. But Jules
Amaru was dead.

Jules Amaru's son, however, was alive and well and operating
a climbing outfitter business on the edge of the village, not far
from the towering *falaise*. Hone Amaru and Didier Turi had gone
to school together in the one-classroom school in the center of the
village, although Didier was two years older than the old mayor's
son. The two had liked each other well enough growing up, in
the rivalrous way of boys playing on different teams and going to
different churches.

But even dislike would not have kept Didier from seeking out
Hone Amaru's counsel. The man's climbing business was one of
few ventures—alongside the pair of tiny *pensions* and the crab
and copra exports—that the island had for making hard currency.
Hone's business was the island's great hope. In Didier's eyes, Hone
Amaru should have been Makatea's *tāvana*. The mayor's sincere
desire was for a peaceful transfer of power, any month now.

Hone Amaru was otherwise engaged. He had spread the word
on the Internet that Makatea offered the best rock-climbing challenges in the South Pacific. Every month or two, a beautiful, sleek
catamaran would sweep in and discharge a Zodiac or two of beautiful, sleek young *Popa'ā*—thin, tall, strong, desirable white people
possessed of the most impressive arms and legs. These kids with
their bottomless purses would proceed to scale Makatea's spectacular two-hundred-foot cliffs. They'd stay a day or two, probing new ways of getting up to the top of the plateau, sometimes
without ropes. They'd tour the ruined towns lost to the jungle and
marvel at what the island had once been. In those two days, the
children would spend like gods, and all the local boats would go
up. Then they'd reboard their massive catamaran and head off on
their next adventure, somewhere in the wide and lucky regions that
composed their playground.

But the latest party of climbers had come and gone a few weeks before, and no new sleek catamarans loomed anywhere on the horizon. No danger of interrupting Hone Amaru by dropping in unannounced. Didier hopped on the mayoral motorbike—the one great perk of his office—and sped down the gravel path from Town Hall to Makatea Climbing Adventure. The slick new sign, hand-painted onto gesso-primed particleboard, even listed an email and hashtag, on the chance that some wandering adventurer uploaded a photo of it to social media.

Didier found Hone rearranging the wall of ropes, carabiners, quickdraws, and belay devices as if to reassure the impeccably maintained gear that dazzling young foreigners would soon be by again.

"Eh. Hone. *Ia orana*. You busy?"

The old mayor's son shrugged and gestured all around him. A tough place to stay busy. "Eh. You know. What's up?"

"A call from Papeete."

Hone Amaru grimaced as Didier fed him the details. The old memorandum of understanding. The President of French Polynesia's intention to lease Temao, Makatea's ruined port. The California consortium's shiny new permit to build a factory to manufacture modular floating-city parts. Didier poured out his fears and doubts on his old soccer rival and teammate, hoping Hone Amaru might give up his marginal business and take hold of the reins of power, if only Didier could make the looming crisis clear enough.

The news caught Hone on the chin. He sat down on the top of the wicker desk that was command central for the commercial doings of *Makatea Escalade Aventure*.

"Incredible. It's really moving forward, then? I thought the Americans were just . . . shitting around. You know how they do."

"It's real. They want to start the proof-of-concept test project next year."

Hone squinted at his shelf full of ascenders and descenders, as if Makatea's future lay just beyond it. He shook his head. "And you are asking me . . . what, exactly?"

Didier flinched. He would lie in his bunk that night, still smarting from the question's harshness. Wasn't it obvious? He needed help. And he was humbling himself to get it.

"I'm wondering how Le Maire . . ." *Le vrai maire*, he meant. "How would your father have handled this?"

"Handled? My father?" Hone stared at the question as if at a pig that had wandered into his shop. "My father would have been all over this. He'd be making giant welcome banners and raising them on all the beaches!"

"But isn't it . . . just more colonialism?"

Hone grinned and whistled like a sandpiper at the fanciest word ever to come from his old schoolmate's mouth. "For us? Always. Everything. My father just tried to pick the colonizers who offered the best terms."

———

DIDIER MOTORED PAST the solar farm on his way back to the Mairie. The four hundred new high-efficiency panels tilted themselves to the sun in a clearing in the vegetation along the old gravel road where the mining train once ran. A single-story battery plant and maintenance shed stood behind the panels. The facility eliminated the need for diesel generators, except in emergencies. The island's savings were immense.

Manutahi Roa stood outside in the lane between the two installations, cleaning the panels yet again with his special formula and his custom squeegee. He was, by Didier's calculations, cleaning the panels about three times as often as they needed cleaning, and all the attention was starting to hurt power production more than it helped. But the mayor figured that the secretary of energy's pride justified the energy overhead.

Manutahi waved and shouted as Didier dismounted, glad for the surprise company. "Hey, Chief! Making the rounds? Not a bad morning for it."

Didier agreed. A little muggy, too many mosquitoes, two degrees too warm, but as always, a fine morning, all things considered.

Manutahi was excited. "Come see this. Good news is raining down on us!"

They went into the house at the back of the installation, where Manutahi popped open a tiny laptop and pulled up a spreadsheet. "Check this out. We set a record last week. Meeting or beating the estimates, every day. It's fantastic, Chief. Showered with energy, and *we* own it."

The numbers were indeed terrific. "Ah, good work. Bravo! Well done." The mayor's need to consult one more confidant before dropping his bombshell on the entire island shriveled inside him.

Manutahi didn't notice. "Such a good feeling. Farming the sun! With our own freshwater springs and the most fertile soil anywhere in the Tuamotus. . . ."

It was a bold claim. The Tuamotus spread across an area larger than Western Europe from Portugal to Germany. But crops did grow better on Makatea than on the other seventy-some islands in the chain. Vegetables sprang out of the ground, because of the magic rock. The rock that had all but killed the island.

"You're getting us there, Chief. You're going to save us. Even the fishing is starting to come back. With a little tourism, and now that we're making our own energy, we can turn our backs on those collaborationist bastards in Papeete. We can finally tell the Australians to go fuck themselves. *Vive l'indépendance*, am I right?"

Didier wanted to tell his former co-captain of the Makatea starting eleven that fending off the Australians now seemed like fun and games. Compared to the Americans, the Australians were old friends.

The mayor looked over Manutahi's spreadsheet numbers and again applauded them. He stood up to leave. Overwhelmed with loneliness, he sat back down.

"You okay, Chief?"

"I'm fine."

"Was there something you wanted to talk about?"

"No, nothing special." Why spoil a good man's happy day?

He already had the answer he'd come looking for. "Just thought I'd drop in."

"Glad you did, Chief." Manutahi Roa grinned like a man whose dreams of world domination were coming together perfectly. He held up his squeegee and bucket. "Now, if you'll excuse me, I'm going to go raise the yields a little bit more. Power to the people!"

Didier raised his fist, grinned his mayor's grin, and mounted the motorbike.

"You should ditch that old gas-guzzler, Chief. They make electrics now, you know."

The world's cheapest electric motorcycle would bust the mayor's budget for the next two years. Didier gave the starter of his Chinese knock-off a kick, twisted the throttle, and skittered away back to his solitary office in the Mairie.

————

HE THOUGHT ABOUT STOPPING IN to find some solace with the Widow Poretu. He went to her at long intervals when he couldn't hold out any longer. He'd gotten clearance on the pragmatic sin from all the stakeholder parties, even the angels. Didier loved his real wife, Roti, as he loved the island, but she had gone off sex altogether long ago. A few years into the marriage, it had become for her both painful and unseemly. They had tried for a while longer, but the attempts at perseverance just made them both miserable.

They still shared a bed at times, though less and less often. Roti could rarely sleep next to his constant twitching.

"I've failed you," Roti told him. "I made a promise that I can't keep."

"You've failed no one," he insisted. "I'm failing you, by still asking you for it!" But he was too young for celibacy. The stress of it would poison him. And he would not make himself come, like some crazy person living in a self-invented fantasy, faithless to her anyway, in his mind.

Roti let Didier know, through oblique but unmistakable suggestions, that he was to do what he needed to get by. All she asked was to be spared the details. This was not easy, on an island of eighty-two people, most of them honorary aunties and cousins.

The idea wrecked Didier. A hundred years ago, Makateans were as healthy about sex as any culture ever had been. Like climbing or running or body surfing, but seasoned with love. Possession was not the thing. You could no more own a person than you could own land or the sky above the land or the ocean off the edge of the island.

Then the *Popa'ā* happened. And there was Didier, crossing himself and kneeling in the pew of one of the island's two churches. Two churches for eighty-two people! Catholic and Mormon, and in the former was the mayor, head down and praying to the angels (because he couldn't make eye contact with the Virgin Mary, whose perfection embarrassed him), saying, "It's still adultery, isn't it? Even if my wife says it's okay?"

To his astonishment, the angels said, *Emergency adultery.*

So, for the better part of a year, the lovely and long-suffering Widow Poretu, ten years his senior, had been the cure for pretty much every ailment life could throw at Didier Turi. She made no claims on him. She liked that he came and never stayed long. She did not mind the judgments of others. Her mild contempt for most of her human neighbors made her the most discreet person in the Tuamotus. If her beloved songbirds were happy and well, the larger bipeds could rot in the hells of their own making.

But in recent weeks, the widow had had less time for Didier, unless he was armed and dangerous. The call from the President's office had disarmed the mayor, and under the stress of the impending catastrophe, he would have been hard-pressed to be dangerous to any woman, even Auli'i Cravalho.

What he really wanted was to *talk*. To ask the widow her opinion about the Americans, and how to proceed with the matter. But that he would never do. To talk to the Widow about such a deep concern would be true infidelity to Roti. But he could not talk to Roti about the crisis, either. She would simply tell him to do what he knew in his heart was right.

What he really needed was someone to tell him what that might be.

He took the long way home, along the cliffs. Power, the mayor decided, was an isolating thing, especially when power was powerless. For the rest of the day, he told no one else about the call from Papeete. He spent the afternoon keeping the wheels of government turning, which on that day meant listening to a dispute over a flock of marauding chickens.

He went to the evening's gathering at the community center, but he couldn't enjoy the music, let alone sing along. That night he lay in the middle of his kapok wilderness, listening to the sound of the surf a hundred meters outside his window. *Of course. Of course not. Of course. Of course not.*

Still half under the drug of sleep, he got up before the sun and sat down at the Mairie's laptop. He wrote and rewrote and deleted and then redrafted a letter to the President's man in Papeete, cc'ing the representative from the Tuamotus. The finished letter read, in full:

> *We the people of Makatea cannot move forward with this*
> *plan without a referendum involving the entire island.*

It was the boldest message Didier Turi had ever sent, either as mayor or as a private citizen. He doubted he had the power to dictate terms to anyone. He couldn't imagine that the President or the French or the Masters of the Universe in Silicon Valley cared two shits what the few dozen people in Didier's electorate thought. *The ministers believed they had your approval.*

Jules Amaru used to say that power was a thing more given than taken. But the old mayor had also known when to bluff.

Didier changed and unchanged a few words, hit send, and instantly wished for an unsend button.

He sat back in the teak chair, having just bet his political career on a few words. In fact, he had bet considerably more than his mere career, which he would have happily traded away for a couple of six-packs of Hinano. He had also bet the island, all on the unspoken threat that Makatea now had a state-of-the-art cell tower. If need be, he could tweet out an SOS to the community of nations. Governments of countries much more real than his had been hung out to dry by the collective outrage of so-called social media. Should Papeete decide to call his bluff, Didier Turi's lone ace in the hole was the planet-sized megaphone.

....

ON THE DAY I GOT MY DIAGNOSIS, I took myself out to dinner at the best Ethiopian restaurant in San Jose. I felt like eating
with my hand. Maybe I wanted to do that one more time in public,
where it was socially acceptable, before I started to do it in places
where it was not. I had no idea what the disease would bring.

For a long time I'd ignored the symptoms: constipation, dizzi-
ness, loss of smell. Shortness of breath after climbing the stairs—
first three flights, then two, then one. Tremors. Stiff joints. Muscle
spasms. Lots of little things that might have been nothing at all.
I suspected Parkinson's. But when the transient visual hallucinations began, and when I got lost in the cereal aisle of the neighborhood grocery store, I had to admit I was in trouble.

Even an old Debate Club champion who could turn black
into white and peace into war couldn't argue for long with an
MRI, a polysomnogram, and single-photon emission computer-
ized tomography. I've always trusted machines more than I trust
people, and the machines laid out a strong case against me. Of
course, they say the only definitive diagnosis is an autopsy. But
I'm not holding my breath for that reprieve.

By the time I sat down to that memorial Ethiopian dinner, I
was done with Denial and was working my way through Resentment. I'd rolled enough dice in my life to know how chance
works. My life's luck had defied the odds. It was time to regress
to the mean.

Dementia with Lewy bodies: One out of every three-hundred-
and-some people in this country suffers from it. One in thirty
Americans with dementia of one kind or another—one in ten my
age or older. If you count all kinds of cognitive impairment, one in
five. That's not an exclusive club. Too many members for a math-
ematically literate person to bother asking, Why me, Lord?

The social worker suggested I might want to get my affairs in
order. In the next breath, she warned me about a temptation to

isolate myself. She didn't seem to know who I was or how hard that would be.

Anxiety? Agitation? Anger? A feeling of bottomless loss? Maybe if the news had hit a few years earlier, when it wasn't yet clear whether my life's greatest gamble would pay off. But I've seen my work fulfilled beyond my wildest dreams, and who gets that? I'll go out on a high note, while my parting gift to the world still feels like a miracle.

The social worker also warned me that DLB often involves apathy and declining interest in ordinary activities. So I figured my peaceful acquiescence that night was just another symptom.

That evening at dinner, my chief feeling was odd relief. Relief that my symptoms made sense at last. Relief that I now knew what was coming. Relief that I'd brought in the harvest before winter. Relief that I didn't have to stick around to witness the grim consequences of my team's total triumph or confront those many people who would want to kill me for bringing that triumph into their lives.

I admit to feeling a fair amount of fear. I've always been a coward about the unknown, and the unknown now ambushes me every few hours. "Fluctuating cognition," my health team calls it. Spontaneous variation in my ability to tell what the hell is really going on.

They say I may die of pneumonia, the complication of no longer being able to swallow. Lots of folks with DLB die from falling or losing control of their body. I may die of sepsis or a heart attack. But no matter how I go, it will be the death of a dazed animal.

"We've detected this early," my neurologist told me. "You may have plenty of good time, still." She did not say whether that meant weeks or months or years.

She warned me that no two sufferers from dementia with Lewy bodies can expect the same fate. She hinted that there were plenty of people whose symptoms were worse than I could imagine. "This is one of the strangest diseases there is, and we know so little about it."

I pushed her until she confessed that the mean run is five to seven years after diagnosis. She worked up my meds, had her staff give me the list of local support groups, and told me she'd see me again in six months.

So I sat that evening on the terrace of one of my favorite restaurants in San Jose, looking out on the foothills of the Santa Cruz Mountains as the Teslas hummed up and down Saratoga. I made a list in my head of all the loose ends I needed to wrap up while there was time. And I tried to estimate how much wrapping-up time I had.

I folded the sheet of injera and used it to scoop up the most delicious wat I'd ever tasted. Just yesterday, I was at the height of my powers. One of my companies was about to reveal a product that would rock the world. Life was beyond satisfying, beyond enjoyable, beyond good. And today, I had dementia with Lewy bodies.

Who could I tell how inexplicable this all felt? I only had this instant. The next day this impossible feeling would begin to seem ordinary. The week after that, I'd begin to forget that anything needed explaining. Then more episodes, lasting anywhere from three seconds to days at a time, when explaining anything to anyone would be harder than I could manage.

I needed to start recording everything. Telling someone. That's where you come in.

The waiter, whose name I once knew, came by to check on me. "How is everything?"

"Remarkable."

He smiled at my satisfaction. "Will there be anything else?"

I closed my eyes and shook my head. "Probably not."

Later, he followed me out to the parking lot to see if the size of my tip had been an accident.

Halfway through the twentieth century, in a cold northern city on the other side of the globe from Makatea, a father threw his weighted-down twelve-year-old daughter into the water, hoping she would sink to the bottom.

Forty pounds of metal pulled the girl downward. Twisting in animal dread, she looked from the world she'd fallen into back up into the world she came from. Through the shimmering layer in between, the girl saw the quicksilver outline of her father stabbing a finger toward his own face and mouthing, *Tu n'as qu'à respirer.*

All you need to do is breathe.

———

MONTREAL, 1947. LATE NOVEMBER, bleak winter, when every trip outdoors after five p.m. felt like suicide. On that night, an engineer for the Air Liquide Company, Canada, drove his daughter from their Vieux-Rosemont apartment to the corporate offices in the Quartier Hochelaga. Back then, it took no more than twenty minutes. They drove in a prewar McLaughlin-Buick, with Evie Beaulieu riding shotgun next to her excited father. A timid child, a child consumed by dread, she shouted at her father every few minutes.

"Papa, too fast. Watch out for the streetcar."

Even seated, the girl stooped over. That year's growth spurt had left her half a foot taller than her classmates, so she hunched forward, shrinking herself. Every other day her mother berated her. *Stand up straight. You'll turn yourself into a hunchback.* The word curled her spine even more.

A constant bruise purpled the right half of the child's upper lip, where she chewed on it. Everything frightened her. Almost two years after VE Day, she still imagined German tanks rolling down Rue Sherbrooke the way they rolled down the Champs-Élysées in the Pathé newsreels. She feared that another telegram like the one about her uncle four years earlier would send her mother back into shock treatment. She was sure that her little brother Baptiste would die of pneumonia. At night, she went to bed terrified that the Virgin Mary might explode out of her armoire while she slept and spatter her with revelations.

Her father's work spooked her, too. His boss, Monsieur Gagnan, had left Paris for Montreal after the war, for reasons no one would say. M. Gagnan was kind to Evelyne, but she found him scary and brooding. During the Occupation, when the Germans stripped France of fuel, M. Gagnan's gas generator regulator had attracted the attention of Captain Cousteau. Together the two men built the CG45 Scaphandre Autonome.

Evie liked Captain Cousteau—his playfulness, his singsong voice, his tobacco scent. But his invention felt sinister. Just the name of it: like some mechanical kraken living in an underwater cave off Newfoundland, feeding on cod fishermen.

Maybe she was jealous of how much attention her father lavished on it.

"We're opening three-quarters of the planet to human beings. We've cut the umbilical. The whole game of human life is changing!"

"Shh! Papa, please. Just . . . drive. *Chauffez le char.*"

Her father chuckled, sledding down the borough's boulevards. The dull, brute hum of the city outside the windows assaulted the girl. *Déneigement* crews were out, stacking the snow into great canyon walls on both sides of the streets. All the way down Rue Rosemont, Evie gripped the dash and steered the car through patches of *verglas* on nothing but her twelve-year-old will.

"Every month, we make it better. Lighter, smaller, safer, longer lasting. And that's where you come in, *mon chouchou.* We need to see whether even a willowy girl like you . . ."

Willowy meant *scrawny.* Too skinny and too tall. *Stand up straight. Be proud of your height. You'll turn into a hunchback before you're a teenager.* Hunchback and teenager: the twin sides of that monstrous coin of her future.

And now her father wanted her to be the first girl ever to test the Scaphandre. "You'll be part of history!"

The thought hunched Evie over even more.

She got them down Rue Viau to the corner of Rue de Rouen on sheer telekinesis. Her father steered the car into a snowbank. Evie opened the passenger door and plunged out to the curb. Winds from the high Arctic hammered her. Father and daughter punched their way through drifts to the Air Liquide building and entered the maze of offices, storerooms, and labs that formed her father's warren.

The test pool waited for them. Her father retrieved a pile of equipment from his workbench in the corner. Evie took off her coat, jumper, and dress, stripping down to her swimsuit. She piled her shed clothes in a heap by the wall. Every item, wool. *Pure laine*, like her mother, Sophie Dupis Beaulieu, a poor Catholic girl from Saint-Henri, *de souche*, old stock, with a family tree rooted in earliest New France. But her mother had married a mongrel engineer.

Emile spoke English like an Anglo, had Anglo friends, and traveled to the States a few times a year. Sophie, though, forever bad-mouthed Ottawa, lobbied for a new provincial flag, and voted for Camillien Houde even after the city's mayor went to prison. Emile thought Houde should have been shot for what he did to the country. Family dinners were tense affairs, with Sophie Beaulieu wandering nightly into soft sedition while Emile carried on about the promise of the aqualung and an open ocean beyond all politics. Evie and Baptiste stayed mute and nonaligned.

The small pool was warmed by the heat of generators on the floor below. Evelyne dog-paddled while her father fiddled with the Scaphandre's hoses and regulator. The girl had a swimmer's build, with surprising strength, but her rapid growth hobbled her. She hated swimming laps, afraid of crashing into walls she could not see.

Evie sat on the pool's edge, where her father helped her into the mask, tanks, and hoses. She eased back into the pool, still clutching the rim. In the water, the tanks were more manageable. Emile Beaulieu mimed to his daughter to insert the mouthpiece. "All you need to do is breathe."

Her lips tensed around the hardened rubber. She whimpered into the mouthpiece as her father coaxed her fingers from the pool's edge. Her brain bucked, and the mass of steel strapped to her back dragged Evie down. She lay on the pale blue tiles, opened her eyes, and surrendered to drowning.

Through the membrane that separated the two worlds, her father signaled madly: *Tu n'as qu'à respirer.* Lost, she inhaled. And with that breath, she drew in all her life to come. A miracle: her lungs did not fill up with liquid. Trapped beneath a dozen feet of water, she was breathing. She had grown gills. She had turned fish, eel, octopus—some submarine creature that had never given the idea of water a second thought.

Her lungs expanded on command, and for the first time she knew how glorious it was to breathe. To breathe *underwater.* Her gangly body uncurled, surprised that it worked better down here. A whole new grace came over her, confirming something she had long suspected. She had never felt at home up there, above the surface, with its noise and politics and relentless verticality. She had been made for water, gliding through a place edgeless and muffled, free of the blows that had always assaulted her in the world of air.

Water cradled her in its great, kind palm. The tanks she carried now felt weightless. She rolled over on her back like a playful porpoise and looked up. Everything she needed lay down here, and she wished to stay submerged forever. She could move with the smallest flicks of her limbs. She did not have to do another thing. Only breathe.

Her body rose and pierced the surface. She grabbed the pool's edge and spit out the rubber mouthpiece. A sob of joy rose in her throat. Life had just revealed itself, and she was in a hurry for more.

"Oh, Papa. It's perfect. Don't change a thing!"

Pleasure on her father's face turned into confusion. "What do you mean, don't change anything? I'm an *engineer*!"

YEARS LATER, EVELYNE BEAULIEU would learn what her father didn't tell her that night at the Air Liquide test pool. Only weeks before, Cousteau had sent a diver down in a test in the Mediterranean off the coast of Toulon. One hundred twenty meters down, First Mate Maurice Fargues gave in to the euphoria of nitrogen narcosis, the high-pressure derangement that leaves a diver indifferent to the real. Fargues lost consciousness and never recovered. He died in the "rapture of the deep." The infant aqualung almost died with him.

And yet, Emile Beaulieu had sent his daughter on her own test dive. Half the age of the youngest person to have used the equipment, a girl afraid to step on the cracks in the sidewalk, and he'd tossed her into the water strapped to a prototype.

That night, on the other side of the Atlantic, a Norwegian was writing a memoir about crossing the Pacific on a handmade raft. Four hundred miles down the Atlantic coast, a pair of men working late stumbled upon the portal to the electronic age. And a little girl who would help save the ocean came up from her first dive.

IN THE CAR, EVIE NO LONGER policed her father's driving. She looked through the windshield onto a city that glinted now like the most magnificent bauble. She was thinking of that astonishing book she had read with her father the year before—William Beebe's *Half Mile Down*. The terrifying, fantastic adventure story had just turned real.

"Papa? Most of the ocean must get no light at all."

Emile Beaulieu made the calculation. He nodded in happy agreement.

The girl frowned. "It will be pitch-black down there. Full of strange things."

"That's certain. We know nothing about the ocean. . . ."

"Not even the shallow parts. . . ."

"Because no one has ever been able to stay down there and look around!"

Father and daughter fell silent. Their eyes dodged then found each other. They burst out in a shared, manic laugh. No one, until now.

They stormed back into the apartment on Vieux-Rosemont, still giggling in conspiracy. It was past Evie's bedtime. She should have been creeping off to sleep, timid even in the safety of her home. But the girl had changed, underwater.

Her mother was alarmed. "What's gotten into you two? Secrets and laughter. *Eh ben, vous voilà comme larrons en foire.*" You two are as thick as thieves!

"It's incredible what they've made, Maman. Papa, more testing, please!"

Her parents shared a look that should have told her everything. "Yes. We'll do that soon."

"Tomorrow night. *Je t'en prie.*" Pretty please.

She dove again, sooner than that. She dove and stayed down, under the waves, all night long in her dreams.

———

EIGHTY YEARS LATER, on a crystalline afternoon in a calm patch of the South Pacific with the sun coming hard across the sky and nothing on any horizon but endless saline blue, a gangly ninety-two-year-old woman pitched backward over the gunwale of a five-meter dive boat and sank wakeless into the sea.

Curled up like a fetus from the plunge, she relaxed, unfolded, and surrendered to sinking. She dropped face-upward through the bright top layers of the photic zone. The weight around her waist pulled her down. Pressure built against her frail frame, and the surrounding water darkened.

She looked upward through that undulating membrane between two worlds as it receded ten, then twenty feet above her, and she realized what should have been obvious to her, that first night, eighty years before. Her father had lied.

He had not brought her to the Air Liquide test pool that night because he and M. Gagnan needed someone her size and weight to test the company's lighter, better CG45 Scaphandre Autonome. He had tossed her into the water in the simple hope of building her confidence.

The experiment worked. In the run of her long life, she had addressed the UN and pressured two Presidents into taking emergency action. She'd overthrown more than one of humanity's cherished beliefs about the ocean and confessed her most private stories to a million strangers. Confidence had long since ceased to be her problem. Her only problem now was time. She needed six months of dive-ready health and her work on this water-world would be done.

For decades, Evie Beaulieu had nursed a secret wish to die diving. But not today. Today, she had one last task to finish. She was on this island for a single reason: To compile another book before she died. To try one more time to make the land dwellers love the wild, unfathomable God of waters. To give the smallest hint of creatures so varied and inventive and otherworldly that they might compel humility and stop human progress in its tracks with awe.

One of those creatures had brought her to this reef, a massive-brained, flattened torpedo with a skeleton half the density of bone, a fish who achieved stunning speeds with one beat of its huge wings, who put its truck-sized body through graceful loop-de-loops, grazed in geometric formations, lofted its thousands of pounds into the air, and played in curiosity with the world around it as with a toy. A creature born swimming, and swimming ceaselessly every moment of its life, even as it slept. If she could tell someone, evoke even one reader's wonder and love . . .

Eight years shy of a century, the last person ever to have used the earliest aqualungs sank faceup through the sunlight zone. The girl was trapped now in a failing body, hammered thin by use, her muscles wasted, her bones ready to snap at the slightest impact.

But here, in water, she was strong and well. Here, in the warm seas of the Tuamotus just out of sight of land, all she had to do was breathe.

She did just that, sinking down toward the edges of the submerged seamount. Below her, an active cleaning station she called Makatea Spa teemed with more workers and clients than most successful urban businesses. Cleaner shrimp and wrasses removed the parasites, while dozens of customers waited patiently in the lobby of this combined surgery, dental office, and health resort. How a parliament of so many varied species managed to form these ad hoc, mutualistic communities Evelyne still didn't know, despite a lifetime of watching. But, gliding into the site, she could see the subtle acts of retaliation and self-policing that stabilized the rules of the win-win game. Despite occasional cheating—more by cleaners than clients—the honor system worked. Creatures that anywhere else would have ended up as prey swam unharmed into the jaws of predators who held still while being serviced, even letting the cleaners steal little bites out of them. To Evelyne's eyes, the safe boundaries of this neutral DMZ resembled the magic circle of children's play.

Her pulse rose: a handful of reef manta rays—*Mobula alfredi*—hovered above a coral outcrop, faced into the current, waiting to be cleaned. A few more traced graceful circles farther back in line. Evie made out many old friends. Kaute, Sandy, Tomo: every manta had a unique pattern of spots on their white underbellies, ventral patterns as distinctive as fingerprints. A serpentine mark just above the right pelvic girdle confirmed Mona, one of her favorites, who turned and floated up to say hello.

It happened more often now, when Evelyne came to the Spa. One of the mantas circling for their turn would sniff her out, curious to learn what this strange daily visitor to the seamount wanted. The lateral lines that ran along the sides of their bodies detected Evelyne's presence at a distance. Jelly-filled canals beneath pores just behind their eyes could feel her magnetic field.

Whatever senses were at play, more than one manta recognized her. Evie was sure of that. After all, these were beings who recognized their own selves in a mirror, something that dogs and cats and even some of the smartest primates failed to do. Mona slowed down around the familiar visitor, beating her fins. She banked and came about, wanting to socialize. Beaulieu, for her part, waved back to Mona, settling on a series of repeated gestures that she hoped would convey, *Yes, it's me, hello, I know you, too.*

She lost herself in watching, the great pleasure of her life. So her whole body jerked in alarm when a great shadow passed over her, darkening the water. She twisted around and looked up to see a creature with a wingspan wider than the house she now lived in gliding above her head: *Mobula birostris*—the giant oceanic manta ray—perhaps thirty years old and six meters across from tip to tip. Beaulieu watched it through flawless tourmaline—a massive male whose clasper extended well past his pelvic fins. She had glimpsed this leviathan two days before, but from a distance. Here he was, so close she could feel his wake: a great chevron-morph goliath she called the Loner.

She held her breath. He drifted above her, a floating refuge for scores of other beings. Two species of remoras clung to him, hitching rides. Copepod colonies camped out all over his surface and inside his gills and spicules. Young golden kingfish surfed the pressure waves pushed forward by the great ray's bow.

So little was known about the giant oceangoers. They were much larger than their reef cousins. Near to land, at a way post like this, they were often solitary. They roved throughout the band of tropical waters that circled the Earth. Their ampullae of Lorenzini sensed the Earth's magnetic fields and the fields generated by great currents, keeping them on a straight course through vast tracts of featureless ocean. But how far they migrated and the paths they took were so much mystery. Sailors talked about great feeding aggregations in the middle of nowhere, thousands of miles from land.

It saddened Evelyne that she would never be able to verify that. But this one, the creature in front of her at this moment: this gigantic Loner, she could verify. The ray hovered above Evelyne in the water column, blotting out a disk twenty feet across. He drifted like a stealth jet in the world's slowest flight. Impossible not to see him as a gigantic, oceangoing bird flying through the water. No wonder that the people of these islands had long considered these creatures sacred—the spirit guardians and promoters of grace, wisdom, and flow. From underneath, looking up into the filtered sun, she found the Loner's pale belly surprisingly hard to make out—a ghost as diffuse as his black dorsal silhouette would appear to anyone looking down on him through the darkening waves. Countershading—Thayer's law: a trick that fish had used for the last hundred and fifty million years to make themselves disappear both into and against the light.

The camouflage that had worked for millions of years was no longer enough. Left alone, a manta might live for four decades or more. But life expectancy was plummeting. The odds were good that the gills of many of the creatures now grazing off this secret seamount would end up in sacks sold in markets in Guangzhou and other Chinese ports, peddled as medicines, but which did nothing at all. What was left of a ray after its chunks of feathery gill plates were cut out would be used as bait or fed to increasingly hungry coastal humans. Mantas were disappearing from places throughout the Pacific where they had once been numerous. Even now, not far from where Evie swam, shadowy boats with captive crews were busy poaching rays, and the impoverished country had no money to police the illegal trade.

So stunning was the Loner's silhouette as he passed overhead that Evelyne gasped into her air hose. Her gasp turned into bubbles that rose through the water and tickled the manta's underside. The bubbles trickled upward into his gill slits. The Loner proceeded to cough the air through his branchial filaments and out of his own mouth. The burst of bubbles dislodged all kinds of stuck particles, sending the cleaners into an orgy of feeding.

The ton and a half of cartilaginous fish circled back and slowed just inches above Evelyne's head. Startled, she blew another burst of bubbles. The ray drew them into his gills and blew them back out. There were no more trapped particles to dislodge, but the Loner persisted. What had been a purely functional maneuver became something else: novelty-seeking, or enjoyment of the feel of the air's caress.

The fish banked back around for one more go. Approaching, he studied her with his huge doe eyes. Evelyne exhaled another column of bubbles. This time, the Loner simply swiped at the bubbles with his left pectoral fin for the sheer pleasure of dispersing them.

The behavior floored her, although a part of her knew it shouldn't. Mantas had a brain-to-body ratio far higher than most fish, as high as many mammals. A giant oceanic manta ray brain was the largest and heaviest of any animal that breathed water. The telencephalon and cerebellum—parts of the brain devoted in mammals to higher functioning—were enormous. And this remarkable brain was wrapped in a *rete mirabile*—a "miraculous net" of blood vessels that would keep the Loner's neurons warm to depths of almost half a mile.

Years of study had convinced Evelyne that mantas were far smarter than the world suspected. She had spent too many decades of close observation to be cowed any longer by the prohibition against anthropomorphism. What began, centuries ago, as a healthy safeguard against projection had become an insidious contributor to human exceptionalism, the belief that nothing else on Earth was like us in any way. At her age, Evelyne Beaulieu had no more time for demure self-censorship. A good empiricist, she felt no qualms about giving the behavior in front of her a name. The way the Loner toyed with her air bubbles was clear enough. Call it what the evidence suggested. Call it what it looked like: the giant bird-like fish was *playing*.

Play was evolution's way of building brains, and any creature with a brain as developed as a giant oceanic manta sure used it. If you want to make something smarter, teach it to play. No one denied the play of mammals. She had played keep-away with dolphins off the Caymans. She'd watched bears wrestle and lions dance, a colt and an elk calf play catch, and chimps bluffing each other in something that looked like three-card monte. For years the family dog had bowed to her, begging her for a romp.

But even fish played: She needed to tell the world this, before she died. Captive cichlids played hockey with pebbles in their tanks. Bettas enjoyed tag. She'd seen cuckoo wrasses chase laser pointers around long after the sport offered nothing but exhaustion. And now a manta with no more need of her air was coming back for more.

Above Evelyne, the Loner climbed so steeply that the flat disk of his body curled over into a full backflip. The flip allowed the titan to see behind and above him, but surely the acrobatics were also fun. The great beast slipped from the loop into a barrel roll that brought him back around and pointed him at Evelyne. *Ready or not, here I come.*

Evelyne steadied herself as if for a pick-and-roll, and as the fish passed by once more above her, she spoke into her mouthpiece, "Your move!"

The Loner caught the bubbles of her words under one fin and held them there for as long as he could. Evelyne could almost hear the creature echo the giggle that tore out of her. Nothing in life matched a game of catch between cousins whose last common ancestor had lived 440 million years ago.

....

IT's BEEN SIX WEEKS SINCE I learned the name for what's happening to me. Hours will sometimes pass in a handful of minutes. I'll block on a word, then I'll wait so long to retrieve it that I forget that I was waiting for anything at all. My car keys seemed strange to me when I held them the other day. Uncle Lewy had me in his grasp. A moment later, I was fine again.

They'll suspend my driver's license soon.

When I'm lucid, I'm quite myself. If I went in for a clinical exam right now, I could fool any examiner. But my ability to speak or organize my thoughts fluctuates, with big spreads between my best and my worst.

I'll disappear into mild delirium, not always unpleasant, like diving into a dark lagoon. "Zoning out," a normal person might call it. I'll find myself shuffling, my legs turned into that heavy clay that Ina liked to work with back in college. I'll take a three-hour nap in the middle of the day, only to thrash around and vocalize all night, laughing and crying, acting out my dreams in a body that sleep no longer paralyzes.

"My memory is great," I tell Isabel, the caretaker I've hired. "When I'm good, I have no trouble with words at all."

"You're confusing this with Alzheimer's," she says. I suppose I am.

I've discovered that I can't smell a thing. The day before last, I had to stop while walking down the stairs. I couldn't tell if they were going up or down, left or right. The whole room looked as if it had just turned into an Escher print. I see things that aren't there. Not the popular "little people" or the scenes that resemble animated Dalí paintings. Twice I saw small mammals rounding the corner into the next room or scampering down the hallway. Once I saw an anaconda slithering across the oak floorboards in the kitchen.

None of these symptoms bother me as much as they should. Which means my personality must be changing. They say I'll *gradually lose my ability to think abstractly. Funny: abstract was the only way I ever could think. They tell me, too, that my executive functions will diminish with time. Probably not good, for a chief executive officer.*

I can no longer play complex games or solve intricate puzzles. That much does plunge me into a deep blue depression.

Then again, some days, the cold front blows through, and my mental skies clear all the way to the brilliant horizon. On those days, I can batten down with you and talk like this for hours at a shot. I feel fine today. Better than fine. Like I could tell you the story of everything that humans ever got up to. Like I could beat even you at the most complex Eurogame there is.

I'm still in the early stages, my hospital team tells me. The hallucinations and cognitive fluctuations won't last forever, they say. I suppose they're trying to be supportive. But they don't talk about the stages still to come.

Of FIRST GRADE AFTER THE INCIDENT WITH THE FLAMING orange cap and coat, Rafi Young later remembered little except his teacher Miss Ebberson's astonishment at how well he could read. The classroom had a bright box filled with laminated cardboard pages in all the colors of the rainbow, each one printed with a one-page story. Most of the other kids struggled along through the Red level. A few pushed up into the Oranges. His cousin Keesha could read the first few Yellows. His bud Janard, from across the way in the Grace Abbott Homes, simply tried to memorize what the other kids read aloud and repeated that when his turn came.

But Rafi Young: He jumped all the way up to Violet, including the one about the virtues of Thomas Jefferson, the page that no one was supposed to be able to read until fourth or fifth grade. The performance signed his death warrant with the other kids. But Miss Ebberson—she of the baggy knitwear, cinnamon-clove perfume, and long, relaxed locks parted in the middle—Miss Ebberson caught on to him.

Rafi's reading skill upset her. "How did you get so *good*?"

He lifted his shoulders and looked away.

Though it made him furtive, the reason was simple. His father drilled him. Whenever Rafi stayed at his father's there were forced marches of reading. Donnie Young wouldn't tell his boy the words. He made Rafi sound them out by himself. Rafi worked through stories way above his head; and then his father would quiz him: Why did the white men want to cut down the Logan family's trees? How did Mr. Fox outsmart the three white farmers, Boggis, Bunce, and Bean?

No father anywhere in greater Chicagoland ever spent more time reading with his preschool child. And for good reason. Six years before his son was born, eighteen-year-old Donald Young, starting out at University of Illinois Circle, handed in his first theme in freshman composition, a fierce defense of the Nation of Islam against its treatment by the *Chicago Tribune*. The paper came back with a failing grade floating above a sea of red ink. Donnie stormed into the office of his teacher—a white grad student from Lake Forest only three years older than he was—and demanded to know why.

"Because you cannot write a proper English sentence."

An hour of conference proved to Donnie Young that the white man was right. The discovery humiliated him. That humiliation led to a vow, the vow led to drilling his firstborn son, and the nightly drills resulted in a boy who could read at the Violet level, three years ahead of time.

———

TO RAFI YOUNG'S ASTONISHMENT, his father did not kill him when Rafi and his sister went away with their mother. If anything, the man was gentler for a while. They went out for milkshakes together, unheard-of luxury. They rode bikes in Addams Park. They saw *Star Wars* three times, and other movies, too, though none as good. But they still read for hours, and his father still grilled him on every page.

"I'm telling you, son. Playing field ain't level. A black man's gotta read twice as good as any white, just to get half the recognition. Four times better, and you'll beat them."

A black man had to be faster, stronger, and shrewder, too, just to get by. Donnie Young had been the third of seven kids, and he took care of them all, even the mentally ill one who set fire to the house. And he did that in a neighborhood tougher than any Rafi ever biked through.

"I had to be the enforcer. A fight, every day. You gotta be ready for anything, Rafi. Hit by a brick in my lower back when I was ten. Coulda killed me. Shot at twice as a teen. Two acquaintances of mine, man named Hampton and a man named Clark, slaughtered by the police the year before you were born. Just over on West Monroe! If the Revolution comes down tomorrow? You gotta be able to take on anyone."

Though his wife had washed her hands of him, Donnie Young continued to help raise his boy. He kept on coaching the tee-ball team—the Abbott Afros—so that his son would have a team to play on. The team was pitiful, in large part because of Rafi. The boy could run fast. He could throw hard, but not remotely at anything. He could hit okay from the tee, but when it came time to hit off real pitching, his aim went up in flames.

His father exploded. "What's wrong with you? Don't turn your back every damn time the ball comes at you! Just keep your eye on it. Meet the ball. Don't be such a coward. That little ball ain't gonna kill you!"

They tried again. Several more times.

"Okay," his father concluded. "We'll stick to reading. Nothing to be afraid of, with reading. Books never hurt nobody. Not even a 'fraidy cat."

Rafi Young learned that lesson four times better than anyone.

———

AFTER THE DESTRUCTION of the orange coat, after Rafi's fateful lie, after his mother smuggled Rafi and his little sister away into a new life in a new neighborhood while his father was busy fighting the South Side's fires, the lessons continued. When his mother started up with her new friend and neither Drunk Gramma nor Evil Gramma would take the two kids, they went to their father's. And that meant two more hours of reading every night, with quizzes every thirty minutes.

He was at his father's in the winter of second grade when the man came into his bedroom for the nightly exam. "Whatchu readin', son?"

"*The Lion. The Witch. And the Wardrow-bee.*"

"It's *wardrobe*, Rafi."

"What's a wardrobe?"

"Just a clothes closet with a trust fund. What's the book about?"

Rafi tried to tell his father about the four English children stepping through a hole in the side of reality into another world. His father took the book from his hands.

"Where'd you get this?"

Rafi's cousin Keesha had traded it away for two Bit-O-Honey bars. The book was beyond Rafi, but his father had told him that if a book was too hard, it just meant he had to read fiercer.

"I don't know."

"How can you not know where you got something?" Donnie Young chucked the book into the corner. "You a little old for fairy tales, aren't you? Let's learn something useful. What do you say?"

Donnie had found a used set of children's *Golden Book Encyclopedias* dirt-cheap at Maxwell Street Market, in reasonable shape, missing only two volumes. Rafi didn't like reading them; each time he turned the pages, he felt the ghostly fingertips of the child who'd abandoned them.

Rafi dragged over to the shelf. "Which one?"

"*Which one?* What kind of question is that? Any one. Sometimes I don't get you, Rafi."

The boy grabbed one of the slender volumes and slunk back to the couch. He sat against the armrest. His father sat next to him, not touching. No false comforts, until the quiz was over. Rafi propped the book up against his raised knees. Volume Five: Daguerreotype to Epiphyte. A coal burned in his stomach, and he tasted the first hints of vomit.

Spooky things spread across the volume's cover. An ear grew out of the side of a rock. A vacuum tube on the top of the rock looked like a glass-domed colony on the surface of another planet. A sinister secret formula—$E = mc^2$—floated on a scrap of paper. Pinned to the wall under that paper scrap was a picture of an octopus attacking a near-naked white scuba diver. Just to the left, a terrifying white baby doll-clown in a half-blue, half-pink costume hung in the air. It stared out at Rafi with glossy black button eyes.

"What's wrong with you, boy? Get on with it."

Rafi pointed to *daguerreotype*. "What's this word?"

Ordinarily his father would have blasted him: *That's your job.*

You tell me. But Rafi knew how to play on his father's weakness, and pride brought Donald Young down again. He took a stab at it, never wavering. A decade later, in Father Terry's class at that Jesuit high school that would save and ruin his life, Rafi would reproduce his father's bungled pronunciation of the word and become the laughingstock of junior-year Modern History.

He pointed to *epiphyte.* "What about this one?"

His father cuffed him just above the temple. "Quit stalling and get reading."

The swat hunched Rafi over. He puffed out his lip and pulled at his earlobe. He opened the encyclopedia volume at random. Holding it close enough to see, he read at a good clip, to score points with the judge.

"DUNES. A dune is a hill of sand. Dunes are found along the shores of lakes and oceans and in sandy deserts. Some of the biggest—".

His father smacked him again. "Slow down, hotshot. You even know what you're reading? Where are dunes found?"

Rafi couldn't answer. He started again, one word after another, like a long string of boxcars clicking down the track behind his father's apartment on the south side of Fifteenth. His knee bobbed up and down like the needle on his mama's sewing machine, and his hand kept whisking at invisible spiders.

"Some of the biggest dunes in the world are on the shores of Lake Michigan."

He stopped, amazed. How did the *Golden Book Encyclopedia* know where they lived? Earlier that season, he and his father had biked along the lake from the Museum of Science and Industry almost to Navy Pier and back. Rafi struggled; his father sneered at him for stopping so often. They took a break near DuSable Harbor to look at the boats. His father gazed eastward across the endless water. He hid his face from his son. But Rafi saw, and it scared him. The man who used to slap around his mother for failing to raise her children right was crying.

"You gotta understand. . . ."

Rafi didn't understand.

"I got to teach you where in this city you can go and where you can't. That's just how it is. Sooner you get that, the better. There's Polish and Russian and Mexican and Jews and Irish and Arabs and Chinese, all with their own territories, and you go where you're not wanted, they'll kill you. But the lake. . . . this lake. . . ." His hand, helpless, reached out toward the level immensity stretching out of sight. "The water belongs to nobody. It's no-man's-land. Anytime you need it, it's here."

Rafi finished the article on DUNES and waited for the quiz. It never came, so Rafi went on to the next entry. "DUST," he read. "Housekeepers spend a great deal of time dusting. Dust settles from the air and may make a gray coating over everything in a house. How surprised many housekeepers would be if they knew that part of the dust they wipe off the floor and furniture each day is alive!"

He reached the end of the article on DUST. See also BACTE-RIA, DISEASE, GERMS, FERNS, MOLDS, MUSHROOMS, POLLINATION, YEASTS. He waited once again, but his father held still, head tilted, eyes fixed on something distant. At last, the silence snapped him from his trance. He spoke as if far away.

"That's good, Rafi. You keep it up. Never let the Lilliputians bring you down."

Rafi had no idea who the Lilliputians were. Probably another Chicago neighborhood he had to avoid.

By way of reward, his father jiggled Rafi's kneecap, gave his leg a congratulatory slap, and slipped out the door. He did not go to quiz Little Sondy. Rafi's sister's reading skills did not concern their father.

The minute his father disappeared, Rafi headed into the room's corner and went back through the wardrobe, stumbling into the brute particulars of another, more forgiving and beautiful world. A world, like the lake, that was endless, open, and free, belonging to no man.

———

EVEN EVIL GRAMMA SCORNED the boy's lack of manliness. For his birthday, she gave him a skateboard. The first time he put a foot on it, he slipped and fell and lacerated himself on the concrete. He tried again, and the board squirted out from under his feet. This time he twisted his wrist breaking his fall.

The skateboard turned the sidewalk alongside South Morgan into the Edens Expressway—nothing but headlong wreckage and flaming bits of death threatening every square. Rafi trickled along, both feet solidly on the board. He tried sitting down, sidesaddle, propelling himself with both scuffling feet.

That Christmas, Evil Gramma gave him a doll. "You don't like my skateboard? Too scary for you? Here. Play with that. You can't get hurt by a doll."

Perhaps his grandmother had never seen a horror film.

———

THEY MADE HIM SKIP A GRADE. Rafi didn't want to. He knew how much more misery the jump would bring. Half the school already called him *Poindexter*, for reading in the lunchroom between bites of grilled cheese. The other half preferred *Preach*, because of the crazy words he used. *Preach speakin' in tongues. Preach comin' through, again.* Between the second-graders he would abandon and the third-graders whose party he would crash, the daily slaughter of his life was about to ramp up several notches.

His mother insisted. "The school says being bored ain't good for you. You need challenge."

Dragging his skinny ass out of bed every morning and parking it in a chair bolted to the schoolroom floor was already more challenge than Rafi Young knew how to manage in this life.

"I'm not bored, Mom. Everything's hard."

"Your teacher says you already know it all, and you sit there fidgeting, pretending you don't."

His mother had gotten a job driving city buses. He'd heard her tell her friends that if the CTA made her drive the Racine route for one more month she was going to spin out and hurt someone. Rafi knew that that someone might be him. She had given him a coat, he'd lied about it, and now his father was alone fighting fires and his mother was raising two kids by herself and working a job she hated.

"You got special abilities, Rafi. No one can stop you. You can do anything if you just apply yourself. Otherwise, you gonna be trapped in a job too stupid for you. You don't want that, do you?"

It didn't sound all that bad. "The kids are going to hate me, Mom."

"They're gonna admire you. They're gonna wish they *were* you."

The plan gave him nightmares. He would wake up screaming, "I'm fine, really! *Fine!*"

They kicked Rafi Young up into the third grade, and his whole shaky existence took a sharp turn south.

His performance nosedived. His mother confronted him. "You pretending to be stupid so they drop you back down into the second grade? 'Cause I'll tell you right now, mister: that's a bad plan!"

"It's not a plan. It's . . . my new teacher."

"Miss Rapp? What's wrong with her?"

"She writes funny."

"What do you mean, 'funny'?"

"Like Chinese. Nothing she puts on the board makes sense."

The boy failed to tell his mother that skipping a grade had rearranged him. In second grade, he sat up front, near the chalkboard, in the seat he chose. But his new teacher slapped the instant third-grader in the back row of his new classroom, from where the chalkboard lay wrapped in fog. That plunged Rafi into a misery that he figured God had ordained.

Then one day during morning recess he found a pair of glasses on a playground bench near the tetherball pole. As a joke, he tried them on. In an eyeblink, all was light. He kept them on when the class went back inside, and from one hour to the next, he went from floundering to outperforming the older kids. That state of grace continued all the way to lunch, when the owner of the glasses came up to him, took the glasses off his face, and pushed him down.

Rafi stayed down on the linoleum and burst into tears. Not because he'd twisted his wrist while breaking his fall. He'd *liked* seeing at a distance. He hadn't realized it was possible. He would never in a million lifetimes have imagined that all the other kids had been seeing at a distance all this time, without telling him. And now he was banished to blurriness again.

———

"YOUR SON NEEDS GLASSES," Miss Rapp told his mother.

"What are you talking about? He can see perfectly."

Miss Rapp tilted her head, and Rafi's mother caught herself. "Why didn't he tell me he couldn't see?"

"How was he to know? He only has but that one pair of eyes!"

———

THE CLASSROOM TURNED SAFE AGAIN. From his throne in the back row, Rafi Young took dominion over everything he could now see. Math, geography, science, art, music, history: he excelled in every subject Miss Rapp threw at him. But during reading, he was safest of all. His Oz, his Narnia. Reading left him untouchable on a raft in the middle of an ocean of bright words.

One afternoon they were learning about different branches of the animal kingdom when a commotion outside the classroom window made the kids around him giggle. The boy next to him nudged the back of Rafi's head. Rafi turned to see his father out on the playground pointing both index fingers at him like revolvers. Then his father began waving like a crazy person. Rafi hid at his desk. His father didn't belong here. This was *school*, his safe spot, where if he did well no one could blame him for anything.

His father shouted, inaudible through the glass. He shimmied a little, like a drunk. The kids around Rafi laughed again.

Miss Rapp asked, "Does anyone know who that man is?"

Rafi studied the window as if it were another science lesson.

The room filled with a silence softer than death. Then Darnell, from his old neighborhood, ratted him out. "His dad!"

Miss Rapp frowned at Rafi. Criminal again. It didn't seem to matter how well he did in class.

"Is that your father, Rafi? Well, you better go see what he wants!"

He went outside, perp-walked to execution. Every kid in the third grade and his curious teacher stared out the window at him. He was like some eel in the Shedd Aquarium.

His father jabbed his fingers, pointing at his own eyes. "Your *glasses*, Rahrah. Your specs. Lookin' *good*! Ooo-eee!"

The child braced for punishment.

"I was on my way to the station. Thought I'd stop in and . . . you know. Congratulate you."

Rafi stared, asking God to make the man vanish.

"Look. Son. I just heard. I didn't know you needed glasses."

Rafi pointed back to the building. "I got to go back to class."

"Listen. Rafi. I'm sorry I used to get angry at you. I thought you were a coward. I didn't know you couldn't see the ball."

Something came over the boy. Someone else's idea. "I *am* a coward."

His father's face collapsed. Euphoria flooded through Rafi, as never before.

"I don't like baseball. I don't like getting stronger or learning how to fight. I just like reading."

The feeling was fantastic. Like beating the man at checkers. Like whupping him at his own invented game.

———

EVIL GRAMMA SMACKED HIM when he mispronounced words. "Get it right, child. You're the only one of us who has a chance of making it, in this world."

Drunk Gramma didn't believe Rafi's glasses did a thing. "You just wearing those to get attention. Trying to be somebody special!"

His mother dropped Rafi and Little Sondy off for babysitting on Saturdays, while she drove the Racine route in both directions until her brain bled. Once in charge, Drunk Gramma took off Rafi's glasses and put them on top of the refrigerator. Then she'd send the kids out into the alley to play ring toss or hide-and-seek for hours. With her experiment concluded to her satisfaction, Drunk Gramma would give him back his glasses just before Sondra Young returned to pick up her children.

One Saturday night at bath time, his mother stopped to examine his naked body under the fluorescent sink light. "How'd you get all these bruises?"

"Running into things. Falling down."

"Why you getting so clumsy, Rafi?"

"I only run into things at Gramma's."

His mother pressed him until he told her why. His father's mother never babysat him again.

———

HE MADE A PERISCOPE from two makeup mirrors and a paper towel tube. Lying on the floor behind the upstairs banister, Rafi spied on his mother and Mrs. Jones in the room below. He had somehow done something wrong yet again, and the principal of his school was recommending punishment to his mother.

"You have to get your boy out of there."

"Why? He's doing so well!"

"That's my *point*, Sondra. He's got the goods. He can go all the way. But not from here. If he stays at Medill, he'll be buried like the rest of them."

From his hidden outpost at the top of the stairs, Rafi imagined his school under a mudslide. He'd read of a grade school in Wales being buried by an avalanche, and it sometimes haunted his dreams.

"Is it really that bad?"

"Honey, you have no idea. The city cheats us out of money. They cheat us on teachers. The smart ones want to work anywhere but here. Nothing against our poor kids, and pardon my French, but this place is a zoo."

"What can I do?"

"I've got favors to call in with the Board of Education. There's a magnet school called Green Classical, up in Park Ridge. Western and Touhy."

"Park Ridge? That's not—"

"You won't have to pay a dime. A smart black boy who can read like Rafi will be gold to them."

A magnet school. Rafi lowered his periscope. An immense Classical magnet had grabbed him and was pulling him up to the North Side, deep into the neighborhoods where his father had taught him that blacks should never go.

———

FOURTH GRADE PITCHED HIM headlong into someone else's life. While his former classmates accused him of uppity betrayal, Rafi Young boarded a yellow bus with stiff red upright seats that took him for an hour-and-a-half ride into enemy territory way on the other side of Chicago's great checkerboard, to serve time as the only black kid in Green Classical.

At Green he met his first Jews, people who, until then, had been as mythical as Babylonians. And the Near North Side kids met their first *African American*. They asked to touch his hair. They imitated the way he pronounced simple words like *get* and *sure*. They wondered about the strange sandwiches he brought from home and patiently told him how his shoes were wrong. But soon enough he was everybody's fetish. He could read rings around all of them. They quizzed him about their favorites—Charlotte and Wilbur, the Boxcar Children, the Chocolate Factory. To the amazement of the magnet schoolers, the newcomer had read them all.

Biology, geometry, geography, history, French, social science: Rafi Young did well in every subject. Not so well that the North Siders hated him. Just well enough that they left him in peace. He didn't grasp much about Green Classical. But he soon learned that the smart kids survived and the slow learners vanished.

On weekends he continued to play in the old neighborhood, as if he still belonged on South Morgan with his old friends. With his glasses, Poindexter could throw like Vida Blue or catch a pass like Lynn Swann. But in the unraveling game of childhood, every week pushed Rafi Young further into enemy territory. His life as a permanent infiltrator had begun.

———

GREEN CLASSICAL HAD A LIBRARY that made Medill's look like a fire sale. Green's was two rooms and a balcony filled with books—books of every size, color, and thickness. Books about reptiles and amphibians and the Civil War and volcanoes. Maps and Greek myths, biographies of great athletes, how-to books for building your own radio or surviving in the woods with nothing but a pocketknife.

He went in one day at recess, afraid that the librarian might stop him. He went up and down the aisles of the thousands of books, afraid to touch them. A large white book fell off the shelves as he passed. He snatched it up off the floor and scrambled to put it back before the librarian threw him out. But the contents of the book stopped him. It was all about building a castle in England in the thirteenth century. Every page had a picture filled with tiny people swarming together to dig the moats and raise the walls and decorate the passageways of the immense fortress.

He'd never wanted anything more in his whole life than to possess that book for a few hours. He had seen other kids leaving the library with books under their arms, but he didn't know how it was done. The books were too nice to be free. At last, he mustered the courage to bring the book to the librarian's desk.

"How much to borrow it overnight?"

The librarian laughed. "Oh, sweetheart! It's all yours. You can take it home for two weeks. No charge!"

It seemed like a trap. But he checked the book out and walked through the library doors. No alarm went off. For two weeks, while commuting up and down the Edens Expressway, he lived in medieval England. They were the happiest two weeks of his life.

THE WHITE KIDS HAD EVERYTHING. They had backpacks and metal lunch boxes and erasers in the shapes of cartoon characters. From one day to the next, every kid at Green Classical showed up with packs of some new kind of trading card. They traded and obsessed over those cards until kids started coming to class with shoeboxes of them. Rafi floundered in ignorance.

"Are they . . . some kind of baseball cards?"

The others just laughed.

Kids kept charts and tables of the cards they had and the cards they needed. Rafi asked Eliezer Kaplan, "Can you just . . . let me hold one?"

Eliezer hunched up, the helpless enforcer of reality. "Well . . . they're worth a lot more if people don't touch them."

"Can I just look at one?"

Eliezer flashed him a look at one sleeved card. It was a picture of a cartoon newspaper with a headline that made no sense at all.

The packs of cards cost too much money. Rafi didn't dare nag his mother to buy him one, especially since he didn't know what they were. So he took a pack that fell out of Joey Blackman's side pocket when they were sitting on the school steps. He slipped it into his own pocket, and though it burned his thigh, he didn't look at it until the long bus ride home back to the Near West Side.

He opened the pack of cards and studied them in bed, when his mother and sister were asleep. Every card showed some cartoon— parodies of famous people he didn't know and jokes he couldn't understand. He would never keep pace with the kids from Green. No matter what his father and his grandmother and the principal at Medill thought, he might learn everything the North Side had to learn, and he would still be buried.

The next day they summoned him to the principal's office. Joey Blackman was already there. Dr. Vedral, the principal, looked Rafi in the eye.

"Rafi? Do you have something that belongs to Joey?"

He didn't want to go to reform school. He no longer wanted to go back to Medill. He just wanted to read until he discovered where all the pain of the world came from.

"No," he said, a little injured. "I have my own stuff. I don't need to steal anything."

The righteous protests of Joey Blackman were impossible to deny. But Dr. Vedral, a trusting white woman, studied the best reader in Green Classical and went with her educator's gut.

"Joey, I think you must have just lost your cards. You two both go on back to class."

Now there were at least three things for which Rafi Young would go straight to hell.

———

WHILE RAFI COMMUTED THREE HOURS each day to Green Classical, Little Sondy stayed home, walking the few blocks to Medill. She turned into Sond for a year, and then 'Dra for two more. She had all the teachers Rafi would have had if the magnet hadn't gotten him and pulled him up North.

'Dra was not a prize reader or a prize math solver or a prize picture puzzler or a prize anything. But she and her brother were bound together in a pact against all others. In their mother's tiny apartment every evening, they fought the world to a draw. And on weekends and over the long summer vacations, as their mother drove the bus and their father popped back into their lives at random, they kept each other entertained.

These were their years of radio, when both black and white DJs at South Side stations spun soul and funk and infant hip-hop and all kinds of urban—years of shared late afternoon reruns, where brother and sister learned about the ways of white folks and the things rich people got up to. Their years of Cubs games that taught the pleasure of constantly destroyed hope. Their years of Parker Brothers, of Monopoly, Operation, and Payday. Each of them served as the other's best opponent. Sworn to blood combat, they spurred each other on, growing fiercer and shrewder with every showdown.

In sixth grade, when he was eleven, Rafi discovered Danish snap-together blocks. Something about those standardized, interlocking components in bright primary colors, all meshing tightly into any clean creation he could dream up, made Rafi feel that the mangled planet might yet be fixed. He spent entire afternoons assembling smooth walls and strong towers, fitting the modules together into solid citadels, secure space stations, and cunning subterranean hideouts.

His sister didn't like playing with blocks. But she liked playing with Rafi. They worked together for two days, making a wardrobe with a false back to it. Rafi wanted to make it big enough to get inside of, but they didn't have enough blocks. At least they could make a working prototype.

They talked while they built. Confiding was easier when you could study the blocks and not have to look at each other.

"Do you really like them, Rahrah?"

"Do I really like who?"

"The white kids. The Green kids. Are they really your friends, or . . . ?"

"Why you gotta ask me this? Stop asking me stupid shit."

"Just tell me. Do you really like being with them? Or you just making nice?"

What was there to say? His classmates had so much confidence it made him sick just to think about. But he knew them, now. Knew what made them anxious or excited. He moved among them without too much trouble.

"I don't know. They're okay. Kind of in love with themselves? But people don't come after you so much, up there. They leave you be."

"Everyone talks a lot of trash about you, you know. Down here."

He kept searching for yellow two-by-twos and red two-by-threes. "Who does?"

"Keesha. Little Charles. Janard. Most of the neighborhood. But they don't know you. Nobody really knows you—not us down here or the white kids up there. Not Mom. Not Dad. Only I know you. Only I know the real Rahrah."

He snapped together two wardrobe panels and thought: *At least that makes one of us.*

———

HIS MOTHER FELL IN with Moody Boyfriend, who all too soon became Moody Stepdad. This man was big and wide and dark and bald and worked as a furniture mover. Rafi didn't bother learning too much about him. It didn't seem likely that he'd be around too long.

Rafi and 'Dra got moved again, to a not-great duplex on the edge of the Robert Brooks Homes. The apartment would have been just right for two, as Moody Stepdad often said. Rafi stayed out from underfoot by moving into the public library branch on Taylor Street, while Little Sondy hid at home by making herself very small.

In the temple on Taylor, Rafi played a game. He went to a section—say, old movies, or the Wild West, or boats and submarines. He'd put his finger on a row of books, close his eyes, step forward, and flick down the row until a spine tugged at his finger. He'd take the selection back to his reading desk—they let skinny, preadolescent black boys have reading desks all their own—then read a little, dream a little, and read a little more.

Moody Stepdad didn't like Rafi going up to Park Ridge for school. "What's he need to go clear up there for, to get what he could get easier down here? Put him in Whitney Young. Just makes more sense, all the way around." And in the middle of seventh grade, without enough time to trade phone numbers with his friends from Green, Rafi began life again in a whole new school, once again walking distance from home.

———

FIVE WEEKS BEFORE RAFI'S thirteenth birthday, Drunk Gramma cornered Rafi's father with family news. Donnie Young's younger brother's oldest son had just been accepted at a private school named after Ignatius of Loyola, the founder of the Jesuits, a crazed Spanish Renaissance soldier given to vivid hallucinations.

"Best school in the city. Top three, anyway."

Saint Ignatius College Prep was right in the old 'hood, close enough that Leon Durham, standing in the parking lot of Rafi's former grade school, could have knocked out a window of the elite institution with a well-hit baseball and some help from steroids. Donnie Young had walked past the grand old Second Empire–style building a few thousand times in his life. It was one of only half a dozen public buildings to survive the Great Fire of 1871, but it never occurred to the fireman that the place was anything more than an island of whiteness left behind by history on the wrong side of Chicago's changing neighborhoods.

"Your own nephew. At least one boy in the Young family is going somewhere. Where's your little reading machine going to high school?"

Donnie Young had no idea. His ex-wife handled that.

"What kind of father are you? You got our best hope in the whole next generation in your hands, and you're going to drop him any-which-where, while his own cousin goes to the top school in the city?"

Donnie couldn't afford to send his kid to a place like Saint Ignatius. But now nothing short of Saint Ignatius College Prep would do for his own heir apparent. Donnie took up the matter with Sondra, meeting his ex on neutral turf in a sandwich shop in Little Italy. The proposal smacked her up the side of the head.

"Wait. *How much?* Is that *every year?*"

But Donnie Young went over his columns of numbers, which he'd written out longhand on a sheet of copy paper. "I can swing two-thirds." He didn't say how that would require his moving into a studio and borrowing money from his own mother, who still did not believe the boy really needed glasses.

Sondra Young, now Sondra Johnson, stared at the remaining balance, the only thing standing between her boy and boundless opportunity. If anyone deserved what the Jesuits had to offer, it was her son. And honestly, she wasn't sure Rafi would survive any other high school that he could reach from home.

They were late in the application cycle. Very late. In fact, Rafi had only three days to craft a personal statement, take a general knowledge exam, and write a thousand-word essay. Hearing his parents' rushed plan, Rafi wanted to drop out and get a job washing dishes.

"Three days? Really?" Three days to apply to one of Chicago's most exclusive schools. He got to work, letting his parents draw their own conclusions from his stoic silence. Once the shock of the initial ambush wore off, he began to feel that he'd been preparing his whole life for this one, ridiculous, thrilling long shot.

The comprehensive exam was more challenging than any he'd taken. But he ran through the questions like a champion contestant on an afternoon game show. His nervousness disappeared, and the rare chance to flex his skills turned into the only blood sport he'd ever enjoyed playing.

The personal statement all but wrote itself: *What is your favorite spot in all the world?* He wrote of how he felt the first time he walked into the Taylor Street library—how everything in creation had its shelf somewhere in that building, and how he could travel anywhere in time and space simply by browsing the aisles. *Maybe it's cheating that my favorite spot contains so many others.*

The thousand-word general essay, however, stopped him cold. *What is the most important quality any person could possess?* Whenever he wrote essays at Whitney Young, he knew how the teacher hoped he would answer, and he rose to deliver what was expected. But he could not imagine what the Jesuits wanted him to say. Faith, he supposed. Maybe hope or charity. But when he started writing about those, the sentences turned silly and fake. The words were dead before they left his pen.

By late afternoon on the Sunday before the application was due, he still had only one fatuous paragraph. His father was going nuts, begging him to finish the essay any old way and turn it in. "Don't have to be good. Just *done.*"

His mother said, "Don't worry, Rafi. I love you, no matter what."

Rafi put his head down on the kitchen table, left ear to the

paper, defeated. Just as slowly, he lifted his head again, and before
he realized what he'd written, he had his first line:

> Without the ability to feel sad, a person could not be kind
> or thoughtful, because you wouldn't care or know how any-
> body else feels. Without sadness, you would never learn any-
> thing from history. Sadness is the key to loving what you
> love and to becoming better than you were. A person who
> never felt sad would be a monster.

In two short hours, he had his introduction, his three exam-
ples, and his summary—one thousand words. The argument was
strange. But it felt lively and true, and the words didn't make him
sick to read.

His father demanded to see the essay. When the man finished,
Rafi braced for his fury. It didn't come. His father handed the pages
back to him and looked away. "All right, then. If those folks don't
take you, it's time to move to another country."

———

FOR A MONTH, Rafi had nightmares of his father punching out
elderly white men in long black robes. His sister reassured him.
"You're the best reader in this whole city. Of course they're gonna
take you. They may be white, but they're not idiots." His mother
kept saying, "Whitney Young is a perfectly good school." But
when the letter of acceptance arrived, she broke down sobbing. A
person who never felt sadness would never have been able to feel
such pride.

The only thing remaining was to tell Moody Stepdad. Sondra
had not wanted to raise the matter until it was a done deal. The
man always required a fair amount of finessing. She went to him
waving the letter, the imposing letterhead, the flourish of signature, the glowing words about the exceptional application. "Look
here! Be proud!"

From across the kitchen table, Rafi watched Moody Stepdad read the letter. The man's posture alone made a vacuum of the room.

"How much is this pride going to cost me?"

Rafi listened to the two adults advance from probe to skirmish to full frontal assault. Neither of the combatants cared that he was sitting right there and could hear everything they said. He got up from the table, crossed the room, and went upstairs with no one noticing and his fate still up for grabs.

'Dra was sitting in the dark hallway at the top of the stairs. He remembered his first day of school, the two of them cowering on the floor above their warring parents, Little Sondy begging him to make them stop. But this wasn't Little Sondy. This was another, fiercer person. His sister was only twelve, but she'd had enough of paternal stupidity for one lifetime.

"The man's a fuckin' piglet."

"Leave it. It doesn't matter."

But Rafi sat on the landing next to her and kept on listening to Saturday Night at the Fights. His mother was saying that she had it all covered. Moody Stepdad wouldn't have to sacrifice a thing.

"Whatever comes out of your pocketbook *is* my sacrifice."

"The boy's father gonna handle most of the costs."

This only seemed to make Moody Stepdad moodier.

"You want to send the girl to an expensive school, too? Make the two of us live on bread and water? Our taxes are already paying for his education. He can go to a free high school, just like you and me did."

His mother said, "Listen to me. That child is special."

Moody Stepdad hooted. "*Special?* What the hell are you *talking* about? He's so slow, he can hardly take care of himself."

On the landing, 'Dra shrieked and jumped to her feet. Rafi grabbed the hem of her sweatshirt, but she pulled away and hammered down the stairs. She slammed into the kitchen with such violence that their mother shouted in surprise. Then 'Dra laid into Moody Stepdad.

"Shut your fool mouth for ten seconds. You're too dumb a shit to recognize the smartest person you'll ever meet."

Rafi smashed his hands against his ears. He stood and stumbled toward his bedroom, the closeable door. Before he could make it, the kitchen erupted. A shouted profanity touched off a surprised bellow, followed by the scrape of furniture and the sound of running. A scuffle, a door thrown open, a chase out into the apartment hallway, a rotted railing pulling out of the wall, another short shout, and the sound of a small, flailing body hitting the apartment stairs four times before coming to rest at the bottom. Then his mother's wild howls.

He forced himself back around into the nightmare scene and down the dingy stairway. His mother and stepdad were already at the bottom, hovering over his sister's unresponsive body. He ran back upstairs and called 911. Then the ambulance, the paramedics, and Rafi remembered nothing more until the three of them were huddled in a waiting room somewhere in the endless sprawling complex of Cook County Hospital, on Harrison. His mother kept saying, "You promised to fix that railing." Moody Stepdad said nothing. Rafi talked only to God, four repeating words.

An ICU resident—white man in white coat—came to tell them that three of 'Dra's cervical vertebrae were no longer as they should be and that her brain was badly impacted. Something in the doctor's voice cowered from the suggestion: survival might be the worst of the two possibilities.

Seventeen insensible hours later, Sondy was dead. His mother clung to Rafi where they camped in the waiting room and would not let him go. His stepfather sought his eyes, begging for understanding. No venom Rafi could whisper at the man was as bad as the truth. And in that moment, the thirteen-year-old chose to live in the truth forever.

....

I KNEW OF RAFI YOUNG *early in freshman year, before I even knew his name. Long, thin face, close-cropped frizz, tight-fitting cotton shirts: he looked like a 1950s jazz musician. Although the school was in a black neighborhood, blacks were a rarity at Ignatius, and blacks who walked three blocks to school through those contested streets of the Near West Side were a class of one.*

He was in my freshman World Civ section, and I took notice, especially because he carried around serious-looking books I'd never heard of. Zen and the Art of Motorcycle Maintenance *one week and* The Screwtape Letters *the next. I'd spy on the titles, then go to the library to look them up. I got a fifth of my education that year from a guy I didn't even know.*

I learned his name: the banal, WASPy surname, the given name rich with Black Muslim resistance. Spidery, long-suffering, and affable, but carrying those deep books, he stood out in the halls, even among an eclectic group of the city's gifted kids. He had the look of someone with a long-term plan and a set of protocols for achieving it. His bearing was impressive for fourteen, and his solitary stoicism made me nervous. I didn't like the idea of being the second-smartest person in World Civ.

I was making the long daily commute down from Evanston, coming out of eight years of Catholic mid-century-throwback schools whiter than Carrara marble. But after a few months at Ignatius, I got a feel for how the few black kids divided. The aristocrats moved with grace and intent, ready to conquer the world. All of them were going somewhere. One girl I knew from the home-brew computer club went on to become CEO of a Fortune 500 company and marry the world's twelfth-richest man.

Opposite the black aristocrats were the Talented Tenth, some of them on scholarship, others by way of the precarious middle class from neighborhoods only a little more secure than Rafi's. These two groups sat at different tables in the cafeteria and gave each other shit, when they spoke at all. Rafi often sat by himself

or with a clutch of outcast whites, so I couldn't make him out, at
first. But the first time he spoke up in World Civ, I knew.

He spoke like he was hungry to talk but wasn't sure he had a
right to. A plume of beautiful, improvised insights poured out of
him, after which he hunkered down into his desk trying to disappear. He mispronounced words—but only ones that were esoteric
and recherché. That meant he'd spent his years reading beyond any
opportunity to talk things over with teachers. The guy had blazed
his own trail here.

IN SOPHOMORE YEAR, he won the Keane Fellowship, the school's
most coveted cash prize for underclassmen. It bore my name, or
rather, I bore its. My father, who grew up in the Back of the Yards,
had gone to Catholic schools his whole life. Saint Ignatius himself
liked to quote Aristotle: Give me the child until the age of seven
and I will show you the man. A nun fished my seven-year-old dad
out of his criminal milieu and convinced him that he deserved the
best that Jesuit education had to offer. He got into Saint Ignatius
with the help of one of his junior high school teachers, and he credited the school with saving his life.

As soon as Micky Keane made his first million at the Board
of Trade, he fulfilled a teenage vow and gave a hefty sum to the
school to endow a fellowship for outstanding first-year academic
performance. Because the prize was so coveted, I suffered a fair
bit of collateral damage by association. My classmates figured that
the Saint Ignatius Fathers treated me preferentially, on account
of Micky Keane's largesse. I was under less-than-subtle pressure
from back home as well, because my father thought it would be
keen if a Keane could win the Keane.

But a Young won the Keane our year, and it only remained for
me to congratulate him. I knew he hung out in the library during
fourth period, and often for part of lunch. This was in the years
before the school underwent its massive expansion and renova-
tion. The library was still an archaic relic, a little penumbral, with

that musty marble-and-wood-polish smell of a Gilded Age time
hole. Big oak bookcases stood against the walls, topped by broken
pediments and lines of balusters.

Rafi Young had a favorite study table tucked away in the corner where he could sit out of sight while surveying the entire room.
I found him there, reading a book called Gödel, Escher, Bach. I'd
never heard of it. I later tracked it down and read it from cover to
cover three times. It changed my life.

It startled him, a perfect stranger coming up to assault him.
Kind of a high school faux pas. But it turned out I wasn't a perfect
stranger. He'd been scouting me out as well.

"Congratulations," I said.

"For what?" His sly smile knew full well.

"The fellowship. I guess we're both Keanes now."

"Peachy," he answered. I didn't get the joke until two days later.

"You play chess?"

I blush remembering the question, all these decades later. I'd
gotten good playing against my father, the manic pit trader, when
the pit was closed and he needed something to tide him over until
the insane game he played five days a week started up again. By
the time I was thirteen, we were playing tense matches several
times a week. Then, as with all our other contests, my father quit
chess forever when the best he could hope for against me was a
protracted draw.

Did Rafi know what I was doing, challenging him to a match?
From this distance, I'd guess he saw right through me. But if Rafi
wanted to dismiss the white nerd's gambit or call me out on it,
some part of him could not resist rising to the bait.

"A little," he said. I would learn that he barely knew how the
pieces moved. His game back then was cribbage, which he played
every weekend with his mother's father. The two of them would
watch Cubs games together—the wrong team for South Siders—
while playing mindless cards. Between those two sedate and out-
dated diversions, he had all the games he needed.

"You should come to Chess Club, then."

He pushed his glasses back up his nose and gave me that sleepy bodhisattva smirk that would become so familiar. "Whatever you say, brother."

I doubt he would have taken the dare except that the Chess Club met after school. Any excuse to go home as late as possible. Also, he wasn't about to let a privileged white kid from Evanston who somehow imagined that he was paying the Negro's tuition think that he could best Rafi Young at anything.

Three weeks later, he showed up for his first match. I later learned he'd spent those weeks reading chess books. Three weeks couldn't give him even a basic orientation of a game that had sixty-nine trillion ways of playing out both players' first five moves. He'd learned two reasonable starts as Black—a French defense for kingside openings and Slav defense for queenside. As White, he was hoping to get by with the tried-and-true but old-fashioned Ruy Lopez.

He'd explored the most likely possibilities for these three openings five or six moves out. Impressive, given how little time he'd had. The Jesuit coach, Father Reeves, tried to match him with one of the weaker of the two dozen club members.

"No, Father," he said, pointing at me. "I gotta play this guy."

We sat down across the board from each other, and he wouldn't stand up again until we'd each played White twice. We were the last two people in the room at the end of that afternoon. As Black, he defended with tenacity. His attacks as White showed a lot of creativity. But of course I slaughtered him, four games in a row. This was America, hardly a fair fight.

"Dude," he said, by way of congratulations after game four.

"You played well," I said.

He smiled that bodhisattva smile and shook his finger in the air to each syllable of his answer. "See you next week, asshole. And don't ever fuckin' patronize me again."

WHAT DID HE SEE IN ME? At first, just a smart, cocky North Sider, someone to measure himself against. Someone to beat.

If not the strongest player in the club, I was close to it. Chess made sense to me. Its series of open-information choices and consequences felt to me like clarity itself. It was a heroic adventure where—unlike the torment of daily life—destiny was yours to control. After programming, which I loved with my whole heart, chess was the closest thing to my religion.

I was coding at a high level, for a kid of fourteen. My favorite language was Pascal. In keeping with the times, I cranked out five-hundred-line strategy games and gave them away. Let a thousand flowers bloom, and all that. The gift culture was exploding the software scene, and my own power and competence were exploding along with it.

By decompiling a few of the early public-domain chess programs, I learned how they worked. I copied one and made it my own, improving the user interface, gussying up the graphics, deepening the look-ahead, adding some new openings, and strengthening the midgame strategies with a capture search algorithm. My program still couldn't beat any decent human player. No programs could, back then. But my code gave beginners a workout and a great way to improve their game.

With some effort, my father beat my program. He declared, "You're a fool to give it away."

I lifted my hands, helpless when it came to the real world. "What are my alternatives?"

My father set me up with a business plan. We bought several boxes of double-sided floppy disks, a disk duplicator, and five hundred self-seal plastic bags. For a label, my mother, who could have been a cartoonist, drew a picture of Shams-i Tabrīzī playing a game against a PC. We ran some ads in hobby magazines and sold my program for four dollars less than Sargon. Soon enough, I was making two hundred dollars a week.

That was crazy money for a kid, and all I did with it was buy *faster and more powerful hardware. It occurs to me only now, more than forty years later, that I was selling software that contained large pieces of other people's donated code.*

In short, I had a bit of a head start in what would become a long-running and multistage battle between Rafi Young and Todd Keane. I gave him a copy of version two of my chess program, to help him train. He thanked me, never mentioning that he had no access to a personal computer aside from the ones at school.

AT CHESS CLUB *we were expected to rotate opponents and keep track of our Elo ratings. This was to prepare us for ladders, playing against other high schools. But Rafi didn't want to play against anyone but me. Father Reeves badly wanted to keep his only black kid in the club. So rules were bent while no one was looking.*

Rafi got good fast. He had a stabbing, aggressive style, and he hated to hole up, even when playing Black. He kept reading, beyond the tame and dated books in the Saint Ignatius library. Among my first three dozen wins, we drew a game or two. By spring semester, he was beating me every fourth game.

Nevertheless, I'd find new ways to torture him: simultaneous games, blindfold games. One day, I went past his locker in that crowded second-floor hall and called out, "d4." (I loved to open with my queen pawn.) When he breezed past me on the stairwell on his way to third period, he called out, "Nf6." He'd gotten good at the Nimzo-Indian.

SO LONG AS *we were engaged in a sport that strengthened our minds, none of our parents objected when we stayed after school for hours. Chess Club was our way of avoiding home. Late in the middle of a protracted slugfest one autumn evening at Ignatius, in the papery, chill dark that was five p.m. in a Chicago October, he stopped the chess clock and said, "Hold on. Can I ask you something?"*

His voice hinted at another question that I'd asked myself so often since making friends with him: How much could one messed-up outsider nerd male adolescent trust another with his innermost discoveries?

"You can ask. Doesn't mean I have to answer."

"Whatever, fuckface." His long, expressive fingers splayed over the midgame between us. "Just . . . this. What do you see in this position?"

He was a pawn up, with better structure, but I was two moves away from trapping him in a devastating fork with my bishop, and we both knew it. That wasn't his question, though, and we both knew that, too.

"Why is this silly little game with its poofy little moves so damn addictive? Why is it all I want to do, all day long? Why is it . . . the most beautiful thing in the world?"

He used the b-word, but it didn't embarrass me. I rose to the bait. "It's the logic. Actions and patterns and deterministic consequences."

My willingness to answer in kind relieved him. But he frowned, wanting more.

"I mean: Every board state is like a computer program. Laws of 'If A then B' and 'While X do Y.'"

He shook his head. "Yeah. No. You're a little freakish. We know that about you, robo-man. Okay, that stuff is all in here? But . . . ?"

He slid my rook forward down the file from its safe spot on the back row to a wild outpost in the center of the board.

"Ha. See? Your pulse is going up. It's not logic. It's drama."

My pulse was going up in part because he was moving pieces around in a game in progress.

"But not just drama. Each of these dudes . . ."—he was moving our pieces around freely now—"has a personality. They each have a history. They're all on a path. And every time they move, they become . . . new power relations . . . each one, relative to all the others. . . ."

He looked up. Our game was chaos, but he had his answer.

"That's it! It's a story. It's a poem. It's fucking Gilgamesh. An epic work in progress."

"Fine. But you've wrecked this one."

He frowned again: disappointed in me. "Whatchu talkin' about, mofo?" In another few seconds, he returned the board to the state it was in when he'd asked his question. He was always a quick study. And it occurred to me that shooting the shit with this man was almost as fun as chess.

I GET VERTIGO REMEMBERING everything that happened to us in those years at Ignatius, as adulthood insinuated itself into our adolescent bodies. I see myself standing in front of those twenty-foot tall, massive oak front doors with the embossed lion's head, hearing the teenage frenzy behind them waiting for me as I pulled them open. We were living that epic work in progress, watching it unfold in front of us, move by adolescent move.

The mess of first sex, my timid experiments with pot, the free-for-all of social jockeying, all the changing games of prestige, self-invention, and group loyalty: life would never again be so saturated in possibility. But the teachers who formed me, the girls I thought I loved with such passion, the classmates whose respect I so desperately sought: they're all like characters in a novel that I can barely remember and have no need to read again. Only Rafi's and my running skirmish down those crowded halls—d4! Nf6! c4! e6! Nc3! Bb4!—still means anything to me. Only the love that I bore Rafi Young still needs replaying, before the game is done.

Evelyne beaulieu spent two summers diving with her father, first in Biscayne Bay and points in South Florida, then later off Klein Bonaire. On her very first ocean dive, she vowed to spend her life diving as often as she could.

"What's it like?" Baptiste asked. And she had no words to tell her infirm and landlocked little brother. How could she say? While she was diving, all her senses were deranged. Distance, color, even shape: in the bent light beneath the waves, the simplest forms defied description.

She plunged into the blue country, gliding through hillocks of staghorn and brain and fan corals while mobbed by snappers and soldierfish, grunts, rays, rock beauties, butterflies and angels, gobies and groupers, sergeant majors, blennies, turtles, triggerfish, sponges, tunicates, nudibranchs, and sea stars, too many to identify. Every new tank of air brought sights that might have come from a fever dream. On some dives, the forms were so fantastic that she wondered if nitrogen was drugging her brain.

She read Philippe Diolé's *L'Aventure sous-marine* the month it was published, when she was sixteen. In it, Philippe Tailliez, a friend of her father's and of Captain Cousteau's, said that diving could not be described. It was not like anything. But Tailliez showed Diolé a stanza from Rimbaud's *Le Bateau Ivre*:

> *J'ai rêvé la nuit verte aux neiges éblouies,*
> *Baiser montant aux yeux des mers avec lenteurs,*
> *La circulation des sèves inouïes,*
> *Et l'éveil jaune et bleu des phosphores chanteurs!*

> I dreamed of the green night with dazzled snow,
> To kiss rising slowly in the eyes of the seas,
> The circulation of astounding sap,
> And the yellow and blue awakening of the
>   singing phosphors!

Dazzled snows: yes. The constant white fall of living particles downward through the water column. *The circulation of astounding sap. The singing phosphors!* She had heard and seen them both. How did the poet know?

———

SHE LEARNED SOON ENOUGH that the secret of diving, like the secret of life, was protective coloration. At seventeen, she bound her breasts and cut her shoulder-length hair close to the skull so she could dive near the Lachine Rapids off Montreal's south shore without being challenged by self-appointed male authorities. A year later, she dove off Nova Scotia. The water was bone-crushing cold, even in the thickest wet suit. But she was Canadian. She observed invertebrates in the holdfasts of North Atlantic sugar kelp forests and submitted field notes to the mimeographed newsletter of the nascent international diving society under the name "E. Beaulieu." She let the editors believe they came from her father.

When the society president contacted Emile with admiration and thanks, the subterfuge stunned the engineer. Emile confronted his daughter. His crumpled smile was wide as ever, though the trust had leaked out of it.

"I take you diving, and you pretend to be me? Who taught you to be so sneaky? It wasn't your mother. Your mother never deceived anyone in her life. It wasn't me, was it? I can't even bluff at cards!"

She had no answer that an engineer could grasp. Her father's world was tensile strengths and rates of flow and mean time between failures. He was a creature of scientific rationalism, too moral to suspect what Evie had discovered: eager young girls required camouflage.

"Evolution, Papa." Survival of the most devious. "*Tout le monde le fait.*" Everyone does it.

Worse subterfuge was yet to come. In her last year of high school, Evie got an Anglophone girlfriend to rewrite her substandard

English personal statement for her application to Duke's under-graduate program. The heavily edited letter suggested a level of competence Evie didn't have. But she would have perjured herself again and again, to get into one of the best schools on the continent to offer comprehensive courses in ocean studies. That simple cheat made possible her whole life. How could it not be almost moral?

Her parents couldn't grasp how the timid kid who chewed her lips and fretted her cardigans to spaghetti had become a felon of self-assertion in a few short years. But to Evie, the metamorphosis felt as simple as breathing. Taciturnity was just desire that hadn't yet blossomed. The world of dry land never offered Evelyne Beaulieu a single thing worth her zeal. The ocean merited breaking all the rules.

She had found the secret of liberty and of life: disguise yourself and do what you need to. And all she needed was to dive.

———

DUKE UNIVERSITY ACCEPTED Evelyne Beaulieu in 1953, the first woman ever admitted into ocean studies. She survived four years of classes in Durham and three summer field research trips through ever-more-inventive feats of camouflage. She hid her extensive diving experience, refrained from challenging any of her professors' many errors, and laughed along with her male cohort's Cro-Magnon jokes. It wasn't hard to pretend to be what the Americans called a *good sport*.

Four years of fake naïveté came easily to a six-foot-tall, awkward, carrot-haired girl with a walloping French Canadian accent and errors in idiom that sent the locals into hysterics. She drew her strength from the coast and lived on ocean time. For four short years, Evelyne Beaulieu stood on the edge of the North American continent, feeling the great wave of her future curling over her and knocking her into the sand. And she rose from the froth howling, wanting more.

The safest way forward was to keep to the group. That's why they called it *schooling*. She made friends in the program—diving partners and topside pal-arounds. Boys to study with. Boys with whom to share field notes, grievances, and an occasional beer. Sometimes she missed women so intensely it surprised her. But most weeks she had too little free time to notice the loss.

Her ocean mania ripened into competence. Competence became knowledge, and knowledge—she marveled at this—made a handful of her fellow students fall for her. Certain kinds of scientific young men would always feel drawn to smart extraterrestrials. She doubted that her appearance in a swimsuit could be to blame. Yet somehow she grew into a woman who made her pals nervous and left some of them mumbling little bursts of deniable longing. She grew adept at not hearing—a protective adaptation all its own.

On holidays when she could get away, she explored the coast, sometimes accompanied by one admirer or another, more often alone. One long weekend, she rented a car and ventured out to the barrier islands at Hatteras, where she fell hopelessly in love with Ocracoke. Combing its beaches from noon to sunset made her feel the aimless joy she'd felt years before, diving off Biscayne with her father.

She walked for hours across the sedge-fringed shore, transfixed by the thought of a world after humans. The beach sank from high briar-covered dunes, past pockets of tidal pools, down into a glorious foreshore riddled with burrowing invertebrates and scoured by more kinds of shorebirds than she could name. At the bottom of the long, shallow run, fine sand churned in the breakers. The salt air tickled her lungs, and the wide expanse of wild shore, mile after unbroken mile, felt like a summons from her designer.

A place so concentrated with theaters of crazed production called out for some vow. Her sense of urgency didn't fade when she returned to Durham. Thoughts of Ocracoke helped her through the gauntlet of junior year when a semester too crammed with chemistry and physics left her on the brink of dropping out. School had turned pointless. She just wanted to dive—to be in and among the flocks of shorebirds and shoals of fish that turned and wheeled together as if they were a single life, which she believed they were.

She sat in a lecture on physical geography with seventy other students as the professor mocked Wegener's theory of continental drift. "It's a pretty thought, but nothing more than romantic moonshine."

Beaulieu raised her hand, shocking even herself. The man refused to see her. She was on her feet before she realized. Questions came out of her, stunning the room. What about the newly discovered undersea mountains in the middle of the Atlantic? The odd zebra stripes of magnetic reversal in rock so different from continental crust?

Through her twenty seconds of objections, the professor stood frozen onstage at the bottom of the auditorium bowl. At last, he grasped the fact that someone was interrupting him. "Young lady, there is no force on Earth strong enough to move continents around. Any intelligent high school boy can tell you that."

"Holmes," she said. "Magma cells."

The professor flicked his ear and frowned. "You have some kind of accent."

The whole hall came awake. A sympathetic soul in Beaulieu's row shouted, "Convection cells! In the mantle!"

A cement smile set across the professor's face. He shook his head in pity. "Oceanography is a science. And science requires evidence. As do exam answers in this course. Now, if you'll allow me to continue?"

————

THE AUTUMN BEFORE EVIE'S graduation was a maelstrom. She took an overload of classes and suffered proportionately. But by then her studies focused on marine life, so four or five hours of sleep were enough to carry her.

One course in epipelagic and coastal life culminated in a final project requiring the students to measure intertidal zonation on a sandy depositional shore. That meant performing a species inventory for each bounded region from the lowest tide to the highest. The task would take a pair of researchers two full days.

Her partner for the project was Bart Mannis. Everyone in the program called him Limpet. He owned a 1952 Buick Special in good condition, looked like a well-kept beatnik, had a way of saying "maybe" to almost everything, and exuded a pleasant brackish scent that got brinier the longer he was out in the field. By all accounts, the man knew his snails.

He and Evie had gotten along fine on prior group expeditions. They enjoyed a rapport free from rivalry or expectation. Limpet was that rare boy with nothing to prove except a mad enthusiasm for things that excreted their own shells. Evie herself might even have chosen him for a final project partner if the instructor hadn't selected him for her.

They had their pick of the entire North Carolina coast. Limpet had ideas for a spot, some of them even useful. But Beaulieu was sitting on an agony of possibility. The choice tormented her. She could keep her magic Ocracoke to herself, or she could surrender her secret to this man and spend two full days surveying a place that made her feel as if she, too, were another littoral creature on a migration pattern longer than her own brain could grasp.

She took the measure of her assigned partner. Limpet was compliant. He knew how to do a species blitz. He even seemed a little in awe of her. And he could identify gastropods that to her were stony blurs. Above all, he owned a reliable ride.

The fellow would have to be initiated. She grabbed him by his button-down collar and swore him to secrecy. "If you tell anyone about this place, I will gut you with an oyster shucker."

"Don't want that, E.B. Really don't want that."

Maybe something about the boy's practicality appealed to her as well.

Had they kissed already, before that Halloween adventure? Yes, she would decide, seven decades later, diving off her hidden seamount in the Tuamotus. They must have kissed at least once, and then some. But surely nothing contractual. Nothing that committed her.

She took him to her stretch of wandering barrier island. The gray-blue, moody grandeur of the place survived Limpet's presence. He spun in place in the swash zone for a long time, muttering, "Oh, yes." The boy was no slouch in the perception department.

All that Saturday, they lay on their bellies with trowels, a stack of graded sieves, two 20x triplet loupes, calipers, a tally counter, a slide rule, three field texts, and battered notebooks. Centimeter by centimeter, they worked their way up toward the backshore, staying just above the advancing tide. The surf made it hard to hear each other, and neither one of them felt like talking. They counted every species of lichen on the action-painted rocks. A ghost crab shook its one large indignant claw at them. Limpet turned up half a leathery loggerhead eggshell. It fell to Beaulieu to identify a curling pair of polychaete worms. Going on noon, they pushed their luck in one rich spot and wound up getting lapped in a surge of waves. They only laughed and went on counting.

Throughout the morning, she came across caches of skates' eggs. Something about those weird black horned pillows moved her—the future calling. Limpet found her holding one, lost in a reverie.

"Mermaid's purses."

Beaulieu stared at him.

"That's what we called them, growing up."

And though he hadn't invented the name, although it was in fact quite common, Evelyne's eyes pinned him with admiration. Bart Mannis. Bart Mannis, that stranger who had washed up on this beach with her. Her field lab partner. The oddest thing on this beach.

She turned her head in both directions. The shore ran forever, leaving her in the dead center of a globe-sized paperweight. Bliss was so simple. Just hold still and look.

Their work that afternoon walked backward through the morning's footsteps. They remeasured the zones that high tide flooded and low tide laid bare again. Evie lay coated in seaweed and wet sand. She scraped herself bloody on the edges of broken bivalves, a clicker in one hand and a loupe in the other, counting off creatures neither entirely of land nor water, beings that had to reinvent themselves four times a day.

A few paces upward onto the continent or downward into the ocean, and the mix of inhabitants changed. Five distinct communities spread themselves across twenty meters of beach within a one-meter vertical rise. Five different worlds hitched a ride on the barrier island as that makeshift sandbar itself migrated back and forth between land and sea through the run of centuries.

They camped on the dunes in a gap in the thorny smilax. The sky cleared and spilled out stars. Every breath smelled of silica and iodine. Their fire on the beach was less than minuscule, and its curl of smoke rose into a night too enormous to say. A hunter's moon pulled at the willing water, crashing it against the edge of the continent, and the pulse of that liquid piston was better than any song.

There was so much to life, too much, more than Beaulieu could do justice to, more than any living thing could guess at or merit. She loved it all, even humans, for without the miracle of human consciousness, love for such a world would be just one more of a billion unnamed impulses.

She wondered, in the dark, after their fire was out and they had retired to their tents, if Limpet might come tap on her canvas tent flap, and she was grateful that night to all the uncountable tiny and tidal gods of the coast that he didn't.

———

THE NEXT DAY they were mostly quiet on their drive back to Durham. Something had changed between them after the night's fire on Ocracoke, some shift toward intimacy she wasn't ready for.

His eyes on the road, Limpet asked, "Do you have a life philosophy?"

"Life philosophy?" The phrase felt like a contradiction in terms.

"Words you live by."

She didn't live by words. She lived by life. But the question was sweet, and she did her best. She fed him that classic bit of Quebecoise wisdom.

"*Attache ta tuque et lache pas la patate!*"

"Meaning?"

"Put on your little beanie cap and don't release the potato."

Bart Mannis laughed so hard he almost ran them off the highway. But the meaning was clear, wasn't it? Hold on tight and keep going. Just keep going. Like any good creature of the tides.

———

IN HER LAST SEMESTER AT DUKE, Evelyne applied to the Scientific Diving Program at the Scripps Institution of Oceanography. They wrote back in March. *We regret to inform you that we are unable to grant you admission to our graduate program for next fall. . . .*

Rejected. The letter made no sense. It wasn't possible: no one in her graduating class had a CV to match hers. Two days passed with Evie in a zombie state, unable to get off the sofa of her Durham apartment.

She wrote to the director of admissions and requested an appeal. A letter came back offering her a twenty-minute in-person interview in which to make her case. *Should we not hear from you within ten days, we will consider the matter closed.*

Powerful men were playing a game with her, sure that she had no countermove. And they were right. She lay on the upper bunk of her shared bedroom, weeping into a wadded-up Blue Devils sweatshirt so her midwestern home economics roommate wouldn't hear. She pictured herself returning to Quebec and enduring years of abuse as her mother lectured her about hubris and realistic expectations.

Out of disaster, a plan arose. At last she roused herself and put on her prettiest blouse and culottes. Then she walked two miles down Chapel Hill Road to Bart Mannis's house. The man with the 1952 Buick Special in excellent condition.

It was after ten o'clock at night when she arrived, but Bart was happy to be roused from bed. She knew he would be.

"How would you like to see the surf come in from the west?" She gave the question a little grin, as if there might be other new things to see, along the way, if he was lucky. "San Diego and back, over spring break. I pay for everything."

Her friend stood dumbfounded in his tiny sitting room. He looked her up and down, trying to diagnose this sudden onset of French Canadian lunacy. The only other time he'd ever seen her reckless was on a dive off Diamond Shoals looking at shipwrecks when she almost ran her tank.

"You couldn't have called ahead?"

"*Écoute*. . . . Listen. I know how crazy. . . ."

She showed him her rejection letter along with the follow-up offering her twenty minutes of appeal. Limpet winced. He himself had the luxury of choosing between staying on at Duke to study marine chemistry and heading up to get a degree in physical ocean-ography at Woods Hole. And his GPA at Duke was a quarter point below hers.

He looked up, head shaking. "This isn't right. You're one of the best of our cohort. The best diver of any of us. They don't even say why they rejected you!"

She held his gaze, trying to make desperation look like determination. "I'd like to find out."

His own eyes declared, *Five thousand miles. A whole week of your life wasted on the longest of long shots. You've gone off the deep end.* But out loud he only said, "I really, really like tall girls."

———

THE TRIP MEANT THREE DAYS of nonstop driving. Everything Evie needed fit in one small duffel bag. They brought sandwiches, cookies, and water in a huge thermos. They read out loud to each other from *The Silent World*, although they'd already read that book four and a half times between the two of them. Every other chapter, Bart badgered her again to tell him about the author. His voice was reverent, as if Evie had a hotline to one of the saints.

"I told you, I only met him three times, when I was a child."

"Yes, but what was he *like*?"

"*Câlice!* What do you want? He was kind and smiled a lot and he said he would have become an aviator if he hadn't gotten into a bad car crash. And he had a fantastic French nose."

She knew what the great man was doing for the oceans. She didn't mind that Cousteau was being called the inventor of the aqualung, even if M. Gagnan and M. Commeinhes and men like her father had done the work. But for writers about the ocean, there was an American woman whom Evie loved more.

She had proposed *The Sea Around Us*, way back in Alabama. Bart demurred. She tried again in the middle of the journey when she was back riding shotgun. "Come on, man. You'll love it. It will get us through the rest of Texas."

The title alone made Bart grimace. "Isn't that for children?"

"Children? Your hero Cousteau is the biggest child on the planet!"

"Somebody's crabby. Maybe you should take a nap."

The man exasperated her. Maybe she hated him.

They said little on the long haul from Amarillo to Tucumcari. But by the time they got through the Sonoran Desert, they were giving each other shoulder rubs again. Drunk with sleep deprivation, he made plans. "Let's visit each other next year. No matter . . . what happens."

Then the Pacific lay all in front of them, a third of the world.

From the rocks along La Jolla Cove beneath the Scripps campus they watched the water retreat down the nearshore. The back of Evie's throat tasted of kelp and fog. Even her first glimpse of the planet's greatest ocean—the surf's relentless growl, four billion years old—wasn't enough to lift her hopes, which ebbed faster than any tide. She had put herself and her best friend through days of crazy stress and expense to make a twenty-minute pointless point.

"You're right," she told Bart. But, sitting next to her on the barnacled rocks, he was too brain-dead from the trip to ask her what he was right about.

Nights of sleeping in the car had not improved what 1957 Madison Avenue would have referred to as her sex appeal. She sink-showered in a woman's bathroom in the original Scripps Building and changed into the belted silk shirtdress that had hung from the backseat clothes clip for the last several days.

"Is it okay?" she asked Bart.

The man was congenitally unable to lie. "I'm sorry, E.B. You look like barracuda food."

"Thanks for your honesty, eh?" She patted his cheek and stumbled into her interview.

The office of the dean of admissions was also a working lab. Six-hundred-gallon saltwater tanks formed a U along three walls around Edward Michelson's desk. He stood to shake her hand. The force of his grip baffled her. Was she making him nervous?

She sat in the hot seat in front of his desk and pleaded her case. The facts were unassailable. "My grades and test scores are strong. My letters of recommendation . . . are even better. I am a first-rate candidate."

Having to say so made her sick. Failing to say so would have made her sicker.

"We get many first-rate applicants. The best in the country."

"Yes. But none with more dive experience than I have."

Dean Michelson leaned back in his chair, studying some crib sheet on the ceiling. "Tell me what you know about Langmuir circulation."

She suppressed a scream. She had applied to study marine biology, not physical oceanography. But after counting to three in silence, she leapt into the complex math of rolling vortices and their effects on plankton and nekton. Her interviewer cut her off just as she was warming to the topic.

"Where do you come down on continental drift?"

The snare was obvious, even before it was sprung. The most controversial topic in all the earth sciences had been a hot war long before her lecture-hall shoot-out back at Duke. In the two years since then, her suspicions about consensual wisdom had only deepened. But any answer she gave would be wrong to half the people in the field. Edward Michelson himself might be in the grip of old ignorance. She took a breath and plunged.

"The evidence is stronger, every year. Those who can't accept it are going to look foolish, by the time I'm your age."

The Institute's designated gatekeeper smiled. "You think it'll take that long?"

She looked down at her lap, where she held the oilcloth-covered journal she had kept since the age of twelve. It held a decade of meticulous handwritten diving logs. She had accumulated more hours at depths below fifty feet than the most experienced man on the admissions committee.

"Here," she said, and pushed the journal across the desk. She'd given up thinking that it would make any difference. But she nursed some small hope that it might still shame him.

The dean of admissions smirked at the colorful hibiscus print on the journal's cover. "What's this?"

Beaulieu just tipped her head toward the book, daring him.

The decider of lives flipped through the pages as her handwriting changed from French to English, from childish balloon printing to clean collegiate cursive. While he read, the three walls of gigantic tanks filled with fish of all colors gave Evelyne merciful distraction. A reddish brown, misshapen monster caught her eye as it rooted in the sand at the bottom of one tank. She called out before she realized she was talking.

"*Gadon ço!* Is that *Dactylopus*? I've never seen . . ."

Dean Michelson jerked up from her dive logs. "Yes. From one of our collection trips to the China Sea."

She did not ask permission to stand and cross behind his desk for a look. Permission didn't matter anymore. Nor did impressions.

She had traveled across the continent for nothing. She could at least look at the remarkable creature, while she was here.

The fingered dragonet was so bizarre, so implausible, so grotesque, so beautiful, she could barely credit it. Shocking blue spots on the leading spikes of its dorsal fin waved above the twin bulge of eyes. Its blood-orange lips were the color of her hair, at least when her hair was clean. Its skin was the perfect, mottled match to the pebbled bed it dragged across. A dragonet, yes, with further blue stripes adding a touch of hideous elegance to its flamboyant tail. She was this fish—a spindly horror in a sweet shirtwaist dress. Beaten down by days of sleepless driving, watching her chance to spend her life among the wildest ravings of nature slip away, she let the burn come up her throat and into her eyes.

A voice at her side said, "It's really something, isn't it?"

She turned to see her tormentor bending down and gazing into the tank with the same wonder she felt, as if it were his first time seeing *Dactylopus*, too. She fought to take control back over her own voice.

"Yes. It's something."

Dean Michelson kept his eyes locked on the fish. "Forgive us. We thought you were lying."

She recoiled from the apology as from a slap. She straightened, and the man straightened, too, repentant but looking her in the eye at last.

"We didn't think anyone your age . . . any woman . . . could have been diving as long as you claimed you've been diving."

Silence felt like her strongest suit. She tried not to make the silence sound righteous.

"Do you think you could come back at four p.m.? I'd like to make some calls."

"Yes. I think I could."

When Evelyne went back into Dean Michelson's office late that afternoon, he greeted her with the news. "I'm sorry, but I can't offer you admission into the graduate program for this fall."

She let loose a whispered stream of joual invective so vile that not even her three days of sleep deprivation excused it.

Dean Michelson regarded her from behind his desk in the U of aquariums. "I won't ask for a translation. But I *will* offer you admission for the following fall, providing you agree to serve for five and a half months on a new research dive boat we're sending out to the Coral Triangle."

She blinked. Then blinked again. Her eyes would not stop shuttering, like the eyes of a mudskipper transiting from water to land.

"Not much lead time. I'm sorry. The team sails in a month. We're desperate for experienced divers. There aren't that many of you, yet. One of our best just backed out, and another slipped and fell on a wet deck and gave himself two compound fractures."

Evelyne Beaulieu sat in her supplicant's chair, slack as a bluefin tuna skewered with a speargun. At last she let belief take hold, and her eyes welled up. Dean Michelson sat gripping the arms of his office chair, wondering if he needed to rescind the invitation. But she rallied and thanked him, trying not to be too pathetically grateful.

"It would be . . . perfect. It will be a dream."

"It will be neither, I promise you. Some of my colleagues think it's foolish to offer you this spot. But you seem like you can handle other people's opinions."

He held her gaze. He did not look confident. She tried to stare back, willing him to see that she was, in fact, a force of nature equal to this occasion.

"Before we announce this to the public, you're going to need training in how to handle the press."

Her sniffling stopped, like a needle ripped from a record player. "I'll talk to the press?"

"Thirty-seven young male scientists and one redheaded twenty-two-year-old Canadienne, trapped at sea together for half a year? Nothing that the newspapers might be interested in."

The year was 1957. Pepsi was offering to help the modern

housewife with the hard work of staying slim. Alcoa announced a bottle cap that even a woman could open—*without a knife blade, a bottle opener, or even a husband!*

"Oh," Evelyne Beaulieu said, and bowed her head. "Yes. Of course. I see."

———

EVIE AND LIMPET TOOK egg-salad sandwiches down to La Jolla Cove. A trio of sea lions had come up onto the rocks, and the air was a bouquet of sagebrush, beach aster, and gull guano. The water was the coldest bit of mix anywhere along the whole San Diego coast, but clear enough to see bright orange patches of Garibaldis just offshore. A little farther out, the great upwelling of deepwater nutrients into the photic zone fed one of the greatest nurseries of life on the planet.

Evie pretended she wasn't euphoric. Bart Mannis pretended he wasn't morose.

"Will you take it?"

She punched him in the shoulder. "What do you think? Are you insane?"

"No, you should. Obviously. I would, if I were you. But then, if I were *you* you, not *me* you, I'd have to face the firestorm."

"Who cares about the firestorm? The American newspapers are not going to follow an ocean research vessel all the way to East Timor."

"So . . . what do we do now?"

Her long, narrow frame froze at that syllable, *we*. She supposed he meant the pact they'd made while on the cross-country drive, to see each other next year. He couldn't possibly hold her to that. She couldn't imagine why he would want to.

"What do you mean?"

He studied the sea lions on the rocks below. Mating season was over. No territory needed defending. And yet, agitation still ruled them all. One large cow tipped forward and slid into the

ocean, turning from a terrestrial shambling cripple into an aquatic
prima ballerina.

"E.B. Don't you have to go back to North Carolina? What
about all your stuff? How will you get back out here in just three
and a half weeks? *Fly?*"

She heard everything that was decent in Limpet struggle not to
say out loud what he had every right to say. She had used him. Used
his car. Taken advantage of his good nature and the fact that he
was in love with her. And now that he could do nothing more for
her, she was casting him aside.

Her hands closed around the small change in her jacket pocket.
She looked down at the rocks.

"I have an idea. What do you say? Let's get married."

————

THE FIRESTORM WAS WORSE than she expected. The journalists
at the press conference were relentless.

"You *really* don't think it's anything special, that you'll be the
only woman on board?"

"Listen. I have a degree from Duke University. I trained for
four years in every aspect of ocean science, with a major in marine
biology. My father helped invent the aqualung. I have been diving
for longer than all but a few people on Earth. I am qualified to collect samples, make identifications, keep good records of location,
depth, salinity, current, and sunlight for all the finds, prepare the
best specimens for museums. . . ."

"You won't just be mopping the decks?"

"We'll be gone for more than five months. I imagine we'll all do
plenty of mopping."

"How does your husband feel about your going?"

"Why don't you ask him?"

She pointed out Limpet, standing in the back of the room behind
the seated members of the press. A grin of wild pride took hold of
her face. Life had become great fun. Maybe she did love him.

Another reporter took up the attack. "Some people say that women at sea bring bad luck."

"Some women say that some journalists' bait might not be worth taking!"

The scattered laughter changed into applause.

"But . . . almost forty men at sea for almost half a year. . . . You really don't anticipate any problems?"

The men at Scripps had groomed her with an answer: *science and professionalism*. But the question had come up with such boring frequency that she finally broke.

"If you want to talk about sex life, ask me about groupers. Ask me about coral sex parties. Ask me about the fish that can change from one sex to the other, depending on what is needed. Insane!"

In the end, the worst headline the expedition had to face was:

LONG TALL EVIE SETS TO SEA
THIRTY-SEVEN MEN IN TOW
FORESEES NO DIFFICULTIES

They sailed, the thirty-eight of them, into the wildest place on Earth. For half a year, from the Philippines to Malaysia to New Guinea, the Research Vessel *Ione* crisscrossed five million square kilometers of ocean, skirting the world's largest mangrove forest and hanging suspended above a third of the world's fishes and three-quarters of the world's reef-building shallow corals.

The *Ione* was just over two hundred feet long and crammed with wet and dry lab space alongside the cramped quarters. So many people confined to so small a floating hamlet for so long were sure to have problems. But these three dozen capable men— and one competent woman—were on the voyage of their lives, out on the open ocean, skirting the most fantastic coasts, making daily discoveries, engaged in activity as meaningful as any of them could need. Keeping the ship in shape and doing the daily science left little time and energy for drama.

There had been romance and sex and love on research voyages

since before the Phoenicians. The enlistment of a woman added little to the mix. If anything, Evie's presence on the *Ione* kept the rest of the crew on better behavior than they might have shown otherwise. Plenty of the men fell for her and wanted her, and maybe a couple blurted poetry at her or brazened out a cheeky proposition or two, in rare private moments. Evelyne handled these as she saw fit, and there were no lasting consequences.

But mostly the scientists onboard the *Ione* treated her as one of the gang. They laughed and ate and drank with her, split her shifts and worked her into all rotations, gave her shit, patronized her, were fiercely protective in their awkward male ways, and spent long days side by side, diving, collecting, and analyzing finds, often forgetting her sex for hours at a time.

For Evelyne, shipboard life sometimes resembled Duke field trips. She'd had years of experience remaining docile in the face of mannish explanations, suffering male banter with a smile, doing twice the work for half the credit. She had no trouble playing by the rules until the rule-makers weren't looking.

The RV *Ione* had been built as a private yacht before the Navy bought it to use as a patrol boat in the war. After decommissioning, the ship was refitted for ocean study. The initial plan was for an old-school oceanographic vessel outfitted for blue-water science conducted with salinometers, chemical testers, gauges, cables, dredges, drift and Nansen bottles, Secchi discs, samplers, nets, and water-column profilers—the kind of science where the scientists only got wet in high seas and wild weather. But, overhauled for the long voyage, the *Ione* became one of the first boats kitted out for the brave new world of scuba, where at last humans could thrive for a while in the world they were studying.

Most of the seas the ship explored had never seen an aqualung. Each time Evie, still just twenty-two, slipped into one of these virgin spots she felt a pressure greater than the water. Hers was often the first good look any human had ever gotten. She had to get it right.

Wherever she dove in the Coral Triangle, fish of every shape and stripe and color schooled around her. Curious, they came from

distant neighborhoods of the reef to investigate this novelty that
had come to visit. It took no imagination for Evelyne to understand: these beings were doing their own research.

At times she treaded in place, swarmed by the wildest assort-
ment of Dr. Seuss creations—indigo, orange, silver, every color
in the spectrum from piebald nudibranchs to bright, bone-white
snails sporting forests of spines. The sea buoyed her, like warm silk
on her bare arms and legs. She hung suspended in the middle of
reefs that mounded up in pinnacles, domes, turrets, and terraces.
She was a powerless angel hovering above a metropolis built by billions of architects almost too small to see. At night, with underwater lights, when the coral polyps came out to feed, the reef boiled
over with surreal purpose, a billion different psychedelic missions,
all dependent on each other.

On a dive in the Raja Ampat archipelago, off the islands of the
Four Kings, she forgot entirely that she was doing science. She felt
like a babe in Toyland, set loose in the greatest playground any
child had ever seen. She played hide-and-seek with octopuses and
tag with pygmy seahorses. She reeled from the surreal stripes of
colonial anemones. Her fingers teased the spreading nets of gorgo-
nians. She did headstands to peer into the cracks and ledges at the
base of corals, the hideouts of action-painted mandarin fish and
elegant green eels.

The prurient journalists were proved right. That voyage did
descend into one spectacular orgy, and half the crew enjoyed it
together under the water's surface. On the one night of the year
when the moon's cycle and the temperature of the water both
declared their undecodable *now*, the whole reef exploded in a
heave of joyous sex. All the colonies in every direction for as far
as Evie could see shot their trillions of sperm and egg into the sea
at once, and a handful of humans with dim lights watched the sea
turn into a swirling blizzard of yellow, orange, red, and white. As
the flecks eddied all around her, something in Evie whispered, *I
could die now. I have seen the relentless engine, the inscrutable
master plan of Life, and it will never end.*

———

SHE WROTE TO LIMPET—Bart, *her husband*—and posted the letters from scattered ports of call:

> *It's almost stupid to count species. The cnidarians alone*
> *are probably a thousand kinds, and so many that none of*
> *us have ever seen. How many species still to discover? As*
> *many as you want. I could spend the rest of my life naming*
> *things after you and me!*

He could not write her back, there being no way to reach the wandering boat, and his questions about moving and garage sales and storage and house rental options and deferred education and emergency stopgap employment and their entire improvised future went unanswered.

No one, of course, ever discovered a *new* species. But when Evelyne did commit to documenting her own large, unknown creature, it was an unearthly amphipod that she named after her father, that tinkerer with the soft laugh, an unearthly man who pitched her into this unearthly place and who left the Earth in the fourth month of her first expedition: *Ingolfiella emilea.*

———

FIVE MONTHS ON, she returned to land. She and Limpet fell into each other's arms in a cheap hotel two blocks from Harbor Drive in the Gaslamp Quarter of San Diego. It was only the tenth time they'd slept together. The bed pitched and rolled beneath them, for him on account of his long-deferred passion and for her because her seagoing brain did not yet believe in solid land. It took two full nights and two slow days of laughter, play, and room service before Bart Mannis realized that the sources of their respective excitement were not fully aligned.

Life back on land left Evie in a low-grade depression. The months of terrible food, cramped quarters, pitching decks, sleepless nights,

and a ship's head from hell were over, taking adventure and cama-
raderie with them. But news had cut through her every despair.

"Listen. I must tell you." She tried to choose her words, but her
heart rushed forward. "You won't believe it. It's so amazing."

Bart grinned and rolled toward her, ready for yet one more
fairy-tale account from the queendom where she had reigned for
half a year. His own stories of life on land during her absence had
dried up within hours of her return.

"They have received a wonderful grant. The *Ione* will make
another trip, probably in the spring."

He returned her enthusiasm, one marine scientist to another.
"That's great. Good for them. Good for America. Good
for oceanography."

Then he realized the source of her joy.

"Oh, you're not seriously thinking . . . ? What about grad
school? We talked all this through."

She rushed to reassure him. "I'll enroll in classes for the fall
semester and stay with you in La Jolla until at least the holidays.
Unless the schedule steps up and we sail sooner than planned. I
won't be away for long!"

"How long?"

"A season and a little. A little more. Another half a year."

He rolled over on his back and looked up at his future. She
studied him. He had waited for her. He was so gentle and steadfast,
for a male, and she was lucky to have married so calm and trusting a person.

He spoke to the road map in the cracked ceiling. "This isn't
going to work, is it?"

"What do you mean? Of course it's going to work. It will be
beautiful. We did so well, these last five months."

He had to smile, at least with half his mouth. "You did brilliantly."

"I'll be back before you know it."

"And then you'll be gone again."

She wanted to fight this accusation with righteousness. But a gap had opened between them in the bed, beneath the crumpled bedsheet. She flailed out to find his wrist.

"It will work."

His fingers curled around to find hers. "This isn't the life I wanted."

But it's the life you get, she thought. *And better than almost any other.* But aloud, she said, "One year for me, and then a year for you. We keep talking about everything."

He tossed her hand aside. "You call this talking? This is just an announcement! We've already given you half a year!"

She flinched from the creature shouting at her from the other side of the stained and rented bed. She didn't recognize him. He didn't recognize himself. He lay back down and put a hand across his face. "I'm sorry. Uncalled-for."

"No," she said. "I called for it."

She wanted to take his hand again. Maybe he wanted to take hers. But neither closed the distance between them. The hand over his face slid back and hooked his neck. It took him two tries to turn his breathing into words.

"Evelyne? I think it's me or this trip."

In the sandy afternoon light, her shame was not distinct from excitement. She closed her eyes, and behind her lids, she saw the cerulean reefs of Raja Ampat, the schools of curious butterflyfish in their blazing yellows and blue-rimmed false eyes investigating her, welcoming her back. She said nothing.

He propped himself up on his elbows. "I guess that means it's the trip."

She reached out to lay her hand on his shoulder blade, but he jerked away. Then he mastered himself again, reached out, and grazed her hand. He rolled off his end of the bed and stepped into his dungarees. She wondered if he meant to get dressed and disappear, leave her alone in this dingy hotel room and vanish from her life like a dead person.

"Come on," he said. "Let's get some lunch. Maybe go out to

Coronado. We can talk about lawyers and divorce when it's not such a nice day." Then he crumpled and hid his face in his hands. He held it for a while. When he bared it again, he smiled.

"Of course you'd choose the ocean. Any sane person would."

She felt a calm like the stilled winds at the equator. She took his wrist and cradled it. He didn't pull away. His eyes skipped from hers, refusing everything. Then they drifted back.

"I—I can't. . . . I'm not going to be able to leave you, am I?"

She shook her head so morosely that it made him laugh out loud in pain. He closed his eyes, as if safety might lie in not looking at her.

"Okay. Remind me again? About the beanie and the potato?"

"Put the beanie on. Do not release the potato."

"Don't release the potato."

"Never release the potato."

———

SHE WAS ON HER third research voyage on the RV *Ione* when she heard the news of the *Trieste*.

Bart was home in La Jolla, finishing his doctorate. His resentment at her time away had softened as his own work on the global ocean conveyor grew more interesting and rewarding. Evelyne's first attempt at graduate school was lost at sea. It made little sense to train for a career that she was already enjoying, and her months on the boat made for better entries on her curriculum vitae than the same number of months in any classroom. The ocean was a relentless teacher, and while Evelyne often had to scramble to fill in the gaps of what she might have mastered at Scripps, her million-square-mile school served lessons that no human being had ever learned before.

She and the *Ione* both only scratched the surface. They were cruising off the coast of Guam in the first year of the new decade when news of Piccard and Walsh in the *Trieste* came over the radio. The two men had descended seven miles, into total darkness far below the thermocline, down into the Mariana Trench near the

Philippines, in a pressure sphere attached to a float chamber filled with gasoline for buoyancy. The tiny sphere, barely large enough to contain both men, had a single plexiglass window that cracked six miles down. Piccard and Walsh took almost five hours to reach the bottom of the Challenger Deep. They stayed there only twenty minutes before making the long trip back to the surface.

All the way down that seven-mile column and all the way back up again, they saw life. Wild, bizarre monsters unlike anything outside of nightmares. Organisms that glowed and pulsed, that took on surreal shapes, their amorphous bodies surviving pressure greater than fifteen thousand pounds per square inch. Her whole life Evelyne had been taught that nothing could live so far down, under such pressure, so far from sunlight. But life was never very good at obeying human logic.

Evelyne and her shipmates got drunk on the news. They sat in a circle on deck, tipping back beers around a trio of kerosene lamps, trying to do the math. At night on the open ocean, in the pitch-dark, under several thousand stars: there was no other way to understand the size of the planet, the extent of the universe, the playing field of life.

It was 1960, and the best oceanographers on Earth didn't know the average depth of the ocean. "But say it's between three and four thousand meters," a crewmate said. "Now spread that depth around three-quarters of the planet."

Evie spoke the thought for all of them. "And it's alive, every cubic meter." Alive and alien.

Someone laughed. "Ninety percent of the biosphere is underwater!"

"Ninety-nine!"

No human being knew what life on Earth really looked like. How could they? They lived on the land, in the marginal kingdom of aberrant outliers. All the forests and savannas and wetlands and deserts and grasslands on all the continents were just after-thoughts, ancillaries to the Earth's main stage.

Speculation turned amber as the lanterns burned low. Talk

turned to philosophy, and then to song, as it sometimes did as the boat rocked under a sky swarming with stars. Evie sat forward in a sling canvas chair, smiling and pretending to sing along. But a fabulous truth had her by the brain stem.

She looked out on the black swells and understood. Every main branch of taxonomy was there beneath the waves she floated on, while only a few had made it up onto the land. The mainspring of life would go on ticking, driving the gears of evolution, oblivious to anything that humans got up to above the surface. To the entities down there in a place as dark and hostile as outer space, life on land could come and go. Khrushchev might lob a few nuclear warheads at Eisenhower on Ike's way out, provoking Dulles's "massive retaliation," and life at the bottom of the Mariana would not skip a beat.

The drink flowed, and the celebration with it. The night and the news and the song that it raised among her people made Evelyne feel so beautiful. And the beauty that she took onto herself made her shipmates seem beautiful to her, too. She was propositioned three times after the hootenanny trickled out, and only two of those offers were obvious jokes. She spanked her suitors and sent them to bed, and every shipboard organism on two legs was satisfied.

Evelyne Beaulieu fell into the happiest sleep. Humans had seen living things seven miles underwater, in the bottommost regions of the ocean. She couldn't believe it. *Life* was beyond belief, beyond the capacity for belief that life itself had tinkered into being. No land-based brain could grasp the size of the experiment. Her cryptic water world was nothing but propositions, down to the bottom.

———

SHE TURNED AND FOLLOWED MONA into the heart of Makatea Spa. The manta weighed around a thousand kilos, while Beaulieu, in all her gear, barely broke a sixth of that. But her two-hand underwater camera tugged her down to the spot where Mona glided.

She glanced up over her left shoulder to spot her minder. Wai

Temauri, suspended near the surface, shot her two thumbs-up and issued a stream of enthusiastic bubbles. She preferred to dive alone and had done it often in her long life. But her Makatean dive-boat pilot would not let her out of his sight. No ninety-two-year-old member of the Ocean Elders was going to die on his watch. And Evelyne wasn't winning any quarrels with someone three times her weight and a third her age. She raised her thumb in return and dove deeper.

Business was brisk this morning at the cleaning kiosks. Fish of all sizes and ferocity, desperate to be rid of parasites, were all on their best behavior. Half a dozen batfish queued up, waiting their turn and punishing all cheaters. Even the killer sharks feigned docility and love.

Beaulieu moved in with the camera as one six-foot requiem shark opened his mouth and kept it open as a clutch of wrasses swam blithely between the rows of teeth. Several more mobbed its dorsal surface and swam up into its gill slits. Evelyne did not look to see what Wai thought of her close-up. She didn't need to. She would hear about it back on the boat. Ten times more people died each year from dinoflagellates than from shark attacks. But her friend Wai could not protect her from microscopic protists.

She was not a shark whisperer. Nor did she seek out thrills. She just needed to get up close and see. Her only job was to observe and describe, while the Rule of Men, at every level, was aimed at keeping her safe from that danger. She felt no need to defy that Rule. All she needed was to dive a little deeper and evade it. To learn the game that the creatures down there were playing, then put her amazement into words.

———

WAI TEMAURI PILOTED THE BOAT back toward Makatea, across what looked to Evelyne like a featureless tract. The open sea was a calendar consisting of one blank page—no days or weeks, not even months, really. Seasons of sorts, but no years, not even centuries, unless you happened upon a garbage patch in the middle of a gyre

or caught sight of a ship sailing from China to San Diego loaded
with twenty thousand containers.

That timelessness had driven her to a life at sea. The sun and
wind, currents and waves, the smell and color of the changing air
and water, the tilt of shadows, the roll of the horizon: all these
she could read. But out of sight of land, human time vanished,
and human geography with it. Evelyne loved that, beyond anything
else she'd ever loved: the feeling that the globe was still mostly
unknown, mostly unknowable. That she was in the middle of life,
while still being nowhere at all.

She could decode the surface of the sea as well as most people who'd ever lived. But Wai Temauri could read things in open
water invisible to Evelyne. The whole ocean engine was known to
him. He was an interpreter of the liquid text, and on every trip
they made he pointed out trails: a school of young barracuda, signs
of seismic activity, the slight swell caused by a seamount not on
the charts, patterns of subsurface bioluminescence, the flights of
birds and the runs of fish all around and beneath the boat cutting
through their wake and across the bow. The Teauhaapapeua current between Makatea and Mataiva and the Ara hao current that
ran out to Rangiroa were as clear to him as if the featureless water
were marked with dye. Wai sat on his throne behind the wheel of
the dive boat, a large, round laughing Buddha endlessly at home in
an amusing world, eavesdropping on the ocean's gossip, glimpsing
its intimacies.

"*Vois-tu?*" You see? Wai inspected some faint starboard spot of
nothing. He raised his double chin to point. The blank sea rolled
in all directions.

Evelyne kept under the boat's sunshade in the scorch of the
afternoon. "No. Where? What?"

"This is the channel. The way we came out."

"Wait. Are you saying you can see what's left of our wake?
From *two hours ago?*"

He shrugged, unable to confirm or deny.

She looked long and hard. "*Non, mais . . . tu te moques de moi ou quoi?*" Are you mocking me, or what?

His poker face was perfect, perhaps on account of the thirty hours a week he and the island's two other captains spent playing poker. He shrugged again and made a vague wave—*une vague vague*—as if to say, *It's right there!*

The poker face collapsed. They both burst out laughing.

"Shame on you. Bull-shitting a senile old lady!"

"You're not all that senile."

She slapped him on his massive, tattooed upper arm. Her shriveled hand stung him no more than a mosquito. Wai pretended that it hurt.

"*Quand même*," he said, in his own defense. "Our wake is still there. The way the bubbles still move." His hand swept upward, into the clear sky. "They can see it, I bet. Or smell it, maybe."

She thought for a moment that he meant *the gods*. Tāne, Māui, Ta'aroa. Then a gull flew overhead, a god all its own.

The island grew larger on the horizon, and the current confirmed that Wai had indeed found their channel. He did not use the instruments. He seldom needed to. She shook her head in admiration.

"You are truly something. The best human navigator in the world."

He let his mouth pinch into a fraction of a grin. "*C'est possible. Mais n'importe quel oiseau ou poisson sait mieux faire que moi.*" Any bird or fish is better at it than I am.

Beaulieu was happy to ascribe to Wai Temauri skills that rivaled the fish and birds. His people had done a thing no modern navigator could match. His ancestors had slid into the immensity of the Pacific in tiny, hand-paddled canoes, without astrolabes or lenses, without compasses, with no maps or charts except those in their heads. Even without writing, they had dispersed through an ocean larger than all the continents combined and settled every inhabitable speck of land in it, specks scattered like stars in a mostly empty universe.

And they had leapt across this vastness so fast that islanders spoke languages that could still be understood by distant kin thousands of miles away. The world's greatest seafarers still shared common myths, common tools, common customs, practices, and beliefs. A clan had spread across a third of the globe a thousand years and more before the West's most advanced ships managed a single crossing. They formed the farthest-flung cultural group on the planet. And all the anthropology and genetics and historical science available to Evelyne's own scientific tribe could not say how the feat was done.

Her awe at that was as profound as the Challenger Deep. There were people who could get by on the ocean, who knew how to read it. There were oceanographers and marine biologists and lifelong fishermen and half-pinniped sailors who made their home there. And then there were Wai's ancestors.

Back in the stern, Wai's daughter Kinipela skipped across the deck, coaxing the bilge pump, peering over the gunwales, scrying the course in bits of floating kelp. The girl reminded Evelyne of her teenage self, diving in the Straits of Florida off the coast of Miami in the early 1950s, as the region turned into Floribec. Skinny, naïve, and betrothed to everything in the ocean.

Kini shouted above the engine churn. "There, Miss Evie. That one! What do you call that one?"

A dorsal fin sliced up through the water, then dipped back down again. The wild black tip was underscored with a shock of white. Even a quick look sufficed. *Le Requin à pointes noires.* Blacktip reef shark.

"*Carcharhinus melanopterus.*"

The girl came closer to the old woman and asked for the name again. Then she repeated it twice.

"So beautiful, that one. My favorite."

If there were an upper limit to how many favorite fish a girl was allowed to have, neither of them knew it. Together, their hands animated all the ways that a reef shark floated through the communities that it lorded over.

Beaulieu caught herself. "What is the Māʻohi name?"

The girl's face lit up with expertise. "We call that one *maʻo ereere*, Miss Evie."

In her tenth decade, Evelyne liked being a Miss again. She took her turn repeating the syllables, hoping they would take. But where Kini Temauri was now the master of a new Latin genus and species, Evelyne Beaulieu, in a few more days, would have to ask for the creature's Māʻohi name all over again. She remembered that *tumu raau* was tree and *maa* was food and *Popaʻā* was white person and *motu* was island and *moana* was the great watery goddess all around them. But of the scores of other Tahitian words that Kinipela had taught her, almost all of them had vanished. And of Paʻumotu or Mihiroa words, she remembered almost none.

The fact saddened Evelyne. Still, she was at peace with it. Memory should be vise-like in youth when the emerging navigator needed it most. But no one ever survived into old age who couldn't open that vise and let much of their hard-gripped facts go free. Evelyne simply hoped that the girl might live long enough to grow as forgetful as she needed to be. As forgetful and reconciled to the horror of life as Evelyne herself had grown.

———

THE ISLAND ROSE like a hatbox floating on the waves. Wai took the boat windward, into the stiff trades blowing from the southeast. Kinipela pointed toward the horizon where the *Mareva Nui*, the supplies boat from Tahiti, on its two-week-long, twice-a-month tour, chugged away from the island on its enormous loop to Mataiva, Tikehau, Rangiroa, Ahe, Manihi, and finally back to Papeete.

Wai piloted to the fringe of coral bounding the shallow lagoon. He circled leeward past the island's headlands, along a fifth of the thirteen-mile coastline. Beyond the promontory, shapes emerged: a gutted cylindrical loading silo, an arc of concrete pyramids, two abandoned industrial buildings, twin riprap jetties, and the ghost of an old, cantilevered, telescoping pier that had loaded phosphate onto ships that once floated just beyond the now-ruined harbor. Even after months, Evelyne marveled at the sight of a port covered in barnacles and mold, crumbling down into the rock-strewn surf.

The dive boat motored down the leeward coast. As it approached its mooring between a freshwater spring and another abandoned village, three slight boys waved at the boat from a spot under the cliffs. Kini saw the welcome committee long before Evelyne could. Those formidable young girl's eyes made out the shapes before her father, although the laughing Buddha pretended otherwise. Soon enough, even Evie's ancient eyes could see the figures move along the shore, waving to the boat. All three wore board shorts and over-sized tank tops, one bright red, one blue with a white Nike swoosh, and one camo with black letters reading BE ALL YOU CAN BE.

The trio of boys scampered toward the mooring as the boat pulled in. Kinipela grimaced as the excited gang came up the beach. Wai gestured at them with mock threats that made the boys laugh. Evie waved and called out, *"Ia orana!"* The trio felt to her as endangered as the creatures she had just swum with in the open sea.

Wai tied up to the small dock and rolled out the gangplank. He cut the engines, and in the sudden silence Evelyne heard Kini humming Latin names under her breath, like a little song. Evelyne Beaulieu knew of only one other person who made up jingles to remember Linnean nomenclature. Any creature could become a little tune. *Carcharhinus, Carcharhinus, men have named you.*

But all mnemonic tunes scattered again in the shouts of the marauding boy army. From her place on the crude dock, Evie heard the trio shouting over one another. The thrill in their voices was audible. Something—*anything*—was happening in this tiny world at last. But their words dispersed in the breezes blowing across the beach.

The gang drew close enough to be intelligible. Mori, the leader, traced his ancestors back to Makateans who'd lived on the island for centuries before the French arrived. Taka, his stout advance scout, the son of the island's Protestant minister, was raised all over the Society Islands. Afa, the smallest, was the ward of two foreigners who had lost their way in the world. Together, they roved around the island, climbing the cliffs, exploring the freshwater springs that flowed through underground caverns near Moumu, and excavating abandoned tools and machinery that had been left to the advancing jungle. Evelyne knew all three of them, but the youngest always cracked her heart open to see.

The squad came up to the dock, keeping up a steady shout. *"Les Américains vont débarquer! Les Américains vont débarquer!"*

Beaulieu looked up to the cliffs above the coast where the scar of history ran diagonally across the island. Makatea felt like a great flensed whale, a third of its body scraped away. And yet, as the Makatean Expeditionary Force descended on the dock, they shouted their alarm in the language of the flenser.

"Les Américains vont débarquer, et tout prendre pour eux!" The Americans are landing, and they're going to take everything!

Understanding them at last, Evie wondered: *What in God's name is left to take?*

....

RAFI AND I BONDED OVER *having skipped a grade and being largely self-taught. We bonded over being the sons of fucked-up fathers and erratic mothers who couldn't cope with their mates. We shared a contempt for the hierarchies of prestige and coolness that ran the school, and neither of us saw our outcast state as anything but a massive asset in the life ahead. We were both nuts about Tolkien and* Star Wars *and Ursula Le Guin. But even with all that in common, the only way the two of us would ever have spent so much time together was over a chessboard.*

Something turbulent was warring inside him, a darker, more desperate game. I sensed it but didn't understand it. He didn't bother hiding it from me, but he wasn't about to share. The two of us weren't going to visit the place together.

One afternoon, I surprised him in the library with a copy of a book called The Master and Margarita. *The book wasn't on any syllabus in that school. He tapped the spooky cover.*

"They're keeping the good shit from us, brother. Too dangerous!"

A few weeks later, in humanities class, as Father Kelly was declaiming e. e. cummings's "somewhere i have never traveled, gladly beyond" for the entire numbed class, I turned around to roll my eyes at Rafi in the row behind me. His eyes were wet and he was mouthing along with the words. He saw that I saw that he was crying, but his murderous gaze told me that if I so much as alluded to this, ever, he would cut me dead.

WE PROMISED TO KEEP IN TOUCH *over vacation after junior year. But we met up only once, at the Cultural Center downtown, to play out a handful of lightning chess matches. I was lifeguarding at Lee Street Beach and running my basement software games company. He was shelving books at the Taylor Street library and reading insane amounts of obscure fiction. It simply took too* much time and effort for us to cross the length of Chicago no-man's-land that lay between us.

On the first day of senior year, we spotted each other across a packed corridor full of kids at their lockers. He was not especially tall, but he was up on his toes, looking out over the crowd. Looking for me, I think. I was certainly looking for him.

We approached with our arms out and thumped each other on the shoulder blades—what passed for a hug among male teenagers in Chicago, 1986. He gave me a big, toothy grin and fell into his parody of 'hood talk, ladled on for my benefit.

"Aight! Dope look, mutha! But that shirt be wack."

He tugged at the popped collar of my polo. He himself was sporting a new, sparse, short goatee that made him look a little like Mephistopheles, even in his blue button-down shirt and black pressed slacks. He brought me up to date on his vacation reading—mostly classics—and I told him about the new turn-based space strategy game I'd written that I was now selling through mail order.

He was bubbling over with suppressed excitement, struggling to remain laconic. His fingers did a little air arabesque. "Somethin' we gotta look into. I'll tell you at lunch."

"Tell me now!"

"Later, 'tater."

The morning passed, a buffet of new classes that would see us through the next four months. I truly loved Saint Ignatius. Rafi did, too—all those priests and smart lay teachers trying to fine-tune our brains the way Swiss watchmakers calibrated gears, balanced wheels, and fitted mainsprings. It was only our classmates we couldn't quite stand.

At lunch, we took our trays of sausage and sauerkraut to the end of one table and sat down to the business of getting caught up. He'd started to write poetry over the summer break, and he showed me a few efforts. It was a weird mix of Langston Hughes and Rilke.

A girl I'd tutored in quadratic equations the year before walked by and hissed at us. "Why don't you two just move to San Francisco and get on with it?"

Rafi snapped his head back, baffled in her wake. "What on Earth did you do to her, man?"

"I'm not sure. It's possible I may have flirted with her, once."

He did that thing with his hands: Don't drag me into all your white-people stuff. *"Okay. Brace yourself, mofo. You ready to head through the wardrobe?"*

He reached into his green khaki book satchel, brought out a Bible-sized beaten-up volume, and laid it next to my lunch tray. The Game That the Gods Play, *by Hideo Ohira.*

It was an old gray clothbound book that had lost its dust jacket. The cover showed nothing but the title and the author's name. Rafi had found it on a Sunday on Maxwell Street. It had been published by a West Coast publisher just after the Second World War, when our fathers were kids. The pages were yellowed and moldering, and they smelled of aldehydes, ketones, vanillin, and decomposing lignin—a mysterious, heady scent, almost narcotic.

That's how it started: Rafi's and my trip through the universe of Go. Everything that happened later—the course that our two lives took—everything was launched from the opening moves of that book.

Rafi waved his frantic hands like he was conducting an invisible orchestra. "I was tired of having my ass repeatedly handed to me in chess just because you had a ten-year head start."

"And on account of my superior intellect."

"And on account of your natural North Side arrogance, which makes you perfectly suited to games of aggression and destruction. But this, my friend, is a game of creative exploration and ingenuity. This game is going to take you to the farthest edge of your ability to contemplate. You ready for that, asshole?"

It was not like Rafi to be hyperbolic. I picked up the book and flipped through it. Every other page had poorly printed engravings of Go boards cluttered with inscrutable patterns of black

*and white stones. Something about the growing, shifting, geo-
metric configurations excited me. I could sense the power relations rippling across the board, although I had no idea how the
rules worked.*

He grabbed my wrist. I'd never seen him so theatrical.

*"This game is to chess what singing is to sucking your teeth. It
is the summit of contemplative philosophy. It makes chess feel like*
Chutes and Ladders. *Get this. If every atom in the universe was a
little universe that itself had as many atoms as the entire universe
had, the total number of atoms would still be smaller than the
number of possible Go game states. And I can teach you how to
play in under three minutes."*

*I figured he had to be exaggerating. But both claims turned out
to be true. The rules were simple, as if they'd existed long before
humans stumbled onto them. Place a stone on any intersection of
a nineteen-by-nineteen grid of lines. Try to surround your enemies' groups of stones by occupying their last pathways to further
growth. Connect your stones; control territory. The person who
occupies the most area is the winner.*

It looked to me like glorified tic-tac-toe.

*He'd picked up a cheap board in Chinatown and had it stashed
in his locker. We played our first game after school that afternoon.
We set up outside on the concrete under the pillars of the school's
back portico and went at it.*

*From the start, everything felt odd. Instead of beginning with
a board full of pieces and picking them off, we started with nothing and added one stone at a time. I waded in, confident that the
simple rules would yield to simple play. Within thirty moves, I got
my red-assed self-esteem handed to me on a platter.*

*I understood the rules, and up to a point, I could see how he
was trying to split my stones with wedges, build up his walls, and
surround my poor stones to kill them. But for the life of me I
couldn't figure out how to defend myself or mount any kind of
attack that he didn't easily swat away.*

The vast, empty patches of intersections seemed arbitrary.

Stones that I thought were on the outside line of a battle flipped and were suddenly on the inside of another, larger war. And this was going on in a dozen different board locations at the same time. The grid of the board became the streets and neighborhoods of Chicago. Some local race war in the blocks of Pilsen was going to unfold until it shook the blocks of Elk Grove to their foundations. How could a person hope to command so many subtle and flickering battles all at once?

When we played chess, I always felt guided by a very few core principles. I knew what every piece was worth and when it paid to trade them. I hewed to the known opening moves, developed my pieces, and tried to control the center board, keep a strong pawn formation, maintain the pressure, lay traps, look ahead several moves, and build toward a dominant endgame. But in this little allegory of unfolding cosmic creation that Rafi had dug up— so much older, larger, harder, subtler, and more complex than the already infinite and impossible-to-master game of chess—I couldn't even tell who was ahead.

Calculating the value of a move was impossible. Whatever I did, he had a couple hundred possible replies. Convinced that I had just forced his next move, I watched him blithely ignore my thrust and place his stone half a board away. When we did go head-to-head in an all-out pitched fight—Jesus! The branches of the fray multiplied so profusely that for dozens of moves I couldn't tell what was happening or who was getting the upper hand.

Put a stone on the board. Just put a little pebble on the board. God only knew what byzantine structure it might become or what its enveloping environment might grow into. I couldn't tell which of us owned large swaths of the board, and I still wasn't sure, fifty turns later. A game might last three hundred moves or more. Chess was almost always over in fewer than forty.

I lost that first showdown. Badly. And I lost again immediately after that.

"One summer, and you're already three levels ahead of me."

"Naw, man. I'm still flailing, myself. Making moves just a step or two better than random."

I was stunned. I felt like I was on a tiny raft floating far out on a sea much bigger than any continent. "Why have I never learned how to play this? I've barely heard of it, before today!"

He grinned as I wandered into his trap. "Yeah. It's weird. This thing is the oldest continuously played board game in the world. Billions of people play it. In China, it's part of the four means of self-betterment. In Japan, it's state-subsidized—a way to become enlightened."

"Why does no one play it here?"

"You tell me, brother."

"One more," I demanded. He shrugged. He had nowhere to go but the firehouse where his father worked, and even there, he was hardly expected.

Dusk was settling over us. I hadn't told my parents I was going to be late. I ran out to the pay phone in front of Saint Ig, a block down on Roosevelt toward Racine. I pushed my coins in the slot, dialed, and got my mother. She was furious with worry, shrieking into the phone like she hoped the sound might come out the other end of the connection and slap me in the head.

I went back to the portico behind the school. Rafi hunched over the board, pushing stones around, playing through some positions in a classic game from the early Qing Dynasty called Nine Dragons Playing with a Pearl.

"Sorry, man. Gotta go. I'm toast, up there."

"Whatever, mama's boy."

"Bring it tomorrow, okay?"

"It's staying here. In my locker."

We played a thousand matches that year alone.

ON MONDAY MORNING, INA AROITA WALKED HER FAMILY
along the wheel ruts of crushed coral up to the sala that housed the
one-room school. Madame Martin and the eight students already
present came out to meet them. The youngest children crawled all
over Rafi—*Monsieur Young! Enfin, enfin!* Finally! The older ones
tugged at his elbow, vying for attention. Rafi followed them into the
schoolroom, toys pouring from his pockets and semi-grammatical
jokes spilling from his mouth in three languages.

Hariti, still young enough to be proud of her father, joined in
the fray. Afa, who had reached the age of awakening discomfort,
hung back. He didn't think it right that his father, with a doctorate in educational psychology from a major American university,
should be the assistant of a *demi* schoolteacher half his father's age
who did not even know what crabs' shells were made of.

The knot of happy kids paraded into the schoolroom with *Monsieur Young* in the middle—a thin black scarecrow flocked by shouting brown birds. Afa watched them. Ina Aroita nudged her boy.

"Go on. I'll be back this afternoon to see your match."

Afa trotted off into the schoolhouse. It wrecked Ina to think
that her son would be off before long to Rangiroa, to continue his
schooling. How the island's mothers sent their thirteen-year-olds so
many miles across the ocean to go to high school was beyond her.

Much about the island still evaded her, even after years. Everyone here had some blood pact with *fenua*—the land—forever connected by mystical, umbilical *pito* to the place where their placenta
was buried. And yet they came and went, migrating to new islands
all the time. Countless more Makateans lived elsewhere than lived
on Makatea. The diaspora that had colonized every habitable spot
in the world's greatest ocean was still under way.

Ina herself had grown up throughout the Pacific, in an island
family. But six years in the dead middle of an endless continent
had baffled her soul and left her an imposter to herself. She had no
home anywhere but where she lived, and that was Makatea now.

Makatea: the capital of *métissage* in the middle of the hot mix that was the South Pacific. In some ways she felt more *Makatean* than she felt *American*, a role she'd had so little real experience with.

So it shook her to hear the schoolteacher ask, "Why are your people trying to take over this place?"

"My people? Take over *Makatea*?"

A minute sufficed to prove that Madame Martin was clueless about the gossip she happily passed downstream. *Several Americans with too much money*, as she put it, were going to reconstruct the crumbling port of Temao and rebuild the abandoned railroad that had once run the length of the island. Then the Americans were going to use Makatea to build a floating city.

Ina Aroita chuckled. "Are they mad?"

Madame Martin was not exactly Makatean, either. She had been born in Papeete and took five years of college in Lyon before asking to be posted to the little island where her maternal grandfather had once cut and loaded six tons of rock into wheelbarrows six days a week. But that made her Makatean enough to resent Ina's skepticism. Her wounded look insisted that of course the nine square miles of gutted and abandoned island would be a hot buy for any shrewd adventure capitalist.

"But *why*?" Ina asked. "What do these people want with us?"

The *us* melted Madame Martin. Most people from continents would have said *it*.

"They need a remote base. They want to launch a business venture in international waters. Apparently they call it 'seasteading.'"

International waters: That much, at least, sounded very American. The country's endless desire to escape regulation had driven Ina Aroita to escape America.

"Have they really made an offer for Temao?" The port: traces of a collapsed pier, a few concrete footings, and stone fragments piled up on the end of what was once a jetty.

Bloodcurdling screams of child pleasure came from the open windows of the schoolroom. Ina's husband, Madame Martin's assistant, the only real American on the island, was stoking up the next generation on yet another game of skill and daring that had gotten out of hand again.

Madame Martin tilted her head. "*Excuse-moi, ma chérie. L'éducation m'appelle.*" Education calls.

———

THE CONVERSATION UNSETTLED INA AROITA. Instead of making the rounds in the village and stopping to see if the Queen needed anything, Ina went back to her own bungalow, itself only recently reclaimed from the spreading undergrowth. Her agitation took her straight into the backyard, where the bits of plastic that she and her daughter had retrieved from the belly of the dead albatross lay spread in the sun.

In her hands, the congeries of brightly colored garbage no longer seemed threatening or urgent. She brought the handful of trash to the side of the house and laid the scraps out on her workbench next to her ongoing art projects. There she sat and stared, pleading with them to cut her a little slack and let her go free this once, on good behavior.

But the pieces of plastic were relentless. They nagged at her the way her mother used to scold her from two rooms away, without having a particular sin in mind to reprimand other than childhood.

Ina stacked the bottle caps and film canister and cigarette lighter and daisy-shaped button into a little minaret. The tower did nothing for her, and she knocked it to the ground like Yahweh batting down Babel's Pritzker Prize winner. She arranged the bits in a circle, creating a tiny plastic Stonehenge. This, too, she swatted back to rubble.

She'd always hated plastic. It was ugly, brazen, and obstinate— the opposite of the sensuous, once-living materials she loved to work with. She carried the junk in her two cupped hands and pitched it into the outdoor garbage bin. Then she went inside to start in on the day's housework.

Whisking down the floors of the house with the bristle broom, she several times thought: *Leave it. It's worthless. There's nothing you can make with it that will redeem anything. Besides, redeeming things isn't your job.*

In mid-sweep, she set the broom down on the kitchen floor, went outside again, fished the crap out of the bin, and angrily dumped it back on her workbench. She rooted up a tube of acrylic adhesive and glued the squirt top to the acrylic button and fixed the bottle caps to the film canister. Then she used the monofilament fishing line to tie the two weird clumps together into a misshapen bundle.

The resulting mash-up of shiny shapes and colors was still ugly, still brazen, still unredeemable. Ina Aroita looked at the sculpted clump from every possible angle: nothing but a bunch of plastic bits jammed together.

Yet somehow the stunted assemblage relaxed her a little. She stashed the construction on the top shelf of the garden shed where she didn't have to look at it, out of reach of rummaging pigs or fiddling children. She had no idea what the garish thing wanted to be when it grew up. But she knew that it wasn't done using her.

She walked back to the school that afternoon to watch Afa's game. It wasn't exactly soccer, as there weren't enough school-age kids to field two sides. Four kids of various ages played four others in what amounted to a series of free-for-all scrums. But from this chaos would emerge the next generation of Makatean players who would head out by boat a few times a month to challenge the teams of nearby islands.

She sat with Hariti on the sidelines on her portable folding stool, cheering on the family's champion and waiting for Rafi to finish helping Ms. Martin clean up the schoolroom. In time, Rafi emerged from the school, limping a little from the day's exertions. He looked spent. He was well into his fifties, with two children and a cadre of young islanders who all claimed him as their best friend. Hariti clung to him as he sat down next to them. The girl worried about him when he got tired. The girl worried about him when he woke up in the morning at full strength. The girl worried about the well-being of the mountains, the ocean, and God.

Ina felt the thinning, close-cropped nap on Rafi's narrow head. "You're well, my sweet?"

"I wouldn't mind lying down a little. Maybe just a month or two?"

His robotic voice alarmed Ina. "Go ahead and lie down. The sky is pretty."

"The sky is always pretty. But it would break his heart."

Hariti fidgeted with insights. "Whose heart, Papa? Afa's?"

"Don't sound so hopeful!" Rafi tickled his daughter until she gasped for mercy.

The boy had become a dervish, dashing between both goals now that his father was there to witness. Rafi shouted encouragements in a secret patois known only to the two of them. Ina reached down to take his shoulder, partly to rub it, partly to signal to him in their own idiolalia that he could stop working for the day.

"Did you hear? Did Madame Martin tell you? About the invasion?"

He kept his eyes on the game. "She did."

Ina couldn't always tell the difference between his defeat and his stoicism. Something to do with his upbringing, in a city he hated and a family he couldn't save. She had stopped prying long ago. Childish, of course, but she herself wished for a tremendous typhoon to blow through and destroy all the island's moorings, cutting the eighty-two of them off from all traffic with the world. They would be just fine, for a long time.

Her husband, always her more moderate double, spoke her thoughts aloud. "Please, God, don't do anything more to this beautiful place."

Hariti clutched at him, sensing doom. Her superpower. "Wait. What? God's gonna do something to us?"

....

THREE MONTHS IN, AND THE DOCTORS *are juggling my meds again. It's all a bit of an experiment. Dementia with Lewy bodies has so many symptoms that treating one risks worsening another. Mostly they give me palliatives—drugs to tame the worst of the sleeplessness, anxiety, depression, disquiet, agitation, and aggression for a few more months, without triggering anything worse. Vitamins and supplements and various other magical Hail Marys, because why not? Science needs to try everything, right?*

They have me on something to treat coordination problems and something that's supposed to reduce the episodes of confusion. Ironically (if that's the word), this cocktail itself knocks me on my ass. So I don't always take it. By itself, the disease makes me sleep all day long, and with that drug, I could sleep twenty-four seven.

The first drug my caregivers prescribed for tremors and rigidity made me psychotic. So we went on another. The thing I was taking for the incontinence wrecked my heartbeat, so I went off it. One of the choices for treating hallucinations ran a fair risk of killing me. They proposed another. We spun the wheel, and I didn't lose. But I still hallucinate.

On good days, the problems seem like a fascinating game of five-dimensional chess. On days like today, talking out loud like this is the best possible medicine. I have a story to tell, the story of my friend and me and how we changed the future of mankind. And I don't have many more good days in which to tell it.

I'm glad that I never had children. I saddle only a small troop of professionals who are glad for the employment and livelihood I supply them.

DLB has no cure. My prognosis is as hazy as a San Jose winter day. When do I drop off from first-stage prodromal disease to second and then third? When will my words start to disappear? How soon will I lose my mind? What horrors will I face after that? Lower life expectancy and quality of life, compared to Alzheimer's. Some of us die within a year of diagnosis. Some of us live—if you can call it that—for two more decades. Beyond that, no one can tell me much for certain.

And yet, my doctors exude optimism. New drugs in late-stage clinical trials. New treatment modalities—stem-cell therapy, gene therapy, immunotherapy. New insights into neurodegeneration and the immunological components of the disease. Accelerated drug discovery, thanks to AI. Just hold on!

Because of my work, my doctors hold me in special regard. Or maybe they've just looked up my net worth online. Either way, I'm getting the best attention and treatment a patient could ask for. But as the song goes, money can't buy me neurons.

I used to measure out my weeks on a calendar app shared with four assistants, where every quarter-hour box was filled in with multiple colors of appointment. Now my calendar app is a red plastic stick of seven sequential pill compartments embossed with the days of the week. And even with that handy tool, I sometimes stop and ask my phone: Did we do Tuesday already?

I've started to wander, and not just at night. I'll materialize in the kitchen without having gone there. Or out in the garage. Or in the park two blocks down the street, firing my jets in restless searching. The radius of my wanderings increases in proportion to how hard it is to make my body move. I'm going to need an ID bracelet.

MY DOCTOR TOLD ME about a thing that dementia patients do called "showtiming." In denial, embarrassment, or terror, we perform ourselves in front of other people as if we have no symptoms at all. I'm a master at it. In meetings, interviews, even live behind a podium in front of several hundred people, I can showtime myself into competence for an hour or longer. Sometimes I even fool myself into thinking that I'm as powerful as ever.

All our symptoms are different, but it turns out that memory loss isn't always an early symptom of DLB. It may come, but I'm good for now. I'm free to remember all I want, for the pure joy of it. And the odd thing? Having DLB makes me remember everything. Even the things I've worked so hard not to recall are now priceless.

First in, last out, as it generally goes, even for brains that aren't being eaten away from the inside by runaway proteins. The older the memory, the more textured. I can't always tell how far away a door is or find my way to it without slamming into things. I'm losing governance over my body's provinces. But I can remember the taste of ice cream when I was six—the precise flavor of blueberry cheesecake—a taste they don't make anymore.

When my doctor told me about showtiming, she warned me against it. She said I'd only be able to do it for short bursts. It would wear me out and distress my loved ones. Of course, she had no idea about you and me. I can showtime for you, for hours. It sharpens me for a while, it doesn't distress you, and it focuses my memories on the man I've tried not to think about for so many years and reasons.

I'LL NEED TO RESIGN *from Playground, of course. All my companies. I've handed over everyday decisions to my numbers two, three, and four. And I've made my preferences for a successor known to those who will select him. But making the facts public will be a nightmare. It'll panic investors with Playground shares in their retirement portfolios. The media will be a circus.*

A lot of tech journalists never got over the fact that a single person managed to hold on to a golden share in a company with annual revenues greater than the GDP of any of the thirty poorest countries on Earth. For the founder, chief architect, CEO, and golden shareholder of any information company of any size to announce, My brain is shutting down, *is not what you call good optics.*

But who am I kidding? I may be the public face of Playground, the only person anyone thinks of when they think of the company. But my little experiment in empowering and connecting people got away from me twenty years ago. I haven't been running it for years. No one has. It's a living system, with its own agenda. Every business beyond a certain size grows its own hive mind. The company itself will find a person who can implement its collective will. And the people at the helm will be convinced of their own agency, just as I was.

Add that to your table of definitions for what it means to be a human being. We make things that we hope will be bigger than us, and then we're desolate when that's what they become.

Here's another matter that needs considering. I've begun to have doubts about my last will and testament, which always seemed a bit fictional. My massive act of philanthropy that I never really believed would happen is now looming. I want to keep the sum together, a fantastic force-multiplier that will further the things I've believed in. But you've sown the seed of doubt in me about the forward-looking venture that I'm endowing.

I'm not ready to speak to the lawyers, because any single thing I do with that much money will seem insane. It's more than the country spends on dementia research each year. But I'm running out of time. At what point will I no longer be "of sound mind and body"?

For now, we're keeping my condition on the down-low for as long as we can. To shore up the stock price and keep our competitors wrong-footed, the boards of my companies want me to stay mum at least until after our bombshell press conference, when we will announce the next big step in evolution: a whole new kind of being, one that will make companies seem as slow, small, and powerless as companies make human beings.

The QUEEN WENT UP THE RISE, SINGING.

She didn't call herself the Queen, of course. But everyone else on the island did, and not unkindly. Her neighbors had called her the Queen for so long that more than one person had forgotten that her name was in fact Palila Tepa.

Palila didn't like her given name. But she didn't entirely mind being the Queen. The title came with privileges, among them the right to sing and dance the old dances anywhere and anytime she wanted, even if the song seemed a little crazy and the occasion didn't especially call for dances old or new.

She allotted two full hours in which to wind her way up to the community center for that night's gathering, and the walk only took her forty minutes. But there was so much *community* to attend to on the road up to the community center that it was always best to get a head start. She factored in time for visiting along the way, as well as for holding still and singing, because sometimes the Queen had trouble remembering the second verses of complicated songs, and she needed a little extra time to line up the lyrics and get them sung.

She had over a thousand songs in her memory to help her up the rise. Genealogy songs and geography songs and historical epics and classic *fa'atara* odes. Some of them were hers but most were only on loan from the past, and when she herself went out—this year or next or the year after, at the latest—when the time came for her to stop walking up the rise and sail back out on the tide, a lot of those songs would never again be sung by anyone.

She had a song about 'Ōio, the father of all the Mihiroa, and about all the named currents that he struggled against to reach Makatea in his tiny single-hulled *va'a*. She had a song about the secret words spoken by the kings from the skies when they first set foot on the island. She had a song about how and where to find the foundations of all eight of the marae that once graced the island, although archaeologists had only ever located the remains of three. All kinds of good stuff.

She had songs about how the entire population of the island fled into the heart of the Pōmare empire in order to escape the Pōmare imperial expansion, and other songs about how they came back to the empty island and made it their kingdom again. She had songs and dances about how warriors from other islands came to Makatea in their war *pahī* because they'd heard that the Makatean vahine were the most beautiful in the world. There were verses about how the men of Makatea barricaded themselves in the caves of the cliffs from the invaders and valiantly fought them off until all the defenders died. And that was why people could sometimes still hear ghosts calling from inside the caves, the way the Queen heard them now as she limped along on her way to the center.

Palila knew songs about the arrival of the *Popa'ā*—first the British, then Germans, then French—although she didn't like to sing those much. She did sometimes sing the one about the Mormon missionaries who came to the island and built the Sanito church, to which her family had long belonged and to which she herself felt committed. But she also knew Catholic hymns and truly ancient *fa'ateniteni* about Māui the trickster and Hina the moon goddess and, of course, Ta'aroa, spinning in his egg while dreaming up how to make the world.

She had gotten many songs from other people—from her grandmothers or her aunties or the old nurse from the mining days, who was the first to collect them. Several came from an on-again, off-again lover—an old fisherman she kept going back to over the decades because he knew so many good lyrics. The man was truly crazy. But crazy memorable.

She also knew big band tunes and plenty of hits from the '50s and '60s, her years of travel in the employ of the French. She had learned so many tunes from working in offices, where someone always had a radio going, usually against regulations. She could learn an entire song by heart in only two or three listens. If she was Queen of anything, it was the Queen of song learning.

But the song she sang late that afternoon—dancing a little to it as she walked, even with a hip that had never mended properly following her surgery—was a song of her own invention. It was about a Mihiroa girl born on the tallest atoll in the sea, on the day that Japanese bombs rained down on another former Polynesian kingdom, a mere twenty-five hundred miles to the north. With a father who built and repaired buildings for the Compagnie Française des Phosphates de l'Océanie and a mother who cooked for the CFPO's workers, the little girl was a true child of the island.

The lyrics were long and rollicking. In them, the girl grew up to be good at many things: tennis, pool, soccer, basketball—all the sports that Makatea enjoyed, being, at the time, French Polynesia's most developed island. Stanza five went:

> We had power,
> we had running water.
> We had medicine and fine houses!
> We made Papeete look like
> a cute little pigsty.

That still made her laugh, there on the edge of the empty town, even after twenty years of singing the punch line.

But the girl in the song only wanted to dance. In school, she helped to form the island's TDC—the Troupe de Danse des Conteurs. She became a star, rehearsing and performing the old dances while all the time coming up with new ones. The Storytellers' Dance Troupe went all over the Tuamotus, taking part in dance festivals:

> We outdanced Makemo.
> We outdanced Fakarava.
> We would have outdanced Anaa,
> but those little bitches cheated!

Many verses in, the girl, now a teenager out of school, went to work in the offices of the mine company, the venture that employed almost all three thousand people on the island. In those offices, she typed and filed and handled complaints from the Japanese, Chinese, Vietnamese, and Maori workers. She did a little translating, because she was almost as good with languages as she was learning lyrics.

Many men loved the girl, and she loved some of them. One of the French officers asked her to marry him and move to Paris. He was handsome and kind and best of all amusing, but how could she leave her island? Without *fenua,* the song said, a person was nothing. That was what was wrong with the French invaders in the first place. They had no home.

Singing and dancing farther up the island for the better part of half an hour, the Queen reached the outskirts of town. She wanted to finish the song, so she sat down on a small concrete pylon underneath a vine-covered stretch of the old overhead distribution track to remember what words came next. Sometimes a line or two got stuck, while trying to sing its way out of her brain.

But her memory was damn good, for an eighty-six-year-old old lady. The songs were the reason for that. When people asked her, *How is it that you are so good at remembering?* she always answered, *Because I do a lot of it.*

It took a couple of tries, but she got to the part about the mines shutting down overnight when the girl, now a woman, was twenty-five:

> Then the magic rock ran out,
> taking everybody by surprise.
> For a while we were three thousand.
> Then, not even a thin one hundred.
> How could we fight that? What could we do?
> All the work was on other islands.

And so, in the next-to-last verses, the woman went to work once more for the French, who were looking for skilled labor on the atolls of Hao and Moruroa, at the other end of the Tuamotus, seven hundred miles away. And there she typed and filed some more and did a little more translating, while the French detonated forty-some nuclear weapons in the atmosphere a few miles outside her window.

The Queen finished her song with a little flourish and the fanciest sashay that her problem hip let her make. The lyrics didn't mention the subsequent dark years. After the hydrogen bombs, she went back to Makatea and married a miner who came from Vietnam. They tried for babies, but the babies wouldn't come. No one at the clinic could tell her why. Her husband divorced her and went back to his own country. Then the lumps appeared and they sent her to Tahiti for treatment.

Her body went through things that should have silenced singing. But those years passed, the singing survived them, and she was left with sufficient skin and bone to get her all the way up to the plateau with enough mobility left over for a little stomp and hiproll at the top. There was nowhere on the island she couldn't reach if she gave herself ample time.

It might have been different, of course. The cancer might have killed her, or the chemotherapy. Or the radiation used to treat the handiwork of radiation. She might have survived everything Tahiti threw at her body, only to get crushed by the impossible hospital bills. But she had a guardian spirit that she could summon, and that kept her spirit intact until chance did the rest.

Salvation of sorts came in the form of a surprise settlement. Because the government had kept her working so close to so many of the atomic blasts, Palila Tepa eventually got a bit of money from the French. About five dozen Pa'umotu people in all received compensation, and Palila was awarded the median sum. Nine people Palila Tepa worked with on Hao and Moruroa got cancer, some worse than hers. One hundred thousand islanders breathed the fallout. One hundred thousand people knowingly exposed to repeated radiation, and sixty-three got checks.

The money the French gave her was more than the Queen ever earned. Once she paid off her medical debts, she had plenty left

over for food and upkeep. The rest went toward her house and
garden. She went to Papeete and bought a terrific CD player and
filled it with discs of dance music from Hawaii, New Zealand,
Indonesia, Zimbabwe, and Brazil. She gave a little help to the fishermen and crabbers when the catch failed, as it did increasingly
these years. And she subsidized the group she had helped form to
keep the ever-circling Australians at bay: Paruru i to Tatou Fenua.
Protecting Our Land. Other members included the postmistress
and the representative for the Tuamotus on Papeete. As always, the
defense of the island was being led by women.

Her hip throbbed by the time she reached the Chinese Store.
That was what everyone had called it in her youth, back when
Makatea had more than one store. The store was run now by Wen
Lai, whose father had dug out phosphate rock by hand for twenty
years before Palila started typing for the mining company.

Wen Lai laughed when people called his shop the Chinese
Store. He was born on Makatea, went to high school in Tahiti,
had family in Singapore and California, spoke both French and
the local strain of Pa'umotu better than many, majored in business at the University of Melbourne, and sounded to Palila, when
he spoke English, like Paul Hogan. He had come back to Makatea
after discovering that he really wanted to spend his days reading
science fiction and doing philosophy. The store happened to be
up for sale.

The shop was clean and spare. Wen Lai stocked a handful of
boxes and bottles of the two dozen items essential for life on an
island hundreds of miles from anywhere. Most of the canned goods
and dish soap and rice vinegar and cake mixes and the like stood
on hand-built shelving pushed up against three walls of the shop.
He kept a few bins of bulk grains. A small freezer case stood in
the center of the room, filled with fish. Near it he stacked crates of
fresh fruits and vegetables. The floor was immaculate tan ceramic
tile, which Wen Lai mopped down each night while listening to his
favorite *New Consequentialism* podcast.

The store dealt in French Pacific francs, of course, but some of the trade was barter. Along with choice fish and fresh harvests, Wen Lai also accepted live *kaveu*, offering a hundred francs of store credit per pound of crab. The crustaceans stayed on the floor along another wall next to the batteries and light bulbs, their claws and legs done up in twine. He bartered these coconut crabs away to other customers or sold them to the twice-monthly boat that made the rounds between Makatea and Tahiti. He had little use for pigs and chickens, since most islanders raised their own.

The Queen always stopped in, whether she needed anything from the shop or not. Wen Lai remembered the old days, and she valued that, although they rarely talked about them. They didn't need to. The two of them were Old Island, both philosophers, of a sort. Besides, Wen Lai talked to more islanders on any given day than anyone else. If there was something on Makatea that needed knowing, that man knew it. He was the Radio France Internationale of the island's coconut radio.

She shuffled into the shop. Wen Lai sat by the till, hunched over a substantial volume. She snuck a peek at the title of the work: *An Inquiry into Modes of Existence*. It sounded interesting. She did not read much herself. But everything that people found of interest interested her.

"Hey, mister," she said in English. "How's business?"

"Can't complain, mate." He laid on the Strine accent, just to make her laugh. "Well, I *could* complain, but I won't. *Et tes affaires, ça marche bien?*"

"Business is good," she answered in Pa'umotu. "Never any customers. But business is always good."

She wandered around the shop, although she knew the location of every item on every shelf by heart. The offerings had not changed for a year. She picked up some of the coffee she liked and a small box of cornstarch. A person could always use cornstarch.

She handed him her mesh tote sack, and he filled it with her purchases. As he rang her up, she asked, "Are you coming this evening? It's going to be a good one. Lots of food tonight. And lots of great music!"

She wasn't sure why she bothered saying that. Of course there would be music. And food. There was always music and food. Twice a week for years. But the word *music* was magic. Who could resist?

"Of course! Important business tonight. Haven't you heard? The Americans are coming. They want to buy the island."

She raised one eyebrow and tilted her head—a tiny dance of nonchalance. She prided herself on never being shocked by anything anymore, though every day was a surprise.

"Well, of course they do. Who wouldn't want to buy Makatea?"

———

SHE STOPPED IN TO SEE the nurse and the postmistress and the banker and the couple who ran the three-room *pension*. By the time Palila at last arrived at the center, the ukuleles were ramping up and a couple of dancers were trying out some steps. Half a dozen women inspected one another's weaving and offered each other assistance. The young adults—those few who hadn't yet moved away to places with jobs—were playing something like badminton without a net or rackets on a nearby grassy mound.

The nice dark American man who helped at the school was running a round-robin mancala championship with the children, using beach pebbles and pits dug into the sand around one of the center's open walls. His wife—whatever nationality *she* was—had spread some trinkets out on one of the tables for the older kids to use in art projects. The old Canadian diver woman sat at one of the picnic tables, tapping her papery hand to the music and smiling like the world was already finished. Palila went up and embraced her.

"Good evening, my sister. It's good you came."

The Canadian tried to answer her back, in the Tahitian of a three-year-old. "Hello, I'm happy to thank you for your welcome."

Palila switched to French. "We know everything, don't we, sister? The two of us? People who are about to die know everything."

The Canadian was not rattled. Palila had yet to rattle her, despite several tries.

"*Peut-être*," Madame Beaulieu said. Perhaps. "But I wouldn't mind learning just a little bit more."

A few of the older men had the fire pit going and were heating up stones for the *ahima'a*. What was it about men and fire? Hours from now, a feast would issue from the underground oven: banana and breadfruit and *fafa* and sweet potato, pig and chicken, roast garden veggies, shrimp, crab, clam, sea snails, and parrotfish, bathed in lemon and onion and coconut milk.

The scent of the preparation went straight up Palila's nose into her soul. For unemployed people who lived in abandoned buildings and bartered for everything, they ate better than a good deal of the world.

As she approached the bandstand, the ukuleles broke off their song and started in on a slowed-down, juiced-up, three-four rendition of "God Save the Queen." Palila cackled and clawed at the players in mock revenge. Sallying up to the musicians, she waltzed to her tune, kinking her hips to the beat of what soon mutated into true island music.

She was still sashaying two tunes later, when the mayor arrived. The poor man looked beyond beset. He carried a folder in one hand, his phone in the other, and a century and a half of colonial false consciousness on his shoulders. Everyone felt bad for the man. They tried to get him to join the imaginary badminton or dance a bit. But not even a soccer ball—his old ticket to glory—could induce Didier Turi to play.

As the sun set and the buried *ahima'a* reached full heat, the outdoor games wound down and people came under the sheltering roof to sit in an enormous circle and sing. Palila counted. It was a good turnout, almost fifty people—more than half of the island. Most of the native-borns were there, and many of the more recent visitors, including the North Americans. It had been weeks, maybe months, since so many people had turned out for the evening festivities. The reason was obvious: the great game of Destiny was revving up again, after decades of dormancy. Makatea was up for grabs once more, and people had come out tonight to learn the details of their fate.

At a break in the music, the mayor waved to the ukes for silence and walked into the center of the circle. The folder under his arm shed papers as he went. He stooped to pick them up, then cleared his throat to address his constituency. He spoke in a nervous spattering of three languages with flecks of English shaken in for seasoning. The children kept playing at mancala and making their art. The young adults did not quit their mock-badminton. The craft circle looked up out of politeness, but they kept on weaving.

"I hope everyone is enjoying themselves?"

The Queen made a megaphone of her hands. "We were until now!"

Laughter churned like a wave in a strong beach break. Even the mayor tumbled up in the surf of it.

"And I don't want to interrupt the festivities. . . ."

A cheer erupted across the center, and the ukes revved up again. Didier Turi waited with a pained smile for the antics to pass.

"I don't want to spoil the party, but something big is happening that everyone needs to know about. A group of American . . . venture capitalists are exploring the possibility of building floating communities out of modular parts. These communities would self-assemble in international waters. The residents of these floating cities will be able to come and go, joining any of these cities that they want."

Incomprehension rippled through the group. The Queen called out, "Why?"

Didier had asked himself this same question several times in the last few hours. "They are exploring new political arrangements. It has something to do with the search for free markets. The floating cities will lie beyond the regulatory power of national governments. Apparently it's called libertarianism. Very popular among the American tech billionaires."

Manutahi Roa, the ever-pragmatic secretary of energy, called out, "But what are these cities supposed to *do*?"

The mayor found a passage among his papers and read from it.
" 'Modular cities themselves might be devoted to marine aquacul-
ture or light industry or growing hydroponic crops or extracting
resources from the seawater or mining the ocean bottom.' "

Manutahi shouted again. "Aren't there cheaper ways to
make money?"

Someone in the ukes started strumming Bob Marley's "Crazy
Baldhead." The mayor stared him down. The voice of the schoolteacher called out from the back, "What do the libertarians want
with Makatea?"

"A good question." The mayor held up his sheaf of papers. "The
Californians want to build their first test floating town off Temao,
just beyond the lagoon. And they want us to be their launching
pad—the place where the floating city modules are assembled, dispatched, and serviced."

This, the biggest development to involve Makatea since the discovery of phosphate, left the assembly in stunned silence.

"I have asked Papeete to allow us a say on whether this pilot
project moves forward or not. And happily—excuse me, *please!*—I
said, *and happily*, they said yes."

"The government?" the Queen shouted. "*Our* government? Is
this a trick?"

The whole center laughed. But Didier looked down at his
papers, wondering the same thing. People turned to debate their
neighbors, ignoring the helpless *tāvana* at the front of the room.
Then the questions started up again, confused, hopeful, dubious.
How soon would construction start, and how many jobs would
be created? Would there be factories, apartment buildings, shops
like in Papeete? How would the island be compensated? Were the
Popa'ā planning to beat the hell out of the place and exploit every
soul on the island, like they did last time?

People wanted clarity. They wanted *details*. Didier gave what
answers he could. But for most questions, he had to beg for patience.

"We're going to need more time and a lot more information."

Wai Temauri raised his hand. His usual Buddha nature was

succumbing to concern. "How much time do we have, Chief? Before we hold this referendum?"

Didier bowed his head. "I will get in touch with Papeete about that as soon as I can."

"Eat something first," the Queen said. Many people seconded that suggestion. But before the meeting could break up and the eating begin, Hone Amaru came forward. He'd been nursing a bottle of Hinano and keeping his own counsel by the side of the *ahima'a* pit. The old mayor's son had his father's face, and something of the old wizard's sense of public timing.

"Didier. Friend. This referendum. Will the vote be *binding*?"

The new mayor blushed beyond the limits of his sorrel skin to hide. "I will request that the outcome of our vote be respected."

The utterance sounded so pathetic that Didier was ready to tender his resignation on the spot. Everyone at the gathering, even those few who wanted the Australians to come in and finish the mining, felt pity for the mayor. The island had all but forced the man into a position he hadn't sought. No one imagined that he would face developments on this scale. Now it was their duty to rally around and comfort him.

"Discussions start tomorrow," the Queen shouted. "Tonight, we dance on it."

And because she was the Queen, the decree passed without vote. The ukes started up as if on cue. The Queen made the rounds, refusing to take no for an answer until everyone was either eating or dancing. She got the mayor out on the dance floor, along with half the craft circle, the odd and troubled American couple, all the children, and even the ancient Canadian diver, who turned out to have a move or two, picked up under the waves, no doubt, where all creatures dance with virtuosity every moment of their lives.

With so large a part of the island moving in time together, their bodies a rhythmic surge that synced with the pulsing tide, feeling the freedom of their arms and legs powering the pleasures of their swaying trunks, the dancers began to sing the song that the pickup orchestra had wandered into, the song whose words and melody everyone born on the island knew:

> *O Makatea, poe nehenehe,*
> *Te tamarii a Ta'aroa!*
> *E nunaa tatou no*
> *te hoê fenua mo'a, e fenua manuïa.*

> O Makatea, beautiful pearl,
> child of Ta'aroa!
> Let us take care of
> this sacred land. This lucky land.

It was a good tune, the Queen decided, as she danced. The tune could get a person up just about any climb. It might be the best song she knew. She waved her arms like a swimming thing and sang, *E fenua manuïa, e fenua manuïa, e fenua manuïa!*

....

OUR FRIENDSHIP WAS BUILT ON PLAY. *No game was beneath us. Rafi and I played mindless fillers merely as a break from the cosmic brain-burn of Go. We spent hours down in that ground-floor corridor that connected the Saint Ignatius main building to the annex, playing that high school favorite where you chucked dice and tried to take over the world.*

"Man," Rafi said. "Anyone who needs luck to take over the world isn't really trying hard enough." I remembered that joke years later, closing in on my first hundred million.

We joined up with five other Chess Club nerds to play Diplomacy—John Kennedy, Walter Cronkite, and Henry Kissinger's favorite game. It unfolded over the course of a marathon ten-hour session one Saturday at the home of one of the club members, a Frank Lloyd Wright creation in Hyde Park. I later hired that guy to work for me as a lawyer for Playground, starting him at two hundred thousand a year, based in part on his conniving in that game.

Rafi's powers of deception in Diplomacy were so fine that it took the others all day to figure out the little two-step collusion that he and I worked up, as Russia and Austria-Hungary. I held my own in the covert dual con game. Late that night I won, and Rafi was my kingmaker. Just like he became in real life.

We played another game—years ahead of its time, where seven ancient cultural groups of the Mediterranean—Assyrians, Babylonians, Illyrians, Cretans, and their ilk—evolve from the Stone Age into the Late Classical and beyond. We didn't know it, but that game was an advance scout for the renaissance about to hurtle the whole pastime of board gaming into the modern era. It checked all our boxes: no luck, open information, multiple paths to victory, and incentives for creative play—a game more about the ride than the arrival.

But those games were mere diversions. Nothing had our full love but Go. We took lessons from the only other kid in school who knew how to play—a left-brain genius in my AP calculus class whose father happened to be the consul general to the U.S. from South Korea. We signed up for weekend classes at a place off Cermak in Chinatown. That dojo felt like a monastery whose monks were the secret manipulators behind the course of history.

I looked for Go-playing software to train on, but nothing existed that could do better than near-random legal moves. All the dial-up bulletin boards agreed: Automating Go lay way beyond the capabilities of programming. The play was too freewheeling, the search space too vast, the goals at every level—from the smallest tactic to the grandest strategy—too complex to formulate with any rigor.

Most experts thought a computer Go agent would never beat a strong human. Of course, the experts had said as much about chess, and chess programs now chewed up all but the really great players. For a long time, chess had been the crowning metric of human intellect, the best measure for what set us apart from mere machines. Now it was becoming obvious that the game might be mastered with brute force.

And so, the benchmark of human intelligence shifted from chess to Go. Go required deep intuition, creativity, psychological insight, a spark of indefinable genius. In short: all the things that chess was supposed to have possessed just a few years before. All the things machines would never be able to do.

Of all the things we humans excel at, moving the goalposts may be our best trick. The moment advanced AIs get good at that, they'll have passed the real Turing test.

I was a soldier for the digital revolution. My basement software side-hustle was now netting me a thousand dollars a month. The entire computer industry—hardware and software—was being driven forward at an incredible pace by games, and game programs were among the most complex artifacts ever made by humanity. So it bugged me that programming fell so short when it came to the game that now consumed us both. Rafi was delighted. Any setback to me was a victory for him and all his poet rebel kin. Already the two of us were locked in a zero-sum game.

"You need a little humbling, bro. If I thought for a minute that you might really automate all the things you plan to automate, I'd have to kill you to save mankind's future."

For the moment, our killing was reserved for the nineteen-by-nineteen board, and the beautiful flow of the life and death of stones. We began playing at my house in the evenings. My father had given me a lightly used Audi Fox as a birthday gift after I got my license. It was meant to impress me with his largesse, to distract me from his recent recommitment to philandering and dissipation, and to exempt him from having to chauffeur me around town. I'd drive to Saint Ig and park the thing in a lot on Roosevelt because my father, great Ignatius booster though he was, forbade me to park it on the street "in that kind of neighborhood." Then I'd take Rafi back to Evanston with me after school.

There were ample spare rooms for Rafi at the Castle. He picked out his favorite and semi–moved in. He couldn't get enough of my latest personal computer with the color graphics card paid for by the proceeds from my chess software business. I had upgraded three times already since the days of READY >_, *and the leaps were like those from bacteria to trilobites. Rafi was a computer games virgin. Games were coming into the world that had no precedent in human history. Shooters. Point-and-click adventures. Interactive fictions. Unscripted business sims that gave the user real agency. Puzzle pieces raining down from on high.*

Rafi tried them but didn't like them. "Whoa. That's just like beating off. Where's the love, man? Where's the other human?"

We'd sit together up in the turret near the widow's walk, eating Space Food Sticks and talking French Existentialism. "You know what we are?" he said, sipping his favorite Life Savers soda. "Condemned to freedom. Sisyphus really is happy, brother. Give or take."

After an hour of homework, we'd play through classic Go games until after midnight. His parents didn't care and mine barely noticed. We played short blowouts and long, rolling matches where we couldn't tell who would win until well past two hundred moves. I remember him once slapping down a brutal stone I didn't anticipate. His grin was vicious. "It's all fun and games, huh? Until someone loses an Eye."

We'd head back down to the South Side in the Audi the next morning. If it was Saturday, he never let me drive him to his doorstep but always got out a couple blocks from his mother's apartment. "Listen, honky. You are not driving into that 'hood in this auto-mo-bile."

He knew his way around white people well enough, from having gone to school with them on the North Side for so many years. But he liked to blast the unexamined privilege of my neighborhood, rolling his eyes for my benefit and falling into his Uncle Remus voice: "So tha's how y'all do things up here! I knew . . . I say, I knew you folks was up to some crazy shit and all, but yowza! This beat everything. Y'all know How To Live, know what I'm sayin'?"

I did not know what he was saying. It took me years to realize.

More than once, we played straight through until morning. As dawn broke, our moves grew shakier with brain-blinding fatigue, but our mastery of the game deepened through indulgence, even if my knowledge of myself did not.

I remember Rafi, bleary-eyed after one brutal ten-hour session, sitting in the breakfast nook of my mother's kitchen, holding a frozen waffle to his head like an ice-pack cure for a hangover and groaning, " 'The road to excess leads to the palace of wisdom.' William Blake."

" 'Wasted days and wasted nights.' Fredrick Fender, Esquire."

"I do not think those lyrics mean what you think they mean, friend. Besides: 'Time you enjoyed wasting was not wasted.' John Lennon."

HE WAS OVER ONE AFTERNOON, waiting for me to finish up my physics problem sets. He pulled a book out of his Army surplus knapsack and hunched over it, in that spidery way he had. I spied the title from across the room: The Philosophy of the Common Task, *by Nikolai Fyodorovich Fyodorov. When I came over to where he was sitting, he squirreled it away. I held out my hand, palm up, wagging my fingers. He handed the book over with a shrug.*

An old volume from the 1930s, rebound in a gray monochrome library binding, it smelled of having been buried in the stacks, untouched, for decades. I flipped through it. It seemed to be the esoteric writing of a nineteenth century Russian madman.

"What the fuck?"

"Okay. I admit it's a little out there."

"Where the hell did you find it?"

He was taking a course in European Literary Modernism at U of I Circle, a short walk behind Ignatius, because he didn't want to read The Great Gatsby *and* Lord of the Flies *for the third time each, in our senior humanities course. That college class got him entrance to the university library stacks and all its buried treasure.*

"It's unbelievable! I can get any book I want. If they don't have it, they can get it from downstate. Twelve million volumes down there. Talk about firepower! And if they don't have it downstate, they'll get it from some other library in the system. I don't care what you say, Keane. Life is good."

"And you're planning to read them all? I mean, Christ! Who on Earth . . . ?" I held the book out and spun it around in space. A total mystery.

"You mean, who would write such a thing?"

"Who would read *it?"*

"Who do you think? Young black bucks who do not like the world as it is, Sam-I-Am!"

"All right. Book report."

"Well. It's simple. Very simple, and . . . also utterly, off-the-wall insane. It's a visionary buried treasure. I stumbled on it by accident, but the moment I leafed through it, I felt I'd been looking for it for a long time."

"Fine. But would you please just tell me what it's about?"

"It's about evolution. About where evolution might be going. The way Fyodorov sees it, in the beginning, evolution stumbled around blindly looking for life, and half a billion years later, it found it. It fooled around trying to come up with consciousness, and a few hundred million more years after that, it hit on that. It experimented with intelligence, and soon enough, bingo. And now it's up to us, evolution's most intelligent children, to help it figure out how to engineer immortality. Defeat the design flaw of death: that's the last and most important step of evolution, after which life will be complete. Which Fyodorov thinks shouldn't be any more impossible than any of those other insane things."

Half of me wanted to blow a raspberry. The other half was thinking how much it resembled ideas I'd imagined myself—the fantasies of a seventeen-year-old kid intoxicated with the exponential growth in the world's programming power. I twirled my finger in the air. "Well? Get on with it!"

"That's what he calls the Common Task. The one thing that can unite all the people on Earth, whatever their histories: Working to learn everything there is to learn, so we can defeat death."

"Well. Fuck me with a garden hose."

"Whatever, dude. You asked me what it was about."

I'd hurt him. "No, no. I'm in. It's crazy. Keep going."

He forgave me, in enthusiasm for the topic. "So Fyodorov thinks . . . he believes that the evolution of intelligence gives people the unique ability to introduce reason and purpose into nature. There's no reason why we can't someday learn to kill death itself. I mean . . . evolution has been changing the rules since the beginning, right?"

I lifted my eyebrows and shrugged. "Okay. And . . . ?"

"And one day, through a mix of genetics, neurology, information theory, and simulation—all things that Fyodorov intuited in embryo, before they existed—living beings will be able to resurrect everyone who has ever lived and died, the way you and I

can replay any game of chess or Go ever played, from a system of notation."

The details poured out of him. The precision of his memory impressed me. I'd never seen Rafi Young so voluble.

"So . . . was he a nutjob?"

"Ask me again in a thousand years."

"What did his contemporaries think?"

"A nutjob, mostly. But Tolstoy loved him. Dostoyevsky said it was like reading his own thoughts."

"And what do . . . people think now? I mean, is it all just gibberish?"

Rafi didn't bother answering. My best friend in the world was lost in his own ideas about humanity's *Common Task.*

We didn't play Go that night. But we did fall into a conversation with the rhythm of a match between old 9 dan rivals. Rafi placed a word, experimental, enigmatic, probing some intersection. Then I placed another word somewhere else on the infinite board, changing his probe into two others. Before either of us realized, we were talking openly to each other as never before.

"Todd. Listen. I'm going to tell you something I've never told anyone."

"You can," I said.

"I'm serious. Abuse this and I'm done with you."

"Understood," I said. I knew I could never betray him.

He was quiet for a long time. My idiocy later would know no bounds. But that night, I was wise enough to let him take forever. When he started talking, it was almost to himself.

"The night I got accepted into Ignatius . . ." His body narrowed. "My stepfather wasn't going to let me go. Too white for him. My sister . . . she was the only person who really knew me. She went after him. She called him something. I never learned what. He chased her out of the apartment, onto the landing. . . ."

The coward in me wanted him to stop.

"She died. She told him I was smarter than he would ever

know, and . . . she died. The man chased her. . . . He might as well have killed her with his own hands."

He turned over the old gray library book in his lap, looking at it as if it had just fallen from the sky.

"I can see the future she should have had. She always wanted to go to New York. She thought New York was It. Liberty. She wanted to go to New York and work in fashion. But in fact . . . she's never going to do another fucking thing."

We both held still. I had seen that look on him before, when he searched for the perfect next place to set a stone.

"And I have to go home every night and live under the same roof as the man. My mother . . . defends him. I can't take it anymore. But my only alternative is to go live with my abusive and vengeful real father, who rides me like I'm his personal retribution machine against all racism everywhere."

A crazy idea shot into my head. "Do you think your sister . . . ?" I pointed to the book: The Philosophy of the Common Task. *Resurrect everyone who ever lived. "Are you saying that someday it might be possible . . . ?"*

"No, asshole. Don't insult me." When I recoiled, his tone softened. "Sorry. But trust me. You can't understand this. Anything. You live here . . . in this place. . . ." He lifted his palms, almost amused by the Castle's trappings. "With those parents. . . ."

I wanted to trade hostages, to tell him that my father was a crazy man who liked to fly small planes in thunderstorms and who had taken to acquiring things he could not afford. That my parents hated each other and tortured each other for pure entertainment. But nothing I claimed could match what Rafi was telling me.

"I tend to think that the world is my fault. Maybe that's ego or something. But getting accepted into Ignatius was not my fault. Being smart is not my fault. Not wanting to die in a Housing Authority apartment at the bottom of a flight of broken stairs is not my fault."

When he spoke again, both his skinny shoulders were up near his neck. "You don't know, man. You don't even know how free you are, because it's just like breathing, for you. I . . . can get free. Sometimes. But only when reading. When I read . . . the other place is more real than this one. If the book is wild enough, I can forget that I'm living in a murderer's house.

"So, if you're asking me: Is this Russian dude crazy? I say: Of course. Do I think we're really going to conquer death? Not in my lifetime. Do I think that all of evolution is embarked on an adventure to learn how to undo death and raise the dead? You bet."

"You . . . what?"

The look that froze my face made him grin, groan, and grab his head. "Keane. Dude. It's a poem."

"I don't understand poetry."

"I know. That's why we love you, motherfuck."

I'D SETTLED ON GOING downstate after graduation, but not on account of that twelve-million-volume library that Rafi lusted after. The University of Illinois had one of the five best computer science programs in the country. It had just landed a massive windfall to build a National Center for Supercomputing Applications. It boasted the first real-time, multiuser system of networked graphics terminals, where email, forums, message boards, chat rooms, instant messages, and online games all got their start. My home, before I even landed.

I went down to Urbana to take the tour. The whole north campus was filled with my people. My parents had no objection. My father had lost his golden touch in the octagon, and he was busy breaking all the accumulated nest eggs. He couldn't have sent me to a private school if I'd wanted to go. Illinois was still a bargain, and with the scholarship the university was throwing at me, I'd make money by going there. Hardly even a decision.

I'd gone out three times with a girl I knew from lifeguarding named Jill Simmons. There was something like sex involved. I told Jillie I was going to the U of I, and she laughed. She was on her way east, to Sarah Lawrence, where she'd been headed since the age of ten. College was going to be her ticket out of the Midwest forever. She told me that wasting my Saint Ignatius credential and college entrance test scores to go to a state school was worse than stupid.

I didn't even bother arguing. Right before the holidays, we wished each other good luck and happy trails. It was a relief to us both, to escape our first relationship free and clear without any bloodshed. It all seemed very mature. We were still too young to know how maturity played out, in real life.

Rafi was fighting other battles. Much to my shame, it never occurred to me that merely going to college might throw his whole life into turmoil. He would have been accepted just about any-where. But no choice he made would be accepted by all the other parties in his life. I should have seen that.

He had friends back in his old neighborhood on the edge of Pilsen that he never talked about with me. I don't know whether he was ashamed of them or ashamed of me. Either way, he kept us separate. I didn't even know their names. A couple of these friends were going to Richard J. Daley College on South Pulaski, a two-year community college and part of Chicago's seven city colleges.

"Thinkin' I will, too, dude."

"Rafi! Are you out of your fuckin' mind? Death by live burial. You'd be throwing your life away."

He froze up like a broken spaceship air lock. "You have no idea what you're talking about. White boy."

I spent two increasingly heated weeks trying to argue him out of it. I was doing to him exactly what Jillie Simmons had done to me.

Rafi chose to stand with his homies. "It's done, man. Back off. Besides, it's not that big a deal."

The choice shattered me.

Rafi's mother gave her blessing. She herself had not gone to col-lege. Small steps seemed right to her. She praised his choice to stay in the city. Moody Stepdad told him to do whatever he wanted.

Rafi took his decision to his father. If I had been appalled, his father was incensed. From what I heard later, the man was an inch *from punching Rafi in the face. Donnie Young hadn't poured a good portion of his salary for the last four years into an exclusive private school for his exceptional son just to have that advantage thrown away on a city community college. He himself had gone to Circle, where he had been humiliated, and later to Malcolm X, which he found pointless and exasperating. His son's future was his own last hope.*

Donnie Young had a contact at Virginia Military Institute. He lined up a letter of recommendation from a friend who had a seat in the Illinois House of Representatives, and he started the application process in Rafi's name. Meanwhile, Sondra Young Johnson was sure that if her son disappeared into the savage heartland of Virginia and became a military man, she would never see him again.

Rafi came to me in despair. "They're going to kill me, brother. Between the two of them."

"Your dad wants you in the Army?"

"Naw, man. It's just a threat."

"For what? What does he want?"

"Nothing much. Just for me to save the Black Race by beating the White Man at his own game."

"Huh. Sounds like he's playing Go."

Rafi's laugh bore no relation to mirth. "He keeps giving me these books. Dick Gregory. The Honorable Prophet Elijah Muhammad. Like they're proof that I need to go to a military academy and get ready for the End Times. He's losing it."

"Raff. Come down to Illinois. It'll be close enough so your mother won't freak. It's ranked higher than VMI on almost everything, so it should satisfy your dad's whole uplift thing. And it's a state school, so your friends can't accuse you of . . ."

A vicious smile tugged at his upper lip. "Of what, brother? Accuse me of what?"

I held up both palms. "Okay. I don't know what I'm talking about. Go wherever is best for you."

"Thanks for your blessing, massa."

He applied to several places at the guidance counselor's

suggestions, places with good literature programs, including University of Chicago, Berkeley, Northwestern, and U of I for his safety school. He got into all of them. He put off accepting any for as long as possible. By Easter, he still hadn't committed. But time was running out and he would have to leap soon.

On the Monday after spring vacation, I drove him back up with me to Evanston for a sleepover and as much Go as we could fit into one evening. During the heady rush of that final spring semester, we hadn't played much. We were letting life get in the way of our diversions.

In the car, Rafi dropped his bombshell. "I'll be seeing a lot of your 'hood next year. Can I just have your room while you're away?"

"What? Serious?"

"Goin' to Northwestern. Wearin' my Saint Ignatius blazer and learnin' how to succeed without really tryin'."

I was thrilled that he'd escaped from the pull of Richard J. Daley Community College. But Northwestern seemed a little rich for Rafi's blood. I wondered how he and his atomized family were going to pay for so expensive a school. That's how messed up I was.

"Who am I supposed to play Go with next year?"

"Fifty thousand students. Fifteen percent Asian. Mostly engineers. You'll find someone."

"We could play by mail. Or road trips. It's only three hours."

"You just concentrate on your coursework, young Freshman Todd."

So there it was: our futures, diverging. Deflated, I congratulated him, and all the way up Lake Shore Drive we talked smack about each other's future paths. I couldn't shake my sense of betrayal, and I wanted to retaliate. I chose my point of attack for maximum irritation.

"By the time we finish school, a computer will be writing poems that pass for human."

"That is such a crock of shit. Maybe bad haikus and broken limericks."

"As far as I can tell, half the poems in the New Yorker are already being written by a machine."

"Ah, the joys of illiteracy."

"By the time we die, all our arts will be handled by artificial intelligence."

"How can a relatively smart human spew such shit? Listen to yourself! Listen to what you're saying! You think creation is all just . . . ?"

"Yes. Yes, I do."

He opened his mouth to rebut me, but incredulity stopped him cold. Little machine-gun sounds of astonishment caught in his throat. He threw up his hands in capitulation and began tugging at his tiny goatee. "Whatever, Hal."

We got off Lake Shore Drive and turned onto North Sheridan. I felt how much I was going to miss him, even if only for the arguments. More than any other childhood friend, he was going to leave a hole in my life, like the space of a captured stone.

In another few blocks he rallied and turned invulnerable again.

"Young Todd Keane, heading down into the cornfields to be ordained as a novitiate at the temple for supercomputing . . . where he gonna teach . . . confuters how to write podems!"

"Rafi Young, attending Little Harvard by the Lake, where he hopes to study literature that will evade the coming hostile takeover of the humanities by our digital overlords."

"I like my odds in this game."

A few weeks ago, we had laid ourselves bare to each other. Now I felt him disappearing again.

"You serious about wanting to live in my room?"

His head recoiled from the idea. He'd already forgotten his little joke. "Aw, naw, man. I wouldn't do that to Maestro and Mammy Keane. A black man living in their house who they weren't paying an hourly wage? It ain't fittin'. It just ain't fittin'."

We cut over to Chicago Avenue and then Sherman, alongside the diagonal of the railroad tracks. Cars around us slowed and thickened. Lights flashed up ahead.

"*Lookie there!*" Rafi marveled. "*The popo . . . are arresting . . . some* white folk*!*"

Someone had run into the central pillar of the underpass at Greenwood. The cops were blocking the turn while furiously waving traffic on Sherman to keep moving. Of course, that only made the gapers' block worse. We were half a block north when my brain realized what it had seen.

My hands lost their grip on the wheel and my voice went spectral. I aimed the car toward the curb and slowed. "Oh, shit. Shit. Shit."

Rafi bolted forward and gripped the dash. "What . . . ? Hey— Todd? You okay?"

The car that was wrapped around the concrete bridge pylon—a Silver 450SL convertible—had the vanity plates PIT BULL.

"That was my father."

We left the Audi half-parked and ran back to the accident. The police wouldn't let us through, even when I screamed at them. An ambulance pulled up slantwise under the viaduct. The paramedics took the crumpled-up body out of the car and angled it toward the waiting stretcher. My father was in no pain.

I DON'T REMEMBER MUCH *about the rest of that spring. Anterograde amnesia, my brain erasing all traces of what had just settled over my life. That, plus the medications the shrinks put me on for months afterward. My mother was even more traumatized than I was, and she hadn't seen the paramedics dragging the man out of his beloved car like a sandbag. The twenty-year game of mutually assured destruction she had played with her spouse was over, and they had both won.*

We didn't have a funeral. We took my dad's boat, and along with his estranged sister and a pair of dutiful trader friends of his, we brought his ashes out onto Lake Michigan and spread them on the swells.

Surrounded by water, so far out that Chicago and Gary were just brown smudges on the horizon, I remembered how I once knew I would grow up to be an oceanographer. Nothing but life underwater had been large enough to shelter me from this man's relentless and abrasive escapades. Now the water had him.

On the way back to the marina, I told my mother, "Me, too. Bury me at sea."

She said, "Fine. Find some state that will let you compost me."

ALMOST RIGHT AWAY, CREDITORS *began to circle the Castle. Scrambling to grasp what was happening (although some part of her surely knew), my mother sifted through the check stubs and credit card statements for the last several years, something she'd always had the luxury of leaving to her husband. She found hundreds of receipts from pharmacies all over the tri-state area, as well as prescriptions for oxycodone from at least four different doctors. Only then did I seriously consider the hundreds of orange and white plastic pill cylinders my mother and I had overlooked for so many years, dutifully facilitating the wreck of the man who still ruled our lives.*

What wasn't to be found anywhere in the paperwork my mother combed through was money. Micky Keane, working-class South Sider, trophy child of the Jesuits, self-made multimillionaire, endower of scholarships, steel-nerved virtuoso of trading-pit brinksmanship, audiophile, pilot of tiny planes, had died a drug fiend and left his codependent family deep in debt.

In quick succession, my mother auctioned off the collection of oils, including a choice Jamie Wyeth that my father had bought to celebrate my first birthday. Dad had already sold the Cessna without telling my mother. No trace of the proceeds. The 450, of course, was worthless.

Mom put the Castle on the market, and it sold four days later. Before I knew what was happening, we started moving into a tiny apartment in Rogers Park. In the chaos of my new life, I finished high school borderline suicidal. My father's ghost came into my bedroom at night, sat on the foot of my bed, and asked if I'd like to play tiddlywinks.

I saw little of Rafi, except in classes. I had no desire to bring him up north with me after school ever again. He was solicitous, coming by my locker during passing periods, as if by accident.

"Hold on," he said. "Small steps."

In early May, he sought me out in the cafeteria at lunch, sitting down across the table with his sack lunch that he always brought from home. He seemed way too casual.

"Got a roommate for fall?"

The question irritated me. "It's a lottery, if you don't request one. They tell you who you match with, over the summer."

"I know how they do it, bro."

I stopped eating and studied him. It was always a game, with Rafi. Or maybe that was me.

"What's this about?"

"Well, brother. Turns out Northwestern already has its quota of five black boys for next year."

"What are you saying? You changed your mind?"

He shrugged, shoulders too high, the way that made him look like a comedian. "Same education, at a quarter of the price. Math's not my strong suit, but it seems like your little land-grant school might be a better deal. Man of the people like me don't need no more private, elite institutions on the résumé. Gets suspicious, after a while. Besides, I know some folks who are going downstate."

My mood cleared and my spine straightened like a plant growing in time-lapse. I didn't know what had made him change his mind. It wouldn't occur to me for a long time: He was seeing me through a dark time. He'd chosen to keep an eye on me, as a brother does.

DR. AND MRS. MANNIS, COMBING THE TIDE POOLS JUST
west of Malibu.

They came up for a conference at UCLA, where Evelyne spoke
on cleaning stations in the Coral Triangle. The talk was a hit,
as Evie's talks always were. She was goofy and ingenuous at the
podium, a guaranteed crowd-pleaser with her still-colorful English
and her little-girl's awe, backed by exotic Ektachrome slides that
she clicked through using a carousel projector.

Bart Mannis had sat near the back of the packed room, falling in love with his stranger wife all over again. He marveled at
how unlikely a couple they were, how wildly incompatible. She was
rangy, adventurous, naïve, fearless, irreverent, and crazy passion-
ate, but only about the sea. He had grown more land-bound, practical, work-driven. He still chafed sometimes at her independence,
once even demanding to know where the marriage was headed. But
he was utterly, hopelessly besotted with her, and he had made his
choice. He'd tried to walk away once and failed. Now, even when
her waywardness grabbed him by the throat, when her coming and
going left him bereft, he knew he would never again think of letting go of the potato. Everything came from the potato. Without
the potato, life would be far bleaker.

In some ways, his existence was simpler than it had been. He
worked as academic support staff at Scripps. He had his research
and taught the occasional class. Evelyne stayed land-bound for
almost eighteen months, completing her long-deferred doctorate.
She had become an American citizen, and visas were no longer a
problem. But with every old issue solved, new ones loomed larger.

Bart had learned much in their eight years together. First among
those things was always to wait until she was in her element,
wrapped up in the ecstasy of marine things, before talking about
anything important. So he had put off for months all thought of
broaching the subject that consumed him. He'd waited until this
moment, with her entranced by a two-foot long, twenty-pound

black sea hare crawling through the drowned basalt at Leo Carrillo beach. The tide was out, and everywhere the pools teemed with sea stars, anemones, mossy chitons, striped shore crabs, assorted tegulae, and hermit crabs pursuing their theft-driven home upgrades. Bart—the erstwhile Limpet—should have been as blissed-out as his wife. But once again it fell to him to keep the small craft of their marriage from being lost at sea.

"Anything you want for your birthday, sweet? It's in three weeks, you know."

"Hmmm? Oh. How about one of these?" She pointed at the sea hare's waving rhinophores. "Can we bring one home?"

The word sounded bittersweet in the crash of the surf. She had been home so little in the last two years.

"This birthday is a big one, you know."

"Big one? How?" She did the math and lifted her eyes from the slow-motion drama of the tide pool. "Argh. You mean the zero on the end."

She sighed and stretched out on the pocked volcanic stone, looking up at the sky. He would have lain down next to her, to level the playing field. But the tide was creeping back in, each wave hurling itself closer, and one of them had to keep an eye out.

She pulled her stringy, strawberry hair out of her mouth and addressed herself to the sky. "Ach, I get it. You want to bring up the babies again."

Bart bit down and swallowed his bile. "You told me to bring it up again when you turned thirty."

"Hey! That's not for another three weeks."

In his silence, her hand flopped about like the strangest of sea creatures, until it found his.

"You must laugh at my jokes. Otherwise, I'm going to start thinking I'm not funny. Which we both know is *not* true."

A little tubercular laugh came up his throat. "Which we both know is not true."

Then it was just the surf, just the spray, the beat of the waves breaking up the ancient rock, the deep, slow subduction miles down grinding away at the edges of the tectonic plates. And farther out, the currents' great upwelling.

She squeezed his hand. "Okay."

The sound startled him. "Okay, what?"

"Okay, *my sweet*."

He laughed again, less morosely. "Wait. You mean, you're okay with it? With starting . . . ?"

He stopped, feeling her flinch a little. But his heart was soaring.

The timing was ideal—a window when she was land-bound, finishing up the coursework for the Ph.D. She had all her data for her dissertation: years' worth, gathered over the course of three separate research trips, meticulously recorded and already half tabulated.

"Sure," she said, into the salt air. "Why not?"

Months of anxiety dissolved in the spume. Bart wanted to shout. "Serious? Are you serious?" He knelt on the rock and covered her body in his. "Oh, I love you. I *love* you. You have no idea."

She laughed as he tickled her, and gasped, "Some!" Professional success was making her so much more agreeable.

A wave broke a few feet below them and soaked them in several inches of surge. They bolted up, both laughing now. When they sobered, she said, "It's not a large deal."

Her lightness intoxicated him all over again. She must have been preparing for this, readying and reconciling herself to capitulation for a long time.

"I mean: think about it." She drew his hand over her flat belly, as provocative a gesture as he could remember her ever making. "It's quite cool, really. For nine months, I will be the host of a sea creature!"

———

TWO, IN FACT. She defended her dissertation while eight months pregnant. Then came the twins. A boy Danny and a girl Dora. She held them, one in the crook of each arm, two red, squalling, wild things, their heads not yet recovered from crowning. She had never felt such overwhelming awe, not even underwater. As for Bart, the press of amazement against his chest threatened to kill him.

The twins were like divergent species: hair, size, body shape, temperament—yin and yang, different enough that more than one grandparent wondered if the hospital had been playing games. Almost from the start, the boy liked building things. The Beaulieu engineering gene seemed to have skipped a generation. Danny craved Lincoln Logs, Erector sets, toys that bewildered both his parents. Within a few years, he was building what he called *Base Stations*. He remembered them all, and numbered them, and even months later he could describe *Base Station Thirteen*.

The girl was haunted and withdrawn. Dora wanted only to be read stories. By four, she started to invent them. *Suppose the moon went down into a mouse hole to have a look around. Suppose Gramma's false teeth fell into the telephone and came out the other end and bit your earlobe.*

Separate, these two small sovereign nations astonished Evelyne, and together they blew her mind. Their emotions pulsed like the skin colors of a flamboyant squid. She had no idea that land-based creatures could be so interesting.

Early on, she showed them how to love the sea. But neither of her children loved the same sea she did. Danny stood on the edge of the Tijuana Slough, gazing westward into the vast Pacific with wild surmise. He was building things: boats that could reach invisible islands, outposts on giant pylons rising above the waves, cities in bubble domes colonizing the coral-encrusted ocean bottom. Dora would sit on a rock exposed by low tide, cocking her head left and right, listening to the sound of the waves and the gulls and the sea lions, entranced by the symphony. "What are they saying, Mama? What does it mean?"

Bart was spectacular with them both. There were times, in fact, when Evie envied the strength of his connection, especially with Dora. Of course, he spent so much more time with them both. When they did things as a family now, she sometimes felt like a visiting aunt.

All four of them prowled the tide pools in La Jolla Cove. The children clung to their father's bare legs. She told them, "Did you know that the two of you were conceived in a tide pool?"

"Evelyne!" Bart scolded. "Don't tell them that!"

"Why not?"

"You know why not. It isn't true."

"It is!"

"What's 'conceived'?" the little engineer demanded.

She tipped her head toward her husband. He stammered, "It means what happens to make you get born."

The boy giggled. The girl looked solemn and amazed.

They sat on the edge of a pool large enough to house both children—four giants peering down through the heavens into another world. The children pointed to every living thing they could see, and their parents named them and told them something odd about each creature. Then Danny found something out of place: a glass bottle, no bigger than Evelyne's hand, invisible except for the slight warping of light around the tapered neck. The boy reached to pick it up. His mother swooped in to stop his hand, fiercely enough to startle the child into tears. He looked to his father for explanation and redress. His father took his hand.

Evie apologized. "Oh, honey. I didn't mean to frighten you. But no one can touch it. Look! There are things living inside!"

The boy stopped crying and peered into the transparent cave. Across the underside of the invisible glass wall hung the twisting tubes of annelid worms. Barnacles clamped to the curved outside, floating mystically above the living pool. Three tiny urchins, like spiny black half marbles, crept across the bottle's base. A colony of hydrae polyps budded in chains around the opening.

The bottle had dropped by godly accident into the pool, and life, which never stopped toying with possible next moves, had exploited the miraculous hiding place dozens of times. The more the family looked, the more settlers they saw inside the glass flask. Stems of living sponges, a bright russet color. Wafer-thin crabs no wider across than the girl's two fingers. Grassy mats of algae, sedentary colonies of moss animals, a pair of crustaceans, and a gastropod whose name only Limpet knew.

Danny was thrilled. "It's a whole city!"

Dora stared at the aquarium inside the aquarium on the edge of the largest aquarium on the planet. The girl shook her head, transfixed by an idea. "I wish I could live there."

"Terrific," the father said. "My *two* mermaids."

―――

OCEANOGRAPHY FLOURISHED IN THOSE YEARS, when the Great Society collided with the Cold War and money flowed into all the sciences. Strange projects that the government deemed worth paying for sprang up with each new season. In the year that the land-based world exploded—in Prague, in Paris, in D.C., across Indochina, in Memphis, in department stores in Frankfurt, in a hotel kitchen in L.A., in the streets of Chicago, in the streets of Mexico City, on an atoll in French Polynesia—the year of the first picture of the whole Earth, Evelyne learned of a project ripped out of her own dreams. The General Electric Company Space Division and Seabees from the United States Navy's Amphibious Construction Battalion were combining to construct a live-in underwater laboratory on the seabed of Great Lameshur Bay, off St. John, in the U.S. Virgin Islands. The Tektite lab would study the viability of saturation diving.

Simply hearing about the project transported Evelyne twenty-two years into the past, back to the night that her father threw her into the Air Liquide test pool in Montreal with a prototype aqualung strapped to her back. The future that she'd envisioned so clearly that night had been decades in coming. But now it was finally here.

Some years earlier, in 1963, when Captain Cousteau built Starfish House, a settlement for five people situated four hundred feet down in the Red Sea, she had dreamed of taking part. She ached for a chance to work in the portable submerged dwellings being toyed with throughout the mid-sixties. In 1965, she watched in

agony from Scripps Pier as three teams of male divers lived underwater in Sealab II for fifteen-day shifts, two hundred feet below
the surface in La Jolla Undersea Canyon. Her exclusion from that
project was the most painful moment of her life, including giving
birth to twins. She would not miss out on another chance.

A notice on a bulletin board at Scripps solicited research proposals for the Tektite project. She wrote up one that involved protracted close study of the relations between coral polyps and the
fish that fed on them. It was a quantitative study that could only
be done by saturation diving, with the researcher in the water for
long periods.

Evelyne did not tell her husband about her application. So she
could not go cry on Limpet's shoulder when she was rejected. She
had nine hundred documented hours of diving experience and
underwater research to her name. Yet, the project's gatekeepers
turned her down. She wrote to the organizers in the Department
of the Interior, asking why. The explanation came, phrased as if
it were self-explanatory. Men and women could not live stably
together in close quarters, underwater, for two months at a time.

The claim was true, as far as it went. After all, men and women
could not live stably on dry land, with no constraints on their
mobility. But the truth did not keep Evelyne Beaulieu Mannis from
wanting to take all the men in the Department of the Interior and
put them on a leaking raft in the middle of the equatorial calms.
She wrote back to thank them for their consideration and let it
go at that.

She returned to the business of raising the twins, teaching
adjunct classes throughout Southern California, converting her
thesis into articles, collating, curating, and publishing her years
of research findings from the RV *Ione*, giving talks and attending conferences, cooking and cleaning house for a family of four,
and diving whenever the chance arose. She had no time left over
for any but the most casual bitterness. Underwater research habitats would continue to proliferate. In a few years, she reasoned,

scientists and even civilians would be living in seabed communities across the world.

When the second letter from the Tektite gatekeepers arrived two months later, it blindsided her. The Department of the Interior, with funding from NASA (who were studying scientific teams working in confined environments), were manning the missions for Tektite II, to be run the following year. Would Dr. Mannis be interested in participating in a two-week, all-female mission, under the direction of visiting Harvard research fellow Dr. Sylvia Earle?

Evelyne had learned, years ago, to convey such news to her husband with her euphoria converted into contrition. And still, he took the announcement hard. There would be two weeks of training, two weeks of underwater life, and a few days of various kinds of decompression afterward.

"Your children are four years old, and you want to abandon them for more than a month?"

"Not *abandon*. You'll be—"

"Do you have any idea how long that is for a young child to be without a mother? They'll forget who you are."

"We can speak by phone, right up until I submerge. And again as soon as I surface."

"At three dollars a minute? The bill will cost more than they're paying you."

But Evelyne heard awe in her husband's voice. She simply had to stay remorseful until he gave in. Bart Mannis, too, had given his life to the ocean. Some part of him revered the idea of being married to one of the first five women since the evolution of *Homo sapiens* to live underwater. And he loved his two four-year-olds so fiercely that even the chaos of a month alone with them would be something to savor.

Bart fretted for some days, shaken by the course their lives had taken. Evie proffered her reassurances and begged his forgiveness and his blessing. In time, he gave both. Danny buzzed with all the excitement of a child too young to understand what was happening. His mother was going to live in a town under the sea. Dora hugged herself, in tears. She made her mother promise again and again to come home as soon as possible.

At the last minute, one of the project managers balked at the idea of letting mothers of small children on the project. But Evie and Dr. Earle, the guilty parties, pointed out that several of the male divers were also fathers. That argument alone might not have carried the day, but it was too late to replan a mission already under way. And so, in the summer of 1970, Evelyne Beaulieu Mannis found herself lifting off from San Diego International, letting loose a silent but delirious victory whoop from her seat over the wing of a Boeing 727 as she headed back east.

———

SHE MET HER THREE fellow scientists and the crew's engineer in Chicago for a series of orientations. One of them she knew from the grad program at Scripps. With all of them, Evelyne felt instantly at ease. She would have welcomed any as a friend. There was no posturing or jockeying for status, as there had always been on the all-male research ships she'd worked on. Just simple, mutual respect and shared curiosity, a love of everything marine that soon turned into affection for one another. From the start, they were a working team.

They flew from Chicago to the Virgin Islands. From outside, the team's new home looked like a shotgun wedding between two small oil refinery silos on the roof of a warehouse. But inside, the Tektite Hilton looked like the heaven of Evelyne's dreams. Forty-three feet down in the crystalline Caribbean, the deluxe accommodation delighted her. The bunk beds were as comfortable as any she'd slept in. The temperature and humidity controls worked better than those in her own home. There was a workbench with a good microscope and other essential lab instruments, a sink with running water, a private toilet, and a glorious shower that ran both hot and cold. The vibrant main chamber of the complex boasted General Electric's finest space-saving appliances: refrigerator, range, television, and even a state-of-the-art tape deck. The freezer was filled with prepared meals.

But the area of the town house that thrilled Evie the most was the lower level of the second tower. The pressure of the room kept the water at bay, so she could open a hatch in the floor onto the azure Caribbean, step through the portal, and be swimming with the fishes fifty feet below the surface as easily as if she'd stepped out to sit in her La Jolla backyard.

The crew were to have no face-to-face contact with any other humans for the duration of the mission. That suited Evelyne. She had spent so many hours of her life in aquariums, studying the fish who swam in their constrained homes. Now she and her brilliant colleagues were the aquarium captives, while the fish of the reef swam past the Hilton all day long and peered in the windows at this most curious sight. NASA, too, was peering in on closed-circuit cameras, studying them for every change brought on by their extreme confinement. The space program was eager to study how the women would bear up in long durations under challenging conditions. This was the part of the project that Evelyne couldn't comprehend. Why would you use the sea to plan for space trips? *This* was the voyage.

The press dubbed the crews of the other Tektite missions *aquanauts*. But for the crew of Mission Six, reporters came up with *aquabelles*, *aquababes*, *aquanettes*, and *aquanaughties*. The journalists did not report that the crew of Mission Six consistently outperformed their male colleagues in almost every metric, from the quality and quantity of their underwater research to the ease of their close-quarters cooperation. If an all-male NASA were really looking for proof that women could do research and perform well in space, they had the data on every day of that two-week adventure.

Brilliant new rebreathers allowed Mission Six to enjoy much longer, quieter dives. Evelyne suited up, stepped into a hole in the floor of the apartment's foyer, and found herself treading on the continental shelf, meeting the neighbors up close and personal for many hours at a time.

Two weeks of life in one submerged spot, and the blurry mass of surrounding organisms separated out into individual personalities. Together each evening in their snug home, the five humans watched the changing of the guard as the morning troupe of animals gave way to the night shift. They watched a triggerfish and a squirrelfish exchange a well-hidden bed at dawn. They had frequent visits from an extraordinary green moray that they all called Puff, and a gang of five inseparable gray angelfish who only ever appeared together. They learned to tell one fish from the other, and they named each one of the five fish after themselves, according to their personalities.

For the first time, Evelyne was *inside* the endless creation of the sea. On one outing with two of her crewmates, she discovered a cluster of vertically swimming garden eels who had made camp near the structure's effluent pipes. Even the sides of the habitat were being colonized by whole ecosystems built around *Porifera* and segmented worms. She learned when the longsnout butterflyfish would show up to peer in the windows. She delighted in the bonanza of night-feeding tarpon and amberjack, who feasted on the buffet of fingerlings hypnotized by the Tektite's lights.

She swam at night, in waters full of bioluminescent plankton. The sea sparkled like silent fireworks whenever she flicked a limb. She swiped her hand in front of her face, igniting a living candle.

The days passed in a bliss of research. Often the team logged ten or twelve hours of diving a day. She didn't have to endure long periods of decompression after each dive. There would be just one day-long decompression at the end of the adventure. For the first time in her life, Evie did not need a diving stopwatch. She could go another hundred feet deeper with impunity. No long and slow descents and ascents. No forced evacuations back to the surface when a tank emptied, just as the fish were doing something extraordinary. She could come and go all day, a full-time resident, albeit one with an elaborate shell.

The crew acclimated to the cramped quarters and grew fond

of each other's foibles. The five of them felt as if they were back in grad school, sharing a one-room apartment. They lived in harmony, partly enforced by knowing that NASA scientists were eavesdropping. But after a week, they forgot all about their minders. They became a pod of colonists exploring a beautiful new planet.

In two weeks, Evie and her colleagues did research that would have taken several months of conventional diving to perform. She documented the interactions between two hundred species of fish, corals, and plants, including a few not previously known to the region. By the end of the run, the rest of the group was ready to surface. But Evelyne wanted only to go on living in the Tektite for as long as she could.

The five of them surfaced to discover that they were world celebrities. The noise and swarm of terrestrial life gave Evie vertigo. She stood frozen in front of banks of microphones that picked up every fault in her stuttering English and relayed them to millions of listeners. She made terrified appearances on national television and even coughed out a few words to Congress. She suffered through a ticker-tape parade down State Street in Chicago, where the five *aquababes* became honorary city citizens. The lightning storm of flashbulbs at out-of-control press conferences—*Did you bring a hair dryer down there? Were there any catfights?*—reduced her to a timid, lip-chewing twelve-year-old again.

But they had taken the next step in the unfolding adventures of humankind. The thought gave her power. With each new press conference, she grew bolder in preaching the gospel of the oceans. Becoming a part of them would give the troubled race of men something to aspire toward. Once people witnessed the abundance of underwater life, once they *lived there*, they would ache to take care of the place like it was their home.

"And you can bring your hair dryers, if you like," she told the journalists. Saluting her touché, they filed their stories about the quirky Canadian with her eccentric ideas, her colorful accent, and her amphibious, bilingual brain.

HER HUSBAND AND TWO CHILDREN met Evelyne at the gate as she got off the plane at SAN. She stepped into the gate area feeling out of control. The kids looked so much larger than when she had left. Danny clamped onto her right leg like a barnacle. Dora embraced her shyly before retreating behind the legs of her father. Her husband's new aura of self-sufficiency startled her.

"Hey," Limpet said, bobbing in the flow of disembarking passengers and brushing her forearm with one admiring hand. "You look good."

His voice sounded strange. "I feel good," she said, tugging him out of the human current. She remembered herself and rushed to add, "You look good, also."

The apartment swelled with balloons and bunting. Posters with newspaper clippings hung on the walls. Together, the welcome committee of three had made Evelyne a Froot Loops cake that looked as flashy, nebulous, and toxic as a sea slug. Both kids gave her drawings to celebrate her return. Danny had studied the pictures of Tektite, and drew it with clean, strong pen strokes. Dora's Crayola picture was a child's wild Turneresque storm at sea.

"Tell me about this, honey." Evie had learned long ago never to ask, *What is this supposed to be?* It upset her daughter that Evie could never see what Dora's pictures depicted.

"Well, this is the ocean and this is your home and this is you and these are your friends and this is the eel and this is me and Danny and Dad waiting for you in California." She pointed to a line of wild, spectral runes of alien script. "And this is writing."

"Wow! What does the writing say?"

"It says, *Welcome home, Mommie. Please come back and stay with us on dry land.*"

Something went out of Evelyne. Her heart thudded against her lungs like the long snout of the butterfly fish ramming the window of the Tektite, trying to figure out what blocked the way.

"I'm here, sweet one," she told her daughter. "Here to stay." Although it felt as if staying for long would be her death.

———

THAT NIGHT SHE HAD A DREAM. In it, she and one of her beloved teammates—or, in that more-than-logic only accessible in the deep reason of dreams, two of her teammates blended into one—were sharing one of those snug little beds in the central living quarters of Tektite II. Each of them placed their hand on the chest of the other, feeling their synchronized heartbeats beating like mad. It was like a promise. It was warmth and purpose and heat and the future. It was like diving deep.

She woke up, her heart still pounding and her body on the edge of bliss. Something had changed in her, underwater.

———

THE AUTUMN WAS LONG and difficult. She transcribed her research notebooks and cataloged her findings from the two-week Virgin Islands dive. She taught. She raised her children, delighting in their enthusiasms and doing her best to quiet their nightmares. The notoriety that she gained as part of Tektite II's most visible mission generated offers from expeditions to three different oceans. But Evelyne couldn't accept any of them. She had made a deal with Bart, after disappearing on him for most of the summer. The press continued to pester her for interviews. But she had little time for anything but science, teaching, and raising the twins.

It took no great powers of detection for Bart to determine that something was off. But he kept his counsel and waited for her to say. Evelyne volunteered nothing. She limped along, afraid of the dream each time it returned.

Bart was ginger around her. The mood between them went from polite to even more polite. Their bed life, which had never been vigorous and had nosedived since the birth of the twins, went extinct.

"Limpet. Be patient with your Evie. I just need a chance to catch my breath and get used to being back on land."

"Please! Who do you think I am?"

But she could hear how studious his kindness had become.

One night, as they lay under the covers reading side by side, he put his hand on her bare shoulder and said something tender. He meant it as an act of pure appreciation. But she tensed, and he discharged.

"Oh, for fuck's sake!"

In all their years together, there had never been violence. Just the sound of his four shouted words destroyed their run.

"What is *wrong* with you? I'm not asking for *anything*."

She covered her face. "I'm sorry. Forgive me. I'm not myself."

"I made my choice. I am fine with it. You can go and. . . ."

He heard himself shouting and hung his head, like a dog who'd just bitten its owner in bewildered self-defense when its tail got caught under the rocking chair.

"Please," he said, with more force than he wanted. "Do *not* apologize. That only makes it worse. I'm not asking for—"

"You can ask. It's you're right."

"Arrrhh!" His wild wail tried to end up as a laugh but failed. "Okay. Look. Is there something you need to talk to me about?"

She pulled the sheet up over her face, and the gesture froze him.

"I don't know. I don't think so. No. *Je ne le crois pas.*"

He faced her on his side, his head propped up on his shaking arm. "Has something happened? Something I should know? Have you met another man?"

Pain pulled back her lips into an awful smile. "Oh, no. My Limpet. Not a man. There will never be another man in my life. No other man but you."

....

*I CAN SEE THE ROOM THAT Rafi and I shared during our fresh-
man year in Urbana as if we still lived there. A tiny stall in a dorm
on the southeast edge of campus, it was narrower than the two
of us laid end to end, and not much longer. With our two bunks
pressed against opposite walls, the aisle between them was only
wide enough for one of us to pass at a time. Our pillows abutted
the walls of twin clothes closets, and at the foot of each bed sat a
tiny desk smaller than my childhood desk in Evanston. On mine
was one of the only personal computers in the dorm.*

*Above each desk, two shelves were drilled into the green cin-
der block. Mine bore fat and expensive texts:* Bayesian Analysis,
Decision Trees, Introduction to Graph Theory, Practical Programming in C++. *From where I lay in bed, Rafi's looked so much
more exotic:* The Norton Anthology of American Literature, Self-
Portrait in a Convex Mirror, What We Talk About When We Talk
About Love.

He still had the copy of Fyodorov's The Philosophy of the Common Task, *which he refused to part with. I couldn't figure out why
he, the world's biggest lover of libraries, would steal a library book
that he might never read again.*

"Not stolen, man. I fully intend to bring it back. Eventually."

*He brought almost nothing down from Chicago but a few sets
of clothes. He didn't even own a scrapbook or a photo album.
But he did have that stolen library book. He took strange comfort
from the idea that endlessly unfolding humanity would someday
learn to resurrect every person who ever lived.*

*As for my own dead, I had a photo of my dad and mom and
me sitting in a huge catamaran on a trip to the Virgin Islands that
we took when I was fifteen. My mother framed it and gave it to me
when I left Evanston. I put it in the trundle drawer under the bed,
its home for the next nine months.*

On the wall above my bed, I hung a cheap print of Paul Klee's
Sinbad the Sailor. *We had a wall phone, as well as a good bamboo*

Go set, a cheap travel chess set, two decks of cards, and a box of different-sided dice. Aside from that, nothing. No disc players or sound systems, no television, no guitars, no stuffed animals, no posters of cinema sirens or rock goddesses, no microwaves, no mini-fridge, no bongs in the closet, none of the other aids to Dionysian existence that furnished the rooms of the other 650 students in our little four-story state.

You would think that moving from Chicago to the cornfields would be like dropping down in Kansas after Oz. But that first year at the Big U, surrounded by forty thousand other people on their own choose-your-own adventure, blew the jams out for both of us. We didn't have a lot of spare time to spend on anything aside from our studies. I was carrying five classes; Rafi had six. But we made time out of nothing, eating quickly, sleeping little, and heading to every outside event we could squeeze in.

We went to bizarro underground movies that aired in holes-in-the-wall across campus, four nights of the week. Rafi had to explain them to me. We went to lectures and came out of them schooled in the size of our capacious ignorance. Rafi dragged me to one of the first-ever poetry slams to have traveled down from Chicago, where the whole movement started. On the way back to the dorm in the dark, I kept saying, "Tell me again what just happened?"

Imagine a tiny monk's cell in the middle of a hormonal superstorm. Sometimes, on Friday afternoons, just walking down the long horseshoe corridor of our wing involved tunneling through five or six spheres of roaring music, one wall of sound shading into the next. That, too, was an education.

To escape our deafening dorm, we each found a hideout on campus. Rafi talked his way into a study carrel deep in the stacks of the Main Library, ordinarily reserved for honors upperclassmen and grad students. The place was amazing: ill-lit, archaic, depopulated, badly ventilated, reeking of binding paste and yellowing pages, crisscrossed by girdered shelves full of old, untouched tomes on subjects no human would ever be interested in again. It was a dark portal into previous centuries, dead-silent except for the steam hissing in the ancient radiators. My friend was in heaven.

I spent my time in one of the computer science buildings on the North Campus, the one that looked like Darth Vader's summer dacha. I sat in a large computer lab, typing away in the chorus of clicking around me, downloading tons of public-domain software and open-source code into the storage account that the university had given me. People were experimenting with bulletin boards and chat rooms where you could trade messages in real time. Talk about afterlife! The future was already here: it's just that the people on South Campus—my friend included—hadn't gotten the memo.

The amount of horsepower on offer throughout the engineering campus defied belief. Micros, minis, mainframes, and supercomputers, as we called them back then. Machines were shouting at me from down the corridors: Do something! Make fine things with me! Change the world! *A guy might do anything.*

Rafi and I would meet back home at the end of each day, telling each other of the places we'd just been. He seemed every bit as transformed as I was, but by mysteries that had unfolded a hundred years ago. At night, too burned out for study, we'd play rounds of lightning Go—whole epic matches in a handful of minutes. Even after lights-out, with the last thundering sound system from down the hall hushed, we would lie on our bunks, so close to one another that we could have reached out across the narrow gap and touched fingers, and whisper to each other in the dark about that day's discoveries, finds that dismantled and reassembled our sense of possibility.

RAFI STUMBLED ON A GROUP *that met every Wednesday night in the windowless crypt of the Foreign Language Building, a few blocks from our dorm. These people were playing games we'd never heard of—groundbreaking, low-luck, innovative games from Germany and France and Scandinavia that rewrote the rules of mental competition. Push-your-luck games that explored every nook and cranny of probability. Pick-up-and-deliver games that stretched my planning abilities to the breaking point. Economic engine games that made me feel like an embattled CEO.*

"Can't go anymore," Rafi said, hands in the pockets of his too-thin windbreaker as we walked home from a game night one bitter February.

"Why not? You were having a blast in there."

"That's what I'm sayin'. I grew up in the get-toe. I've seen what crack does to a fella."

He was right. For people like us, a well-designed game had all the allure of life, and, hour for hour, was way more satisfying. Either one of us could have thrown away our futures in that basement, pitted against those ingenious opponents, over those colorful boards, coming up with moves more beautiful and imaginative than ordinary life required.

He pulled his too-thin coat around his too-thin frame. "How many hours have we already sunk into Go?"

In a world where hard work was a virtue and free play a vice, the number was incriminating. I didn't even want to estimate. "Not enough to get to 9 dan yet."

"That's right, brother." He jerked his thumb over his shoulder, back toward Sodom and Gomorrah. "And how many of the dozens of new games that those cave trolls are bringing to the party every week would you like to become the best at?"

"The best?" I grabbed his elbow and stopped him on the icy sidewalk. "Wait. Are you trying to be the best?" When he said nothing, I busted him. "Holy shit. Rafi Young, Man of Ambition."

"Me? Ambitious?" He scoffed. "No, man. Just trying to get my father off my back. Don't want him telling me on my deathbed that I failed all Negroes everywhere."

"You are. You want to be the best. I never knew this about you."

He shot me a middle finger, readable even through his mitten. "Don't have to be the best. Just have to be better than you."

"And why is that? Exactly?"

But he stopped rising to my bait. He stared ahead vacantly,
down the chilly streets of that desolate cow town of learning. "You
know why I love games? For the same reason I love literature. In a
game . . . in a good poem or story? Death is the mother of beauty."
He stopped and twisted to face me. "Know what I'm sayin'?"

"No idea."

My smugness upset him. "Well, okay, Toddy. Your loss, then."

I apologized and asked him to explain, but it was too late. I
wasn't going to get anything more out of him. We walked back to
the dorm in silence.

Rafi stopped going to game night, and a few weeks later, so
did I. All the time we saved we plowed back into booking for our
exams, which, of course, were games by another name.

RAFI COULDN'T ACCEPT THE IDEA *that his one obligation was*
to read all day long. It felt like a trap, something he would pay for
down the line, in life's rigidly scored zero-sum contest. It never
occurred to him that he'd paid for it already.

Remarkably, turning his passion into work did not destroy it.
He lost himself in poetry. He read all the wild stuff that the Jesuits
had hid from us. He typed up the ones that made him feel like a
comet had just screamed across the sky, and he taped those up to
the front lip of his bookshelves as if they were WANTED *posters.*

He hung Amiri Baraka's Preface to a Twenty Volume Suicide
Note *next to Ishmael Reed's* I am a Cowboy in the Boat of Ra. *I*
tried to read them, but my brain had reached its limits of poetry
comprehension back at Saint Ignatius. All the separate words
made sense, but I couldn't figure out what they meant when you
put them all together. I got him to explain them to me.

When he was done he asked, "Capisce?"

But I couldn't decide what would count as a yes.

He'd written back in high school, but that had been child's play.
Now he began again in earnest. Something about being thrown into
classes filled with eloquent, high-minded women while consuming

thousands of pages of the most revered American works from the last four hundred years triggered his PTSD and left him wildly competitive, crazily creative, which came to the same thing. Words poured out of him, his new playing pieces of choice.

He sat at his desk in front of a little portable Underwood type-writer, cranking out poems, prose, prose poems, concrete poetry, bits of plays, memoirs, satirical sketches, and uncategorizable essays. He'd pull the pages out of the platen, red-pen them, ball them up, and shoot jump shots at our trash bin. Then he'd roll another blank sheet into his machine.

He only ever let me see the ones he said were worthless. "Help yourself. That one is a flaming piece of shit."

"It's good," I said, not understanding it. "Why are you so hard on yourself?"

"Because God has been too easy on me."

The rare pieces that he thought might be okay went into a lock-able folder on the shelf in his closet. It hurt me that he resorted to locks. But he was right. I'd have snooped on them all if he hadn't.

THE ILLINOIS COMPUTER SCIENCE DEPARTMENT *was deep in the golden age of symbolic artificial intelligence. This was the heyday of GOFAI—good old-fashioned AI. I was onboard, with all my heart and soul. My people were grilling experts about their knowledge and putting it into clean, powerful, easy-to-use black boxes. We were going to make expert doctors and expert lawyers and expert engineers and expert architects. And then those expert systems of ours were going to clean up humanity's act and whip it into shape.*

My programming powers landed me an internship at the Super-computing Center. I worked on a segment of an enormous project involving several universities and two dozen large corporations. Comprehensive representation of implicit knowledge—CRIK. It was part of America's attempts to beat all comers to a truly intelligent machine.

CRIK's aspirations were mind-bending, and its goals would require many thousands of person-years to come to fruition. It aimed to specify, in rigorous, higher-order logic, all the underlying concepts that went into what humans called common sense. Hundreds of people around the world were spelling out rules that put all existing things in ordered hierarchies. Then they put those rules into machine-usable form. The hope was to specify everything in existence, one fact at a time, telling CRIK about individuals, collections, classes, relations, fields, attributes, and actions. People like me had already spoon-fed CRIK some tens of thousands of bits of knowledge. The goal was to feed it millions—everything it would need to make sense of any question.

I started out on the lowest rung of the massive, multinational totem pole of CRIK's handlers. I fed CRIK tiny news articles and asked it simple questions, to see if all the hand-coded logic was working as expected. After a while, I was allowed to help with the special modules that CRIK used to solve certain classes of problems. It wasn't enough just to tell CRIK twenty million things about the world. We also had to tell it how it could drill hundreds of steps down into that ocean of twenty million facts and chain together inferences.

CRIK knew that all living things were made up of cells. It knew that everything with cells died. It knew that animals were living things. It knew that Homo sapiens was a kind of animal high up in the splitting branches of the Linnean family tree. It knew that humans made friends, that bad things happening to people's friends filled them with grief, and that death was considered a very bad thing. So, by a series of inexorable inferences, CRIK could have told me that I was headed to bottomless grief. Which is more than I knew at the time, even though I won an undergraduate programming prize, made the dean's list that year, and was considered quite the little phenom.

I worked on CRIK for the next three years, adding a flyspeck of results to a growing leviathan. That leviathan would go on growing long after a new and vastly more powerful way of teaching AI *leapfrogged beyond CRIK and threatened it with extinction. In time, I would find myself in one of those stories about a faster-than-light spaceship that comes across an older, sub-light-speed vessel that has been cruising for millennia. How do you tell the crew that their generations of sacrifice were pointless? CRIK's designers were pioneers, and everything that they gave their lives to would be passed by in a heartbeat.*

I TOOK RAFI to my little cubicle in the new supercomputing building. We played with CRIK for a long time, as if that creature were another of the many addictive networked games running on the university's groundbreaking time-share system. Rafi wanted to stump CRIK. He probed it to see if it really understood the concept of "water." Did it know that water was continuous with snow and ice and vapor? Did it know that water ran downhill and could polish granite or break it into little pieces? Did it know what it meant to make a thing "wet"? Did it understand "pouring" and "drinking" and "flow"?

We sat there for two hours, poking our probes into a clunky keyboard and waiting for CRIK to respond on a green, all-text screen. It was the strangest, most exciting, most entertaining thing in the entire universe. And CRIK did reasonably well. Not human, but it could answer questions. That alone felt like a miracle.

It was Sunday, the day when the dorm cafeteria served no dinner. So after playing with CRIK, Rafi and I went to campus town and shared a deep-dish pizza. The pie cost eight dollars—a ruinous expense for both of us. He had grown up on the border of poverty and would never learn to spend money freely. My father had had his own airplane, but my mother now lived in a one-bedroom apartment, selling the last of her husband's prog rock vinyl collection at garage sales to make bus fare. Splitting that eight-buck pizza felt as sinful as flying to New York for a weekend to see a show.

We ate in near-silence. CRIK had shaken Rafi. I kept waiting *for him to volunteer something. Finally, I had to ask. "So, what do you think of my baby?"*

"Fuckin'-a, man. As if I didn't have enough anxiety. Now I gotta decide whether to go on living."

He was still preoccupied later that night, in our broom closet, as we went to bed. He lay in his narrow bunk, staring up at the ceiling. When he spoke at last, it startled me.

"Has it occurred to you that computers might be the thing that makes it possible?"

We'd been living together in such close quarters for so many months that our brains had synchronized. I knew in an instant what he was talking about. His pet obsession. The Common Task.

"Make everybody live forever?"

"And raise everyone from the dead."

I waited for him to say more, but Rafi was already starting his long descent into reticence that would, in time, cut him off from me forever. That night, he fell asleep without another word.

THE NEXT SATURDAY AFTERNOON, THE MAYOR CALLED another island-wide meeting. Most everyone above the age of eighteen was there. Not the Hermit, of course. Didier had ridden the mayoral motorbike down to the abandoned hamlet of Tahiva to tell the solitary man, but Tamatoa was not interested. Almost all the other adults showed up, including the postmistress, the clinic nurse, the priest and the minister, the *pension* owners, the American couple, the ancient Canadian diver, and even Wen Lai, who had to close the shop—no hardship, since everyone else was at the meeting. Mothers brought their children, and a couple of the more curious teens turned up to watch. Life on the island ceased as Makatea convened on the community center.

There weren't enough folding chairs for everyone, so some sat on woven mats in the front of the circle, while a few others stood behind the ring of chairs. Didier opened the meeting with an announcement.

"The government has agreed to respect the outcome of Makatea's vote."

Surprise rippled around the ring of listeners. Lots of islanders began to speak at once.

"Can we trust them?"

"Why did they agree so easily?"

Manutahi Roa was on his feet, shaking his head. "It doesn't sound like them, Chief. They must have something up their sleeves."

Hone Amaru answered for the mayor. "They have plenty of fallbacks. If we don't want to host the pilot, one of the other hundred-and-some islands in the country will be happy to profit from it."

Five minutes in, and Didier felt himself losing control of the meeting. "All the involved parties see Makatea as their first and strongest choice."

Father Tetuanui, who had baptized, confirmed, and married Didier, raised his hand. Feeling like an upstart child, Didier called on him. "Yes, Father, please. Go ahead."

"Forgive me for being slow. Could you please tell us exactly what we'd be agreeing to?"

"Yes. I was just getting to that." Head down, he examined the official proposal. "The Californians will renovate the mining company main offices, tear down and reconstruct seven of the old warehouses and storage facilities, and restore four miles of the overgrown railroad. Building materials and some semi-finished components will be shipped in through the rebuilt port. Two factories will be built—one to fabricate struts and pontoons and one for assembling the working modules. . . .

"In stage one, eight initial floating modules will be constructed— four for habitation and one each for maintenance, agriculture, light industry, and power. Power will be a mix of solar, wind, and wave. These modules will be launched beyond the lagoon, where they will be tested in different configurations. If the initial projects go well, the consortium will submit further proposals for stages two and three. . . ."

This catalog was met by an outbreak of local debates. Didier called the meeting back to order, with limited success.

"Let's do this together, so we all benefit, eh?"

A dozen hands shot up. Didier called on Wen Lai. Everyone respected Wen Lai.

"But what is the nature of the proposal? Have they set a method to calculate our remuneration? The last time a project of this magnitude came to the island. . . ."

"They robbed us blind and trashed the place!" Neria Tepau, the postmistress and cofounder of Paruru i to Tatou Fenua, tapped the mood of much of the house. A wave of agreement propelled her forward. "Never forget how they manipulated us!"

Silence fell over the room for a full five seconds. Wen Lai broke it.

"We will need so much more information to consider this matter. Are they buying or leasing? Did these people promise anything about salaries? We all remember what our fathers and grandfathers earned, for risking their lives on the pinnacles and breathing phosphate dust all day long."

Didier went back to the proposal and read starting salaries for a dozen different job descriptions. The whole gathering gasped. Madame Martin called across the congregation to Ina Aroita and Rafi Young. "Your people are insane with money!"

The promised salaries alone threatened to sway the electorate. The circle buzzed with the sound of people asking each other what was left to debate. The island's poverty would vanish. Makatea's debts would be paid in full. The ruins would turn back into a living town. They could expand their one-room clinic and hire doctors—no more ferrying sufferers across a hundred miles of ocean. They could staff and equip a high school. They could buy the best of what the outside world had on offer: new clothes, furniture, dishes, tools, tablets, phones, books. There would be money enough to grind down and fill in the treacherous pinnacles, to heal the scar of extraction that ran the length of the island.

The chief of sanitation stood up, a man named Tino Fortin. He'd come to the island forty years ago, after some youthful scandal on Mo'orea. Since then, he'd gone native in every way—thought, speech, and custom. People sometimes forgot that he wasn't Tuamotuan.

"What kind of employment numbers are they projecting?"

"Phase one is expected to involve three hundred people."

The laughter fell somewhere between rowdy and incredulous. Every person on the island would be employed, with hundreds of jobs left over. For every current inhabitant of Makatea, three more immigrants would move in. In seconds, the room split between those thrilled at the prospect and those who were terrified.

Muscles spasmed across Manutahi Roa's face. Clearly Papeete was dead set on this project, and he did not trust Papeete. But with that kind of money pouring in, and future phases to come, all 118 islands of French Polynesia might finally be emboldened to cut the umbilical from Mother France. He raised his hand to make the point, then lowered it again. A fair part of the island opposed

the whole idea of independence. Linking the two questions might
be ill-advised.

Puoro and Patrice, the trawler co-owners, waved their four
arms until Didier hushed the room and acknowledged them. Patrice
stood and chopped each syllable into the air.

"Imagine what effect this will have on fishing."

Hone Amaru stifled a laugh. Didier faced the old mayor's son,
waiting for elaboration. Amaru tipped his head toward his rising
right shoulder. "Sorry. *Carry on!*"

Puoru took up the thread. "All those big industrial ships churn-
ing up our reef? It'll destroy the catch."

Hone could no longer contain himself. "We'll be making more
every week than your fishing produces in a year! We could buy all
our fish from other islands and still come out miles ahead."

Evelyne Beaulieu shifted upward in her chair in the back row.
Her body flushed and her thoughts raced into battle, but this was
not her fight. She glanced at Wai Temauri, sitting next to her. The
captain squinted and ran one open palm against his mouth and
chin. She could not read his vote. His daughter Kinipela—the
youngest person in the gathering—twisted on the lip of her folding chair. Her right hand wanted to levitate, but her father held it
gently in his left.

The Queen rose and shimmied to the center of the ring. She held
out both arms as if about to dance. When she started to speak, she
was almost singing.

"Listen. Friends. *Te mau haamaitairaa i ni'a i te mau taata
atoa.* Blessings on everyone. What I have to say is very simple. You
know that I worked for the CFPO, and I did good work for them.
You know that I went to Hao and worked for the French there,
when they . . . did what they did. I have seen this island rich, and I
have seen this island poor. I know what it means to have a job and
to be without one. I know what it means to want things.

"But I know what it means to have things, too. I ask you: Who
among us, right now, is truly unhappy? Who, right now, thinks

we are miserable? Progress tore the heart out of this island. It's enough. Now we are mending. We are mending! Our forests are coming back. The numbers of our beloved *rupe* are going up. We will be a bird sanctuary again, before too long!"

The Widow Poretu, who loved her birds more than any other biped and tracked their comings and goings in twenty years of notebooks, called out, "Hear, hear!"

The Queen continued. "You know, they call us *Makatea l'Oublié*. I say: Fine! Let them forget us. Let everyone leave us be, so that we can live here in this healing place together and enjoy each other all our days."

Scattered applause started up, even before she finished. She dipped her head a little and glided back to her seat.

The mayor nodded. "*Māuruuru*, auntie. Thank you. But maybe it's not quite time yet for the actual arguments. . . ."

His words drowned in thirty different urgencies, all debated at once. People leaned in, faced down, and talked over one another. In the commotion, Madame Martin rose and moved to the right of Didier, who stood stymied at the head of the ring. In the patient voice of a schoolteacher, she called, "*Silence, s'il vous plaît! Un peu de silence!*"

At the sound of that voice, which rang with authority in the ears of many of the younger islanders, the gathering came back to order. In the same slow, well-modulated singing voice she used in her classroom, Madame Martin said, "If we could all please take one giant step back? I want to point out that we have gotten a little ahead of ourselves. There is an important first step we still need to take. Have we decided yet, exactly who gets to vote?"

The simple question silenced everyone. So obvious to ask, and so impossible to answer. Everyone looked to Didier, who studied his sheaf of papers. Hone Amaru raised his hand, and the mayor almost leapt at him for an answer.

"If the government has approved a referendum, surely they're assuming it will be a poll of registered voters."

A voice came from the audience. "But does their assumption matter? Shouldn't we decide who gets to have a say?"

Hone Amaru spun around, searching for the source of the ambush. The challenge came from Wen Lai. The owner of the Chinese Store seemed an unlikely opponent. But the quiet shopkeeper was also a philosopher, one who had seen his father put his life on the line twice, as a *huagong* "coolie," fighting for a say in his own destiny in two fatal strikes against the CFPO.

Who got to vote? Makatea had suffered from history so hard and for so long that it was tough to tell the outsiders from the indigenous. Most everyone was half from somewhere else. An easy half dozen of the island's current adults were not citizens. But the island's guest-friendship ran so deep that no one in the ring could look the more recent residents in the eye and tell them: *This is none of your concern.*

A burst of uncharacteristic political savvy flashed through Didier Turi. For a moment, he remembered how to fast-break out of a midfield scrum and blast the ball downfield. He held up both hands, preempting all discussion.

"This decision will change the lives of everyone on this island. I move that every adult resident who has lived here more than half a year be allowed to vote. All in favor?"

A cheer went up, as much for his decisiveness as for the decision itself.

"All opposed?"

The opposition chose not to die on this hill, this time.

"Papeete has given us a month. I propose that we take that full time before voting. That way, everyone will have a chance to discuss and consider the question fully. Of course, we'll gather again many times before then. So, unless there are any further questions. . . ."

There were always further questions. This one came from Roti, Didier's wife. The mayor dropped a beat, before acknowledging her raised hand. He could not remember the last time his wife had had anything to say in any group of more than three people.

"Yes," he said. "Mrs. Turi?" And the whole island aside from Roti Turi laughed.

Her hands shook and her face paled, but her voice held steady. "Once these people come, with their factories and their floating sea-cities, they won't be leaving again. Life here will change in every way. Nothing will ever be the way we know it now."

Didier lifted his hands. "It is not yet time to argue—"

His wife sailed past his objections. "Long after we adults are dead, our children will still be living with the consequences of this decision. I move that we let everyone who can write their own name vote."

She sat down, flushed with embarrassment. Didier gaped at the woman he had been married to for nine years. And the sala erupted again.

Hone Amaru opposed the idea. "The brains of young children are not yet mature enough to reason well."

Wen Lai said, "Decisions are rarely made by reason but almost always by temperament, and that doesn't change much as people get older."

Manutahi Roa objected. "The children will vote how their parents tell them, giving everyone with children more say in the matter."

Every parent in the ring howled with laughter.

Tino Fortin stood again. "The island has so few children. If they split in the same way as the adults, it won't change the vote. If they don't, it means Roti Turi is right about letting the future have a say in the matter."

Tiare Tuihani, the nurse who ran the clinic, leapt up. "How can any child understand the enormous complexities and consequences of sending Makatea down the road toward . . . toward this seasteading?"

The Queen chuckled. Still seated, she shouted, "The adults understand perfectly, eh?"

The ensuing debate got away from Didier Turi. He was still marveling at his wife's public courage. She had all but blurted out to the entire island what she had struggled to tell him in the privacy of their own bed. The younger a human being was, the more readily she loved them. And life had said that she would never hold her own newborn in her arms. Of course she had gone off sex with him. Any attempt to persevere in it must have felt like being slapped around by God.

Democracy was slower and more erratic than windsurfing. Soon everything that could be said about the wisdom or folly of letting children vote on the future of the island had been said. Didier shook off his fog.

"All in favor of extending the vote to every person capable of writing their own name?"

A cheer went up, and a forest of raised hands.

"All opposed?"

Another cheer and show of hands, close in size to the first. The mayor was tired of politics and wanted this meeting to be over. "The motion passes," he announced.

And to his amazement, no one objected. The only response came from Kinipela Temauri, who leapt to her feet and shouted, "*Yes!*" She fist-bumped her father and hugged his ample belly, to general laughter and applause. Then everyone in the ring stood up to go, and Makatea's month of collective deliberation began.

....

*R*AFI AND I WEREN'T THE ONLY *serious students in our dorm.
But most of the better ones moved out after the required two
semesters. We two lived on in that shoebox for three more years,
long after every other self-respecting pre-professional decamped
to more luxurious off-campus housing. Our miniature, minimal-
ist HQ suited us. The more constrained and featureless our living
quarters, the more it focused us.*

*Those were the early years of the Third Industrial Revolution.
We'd studied the First Industrial Revolution, the Age of Steam,
together back at Saint Ignatius, in AP history. Rafi had fallen in
love with the art and literature of the Second Industrial Revolution, the cultural earthquake of High Modernism that accompanied the Age of Electricity. Now I was joining the revolution that
I'd sided with since childhood, the one that was disrupting everything we took for granted: the Age of* READY >_.

*Somewhere between our freshman and senior years, the magic
boxes went from exotic toys to necessities. Rafi bought his first rig,
and I got one that I could toss in a bag and carry around with me.
Only twelve pounds: I could code while sitting in the shade of an
oak on the Quad. It astounded everyone, even my techie friends.*

*Neither Rafi nor I saw what was happening. No one did. That
computers would take over our lives: Sure. But the way that they
would turn us into different beings? The full flavor of our translated hearts and minds? Not even my most enlightened fellow programmers at CRIK foresaw that with any resolution. Sure, they
predicted personal, portable* Encyclopedia Britannicas *and group
real-time teleconferencing and personal assistants that could teach
you how to write better. But Facebook and WhatsApp and TikTok
and Bitcoin and QAnon and Alexa and Google Maps and smart
tracking ads based on keywords stolen from your emails and
checking your likes while at a urinal and shopping while naked
and insanely stupid but addictive farming games that wrecked
people's careers and all the other neural parasites that now make*

it impossible for me to remember what thinking and feeling and being were really like, back then? Not even close.

IN THE FALL OF *our senior year, when the sweet gums turned burgundy, the maples went lemon and orange, and the oaks all over campus settled into shades of scarlet, when the daylight hours shrank and the air thickened with that sere, weird scent of antici- pation, Rafi came back to our dorm room late one afternoon with an announcement. He smiled his most serene and philosophical smile, with his tongue in the slight gap between his two front teeth.*

"I've just met the woman I am going to marry."

I laughed. "Congratulations. I think?" I didn't credit his announcement for an instant. The Bayesian priors—his track records—weren't especially good. He'd had girlfriends off and on over the previous three years, even ones for whom he'd asked me to vacate the dorm on a Saturday night. But his enthusiasms always went from crazy love to jaded disillusionment in a mat- ter of months. So even though the word marriage rocked me, his threat had no credibility.

"Does she know this yet?"

"Silence, exile, and cunning, man. I gotta sneak up on her."

"With your tachometer? Good luck."

"She's a first-year grad student in the School of Art. Born in Micronesia. Grew up all over the Pacific. Get this: she never stepped foot on a continent until a few months ago."

"Whoa, Rahrah. A Pacific Islander? They're, like . . . half a percent of the world's population. I've never even seen one. When do I get to meet her?"

He froze me with a look from across the narrow gap between his bed and my desk. "That's fucked up, brother. You're a disgust- ing piece of work."

"What are you talking about? What'd I say?"

"You want to see her tattoos? You want her to show you her carved war canoe while she dances you some hula?"

"Jesus, Rafi. What is wrong with you?"

" 'I've never even seen one?' Take your sick fetishes elsewhere."

Ina Aroita had not yet been in our lives for one full day, and already she changed everything.

"All right. Guilty as charged. So what's to love?"

He got that expression again, like he was looking out over two thousand horizons, laid end to end. "She is . . . utterly fearless. Everything is art, to her. I always thought that a person had to choose between safety and freedom. This woman is not letting anyone make her choose anything. She . . . she could teach me a thing or two."

HE INTRODUCED ME. *The three of us went bowling in the basement of the Union. It was the most fun I'd had in public since childhood. The woman floored me. She reminded me of someone, and it wasn't until the seventh frame of our first game that I realized who it was: the famous bust of Nefertiti, minus the headgear. She was short—maybe five feet two in bowling shoes—but she never stopped dancing. She leaned in and did this little thing with her wrists and forearms to try to steer her ball and keep it from going into the gutter. When she succeeded in nicking a pin or two, her victory pirouette was Bolshoi-worthy.*

When she and Rafi talked, I was mystified. They shared some private, allusive language filled with cultural references that left me convinced that the Jesuits had failed to educate me. Rafi: I'd never seen him so at ease or at home with anyone. No put-ons or put-downs or jive talk or funny accents. Just Rafi, open and unashamed, in all his lit-nerd glory. Of course, I was jealous.

Ina made a secret note of our shoe sizes that afternoon. The following Saturday, she rented three pairs of Rollerblades and took us on a wild ride across four square miles of campus. I hit the pavement three times in less than an hour, and I didn't care. I didn't even mind when the two of them, chattering together in their secret fine arts language, sped on like two Olympians and left me half a block behind, flailing to keep upright. Ina slipped through the air like she was swimming, and my best friend paced her, laughing and smitten, as ecstatic as a kid who just aced the final question in God's quiz show.

He must have told her that I needed caretaking, because they adopted me as their mascot. Sometimes on weekends we went to cult movies that the two of them loved and that bored me to tears. Ina took us to the marble-clad art museum—the "whited sepulchre," as Rafi called it—and showed us how to dance in our minds with a painting that looked like food stains on an old work shirt. The thing would have incensed me as fraudulent had I come across it a month before meeting her. Now it became a mirror, a weird cousin to play with, a thing that offered up a meaning that wasn't mine until I looked closer.

IN HER PRESENCE, Rafi became a whole new person—nimble, witty, vulnerable, open. For the first time since I'd met him, he had a real dog in life's fight. I watched him charm and tease and debate her, and I saw him come into his own. With her, there was no more Great Black Hope. No dead sister. No abusive and unappeasable father. He was working for himself at last. Staking out his right to enjoyment. Playing in the world.

Maybe I seemed different to him as well, tagging along awkwardly in their wake, making my goofy math jokes, a beat behind and outclassed by the worldliness that Ina brought to the party. She breathed new life into our stalled friendship, giving us new instances of one another to explore. And she was liquid confidence and fresh eyes to both of us. The three of us, together, became invincible.

I remember her saying once, "Where I come from, the artists came first and all the gods followed."

I could never quite follow her, and it made me nervous. "Okay, fine. But what does that mean, exactly?"

Rafi smiled at my anxiety but did not mock me. "Don't worry, Toddy. We got you. It means love and do whatever you want."

Ina wagged her finger in the air. "It means the artists made the gods!"

Ina was especially good at that. For a few months of our shared lives, she made gods out of all three of us.

I DON'T KNOW WHEN I fell in love with her. Right away, probably. But it didn't feel wrong or painful. I was thrilled for Rafi. I was thrilled for myself. It occurred to me that I'd never before seen my friend truly happy, except perhaps when he was marking up a volume of Rilke or beating me at Go. He was himself with this woman. He no longer had to prove anything to anyone. She made him feel like the game of life was won simply by playing it.

Ina had her own apartment on the third floor of a partitioned-up old American Gothic in West Urbana. Rafi started spending nights over there in early October. By Halloween he was a regular tenant. As fall went on, I felt abandoned, a senior in a dorm filled with noisy and very green underclassmen.

One crisp Saturday in late October, we introduced Ina to German board games. She struggled with the complex rules, but the novelty of calculating odds and fighting it out with the boys kept her at the table for hours, until we were too stiff to stand up. She got cross with Rafi for the way he played.

"Hey, fella. You're not making your own best moves. You're just trying to stick it to Todd!"

"Sticking it to Todd is my own best move."

"We call it the Young strategy," I explained. "It's what has kept the two of us together all these years."

"Hmm New game, then. For all of us. And I'm making the rules."

And she did. For a while, the two of us played every game she invented.

THE SCULPTURE GREW BEYOND HER CONTROL.

She added to the few pieces of plastic that she and her daughter found inside the belly of the dead albatross until there were enough to form into a sinuous double-arc of glued-together shards that now stood taller than the little girl. Ina had no idea what the assemblage was trying to become—only that it wouldn't stop unfolding. She could feel with her arms and hands where each new piece of petrochemical flotsam wanted to go. But beyond that, she worked blind, in the way of a waking dream.

She harvested new pieces for the growing sculpture whenever she was out. On her way to the Chinese store, she saw a cracked cadmium spray bottle that had blown across the path, and she stashed it away in her shopping carry. A tangle of torn filament and fishing floats that washed up near Patrice and Puoro's moorings caught her eye, and she waded out at low tide to retrieve it and add it to the monster growing in her yard.

As the sculpture grew, Ina hunted more deliberately for bright pieces that would fit into the accreting shape. When she and Hariti scavenged the beach for shells and pretty stones, she kept an eye out for synthetic bits, surprised that she now thought of them as pretty.

It surprised her, too, to realize how many trinkets of trash washed up on the island every day. She'd always ignored them or wished them away. On the lookout now, she found them everywhere.

She went to her husband Rafi.

"How about a family hike and picnic Sunday, after church?"

"Sure," he said. "Let's walk to Hawaii."

———

NEITHER INA NOR RAFI ever believed that the universe was guided by an agent that had their welfare at heart. But both the children were crazy about the idea, and on an island of eighty-two people, almost all of them religious, churchgoing had its rewards.

The singing, for one, always did a number on Ina. They went to the Catholic church one week and the Mormon Sanito church the next. It made them popular with both congregations, who vied for their loyalty.

"Is it the same God?" a troubled Afa asked his father that Sunday, after the Catholic service.

"With different capes," Rafi told his boy.

Ina slugged her husband in his thin upper arm and petted her son. "Every human heart imagines God in a different way. A way just right for that imaginer."

"What about *my* heart?" Rafi pouted, rubbing his bruised bicep. His son broke from his mother's arms to comfort him.

"I said *human*."

The children looked away in disgust as their parents began to coo and bill at each other like Makatea fruit doves in the mating season.

―――――

THEY HEADED OUT to find a picnic spot. Rafi loved a good foot expedition. Right up there with playing area-control games with his son or worker-placement games with the kids at school, and just below studying centuries-old Go matches with Wen Lai, walking was now his great pastime.

"Want to walk cross-island?"

Afa shouted, "Yes!" There were crabs up on the plateau. They only came out at night, but a boy could always hope.

Ina hid her plan from the boys. "Let's walk the beach up to Temao. We can head clockwise around the coast and lunch somewhere fun along the way."

"Are you joking? It's twelve miles, all the way around."

"We don't have to go all the way around. When we get to Moumu, we can cut back across on the road."

Still several miles. Rafi pulled a skeptical face. "Okay? But you're treating the blisters when we get home."

Ina gave everyone a pillowcase. "Fill them with any pieces of plastic you find along the way." Rafi raised his eyebrows but set to work. Hariti loved any kind of treasure hunt, and this one had the hopeless idealism that most appealed to her. But Afa soon started to grumble at the chore of picking up trash.

His father asked to see his sack. "How many colors you got there?"

"Green, red, clear—is clear a color?"

"Clear is the wildest of all colors, my man."

"Green, red, clear, white, blue, brown, yellow . . . and weirdos."

"Great. That's eight kinds. I'll race you. By the end of the day, whoever has the most of the fewest of those colors gets half an hour of backrub."

The boy tapped his head, trying to decode those victory conditions. But once he figured it out, he was off and running, finding plastic everywhere and shouting in victory at every discovery. It thrilled him to turn up a bright yellow rubber duck bath toy, stuck in some beachgrass up above the high tide line.

Rafi held out his hand. "Let's see."

Reluctantly, his son handed over the prize toy.

"I've read about this. Tens of thousands of them tumbled off a container ship in the middle of a storm years ago. Been washing up on beaches everywhere, ever since."

Afa reached out to take the duck back. Rafi high-fived him. "Collector's item, man!"

"Sweet!" Ina declared. "Perfect for the sculpture."

"No! I'm keeping it!" The boy took it back and thanked the ocean with a shout.

With the advance scouts down the beach filling their sacks, Rafi put his hand around his wife's waist and matched her barefoot pace.

"So how are we handling this referendum?"

"Handle?"

"Every resident of the island who can write their own name. That includes both kids. This little family officially controls five percent of the say over Makatea's future. It might decide the vote."

Ina stopped and looked out at sea. "Holy shit."

"I mean, do we coach them? Do we just tell them how to vote?"

"Tell them what? I don't even know how *I'm* going to vote! Do *you*?"

He craned back and assessed her. "*Serious?*"

"I'm sorry, Rafi. I really don't know. I can't even tell you what seasteading *is*. Is it the way forward? Will it help to solve . . . ? I have no idea. Maybe it's the next Internet."

"*Ina!*" His voice was tight. "Even if this were a referendum on continuing the *Internet*, I'd vote no."

"Why."

She had a way of saying *why* that he loved with all his heart. More statement than question. Intelligent, clear-eyed, curious, noncombatant, already reconciled to any answer. She'd given the word that note since their first winter together at Illinois. And he'd never once told her how it beguiled him.

"Because. . . ." He waved his hand toward the line where the pale azure of the fringing reef changed to the cobalt of the deeper water just past it. He drew his palm in a great circle, taking in the ocean on the other side of the island. "This place. . . . think of the scars. When we first came here, to be with these beautiful kids . . . I wasn't sure I'd be able to make it. I was so juked up on everything that the human world inflicted on me. But here, there was just . . . *this*." He stared at the cliffs and the surf and the rocky beach as if for the first time.

"It took me about six months to detox. Systemic FOMO. I couldn't concentrate, this place was so quiet. And then . . ."

She put her ear to his clavicle. She could never get enough of listening to what his heart sounded like, when he got worked up.

"Now I think: there are ten thousand little spots like this that the continents can't reach, little outposts of sanity. These folks. . . ." He waved over his shoulder toward Vaitepaua and the seventy-eight other people who were now his whole world. "They're like the inhabitants of a Dark Ages monastery, keeping literacy alive. And now the Outside is coming for them again."

Ina Aroita pulled away as gently as she could. "Rahrah? What if that's condescension? I mean, not that you mean . . ."

He looked stung, but he didn't spin out into a funk. Age and the island had cured him of that impulse. She couldn't remember the last time they'd had a real fight. She could say almost anything to him now, and given a few moments, he'd thank her for her honesty.

Rafi started back up the beach, where Afa and Hariti were joining forces to dig a five-gallon plastic jug out of the water-worn gravel. "Okay. Tell me how it's condescending."

"What if most people here think the proposal is great? What if the island wants it? Meaningful work, fair compensation, the chance to be part of something larger. Healthy, educated kids and grandkids with more future than they have now. Don't you think our friends have the right to all those things? Maybe most of Makatea doesn't want to be . . . monks in your monastery."

He tipped his head and lifted his eyebrows and bent down to pop a plastic bracelet charm that the children had missed into his sack. "What if it's another way to gut the place?"

"Then Makatea will vote against it, and the country will find another lagoon to develop, somewhere in their twelve hundred miles of islands."

"Maybe. But that's why we're obliged to call the matter how we see it."

"Are we, really? You and me? Yeah, for us this place is perfect as it is—a scarred-up tiny heaven. But it isn't ours. We only just came. I'm not sure the *two of us* have a right to vote, let alone Affy and Har."

"Well, the people of Makatea have decided that we have that right, and now we're condemned to choose. Democracy, eh? How many other places would have given us the vote on something like this? Yet another reason I'd like to protect this place from the techno-utopians."

She thought: *That, too, might be condescension.* But she said, "Why do they want to build it here?"

He tipped his head toward the cliffs above them. "As the waters keep rising, we'll be the last island to go under."

They wandered apart and gleaned in a small inlet where pieces of acrylic and PVC accumulated. They filled their sacks to the sound of the surf, the pulse of waves that would bring in fresh crops of bright, hard plastic once their Sunday scavenger party was over.

Ina found a hoard of colored chips worn smooth in the churn of the surf like gemstones in a lapidary tumbler. "Look at these! Perfect."

Rafi knew better than to ask how she recognized *perfect*. He didn't need to know. Never again in life would he let *perfect* be the enemy of good. He had lived that way once, and it almost cost him everything. Combing the rocks now, he stashed away each bit of trash he came across, even the soft, crinkly, pathetic little half-serving water bottle no bigger than his fist. He'd found her again, here, after having lost her forever, found that pair of magic small beings he could see down the shore in front of him. He would never want or need anything more perfect than this.

Ina picked up a parti-colored shelf-stable drink box, now encrusted with the shells of sessile crustaceans.

"What do I do with this? If I take it for the sculpture, the barnacles will die."

"Then leave it."

"But it's still garbage, Rahrah, and I touched it last! Also?" It grabbed at his heart when she looked sheepish. "It has *great* colors."

His hands went up in a declaration of nonalignment. "You do you, Boo."

Stoically renouncing her greediness, she wedged the drink box back into the rocks of its tidal pool home. "Is a thing still garbage, once life starts using it?"

He'd wondered the same thing, while out snorkeling with the kids. They'd seen an octopus who carried around a clear glass jar to make up for the shell it had lost to evolution. The creature ducked into its transparent mobile home at every sign of danger. They'd seen a pygmy seahorse clinging to a plastic drinking straw like it was a strand of host kelp. When humankind was gone, the spin-offs of their creativity would provide a resource management game for the rest of creation for eons to come.

She strode a little toward the children, who were venturing too far down the beach. Rafi strode along beside. He could not keep his hands off her. Something about Ina's willingness to entertain the idea of seasteading left him feeling a little clingy.

"Okay, but forget about everyone else for a minute."

"Hmm. Remind me how to do that, again?"

"You can't really believe that inviting in a massive construction project, with industrial ships and factories and dredgers that are going to dig out the lagoon . . ."

He couldn't even bring himself to name the upgrades that the seasteading experiment would inflict on them. It shocked him that she held her body a little aloof from the question.

"I'm a guest here, Rafi, and grateful to be one. I've never been happier, anywhere in the world." She pulled a strand of hair out of her mouth. The sea wind whipped it right back into her face. "I just want this island to be well again."

"It's getting better. Sixty years since the mines closed, and the plant cover is almost back. The crab-catchers just had one of their best years in anyone's memory. The *rupe* is returning from the brink. The fruit doves, too. All the birds, really. The reef looks more vibrant than it has since the runoff stopped. You can't possibly want to beat everything all back down again?"

"What *I* want isn't the—"

"This seasteading thing could get out of hand fast. In a few years, it could make all those years of phosphate mining look like a Junior Chamber of Commerce exhibit."

Her eyes were on the children, fighting over a piece of bright blue sheathing the size of a sea turtle. "You're right," she said, a little vexed. "They'll have to vote."

"And they were born here."

Their children might live their whole lives in this place. They might grow up to think of America as a crazy fairy tale, the land of

movies and pop music. Chicago might never mean anything more
to them than gangsters.

"We won't even be able to explain it to them without
influencing them."

"Oh, Rafi. I don't know. People are like sculptures. You can
mold them a little when they start out, but not much. A body wants
to be what a body wants to be. I've known who these two souls are
since we first laid eyes on them."

"You think so?" he said. But his body agreed with her. "So how
will each of them vote?"

She dipped her head and grinned at her secret. "Afa will vote
for progress and excitement and bold new things coming into
the world."

That sounded irrefutable to Rafi. It was partly his fault. The
games they played were all about growth and development. Getting bigger faster than your opponent.

"And Hari?"

His wife snorted. "Do you have to ask? She'll vote to please me."

"Which means . . . ?"

"Ha! I see what you're doing here."

Before he could press his point, they came alongside the kids,
who were battling over who had found the coolest plastic treasure so far.

The four of them didn't even make it to the shores beneath Teopoto, on the northern headlands. Long before then, their sacks
filled up and they had to head back. Before they did, they had
their picnic—spicy roasted breadfruit with tomatoes right out of
the *fa'a'apu*.

They dumped out the bags in the back garden, in a pile by the
door of Ina's studio. Plastic in every stage of wear. Afa and Rafi
counted to see who had the most of their rarest color, and the boy
let out a whoop when he won.

The defeated father scooped up two handfuls of trash and let
the pieces drop like a waterfall. It made no difference if the island

approved or rejected the seasteading project. Ever-growing human ingenuity would bury them eventually, either way. Rafi dipped his head and regarded his wife. His smile said, *It's game over for this place, isn't it?*

But Ina smiled back as if she'd just won the lottery and hardly knew how to start cashing in.

....

ON THE SUNDAY BEFORE THANKSGIVING, *we three biked out to a pathetic little pond that Downstate Illinois had promoted to lake status, in the absence of any other serious contenders. Real cold was late in coming that year, but it was chilly enough for sweaters. The wind was stiff, and we worked hard to make it across fifteen miles of open prairie.*

At the lake, the two of them messed around in a leaky dinghy that someone had abandoned on the dock, while I stayed on land, spread out on one of Ina's woven blankets, doing the Times *crossword and looking for clues to the cryptic words in the cloudless sky.*

Over a picnic lunch of peanut-butter-and-honey sandwiches with dried apricots, she came up with our first joint homework assignment.

"We should hold a little lecture series. Just the three of us."

"Sounds like fun," I said. "I'm game."

But Rafi closed his eyes and hung his head in one hand. With the other, he pawed her shoulder. "Oh, God, no, darling. Don't do this to me."

"You know. Like the way that other people have book clubs? Only the book is you. We each take a night. Whoever's turn it is needs to put some stakes on the table. Take the other two of us to their sanctum sanctorum."

I looked at Rafi. "You studied with the Jesuits. What the hell does that mean?"

"I think it means, 'No contest.' No, wait. 'You shall have the body.'"

Ina slapped him on the forearm hard enough to make him squeal. "That's Islander for, Don't be a little prick."

"Aw! Did you hear that, Toddy? I think she loves me."

"For *who you really are.*"

Ina Aroita pressed on, *unflustered. Flustering wasn't her idiom.* She pointed her pinkie at me. "Mr. Spock. You go first."

"Take *you to my sanctum sanctorum?*"

"*Please, bro. Don't encourage this nonsense.*"

Ina linked her arm in Rafi's and pulled him toward her on the picnic blanket. "Do this for your friend," she told me. "We have to build up this boy's immune system."

Rafi seemed desperate. "I don't know about this. Seriously. It sounds kind of precious."

Ina exploded. She pushed his arm away and scrambled up. "Oh, for Christ's sake. Stop being such a self-protecting little coward."

I sucked air. By accident or intimacy, she had found an accusation that gave Rafi as much pain as anything she might have hurled at him.

Rafi sat straightening his glasses with one finger, frozen in dignity. I knew the posture; he was debating whether to ruin the picnic and set the day in flames or hold on to this woman who, only a minute before, had seemed his one best way forward in life.

I looked at Ina. She wavered. She hadn't expected to draw so much blood. She pretended not to notice, which was wise and probably saved the two of them, at least for a little longer.

"Or we could start a weekly pinochle game."

Rafi snorted, despite himself. Something in him understood what the contrived ritual meant to her. She'd never had anyone in her life she could play such a game with, except her two disciples.

"All right. I will do this thing. But I want to go on record as saying that no one in my world either knows or cares what the fuck a sanctum sanctorum is."

He was lying, of course. He had no more world anymore but the two of us. But that world had shifted. All three of us were more than a little subdued for the rest of the abbreviated picnic and on the fifteen-mile bike ride back home.

INA HAD NOWHERE REACHABLE to go for Thanksgiving break. Rafi did, but he stayed in town with her. An easy choice. I went back to Chicago and spent the holiday sleeping on the pull-out couch in my mother's one-bedroom apartment on Howard Street

*near the CTA stop, and working with her on a picture puzzle. It
was the only way the two of us could be in the same room and not
go to war.*

*Hunting for pieces, we were on safe ground. It was a two-
thousand-piece puzzle of Constable's* The Hay Wain. *I can still
remember the strange way that the shapes and colors of the individual pieces would turn into other things than what I thought
they were, when snapped into place. My mother and I were building a time tunnel, not just back to the childhood I never had, not
just to Constable's 1821, but back several millennia, to the first
magic picture puzzles from history's beginning. That's how my
brain works. How it used to work, I mean.*

*Protected by the shared task of the puzzle, I tried to talk to my
mother about my father.*

"He really messed me up, you know? Messed us both up, badly."

*My mother shot me a look, as furious as the looks she used to
train on him. "You shut up. You don't know what you're talking
about. No man should have to endure what your father did."*

*And that was the last time I ever tried to talk to her about Saint
Micky Keane.*

WHEN I GOT BACK *down to school in early December, I took
Rafi and Ina up North of Green with me, to my little carrel on the
second floor of the National Center for Supercomputing Applications. I sat them down in front of my terminal, which had a direct
Ethernet connection to the university's networked mainframes. I
pulled up a window and opened a session with CRIK.*

"Here it is. My holy of holies."

*I put CRIK through its paces, asking it what it knew about
Hawaii. It knew quite a little bit, not surprising, since I'd been
feeding it Hawaiian facts for weeks.*

*Rafi was not impressed. "Uh, dude? 'A collection of pieces of
land rising up above the surface of the ocean'? That's what we
warm-blooded types call 'too obvious to mention.'"*

I was hurt. "There has never been anything like it on Earth."

Ina knit her brows. "Freaks me out a little, Toddy."

"And when it knows everything in the world that is 'too obvious to mention,' when it can draw every commonsense inference that any warm-blooded—"

"I'll still be able to beat it at poetry and Go," Rafi said.

Ina asked CRIK all kinds of homesick questions about Hawaii. Why did the U.S. overthrow the Kingdom? How many Olympic golds did Duke Kahanamoku win? How did Eddie Aikau die? Where was the best place in Honolulu to buy ice cream? Of course CRIK failed me. There were massive holes in what my golem could do, more holes than clay.

I apologized. "It'll take centuries before any machine can answer those kinds of questions." In fact, it took about thirty years.

Ina stared at the terminal, trying to see it the way I did. "But . . . couldn't an encyclopedia tell you a lot more, a lot more easily?"

"We're automating the encyclopedia."

She frowned, wondering how that might be desirable. "You're something, Mr. Spock."

Rafi said, "You see what I've had to deal with, all these years?"

"I chose Hawaii out of tens of thousands of possible domains. It knows things about fish and trees and Presidents and the laws of physics. . . ."

But I could feel my entire sanctum going south.

I opened a new window onto another project I'd been recruited to help on, something the NCSA was months away from springing on an unsuspecting world. I felt sure this one would impress them. I typed a string of arcane letters and symbols into a primitive prompt at the top of the screen. After several seconds, a painting began to form from top to bottom, line by line across the CRT. Underneath the accumulating image there appeared a few paragraphs of text.

A grin filled Ina's face. I was pandering shamelessly to her, but this time it worked.

"*Gauguin! D'où venons-nous? Que sommes-nous? Où allons-nous?*" Where do we come from? What are we? Where are we going?

Rafi flapped his wrist in the air. "*Damn, baby girl! You're impressing me.*"

Ina floated her finger in the air above the image, Gauguin's vision of Tahiti, from 1898. "*I don't understand. Why is this picture in your computer? Did you scan it from a book or something? A little present for me because you knew I was coming?*"

"*It's in Boston.*"

"*I know it's in Boston. At the MFA.*" *She sounded as impatient as I've ever heard her. Something she didn't get about what I was showing her made her anxious.*

"*No. I mean, this* page *is in Boston. This data is coming from a machine at MIT.*"

"*What do you mean? What 'page'?*"

I flipped through a stack of printed notes and typed more arcane symbols into the window's prompt. After a bit, a picture of the famous Nefertiti bust appeared. I had become a little obsessed with the sculpture, for reasons that neither of them needed to know.

"*This one's coming over the network from Berlin.*"

Ina gasped and clapped her hands. "*From the Neues Museum?*"

"*Well, the page is on a machine at Humboldt University.*"

She shook her head in disbelief, beginning to see. Even Rafi sat forward on his rolling office chair.

"*Bro. You could do this ten times better with a CD-ROM. Add a ton of bells and whistles plus a fancy interface, and everything would still load a million times faster.*"

She slugged his bicep. "*Wake up, mister. Don't you get it? From my little apartment on Daniels, on my dinky little Amiga, I could go to any museum in the world.*"

She didn't get it, either. I didn't get it. None of us had the faintest idea what was coming.

Ina turned and looked me in the eye. My heart pounded and I couldn't hold her gaze.

"So this is you?"

"This is me. The innermost of the innermost. Nothing more inner than this."

"This is what you want to give your life to?"

"That's right."

Rafi *looked at me sideways.* "You're lying, man." *And he was right.*

"Why?" Ina *said.*

"Why, what?"

"Why do you want to automate the encyclopedia? Why do you want to send art museums around the world?"

"I. . . . What do you mean, 'why'?"

"Did something happen to you, growing up? Something you're trying to fix? Something you need to give to someone?"

"I loved computers the moment I saw one. I think I was born this way." I'd forgotten, entirely, what I loved before I loved computers.

Rafi *shook his head as I spoke. He knew my roots, every bit as well as I knew his.* "No, brother. That ain't it. But whatever. If it makes you feel good to think so, then think so."

I don't know how it took me until right now, telling all this to you, to see what my onetime friend already saw, a third of a century ago.

Ina *dismissed Rafi's objections as some quibble between boys. The Young Strategy. The Keane Defense. She hugged me and pecked me on the cheek.* "Cool beans, Mr. Spock. You get an A."

My whole body flushed with her reward.

ALTHOUGH HE'D WATCHED ME *humble myself to Ina's ritual,* Rafi *still wanted out.* Ina *clucked at him and wagged her finger in his face like a windshield wiper.* "You promised." *When he still balked, she sighed.* "Fine. I'll go next. Wednesday night. At my studio space in the art building. You two can sit and behave yourselves while I do my thing."

On the appointed Wednesday, Rafi and I left the dorm cafeteria after dinner and walked across the South Quad to Art & Design. We passed the enormous sycamore behind the auditorium, its limbs held up with metal guy wires. We walked alongside the main library, that huge Georgian time tunnel where Rafi spent half his out-of-class hours.

I asked, "You sure you want me around when she shows off her sanctum sanctorum?" But Rafi wasn't playing. Or rather, his mind was toying with something else. He shook his head, not quite believing what he was going to say.

"I don't know how or why. I don't know in what way it's gonna happen. But I'm certain of it. This woman is my destiny. She is cracking open my chest, man. Teaching me how to be good with everything."

I waited for more, but there was no more. We crunched through the dried leaves on the sidewalk and entered Art & Design in silence.

The building was deserted except for a few souls scattered over its four floors, working on their private projects. Rafi and I found Ina's studio down in the basement, a large, open room divided into several workspaces each cluttered with color and creation. The air stank of mineral spirits, canvas, wet clay, wood shavings, and dried plants.

Ina was waiting for us in front of a sculpture twice her height. It consisted of hundreds of different pieces of wood all glued, screwed, bolted, nailed, or lashed together. From up close, it looked like chaos, with two-by-fours fastened willy-nilly to beautiful old hand-carved bowls, picture frames, birdhouses, and decorative boxes. Pieces of bookshelf, toy tops, wooden cooking utensils, and even an inlaid chess set were thrown together as if by chance into the massive 3D collage.

But from a few steps back, the patchwork of junk resolved into a woman's face. Two wooden ship's wheels were its eyes. Its nose was a great wooden sled like the kind I used in Caldwell Woods, when I was little. The solution to the optical illusion jumped out at me, and I gasped. Rafi paced around the ten-foot-tall wooden countenance. He studied it, holding the lower half of his face in place. He was discovering his destiny's destiny.

It looked like a life-sized tiki. She had painted over the entire sculpture with some kind of gypsum mix that turned all the different shades of wood a dark cream. Every inch of that whited surface was painted with fine spectral lines and repeating geometric designs in red and pale green, giving the entire wooden visage a Māori tattoo. The tiny veins were so intricate, so small, and so numerous that I choked on the labor involved. I couldn't see how she had been on the mainland long enough to have painted that many tiny tendrils across so huge an expanse.

"I can't believe what I'm looking at. Did you use a magnifying glass? How many hours did you put in on this?"

My astonishment only amused her. She raised a bushy eyebrow and in her most matter-of-fact voice she said, "A few."

"Is this you?"

Ina ignored me and herded us into folding chairs six feet in front of the sculpture, so close that the assemblage turned back into jumbled pieces of painted wood. She held up a finger, opened her mouth, then closed her eyes and waited. Something like inspiration must have arrived, because she started speaking and didn't stop again for a long time.

"I'm simple. So simple. You only need to know a few things about me." She closed her eyes again and counted on her fingers. "Five. If you get those five things, you get me.

"First: My father is a patriot who is going to finish out his days as a lieutenant commander in the U.S. Navy. He was away on ships for most of my childhood. He has one shriveled hand and one gold-edged tooth, and a brilliant, trusting smile, and he puts on one of his several uniforms every day and goes to work helping to bring stability to a volatile world. He likes beer a bit too much, and Dave Brubeck, in small doses. He worships, worships, worships me, but I scare the shit out of him because he knows I don't believe in his world, and he'll never understand mine."

I looked at Rafi. His head was bowed and his two fists sat in his lap like stones.

"Second: My mother was from the Tahitian underclass, poorly educated, badly fed, and robustly indoctrinated by the ruling elites and the full-blood French. She worked for many years as a maid at a luxury Western hotel, pushing the maid's cart around, changing the bed linens, refreshing the little soaps and tiny shampoo bottles. What she saw in those rooms changed her. She never trusted strangers again. I tried to talk to her about it once, and she waved me off. 'People with money do scary things.'

"My father came and swept her away. She devoted herself to him. But devotion meant hiding. My father loves my mother like he loves America, but she has hidden most of herself from him and from her children behind a mask of efficient competence. She has always been kind to us, but I have no idea who she is, in the life underneath the one she lives."

By this point, Rafi had the middle two fingers of his right hand pressed to his forehead, trying to stuff his frontal lobe back into his skull. I turned my eyes back to the Ina show.

"Third: I'm the first of five children. We grew up as military brats, moving to yet another naval base in yet another country every two years. You make friends fast, living like that, and you lose them even faster.

"I was a gymnast before I became a bohemian. My sister was a singer before she became a phone receptionist. And the three boys. . . . I don't know what they are. They eat mountains of starch five times a day and still go to bed hungry. They plan to make a living by surfing. I've watched them get buried in waves as high as an eight-story building. I wonder which of them will survive into adulthood."

She stopped to stir a stick in an open can of blue housepaint sitting on the stool behind her. It was like the can was alive, a pet of hers, and she suddenly remembered that it needed feeding.

"But here's the thing. Number four. I'm not from the same planet as you. On your planet, there's always more. More growth,

more land, more possibility. You can get in your car and drive for three days, and still not get where you're going. And when you do get there, it's time to get going again. I've lived in eight different places growing up, and I could have biked from one end of those worlds to the other without too much trouble. This is the first time . . ."

She stopped and swiped her hand out toward the wall, at the endless, level miles of corn and soybean desert stretching away from us in every direction. She pointed her disbelieving fingers at the Rockies, the Grand Canyon, the Great Lakes, the Gulf of Mexico—all the places connected by land to our little town.

"This is the first time in my life when I've had no idea in creation where the hell I am."

She gave the paint can another stir, and when she started talking again, she addressed herself to that curious shade of cobalt-blue.

"Finally: Five. Everything in my past, all the collective memory of the people I come from, all the native creatures of the places where I've lived—all of it has been blown away. There's almost nothing left but picture postcards, a few stones from ruined marae, and hula dancers putting leis on the shoulders of tourists.

"What does it mean to be a 'Pacific Islander'? I haven't a clue. I dress and think and behave like an outsider. I speak the languages of the Western invaders. The planet that I came from is gone forever. And I don't belong in the one where I've landed. The only way I can find out about where I came from—who my people were—is to read about it in books.

"Well, okay, then. This is what I read. For centuries, my ancestors kept hundreds of islands spread across several thousands of miles of ocean in song-maps stored in their heads. All those islands and the paths of all the stars and the swirls of hundreds of currents and the behaviors and migrations of every sea creature. . . . Now all those maps are gone, and my generation of islanders are wandering around on the beach in a daze, concussed by history."

Rafi called out next to me, his voice sharp enough to make me jump. "I hear you, girlfriend."

But she didn't seem to hear him. She waved at the ten-foot-tall self-portrait next to her, as if it were one of the vanished maps.

"Our first god made the world from eggshells and tears and bone. Then our artists made the other gods out of shells and coral and sand and the fiber from palm fronds. All those gods are dead, now. What am I supposed to do? What am I supposed to make?"

I think I would have given my life for her, had she asked. And she would have made the sacrifice into an adventure.

She picked up the can of paint in one hand and the stirring stick in the other. A sick feeling came over me. Rafi, too. He rocked forward, as if to leap from his seat.

"Wait!" She swung the blue-coated stirring stick at us, freezing us in place. "One last thing. Number six. What you call the ocean is nothing but the coast. You can go visit it for a long weekend. You can even live alongside it. But you never get much farther than a mile or two from the shore. Your ocean is just the continental shelf, a little bit of spill over the rim of the cup.

"The real ocean . . . the deep one . . . the one that doesn't end. . . ."

She dipped the stirring stick back into the can of blue and closed the distance to the sculpture. A weak, incredulous, "No!" came out of Rafi's mouth, but it didn't stop Ina from swiping thick blue streaks onto the surface of the giant face. Every slash of blue annihilated a few feet of the intricate web of tendrils that had taken her so many hours to paint.

I wanted to jump up and pin her arms, but I couldn't move. Rafi's head was between his knees. He whimpered, "Please, stop." By the time Ina set the stirring stick back into its paint can, he was a wreck. She had to come and kneel in front of his chair. She grabbed his knees.

"Buddy. Bud." Her finger lifted his chin. "Look!"

We all three turned back toward the defaced face, now streaked top to bottom by three layers of joyful blue cartoon waves.

"Hey!" She patted his thighs. "Come see." She tugged his hand and made him stand. She brought him up close to the vandalized sculpture. I tagged along. She found a spot at eye level where the splash of blue paint covered the elaborate webs of lines and dots that had cost her so many weeks to lay down. She put her finger in the boundary between creation and destruction. "See? Isn't that the coolest effect you've ever seen?"

Rafi took off his glasses and pushed his face up close. His head was moving, somewhere between a shake and a nod. His teeth showed a little, and the tiny rictus of his lips confirmed that she was right. The messy waves of blue did not destroy the patterned precision that must have required a loupe to trace. In fact, the slashes of paint intensified the lines and colors that peeked out from the obliterating blue. Most everything was now submerged. But what you could still see hinted at all the invisible amazements hidden under the waves.

"Okay," he announced. "But never do that to me again."

His devastation amused her. "Hey, that's art, baby. I was waiting to do it until someone could watch."

It stunned me that the two of us were someone enough for her. "It should have been a roomful of people. You should have filmed the whole performance."

"What? And commodify it?"

Rafi was still shaken. "Girlfriend, you're gonna kill me. What do you want from me?"

"No-thing," she said, singsong. "Every-thing."

HER PERFORMANCE FORCED HIS HAND. Three days before Christmas vacation, Rafi got us past security and into the closed stacks where he had his study. I hadn't been there since he'd gotten promoted to a lockable carrel up on deck ten. It surprised me that he hadn't yet asked this woman, whom he meant to marry, to visit the spot where he spent his days.

"*Wow,*" *Ina said, winding through the old passageways of steel-girder shelving. "It's heckin' dark in here. No wonder you're so pale.*"

My friend was too preoccupied to play. The deck full of a hundred thousand books felt as if it hadn't been visited by humans for years. He led us to the back corner where his carrel sat, an eight-by-five-foot box built into the wall, its door cut out with one large wire-reinforced, frosted window. It was a cage for scholars, and no one could enter it but the monastery staff and him.

He unlocked the door, and the three of us squeezed in. There was barely enough room for the oak desk, his armchair, and the flimsy metal table on which stood an old Remington typewriter still in its flip-up portable carrying case. One little window, also laced with chicken wire, looked out on the south farms beyond the edge of campus.

Books were everywhere. Old books with solid black, green, tan, and burgundy bindings. Quartos and folios that I was surprised the library let circulate. Pamphlets bound in weird brown material neither cardboard nor plastic. Books lined the shelves above the desk. Dozens of them spread open across it. Books piled on top of one another in a semicircle, as if he had spread the parts to a symphony all around him and was trying to reconstruct the full score. There were books on history and race and Chicago and inexplicable subjects like boat building, table tennis, and marsupials. There were books of poetry by poets whose names meant nothing to me. At least twenty lay sprawled open and waiting for him, as if he'd just stepped out to get some more.

"The best thing about having this place? You can just wander around the stacks, check books out to the carrel, and squirrel them away back here, where only you can touch them."

Ina cleared a space on the desk and sat. She had to hike up her purple pencil skirt, and I had to look away. Rafi took the chair, and I, Mr. Spock, stood behind my captain.

*Rafi scowled and gripped the arms of his chair while avoid-
ing all eyes on him. "We don't do this kind of shit where I
come from."*

*"So you've told us, a few times already." But Ina's voice was
soft and sympathetic. It just wanted to know what drove him.*

*He reached out for his books as if they were a life raft. But his
hands went instead to a stack of nine-by-twelve brown envelopes,
the kind with a piece of string looped around two disks near the
lip flap. He took the top one off the stack, unwound the string,
opened the envelope, and removed a sheaf.*

*I saw over his shoulder. Dozens of copies of the same poem,
typed out again and again, were peppered with minuscule red-
penned edits. The poem was evolving, but in steps so small they
seemed trivial. He riffled the stack, looking for the cleanest, most
recent version.*

*"You know, I bluffed my way into the highest-level poetry
class this university has on offer. I sat there for an hour in the
office of this enormous, balding man who looked like a giant-sized
jokester version of Allen Ginsberg. I talked a steady stream of
utter bullshit about poets I didn't understand and poets I'd never
heard of, until he waived the prerequisites. That's how badly I
wanted membership.*

*"In the class, he told me to 'speak to your color.' I told him
to 'speak to my ass.' He's a total asshole, but I love the guy.
He wants to be my surrogate father. He has no idea what that
means. He made us all write a sonnet. This was mine. He told
me, 'You realize this is broken.' I said, 'The fuck, man. Not
broken. Liberated.' It turned out okay, between us. Like, 'Kum-
baya' and all."*

*He heard how much he was saying. Everything he said was
news to me—to me, his roommate and best friend, who once
knew everything that happened to him over the course of every
day. Rafi grinned, wolfish. He waved one hand in the air, dismissing his introduction, dismissing any feeling we might have about*

*what he was about to read. Dismissing the poem in advance.
Then he read it.*

TRANSCRIPT (A LIBERATED SONNET)

*She sent me off to my first day of school
Wearing a screaming orange coat so that
She could see me however far I walked
To school that day and know that I was safe.*

*Her face was bruised so blue that even I
Could see those colors from as far away
As school, and every school since that first day,
However far I walked in space and time.*

*What lesson did I learn on that first day?
That being safe would always get you killed.
And so I traded safety for more school
And when I had to make a choice, I chose*

School and freedom over home and race.

*All that schooling to teach me how to be
Another bruise on my mother's unschooled face.*

He must have practiced the poem out loud many times, sitting in this carrel on school evenings, reading his work for an audience of no one. He could have been a voice actor. His left hand moved as he read, an involuntary stream of gestures not quite explicating the words—more like a parallel poem alongside the one he recited. The words went right through me. I didn't understand poetry, but I understood this. And when he finished, distracted and spent, I swiped a copy from his folder of drafts. The one I still have and the one he ended up with were surely different.

He read us two other poems that day, each tied up in its own manila envelope, hiding among scores of drafts. One was called "Acceptance Day." I don't know what Ina made of it, but knowing what Rafi had told me about getting into Saint Ignatius, I felt the poem like a hot poker. It was long, witty, furious, and sad, and I can't remember a word of it. I must have buried it from myself. The last one, addressed to his father, was called "Blumenfeld Countergambit." Ina couldn't know this, but I did. It's an opening by Black that depends on sacrificing a pawn to gain an unstoppable advantage. That one was written to be remembered forever:

> *"Read," you commanded. "Read alone,*
> *read with no help from anyone until*
> *you have their power—the means to be."*
>
> *How is it that you hate me for winning*
> *a game that you wouldn't let me lose?*
> *Daddy, abuser, I did as told. Thank you.*

The three of us stood in that cage of books, the words still in the air. Seconds later, Rafi took a red pen from the desk and began working over the poem, crossing out and circling words, sending them to other spots using carets and long arrows. In another minute, the page looked like the drawing of a football play. So, once again, the poem I can recite for you is not the one he ended up with. Who knows what version he ended up with?

Ina said nothing as Rafi disappeared into his edits. She had asked to see his innermost place, and this was it. Rafi, at twenty-two, bent over the paper, fixing the deficient words, changing and changing, even after reading their perfection to us. He edited them as patiently as he'd edited himself. He spoke head bowed, addressing the page.

"Toddy had like a million things we were supposed to know about him and his machine. Een had five. I feel like a slacker,

with only two. First: I am working to revise some early lessons. Second: That takes a lot of drafts. Fortunately, I do enjoy keeping the game going."

"That's three things," I said.

He set the pen back down on the desk and looked up. In a goofy, cartoon voice, he said, "A th-th-th-that's all, folks!"

"Rafi," Ina said.

He heard the pleading in her voice. His own voice turned earnest, trying to interpret and to forestall, which I suppose comes to the same thing.

"It's the first mystery of my existence: That to get their revenge on a culture that's killing them, my parents pushed their child into a place that they themselves can never understand. Poetry, for God's sake. They got what they wanted, but now they want the old me back."

"Rafi," Ina said again. She slid off the desk and stepped toward the chair. Involuntarily, he put up his palms in self-defense. She took his hands in hers, held them down to her side, and kissed him. He kissed her back, amazed. Neither of them cared that I was standing right there.

The kiss went on, motionless and exploratory, until I couldn't stand it anymore. I eased myself out of the cramped room, opening and closing the door with its frosted window, and neither of them heard me leave. I threaded my way back through the maze of shelving and down to level five and the bookstacks exit. I waited for an eternity on the other side of the turnstile.

When the two of them came out at last, they looked flushed, happy, and more than a little nonchalant. Rafi spied me sitting on my haunches against the wall, outside the exit.

"Mr. Keane, I presume."

Something about our friendship had changed. And something much diminished was growing up in its place. The three of us went down the double-height flights of stairs to street level. Outside, the cold air smelled glassy and metallic. Winter on the prairies.

We went to a Korean restaurant in Campustown. The things

we were not to talk about were as clear as if he'd spoken the pro-
hibition out loud. Instead, the early dinner conversation was filled
with insipid chatter. Ina described what sea slugs tasted like. Rafi
explained why he would always be a Cubs fan, hoping without
hope, the masochism of each new season. I was done with them
both and couldn't wait for the meal to be over so that I could go
back to the NCSA and be with CRIK.

But when I made to go, Rafi wouldn't let me.

"No, you don't, friend. Did you forget that we're going to see
Willy the Shake?" He had gotten us tickets to that night's student
performance of The Tempest. *"Greatest play ever written by a*
dead white dude."

THE PERFORMANCE WAS ATHLETIC. *Characters and words*
and books and magic spells and hopes, fears, dreams, and crazy
untamable desires were flying around the stage, hitting various
targets and sending them careening. For the first time, the penny
dropped, and I realized why we call them plays. I sat there in the
middle of the most amazing dungeon crawl, watching the adven-
ture unfold as if the dice were still being cast.

I was mostly lost. The story seemed to be about a hermit wiz-
ard of great powers who has taken over the island of his banish-
ment, and when outsiders land, he plays out the finale of a vast
and patient game for his own artistic purposes. Halfway through
the play, the tortured monster Caliban, who has a strange S&M
relationship with the wizard, comes out onstage and reassures
his fellow revolutionaries with whom he is plotting a coup that if
they hear things in their heads, it's all magic and they shouldn't be
afraid. It's just the wild island talking, and all the sounds are more
enjoyable than dangerous.

You tell me. You're the one who's read everything ever written.

As the tortured slave creature spoke those words, Ina, the
island girl, sitting between us, let loose with a tremendous sob
and grabbed both our hands. I had no idea why. You, on the other

hand, can probably make the connection in whatever passes in you for a heartbeat. The island really is singing. And the song really is good. It only sounds terrifying to us humans.

Ina's sob echoed through the theater. It embarrassed us both, and Rafi tried to hush her. But she cried through the rest of the play. When the spell broke and the play ended, she was wrung out. She didn't want to leave the empty room. Her eyes looked rubbed with salt. It had been some day.

Rafi and I walked her home across campus and into the cold, square residential blocks that so disoriented her. Some of the houses were lit with strings of Christmas lights, which she marveled at as if they were bioluminescent deep-sea creatures. She stopped to regard the cloud-streaked moon, a gray squirrel shooting up a tree, a crow settling to roost, as if she had never seen anything like them before.

Increasingly foulmouthed, she kept cursing the cold. "How do you fucking live here? This place isn't fit for human habitation." Rafi and I wedged up on either side of her, trying to warm her while still walking. The three of us, moving through that frigid night, and the isle full of noises.

Then: "Would you look at that? Look at that! You stupid shits!" It took us too long to figure out what she was talking about. It was too ordinary a thing for us midwestern boys to notice. "Why didn't you tell me about snow?"

ON HER DOORSTEP, she hugged me to her and kissed my earlobe. Rafi, too, in his puffed-up coat and knit elf's cap, uncharacteristically clapped me on the back and wished me a merry Christmas. But it meant the night was over, they were going upstairs to finish it together, and I was banished.

I headed back to the dorm alone, then up to Evanston by myself two days later, for more picture puzzles with my mother. Later that holiday break, while I was putting in a piece of bluish steam coming out of the train engine smokestack in Monet's The

Gare Saint-Lazare, *I had the brainstorm that would shape the rest of my life and earn me my first hundred million dollars.*

IN THE SPRING, *Rafi moved out of the dorm and into Ina's equally tiny apartment. Full of final projects, my semester passed in a flash. I saw little of them. We did celebrate graduation together, me with my BS in computer science and Rafi with his degree in creative writing, Ina presiding as toastmaster to us both. Our parents did not come down.*

We each decided to stay at Illinois, Rafi to be with Ina and pursue a master's degree in American literature, and I to form a little start-up and realize my brainstorm. We rarely crossed paths. The one time that felt most like old times—with Rafi and me both dipping joyfully into the old playbook—turned out to be the meeting that would kill our friendship for good.

THE THREE OF US *remained in that endless cornfield for two and a half more years. Rafi and Ina grew more inseparable with each passing month, more inclined to hole up and see no one. I didn't know what was really happening to them until too late—too late to avert the disaster or even understand it.*

My island girl. My tormented friend. They should have ended up together.

SHE LOVED WOMEN.

That fact made Evelyne's thirty-six-year-old heart beat hard.

It was, in retrospect, a most obvious discovery. Not even a discovery, really—more of an acquiescence. Obvious, and yet a total shock. The shock of that shock made her thirty-six-year-old heart beat harder.

Had it been a different year and she a different person, she might have started her life over. But it was 1971, and she was Evelyne Beaulieu Mannis, married to the world's most gentle and accommodating man. She had two children who looked to her to protect them from a world that neither child understood. And she still had a mother in her sixties, a status-conscious woman living in a bygone age. Evie could not humiliate or hide from her.

Above all, Evelyne had her career. Against all odds, she'd worked her way into a field she shouldn't have been able to break into, a life that she was made for, in a profession run by standards-maintaining men who would exile her at the first hint of impropriety.

Maybe if she was devious; maybe if she could sneak and hide. Maybe if she loved one single woman, and not a mix of several. But even then, she would not have known how to leap from her solid and rewarding existence into the terrifying unknown. She loved women. But there were all kinds of things she loved and could not have. Best to have the things that already overwhelmed her with their amplitude, the things she already could never exhaust. She had the ocean. And the ocean absorbed all her hope and excitement, all her panic and pain and love, into a place far larger than anything human.

————

THE WORLD'S MOST FAMOUS picture magazine asked her to dive off Truk Atoll, a thousand miles north of New Guinea. The editors wanted her to explore the war machines destroyed in Operation Hailstone, one of the Pacific War's biggest battles. She was to take pictures with a new underwater camera and write up her impressions of the immense graveyard, submerged for almost thirty years. Few divers had explored that sunken cemetery. An article by her with state-of-the-art photos would bring the wrecks into millions of living rooms.

Evelyne was fond of the yellow-covered magazine. The French edition had fed her hunger for adventure when her family's ideas of an exotic expedition had been driving to Mont Tremblant. She and her little brother Baptiste used to stare for hours at the magazine's pictures of garish rain forest frogs. Its coverage of Cousteau had strengthened her resolve to become a diver.

The Tektite II mission put Evelyne on the geographical society's radar. They came after her with a proposal: You dive and take pictures of the underwater astonishments. We'll take pictures of your long, trim body in its wet suit, complete with its mermaid flippers. The deal was innocent enough, for the early seventies. But Evelyne wrestled with it. Serious science looked askance at any writing that smacked of mass-market fluff. Publishing in the pages of a popular magazine might be professional suicide. Once her body appeared on millions of coffee tables around the world, her peers would never take her seriously again.

It took three agonized weeks for her to say yes. She hoped that a byline in that old, beloved magazine might finally convince her mother that Evelyne wasn't just some oceangoing tramp. Also, her uncle Philippe had served on one of Canada's few Pacific warships, the HMCS *Uganda*. He died the year after Operation Hailstone in Operation Inmate, a cat-and-mouse game off Truk, and his crew buried him at sea. Evelyne had only dim memories of the man, last seeing him when she was six. But she remembered well enough her mother's nervous breakdown and the month she spent in a "rest home" following the cable of Uncle Philippe's death. Perhaps it might give Sophie Beaulieu belated closure if a family member presided over his funeral, decades after the fact.

Leaving home for another long trip was less of a problem than it had ever been. The kids were getting older. They knew now that their mother came and went, always bringing them back shells, corals, and other treasures. Their father found his satisfactions in raising them and in the endless, unanswered questions of his own work. As his wife dove in the world's faraway oceans, Bart Mannis set up his kingdom in a twenty-by-twenty-six-foot dry lab at Scripps. He had staked a claim to physical oceanography, using the rapid expansion of computing power to model the transfers of heat and energy flowing between water, air, and land. The great ocean engine ran the world and decided the fate of all life. Most of humanity had no idea how beholden they were to the interplay of salinity and temperature. Bart found tremendous pleasure in being part of a global community of scientists discovering how that engine worked.

When Evelyne told him that she was leaving again, a cold current passed through Limpet's own circulatory system. The old, familiar hurt had come to feel almost proprietary, even exciting. Through his work, Limpet had learned to see all the hurt they caused each other as part of an enormous system of fluctuating currents that worked on scales too large to grasp. In their recirculating pain, he and Evelyne were united again. Even saying goodbye to her, again and again, was thick with meaning.

EVELYNE DOVE IN THE LAGOONS near Truk, unsure what she'd find. More than 250 planes and 50 ships spread across a patch of ocean bottom seventy square miles large. Most lay between fifty and two hundred feet down, no more than a mile from the mangrove-fringed shores.

Before the battle, the lagoon around the islets had been a smooth, shallow slope of sand and mud colonized by half a dozen species of algae that grew in meadows a foot high. Injecting hundreds of planes and scores of ships into this pastureland was like dropping a city down into an endless cornfield. Truk had become a series of living caves, causeways, and canyons—the largest manmade reef on the planet. The stacked decks and spiral stairways of the ships, the gun barrels and batteries, the signal bridges and chart houses, the lower decks filled with engine rooms, the passages lined with officers' state rooms and galleys and crews' quarters created every imaginable kind of neighborhood: hundreds of biomes where there had been just one. Even a single-person plane, with its cockpit and propellers and shattered wings, was an intricate apartment building for kinds of life that would never have gotten a foothold without the carnage.

Every time Evelyne and her partners from the magazine dove, they came across astonishment. A kelp-coated Japanese submarine lay on its portside in 125 feet of water. It had dived in haste to avoid American planes and failed to close all its valves. Everyone on board died a slow death on a craft that could no longer surface once the danger passed. Not far from the sub lay a transport loaded with trucks and tanks, each vehicle done up in living, vivid crepe as if they were floats in the Rose Bowl parade. In the officers' mess of an auxiliary water tanker, Evelyne came across a rack of deer antlers hanging on the wall.

These haunting scenes all but wrote Evelyne's article for her. But not until her fourth descent did she come across the wreckage that would form her centerpiece. In an area no larger than the heart of the Scripps campus, her team found a warship split down the middle nestled near an armed aircraft carrier transport, while one auxiliary ship and one cargo vessel kissed each other on a nearby sloping shelf. The whole surreal tableau was peppered with Zeros and other planes. Machine parts lay everywhere, twisted into shocking shapes, their intricate purposes now indecipherable.

Evelyne dove, trailed by the two divers who photographed her. The warm water was clear to fifty feet. She held her underwater camera in front of her as if it were a shield. Between fifty and a hundred feet, she entered a rainbow garden painted by Bonnard. She could not believe that so many different plants, animals, and in-between creatures had found their way across open ocean and colonized each custom-made spot in a matter of mere decades. It was as if the designers of the world's greatest aquarium had gotten together and stocked their exhibits with two of everything.

The hulls and decks were so mangled by shells and collisions with the ocean bottom that Evie struggled to tell which way some ships were facing. One of the vessels lay on its side with large pieces buckled in every direction. Another of the larger battleships, repeatedly bombed and torpedoed, had shed its turrets and cranes, conning towers, funnels, antiaircraft guns, and gun directors across several hectares. Everywhere a cluster of parts landed, it spawned a new reef.

Life covered every inch of the twisted surfaces and turned them into high-rise dwellings. A brass ship's throttle, its handle stuck to a speed that failed to save it, lay like some wild Miró sculpture caked in starfish and worms. Morays nested in the gun barrels. One ship's crumpled mast was so coated with swirls of whip coral and anemones that it, too, branched as if alive. Troops of porcelain crabs skittered in formation. Nudibranchs slithered across bits of blasted deck as if some wedding had scattered hallucinogenic bouquets.

Evelyne felt herself swimming inside a giant glass bottle like the one her son Danny had once found in a tidal pool in La Jolla Cove. The wreckage of war had seeded the greatest nursery she'd ever seen.

She focused her dives on the carrier transport. Most of its half a dozen holds were punctured. The steep cliffsides of the hull, four hundred feet long, were encrusted with sessile animals. All around the wreck grew several dozen species of plants. She did a quick tally of corals, but lost count well before a hundred. The fish were even more various. Sharks, barracuda, trevallies, snappers, and other top predators abounded.

The colors alone defied belief. Black coral decorated the hull and visible deck. Spectral sponges in crazy numbers—silver, pallid, and alabaster—encrusted the gunwales and waved in the current. Milky glassfish patrolled the wreck's burst holes. Clouds of nacreous pearly dartfish and blue-green chromis damselfish schooled around her, running their own investigations. The reds, burgundies, and oranges of marbled shrimp in all their stages clattered through the hidey-holes of the jumbled metal, looking like animated Christmas cards. Parrotfish, groupers, cardinalfish, gobies, two-tone darts, wrasses, blennies, scorpionfish, jellies and other cnidarians: she couldn't begin to name all the colors.

The new camera functioned well, clicking off pictures of the constant wonders. Evelyne swam closer to the main mass of the shattered ship. She grabbed hold of the tangled cross-braces of an antenna tower. Her hand came away crawling with living things. Skirting a ruined bulkhead, she approached the rail above the gang-way. She gestured for the other two divers to follow, then passed through a blast hole in the hull deeper into the wreck.

As she entered the obscurity of the enclosed staterooms below, plants and corals, creatures of the light, gave way to those that dealt in darkness. In the lower forward hold, she came across two flights of disassembled Mitsubishi fighters, and farther aft, a machine shop filled with cryptic tools and devices, their purpose no longer readable under the layers of accreting life. In one cor-ner stood what must have been an air compressor. Pipes snaked like limbs around its cylindrical body, and its twin circular gauges looked like goggles on a robot from a dark and silent future.

She pressed deeper into the ship, forcing her body through smaller crevices. Her path began to agitate her minders trailing behind her. Reef sharks were everywhere—whitetips, blacktips, and greys. The other two divers watched in horror as a two-meter-long grey reef shark tore into a school of jack and made a kill. The scene so entranced Evelyne that she forgot she was holding a cam-era. By the time she started shooting again, the shark was gone, leaving nothing behind but a cloud of entrails.

More worrying than the emboldened predators were the mines and unexploded munitions—stockpiles of live projectiles that had gone down with these ships. No one had inventoried the dangers inside the wreck, the gash hazards and leaking toxins. Tangles of shredded steel and debris might shift with contact, blocking an exit or snaring a diver. Her dive mates beckoned to Evelyne, begging her not to go any farther into the encrusted, murky maze. But she pressed on into the next room, whose marvels exceeded the ones that had already engulfed her.

On the floor of the alcove stood a suite of upright flasks and wine bottles covered in coral starts. Near them, dishes and utensils spawned a swarm of gorgons. A school of cardinalfish came and went above the living picnic. Garish worms and other invertebrates crawled over everything, kinds of life she couldn't identify. She snapped pictures like mad, not just for the article's future audience but for her own chance to discover what she was looking at, later, on the surface.

Then her eye settled on a thing she knew in a flash, even with almost nothing left to go by. The remains of two sailors clutched each other underneath the eternally renewing bouquets that had sprung up on their ad hoc grave. Evelyne hung in place above the pair of skeletons. The eye sockets of one stared up through the cracks in the ceiling above.

She was likely the first to see this pair of corpses since their world ended in a play of waves. It fell to her to consecrate the deaths of these men whom her people had hated with a hatred that had felt pure and righteous, men who had killed her uncle. Thousands more dead lay scattered through this crypt, and the sea had turned them all into new experiments. They all called out for her benediction.

She took no pictures and spoke no blessings. She left them to their continuing conversion. They had become a reef. The muffled hum of fish was their equal music. The surprise of death was their equal possession. The sea was their equal eternity.

The canted corridors led deeper into the bowels of the ship. Evelyne followed, until one of her minders swam up next to her and tapped his watch. They were pushing their tanks hard and had to start heading back up.

But the way out proved harder than the way in. The passages tilted at crazed angles, and the maze of twisted braces and ruptured plates confused her. Her diving partners got turned around. The trio gesticulated at each other, pointing out their preferred routes with forced calm. One tapped at his dive watch and drew a finger across his throat. Kicking away in exasperation, Evelyne caught herself on a piece of broken railing, and for an instant she thought she had ripped her air hose. She held her hand in front of her mask to see a gash on her index finger oozing blood. In the filtered light of water at this depth, the blood trickled inky green.

A small adjustment cleared the hose and her air started again. But in that instant, Evelyne Beaulieu had a premonition. She would die, not here, not today, but in some place and time that could be reached from this one, entirely by swimming. She would die somewhere down in the world's one, continuous ocean, and she was at peace with the idea. More than at peace. After this day, dying on land would feel repugnant. She needed to be a reef.

––––

THE DAY AFTER SHE GOT BACK to California from Truk, she wrote her mother. *Chère maman*, she wrote. *Je viens de rentrer d'une aventure des plus remarquables. . . .*

> *I have seen Uncle Phillipe's final resting place, and you*
> *were so much with me while I was there. . . . I remember*
> *how hard the news of his death hit you and how horrified*
> *you were that there was no body for us to gather over and*
> *put into the ground. You thought it was terrible, his burial*
> *at sea. You called it a nightmare. . . .*
> *But I have been there, Maman, and I can tell you that*
> *if any place on this entire planet can be called paradise,*
> *Uncle Phillipe is in it. Heaven is growing out of him. . . .*

Evelyne went on to tell her mother what she had seen, and those first attempts to describe Truk became the article she would publish five months later.

FOR A LONG TIME after her article appeared, she was showered with letters from strangers. Maybe it was the stunning photographs, culled from the dozens that she took. Maybe it was the simple prose of someone neither a writer nor a native speaker. Maybe it had something to do with the Shakespeare quote she used near the end of her piece, Ariel's famous song from *The Tempest*:

> Full fathom five thy father lies;
> Of his bones are coral made;
> Those are pearls that were his eyes;
> Nothing of him that doth fade,
> But doth suffer a sea-change
> Into something rich and strange.

Whatever the reason, her piece about the perpetual sea change being worked on the dead of Truk Atoll cast a spell on readers, and it went on doing so long after Truk turned back into Chuuk and the forty-mile-wide grave site turned into a popular tourist diving destination.

FOUR YEARS LATER, when Evelyne went to clean out the house in Vieux-Rosemont after Sophie Dupis Beaulieu died of a burst aneurysm, the issue of the magazine with Evelyne's article stood on the wicker bookshelf by her mother's bed alongside half a dozen slim volumes of light reading, a missal of daily devotions, and the *Bible de Jérusalem*. And the letter of attempted comfort that Evelyne had written her mother, decades after her mother's grief had hardened into a dry cyst, was tucked inside.

....

*T*HOSE TWO AND A HALF YEARS *were the best of my life. Looking back now, I can't believe my golden age lasted only thirty months. Thirty months of constant work that felt like an endless holiday.*

Down the hallway from my office in the NCSA building, my colleagues launched a piece of software that would evolve into the most powerful human creation since the steam engine. The people I worked alongside of at Illinois went on to create Netscape, JavaScript, Oracle, and YouTube. Huge empty continents were thrown open for homesteading. The world slipped from one age into the next.

I now had the tools to create a way of playing in this life that human beings had always wanted. I fell asleep at night barely glimpsing what that place would look like. I woke up in the morning with multidimensional arrays dancing in my head. I couldn't wait to get coding, sometimes cranking out scores of lines of subroutine before breakfast. I typed with one hand as I drank my orange juice from the cardboard carton and ate my wheat flakes in dry clumps straight from the box.

By afternoon, I often worried that some other creative visionary somewhere in New England or California would beat me to the starting line. In those days, only a thousand people on Earth understood what was happening. But that still left nine hundred and ninety-nine other adventurers who might steal the grand prize out of my outstretched hands. I teetered between rushing my creation into the world half-baked (risking that someone would do it better a few months later) and waiting until my creature was perfect (risking being scooped by a similar platform that was good enough).

But if the late afternoons sometimes gave in to a competitive panic, by evening I was shooting down the whitewater cascades of creation for the sheer joy of it. I didn't care who got anywhere first. I was just so grateful to be present in the first days of this new kind of life.

Rafi turned me on to a thin little book of gnomic aphorisms called Finite and Infinite Games, *by James P. Carse. I read it in bits late at night, as a reward for twelve hours of coding, and it seemed to contain the key to all meaning. "A finite game is played for the purpose of winning, an infinite game for the purpose of continuing the play." Up until about five p.m. each day, I was playing to win. From then until well after midnight, when my best work got done, the game turned infinite. I wrote out a little slogan in stick figures on an index card and pasted it on the bezel of my monitor:* Find the moves that the rules forgot to outlaw.

In those years, we coders were still committed to the digital gift economy. Wealth meant giving away treasure, hand over fist. The university gave away their epochal web browser when they might have made a fortune for decades to come. I'd always planned to give away my creation. But even before I finished my first alpha version, I came up with a way of giving away and holding on to my prize at the same time, while maybe even becoming unthinkably rich in the bargain.

It's still the stuff of legend how the first several versions of what would become Playground were all handwritten by a single person. When the team at NCSA that built the first graphical browser left Illinois for California, it dawned on me that I would need to bail out from the university as well, if I wanted to keep legal ownership of my creation.

I left graduate school but stayed in town, living in an efficiency in a cinder-block building, spending nothing, and eating half-price day-old donuts. I owned one hide-a-bed sofa (secondhand), one rust-colored recliner (thirdhand), a pressboard desk, and bits and pieces from several different sets of kitchen utensils. I never got around to buying a shower curtain. I'd saved a little war chest from my assistantship, and it was enough to keep me afloat. When I needed cash, I freelanced on CRIK and took on other small programming jobs. I still had access to the university network, and that saved me thousands, too. My use of their systems was not entirely legal, but no one cared. The more everybody gave away, the more we all had.

The days were as long as those two and a half years were short. I created Playground. In all that time, that's all I did. Today, they'd call me an incel, but that would be wrong. Celibate, yes. But not involuntary. I made a choice, and while I had it, the thing I chose was better than sex or love.

I didn't see much of my two friends. They were busy, too, making their own new worlds. Ina had her public obsession—carving a boat out of a massive maple that had fallen on the South Quad. No studio on campus was large enough to house the project, so she carved it under a tent outside the Education Building to much gawking and fanfare, covering the hollowed-out wood with sea turtles and fish and water gods and all the icons of a home she didn't really have. The giant canoe was her final thesis project, the one that would make her a master of art.

Rafi was hard at work, too, doing everything in his power to evade his own master's thesis. All he needed to do was knock out four term-paper-sized articles on four different twentieth century American poets, sprinkle those pages with footnotes, and lard it all with fashionable criticism. A hundred and fifty pages would have done the trick. He put in days almost as long as mine. He was writing up a storm, cranking out several thousand words a day. He just wasn't keeping any.

Even the artists and humanists were using email by then. Rafi sent me one every week or so, just to prove that he was still alive. Sometimes he wrote to say that he'd altered his lineup of poets again. He only needed four, but finding the right four was taking him hundreds of permutations. Now and then he would mail me an original sentence that he liked, or even a whole paragraph— words that managed to escape the relentless editor that he'd become. But if I made any comment, if I responded in any way to his trial balloons, he would go dark, and I wouldn't hear from him again for a long time.

He liked to send quotes that had nothing to do with what he was writing. He sent along cobbled-up translations of the Tao. He mailed quotes from James P. Carse: "A prediction is but an explanation in advance." He pulled passages from Johan Huizinga's classic, Homo Ludens: *"At the root of this sacred rite we recognize unmistakably the imperishable need of man to live in beauty. There is no satisfying this need save in play. . . ." Judging from the lines he'd sent, a stranger would have thought that Rafi was writing a thesis about games.*

The two of us tried to meet once a month for lunch, but Rafi was a fussy eater and didn't like breathing the aromas of any food more exotic than roast beef. He had one or two greasy spoons he was okay going to, but I was addicted to novelty and hated stepping into the same restaurant twice. So finding a place that pleased us both turned into a bidding game all its own.

On the day of the lunch that would ruin us, we went to a Greek dive. For some reason, Rafi would eat gyros, and the other Mediterranean smells didn't bother him that much. I had moussaka. I will die believing that eggplant is the only remotely believable proof of intelligent design.

It was July, the dog days, a time of year that the Midwest did brutally well. On the other hand, school was out and the town was empty, and that was always magical. Rafi wore a Cubs cap, jeans, and a T-shirt bearing a column of typeface that read:

THEREAFTER

NOTHING

FELL OUT AS

IT MIGHT

OR OUGHT

He wanted an update. He bared his hands on the booth table as we waited for our orders.

"Just tell me, in words a poet might understand, what is so compelling about your . . . whatever it is?"

Rafi still used the newborn web only gingerly. He didn't have much call for it. Nobody really did yet, except for explorers and adventurers. And while he was adventurous in his own way, my friend was not exactly a public person. The idea of giving human beings yet more ways to get together and be argumentative horrified him.

"I'm very close to launching. I've settled on having twelve top-level topics—Science, Politics, the Arts, Recreation, Society, Business, Family and Friends, et cetera. I'm calling them Domains. Each of those Domains will be broken out into several Kingdoms, with Phyla and Classes below these. People can post their thoughts on any topic under the sun. They can comment on the thoughts of others, or on other comments. They can ask and answer questions. They'll be able to upload pictures and sounds. Everyone can vote on the value of any post that anyone else has made. . . ."

Rafi sank lower into his side of the booth. He hunched his shoulders and pulled the collar of his T-shirt up and over his mouth and nose. At last, I stopped talking and laughed.

"What? You got a problem with this?"

In a tiny, terrified, little-kid's voice, he said, "Please, God, take me now!"

I swore at him. He sat up and waved his paw through the air.

"Naw. Just funnin' you, bro. I mean, why people would want to shoot that kind of shit with total strangers is beyond me. But, seeing as how you're doing this, I think you're missing a huge opportunity."

Our food arrived, but even the moussaka suddenly seemed like an imposition. "Do tell."

He smiled the way he used to smile just before making a brilliant Go move. "Come on, Toddy. Isn't it obvious? You gotta gamify it."

My hands flew up. "It's already gamified! The whole thing is a giant sporting event. A magic circle for amateur theatricals. That's why it's called Playground."

"But where's the game?"

"The voting. Get more upvotes and fewer downvotes than any-one in that Domain."

He shrugged. "I suppose. Accumulate prestige points. It's a start. But if I can vote on anything anybody posts without any cost, it's not much of a vote. That's like Miss Ebberson back in first grade, dishing out gold stars for free. You know: 'All you kids are so special. You're all winners.' That ain't capitalism, Boo. Who's going to stick around to play if no one has any real skin in the game?"

He picked at his gyros as my annoyance mounted. My brain reeled from the idea that all my months of work had overlooked something huge. But it was also lit up by the possibility of a brand-new kind of sport coming into the world—a communal proving ground where real natural selection shaped by real profit and loss resulted in the real evolution of ideas.

"Since when did you become the great philosopher of capitalism?"

"Ever since my daddy started fighting fires and my mama started driving buses. Ever since the whole system chewed them up and spit them out like an owl pellet. You can't pay for the edu-cation I got without becoming a philosopher of the shiny."

"So . . . what are you suggesting?"

"Just that you're missin' something, brother man. I think you need a genuine, primary currency. Something people have to sur-render if they want to vote."

He fiddled some more with his food. He rarely took bites, but there was much ritual rearrangement of the cutlery and condi-ments. I almost wanted him to shut up. I was on the verge of working it out by myself. But he lifted his head and looked around the restaurant. His eyes settled on the dollar bill that the Greek owners had framed and hung on the wall behind the cash register—presumably the first that their gyros ever earned them. Rafi brightened and put his finger in the air.

"Playbucks!"

The word was like a starter's gun launching us into two of the

*best hours of conversation we ever had. We invented and inter-
jected, talked over each other, and finished one another's sentences. We scribbled designs on napkins and drew ideas in the air.
We shouted and overruled and dismissed each other, every one of
our ideas touching off two more.*

*It was the most intense match Rafi and I had ever played, but
a match that belonged to a genre that wouldn't mature until years
later: the cooperative, save-the-world-from-pandemics game.
What we did in those two hours would set Playground apart from
all the other glorified bulletin boards, chat rooms, and white-bread
social networking sites springing up across the infant Internet.
Those places were meeting rooms. Playground would enter the
world as a full-fledged country, complete with its own resources
and economy—a marketplace for building reputation and culti-
vating net worth. The breakthrough was simple, and it could have
been implemented ten years earlier on any of the primitive online
communities that existed before the web: scarcity.*

"Give it stakes, dude. Make 'em pay to play!"

*Every ten minutes that a user spent on the platform earned
him one Playbuck. He could spend this money in various ways,
most notably by upvoting the posts of other users. Every Playbuck
spent went to the voted-on poster. But the amount spent increased
the tipper's odds of seeing future content from that source. It also
increased the odds that the tipper's own content would be seen
by other people who tipped that post. So both tipping and being
tipped increased a player's influence. There were leaderboards
in various categories. People could participate in other influence
contests and buy cosmetic trophies in each of Playground's different Domains—expenses that would curb inflation.*

But all playing had a cost: that was Rafi's golden insight.

*In two hours, we worked out all the interlocking moving parts.
The only thing we couldn't figure out was how to monetize it for
real. But I never doubted that would come. In the future, there
would be no "real" money. There would only be your standing in
that new Wild West free market called the web.*

*The Greeks wanted us out of their restaurant so they could put
our table back in circulation. As newborn purveyors of capitalism, we understood completely. We were still refining and inventing and shouting at each other all the way across campus and up
to that intersection where our paths diverged. Rafi was having a
great old time. I hadn't seen him so animated in months. It was
like we were back in high school, racing each other to the next
level of Go.*

*I grabbed him by the shoulders and stopped him on the corner
of Green and Lincoln.*

*"Rafi. Dude. Listen to me. This is going to be huge." Far big-
ger than any prize he could hope to reach on his current life's trajectory, though I didn't say that out loud. "Come onboard."*

*Like there already was a company to join. He flashed his con-
siderable teeth. "What? Work for you?" He looked down at the
sidewalk, clearing his visual field so he could think. For a moment
his face looked like a little child's. The hint of a smile played on
his lips as he imagined what it would be like, the two of us going
into business, making our own rules, creating a new living thing.
I agonized over whether to press him—to pitch how fun it would
be, win or lose, to try to change the world together. He always
bristled at my slightest attempt to influence him.*

*"You could write your own job description. Lie on a couch all
day long and be the idea guy. All the time in the world to write
poetry on the side."*

*"Huh. This gonna be a real biz, or just—you know—a couple
of guys with toy trains?"*

*Nobody on the Internet had a real business plan. I didn't even
have a real business yet. But there were fortunes to be made. That
was obvious to anyone who was paying attention.*

"Toy trains have made a lot of people a shitload of money."

*He pushed his glasses up with his left index finger while shov-
ing his right index into my chest. "And if we go down in flames?
If this whole cockamamie brainchild of yours goes belly-up in
nine months?"*

"Then you slink back to graduate school."

Something about that reply angered him. He tightened his lips, tugged at his T-shirt, and turned all business.

"No, man. You know what the flight attendants say. 'Put your own mask on before assisting others.' "

I stood there on the corner of two summer-emptied streets, gaping like a fish and feeling like he'd just slapped me. I wanted to fight back. I started to shake. I wanted to say that our destinies had been connected ever since he won my father's scholarship, back at Ignatius. The one named after my family.

"Fine," I said. "Thanks for lunch." I had paid. "And for the ideas. See ya."

I spat out these words curt enough for him to know that I was hurt. He lifted two fingers in a dismissive blessing. "Yeah. See ya."

I walked away and did not turn around to see how long he stood there or what look played on his face. I went home and worked for hours, more driven than ever to take over the world.

HAPPILY, MY EXISTING PLAYGROUND CODE *proved sufficiently well designed that the additions to the platform Rafi and I had come up with over lunch required no major surgery to implement. The upgrade went fast.*

I'd been running a closed beta version for months, using about eighty trusted former colleagues and virtual acquaintances to test the work. When I pushed out the first version that used Playbucks, the response was dramatic. Several beta testers grew obsessive. Usage went way up, both in hours spent in the sandbox and numbers of words posted to the various Domains. Users sent me rave messages, begging for new features.

I studied what worked, tweaking and fleshing out the economy. People badgered me for a public launch. They wanted thousands more people to play with, to rate, and to make Playbucks on. In those days, coders put things out there in embryo and let the community mature the product. Even the early browsers went through many public versions before they stabilized. I refused to do that, and my users couldn't understand why I was holding back.

AROUND THAT TIME, *I got an email from Ina. I'd had little contact with her since her graduation. She was working as a barista at a coffee shop across from the performing arts center. She wrote:*

> Can you please get him to finish up his thesis? Tell him no one is judging him. Tell him to take the last hundred pages that he just threw out, put his name on it, and turn it in.
>
> Todd, I'm desperate. I don't want to spend the rest of my life in this sinkhole.

My heart fell when I read her words. It was the first I'd heard that she meant to make a life with him, beyond school, somewhere else. Of course she did.

Any word I tried to "tell" Rafi would only make things worse for everyone. Still, I could have gone to see him. She asked me to, and I didn't. I was still bitter with his rejection. The lowest part of my brain was thinking: Put your own mask on before assisting others.

A LATE-NIGHT CALL FROM HIS MOTHER, AND RAFI'S FIRST thought was: *Who died?* When it was clear from her first few words that no one new had, he put his hand over the receiver and sighed.

"Can I call you right back, Ma? No—I mean right back. Like, thirty seconds."

He hung up and slipped out of the bedroom, heading toward the phone in the kitchen.

"It's fine," Ina mumbled, her face in the pillow. "Don't go. I wasn't completely sleeping."

"Sorry, love. Mama. I'll be just a minute."

"Say hi from me."

"I will."

He hadn't yet told his mother about the woman he intended to propose to any month now.

In the kitchen, he dialed the number stored in his fingers since childhood.

"Ma! You good? Everything okay?"

"I'm doing fine, Rafi. Little lonely, is all."

Moody Stepdad had disappeared the year before. Rafi's first fear was that he was threatening to come back.

"It's kind of late, Mom. Is there a problem?"

"You, Rafi."

"Me? What *about* me?"

"I had that dream again."

"Well, I told you already. Stop having that dream."

"Maybe if you came home. Maybe if I could see you more often."

"I'm working hard here, Mom. I've got an advanced degree to finish up."

"I know that, Ra. And I am so proud of you."

"But . . . what?"

"But . . . you got what you need already, don't you? I talked to Mr. Charles again."

The managing director for buses at the CTA.

"Mother. We've discussed this."

"I told him how smart you are. I told him how well you get along with white people. He says you don't even have to finish your whatever you're doing. Your master thesis. He can start you right away as an assistant manager."

It was a mystery to Rafi: Why did his breathing always slow down whenever his heart sped up?

"That's great, Ma. I . . . really appreciate it. It's just that . . . I've got my work to finish here."

"So when you gonna finish?"

"Soon. It's all going really well."

"It's taking so long. How come you need a master thesis? Didn't you just hear me? Mr. Charles says he'll take you right now."

"I heard you, Mom. Are you hearing me?"

"How much student debt do you want to keep accumulating? How you gonna pay off what you already owe?"

The bleak, crowded, dismal blue-gray rat warrens of the CTA in the bowels of the gargantuan Merchandise Mart flashed on the back of his closed eyelids. The one time he'd gone there with his mother, he barely lasted ten minutes. Eight hours a day would kill him before his first paycheck. He could never go back now, after where he'd been.

But neither could he tell his mother why. He had stepped through the wardrobe into a place where he was free to do what he did as well as anyone. That thing his father had drilled him all childhood long to excel at. He had an answer for little Sondy, ten years too late. He did not love whiteness, per se. He only loved what whiteness gave him.

Why did no one get it? Not his mother, not his lifelong friend, not even the beautiful woman sleeping in the next room, whose love had taught him a new kind of liberty. He was happy. More than happy. He was utterly fulfilled, rolling the thankless stone forever up the hill. The many demons of his past, his lifelong sense of guilt, his fear that he would never be *good enough*: he could hold them all at bay, so long as he was free to go on revising. The Lilliputians could not touch him; he could outread them all.

His mother was speaking, but he didn't hear. His mind was busy retrieving the stoical quote—Camus again: "If I had to choose between justice and my mother, I'd choose my mother." Sure. But what about choosing between your mother and *freedom*? No choice, really. Of those two options, only one would let him go on breathing.

"I appreciate it, Ma. And I'll think about it. You thank Mr. Charles for me, okay? Okay? See you. Yeah. Love you, too."

In bed, Ina murmured, roused herself, and rolled over to spread herself against him.

"Did you say hello?"

"I did. She says hi back. She wants to meet you soon."

———

THREE MONTHS LATER, Sondra Harris Young Johnson's aorta came apart. She had just finished her third Racine run of the day. She was dead before they could get her out of the drivers' coffee room and into an ambulance. A devastated Rafi went back to Chicago for the funeral. Ina went with him to prop him up and walk him away from the grave.

His cousins and aunts and uncles and grandparents cleared a space in their grief to welcome Rafi and his surprise guest. His father didn't show. Rafi and Ina stayed two days. It felt much longer. She wanted to see the neighborhood. He wasn't giving tours.

Back downstate, they had another wake, just Rafi and the two people he was closest to in the world. He told them stories and read a poem.

"I always admired her," his best friend said.

Rafi bit his tongue. It didn't seem the moment to fight. His friend was so clueless, you had to love him. And who knew? Perhaps Todd really did. Really did admire, in his own Keane way, a woman he'd met all of three times and didn't know from Eve.

....

THE MOMENT I LAUNCHED, *all kinds of clones were sure to spring up like weeds. I wanted the largest possible head start with as many features in place as I could nail down. When the imitators started chasing me, I'd have a commanding lead with a large, loyal user base who had no reason to leave and lots of reasons to stay and play.*

Once the project went public, I would need several programmers to develop and maintain the code. I needed servers, along with an ops person to do the constant maintenance and upkeep. I needed a real graphic designer to make the thing look beautiful. And for all of that, I needed to play a shiny strategy. Not Playbucks—real money. The kind that people used in the playground above my Playground.

I went to Professor Handler, my former supervisor. The CRIK project was still chugging away, making tiny gains in its goal of fitting everything ever known by anyone into the structures of symbolic AI. Professor Handler liked to joke that every year, they succeeded in formalizing another week of human knowledge. Meaning they'd just slipped another fifty-one years behind.

Handler had started a couple of companies of his own, and he knew angel investors in the Valley. I walked him through the Playground beta. We browsed several of the top-level Domains, then drilled down into Politics. We drilled down again into American Politics, then American Political Current Events, only to arrive at a flaming hot discussion about the recent Oklahoma City bombing. When Professor Handler interrupted his running critique of the interface to spend his pile of complimentary Playbucks on rebutting the currently most popular post, I knew my creature was going to have a long and happy life. I had to pull him away from the thread and remind him why we were there.

He said, "Let's take a peek at the code."

I didn't want to show him. It was like disrobing in front of a panel of county fair judges. I didn't mind him seeing my work. The work was strong; I'd learned well from him and scores of other greats, in my years of school. I just didn't want him to discover, in twenty minutes, all the ingenious inspirations that it had taken me two years to come up with.

He liked what he saw. "Why don't you create a couple dozen guest accounts, and I'll distribute them to a few venture capitalists I've worked with. This is exactly the kind of ambition everyone is looking for."

Three weeks later, I got a call from a group named the Seedbed Partners. They wanted to front me three-quarters of a million dollars. The figure was so unreal that I barely heard the terms. But the terms were favorable. I almost said yes right then, over the first phone call.

My advisor reined me in. "Sit tight. Buy time. Play coy."

Two days after that first miraculous offer, an outfit called the Honte Group called and offered me three million to buy the entire project out from under me. They would keep me on as lead programmer and project manager at a crazy salary if that interested me.

Again, I almost agreed before they finished their proposal. Any firm named after a Go term had my trust. I mean: three million dollars, thrown at someone who was still in his mid-twenties? I could have invested it in conservative long-term bonds and lived off the interest forever. Free from the messiness of making a living and accountable to no one, I could have spent the rest of my days tinkering on new projects and hustling chess games in Grant Park.

I went to Handler and begged him to tell me what to do. "It's worse than training CRIK," he said with a sigh. "We teach you everything except how to know yourselves."

"The Honte people say they need an answer by the end of the month. Seedbed Partners are about to withdraw their offer. I'm melting down. I can't sleep. I just want to curl up in my room and play Unreal."

"Aristotle said that happiness is the settling of the soul into its most appropriate spot."

I doubled down on my belief that computer scientists should never dabble in philosophy. "What does that mean, exactly?"

"What makes you happy, Todd Keane? What's your work? How do you define a day well spent?"

My mind flashed on that day many years ago when Rafi and I had looked at a Go board for the first time together in the basement of Ignatius, trying to learn the life and death of groups of stones. I watched the clusters creep and connect across the board, joining up like the neighborhoods of a great metropolis. The years since that day had unfolded one stone at a time, chaining and laddering, from the moves of that opening Fuseki to this vital point, this Tsumego, when I found myself facing a moment of life or death.

The words of the book that Rafi had given me sounded in my head, as if they'd been waiting for this moment. A finite game is played for the purpose of winning, an infinite game for the purpose of continuing the play.

I looked at Professor Handler. It was all so obvious.

"No one is going to run my company but me."

He smiled and sank deeper into his Aeron chair. "Well, all right, then! Now: Do you need a consultant?"

I stared at him, but the old man was joking. His revolution had run its course. Mine was just beginning.

I called Seedbed Partners and took the three-quarters of a million. It was more than enough to get me going. It was also an insane amount of debt for a child with an uncertain prospect and no sense of business. But my father had told me once that a man's worth was measured by how much money other people were willing to let him lose. And a corollary: the strength of a man's character was measured by how much he was willing to lose on others' behalf.

I suddenly had character to spare.

WHEN PLAYGROUND LAUNCHED, *I had five people on payroll. Two months later, we were eight. And that was nothing compared to the growth of the user base. In those same two months, the closed beta of eighty users swelled to more than ten thousand, on word of mouth alone. Remember, real search engines were just appearing, and people still published paperbound books listing all the most interesting website addresses to type into your browser.*

Everyone I hired had to have a little ludic lunacy in their heart. I ended every hiring interview with a question: "What's more important: the journey or the destination?" Either answer was fine with me. I was just looking for how much bounce the candidate was willing to put into it. Soon enough, we had a corporate culture, one that is still at the heart of the thousand-headed monster that long ago got away from me. We believed in rapid prototyping, in playing hard and getting hurt, in finding everything that the rules never thought to prohibit, and in letting the users tell us what to build next.

How so many users found our site so fast still mystifies me. But why they stayed was obvious. We humans are built to compete, built to spout opinions, built to seek prestige and shiny, built to watch our accounts and ratings grow, built to impress our friends and vanquish our enemies. Or maybe we're just built to play.

We had a payroll now, and operating expenses, but not even a trickle of revenue. Internet commerce was still pitiful; banner ads were crude and paid almost nothing. How the site might ever generate a positive cash flow remained a mystery. But Seedbed Partners threw another two million at me before the year was done.

SO MUCH HAPPENED in those months that when Ina knocked on my apartment door on a cold Thursday night late in spring, I felt as though I hadn't seen her since childhood. I greeted her with a burst of joy before seeing her distress. Stupidly, I asked, "What's wrong?" as she stood there grieving in the hallway. She pushed past me, into my efficiency.

It was almost eleven. I sat her at the table. "Can I make you something hot?"

She sniffled and nodded. Her eyes were red and her face was flushed. She held out one palm, asking for time, and cupped the other around her trembling throat. I boiled water in silence and made two mugs of lemon and ginger tea.

I sat down across from her at the folding card table in my kitchen, cupping my hands around the mug's heat. I had a pathetic desire to brag about Playground's launch and impress her with the fact that I was on my way to becoming a millionaire. I managed to say nothing, pretending to sip my tea. So did she. It took her some time to collect herself. Her composure rose and fell in her face like the tides.

At last she said, "We had a fight."

My heart flung itself all over the room. I wanted lots less and so much more. "What . . . ? What happened?"

"He's been far away, Todd. Ever since his mother died. He writes and writes, sometimes twelve or thirteen hours a day, and there's nothing to show for it. Nothing! It doesn't seem to bother him that he's stuck in place. I can't take it anymore."

I should have been impatient. I should have demanded details. But Ina Aroita was in my apartment, across the table from me, and I was in no hurry for any change. If she was buying time, I was selling.

She blew on her tea and studied the ripples as if the surface were the open Pacific. Her eyes were the weirdest mix of ferocity and fatalism. She wanted to be as far away from this continent as she could get. But I gathered that he would not go with her.

"He's never going to let that thesis go until it's better than any thesis anyone has ever written."

"Better than any North Sider's," I corrected. She looked at me, not understanding. "Better than any privileged person's thesis."

The explanation puzzled her as much as Rafi's behavior. "What do you mean? What are you saying?"

"It's his dad," I said. "The man's a competitor. I've met him several times, and he was always trying way too hard. Do you

remember that poem . . . ? From childhood, Donnie Young set him on a course to beat the white race at all its own games. Rafi has gotten past a lot of that. But if he can't win over all his peers and all his professors and anyone who might read the thesis even by accident, he's not going to show anyone a word."

She looked sick with recognition. "That's exactly what's happening. He's convinced that nothing he writes is good enough. And he won't believe me when I tell him that it's fine."

"Oh, my. Don't do that. That's not a good idea. 'Fine' is as bad as it gets."

Her eyes lit up. Horror at what she was coming to understand, and horror at what, in her ignorance, she'd already said to him.

"Wait. Do you think he thinks I'm a white person?"

"I have no idea." I didn't know how Rafi saw anyone, least of all himself.

"What has he told his father about me?"

Of that, I knew even less. "I don't think they talk much these days. That doesn't matter, anyway. Any objections his father has will only make Rafi more loyal to you."

Her fingers drummed on the lip of her mug. She kept looking at the apartment door, ready to rush back across town and work things out. Then she would melt down again. I sneaked a look at my watch. We still wore watches back then. Half an hour to midnight.

"Okay," she said, like she was the one on trial. "Some of this may have been my fault. I told him that he had to finish up the thesis or I would leave town without him. . . ."

I waited until I could fake a normal voice again. "That's harsh."

"And he said . . . 'I think you better leave, then. For your own sake.'"

"Harsher."

"He was just getting warmed up."

"What . . . exactly did he say?" I was afraid of her answer. I pictured Rafi weighing out the lightning strike, toying with a

*stunning move that would turn a weak position into a strong one.
If Rafi had uncorked on her, if he'd truly gone up into the heaven
of his fluency, he might have said anything.*

*"He said he could never make a life with anyone who laid
down ultimatums. He told me to go get myself a better Negro."
She looked at me, to see if that might be sufficient. Numbed, she
added, "Except . . . he didn't say 'Negro.' I told him I was sorry,
Todd. Over and over. I told him I didn't mean it. That I'd stay
with him until he finished, however long that took. I begged him.
I groveled. But it was like my words had flipped a switch and he
was just . . . done."*

*I saw it as if I were looking at myself. Ina wasn't the one Rafi
couldn't forgive.*

*She started crying, but tentatively, as an afterthought. "It's like
he always knew we were doomed to blow up someday, so he's
decided to blow us up in advance and get it over with."*

*I wanted to tell her: His act was his artwork—an act of poetry.
He was slashing at what was best between them, much the way
Ina had once defaced the sculpture of herself. I couldn't look at
her, so I got up and started fussing with the teakettle. Someone
somewhere surely wanted more hot water.*

*I spoke to the sink. "You know that he's convinced he wrecked
his parents' marriage?"*

"He what?"

*I turned to see her looking at me as if I'd struck her across the
face. "Do you remember the poems? The one about the orange
coat and Rafi's first day at school? That was real. His parents
fought about what happened that day. His father hit his mother. It
was a repeat thing, and she'd had enough. She left him, and Rafi
took the blame."*

"That's insane."

*"Yes. But it gets worse. Remember the poem about the day he
got accepted into high school? He also thinks his sister's death was
his fault."*

She raised her face to mine, uncomprehending. I sat back down

at the card table and told her what I knew about the night of his
sister's death. I gave her all the details exactly the way that I told
them to you. The absurd conclusion. The crazy conviction lodged
in the heart of my very sane friend. I told her about Rafi's obsession with Nikolai Fyodorovich Fyodorov. She'd seen the stolen
copy of The Philosophy of the Common Task on his bookshelf and
never opened it.

She laid her hand on my wrist. I did not pull away.

"Wait. You're telling me he thinks . . . that if he writes a good
enough thesis that . . . it'll bring his sister back from the dead?"

It was now after one a.m. Time meant nothing to her, and she
showed no intention of going anywhere.

"I. . . . he. . . . how did it end up, between you two?"

"He said I should leave. I left."

She said the words soberly, as matters of fact. But the feelings
were those of a frightened little girl, fighting fire with fire.

"You're not going back? I mean, tonight?"

In a heartbeat, she was all apologies. "Todd, I'm so sorry. I can
get a room at the Lincoln Lodge."

"Don't be silly. There's plenty of room here." I waved my hand
across the efficiency, and we both laughed at the size of my lie.

But there was room enough. I lent her my robe and found her a
fresh toothbrush, and while she showered, I pulled out the sleeper
and changed the sheets. She came out of the bathroom wrapped in
the robe, which reached down to her ankles. She studied the bed as
if it were a math problem on the Graduate Record Exam.

"I've got the floor," I said.

"Now who's being silly, Todd? We're adults."

"Exactly. I've got the floor."

She studied me, discovery dawning. How could she not have
known? She seemed more puzzled than alarmed. I made a little
rat's nest with the sofa pillows by the far side of the pull-out bed.
I'd slept on worse, but the recent big jump in my prospective net
worth added a touch of burlesque to the arrangement.

Ina switched off the overhead light and climbed into bed. For her own burlesque touch, she peeled off my robe and tossed it on top of me with a pained little giggle. She knew now, but she didn't really believe. I was her great love's great friend, and she still believed that I would save her. She was an optimist who thought she could correct her small mistake. That's what doomed her.

I dreamt that an island rose in the middle of the ocean, and Ina Aroita was on it. As in the best dreams of my childhood, I could breathe underwater. I swam all around the foundations of her island, and what I took for the crenellated towers of coral reef were in fact intricately carved statues, made by whatever sculptor had made her island. When I woke, I was curled up halfway under the bed she slept on.

I put away the bedclothes of my rat's nest, and as quietly as I could, I began to make breakfast. As I sliced into a pink grapefruit, two soft knocks landed on the door and Rafi let himself in.

Ina scrambled out of her dazed sleep and shouted his name in joy. As she sat up, her breasts popped out above the sheet, and she hurried to cover them.

Rafi hung in the doorway, surveying the scene. "So . . . the fuck is this?" He spoke to himself. Ina and I were there only as state's evidence.

I stepped forward, pointing the tiny grapefruit knife to the far side of the sleeper where the rat's nest had been. "I slept down there."

A dry chuckle came out the side of Rafi's mouth. "Don't insult me, fucker." He didn't care about the sleeping arrangements. Our real act of disloyalty cut him deeper than that.

He closed the door to the apartment and backed into the corner next to it. He held his right elbow in his left hand and pressed his right hand to his mouth, as if looking at an art installation. From the sleeper, with the sheet pulled up to her neck, Ina said, "Rafi. Rafi. I'm so glad you're here."

He didn't hear her. He pointed one crooked index finger at me. "So . . . you. . . ." His finger swung to the bed. "You came to

*him. . . ." His finger swung toward me. "To tell you what's wrong
with the Black Guy?"*

*I might have denied the charge if Ina hadn't been there to force
my honesty. How did I not see it the night before? We had confirmed for him his enduring nightmare: people he trusted were
judging him.*

"I was scared, Rafi. I was hurt."

He turned toward me. "And what did you tell her?"

*I said nothing, and my silence was an admission of the worst
kind of guilt.*

*He sat down on the foot of the bed where the woman he thought
he would marry sat with a sheet held up in front of her nakedness.
"What did he tell you?"*

*She was desperate. She blurted out, "He told me about your
sister. Rafi . . . that's not on you!"*

*He swung his head back toward me. The oddest look crossed
his face. It seemed like good-natured amusement, like someone
had played an obvious prank on him and he had fallen for it. It
seemed to say that he had known, all those years ago when he had
confided in me, that I would betray him someday.*

"Didn't I say? Didn't I . . . ?"

"Man," I said. "Listen. It wasn't like that."

"No? What was it like?"

*All I could manage, again, was nothing. Silence, with all
its concessions.*

*"Well . . ." He nodded. One hand reached out and patted the
foot of the bed. "All right, then. . . ." He stood up.*

"Rafi?" Ina said, her voice spectral.

*He opened the door and turned to study us. He addressed us
like he was arranging plans for later that afternoon. "I will not be
analyzed by two people who have no clue." The door clicked shut
behind him, and he was gone.*

*Ina started to wail and make strange motions with her hands.
I thought she was going to decompensate. It took me too long to*

realize that she wanted me to turn around so she could get out of
bed. I did, and she was dressed in a flash.

"He'll be all right. Just give him a few hours."

She ignored me, pulling herself together and rushing to collect
her things.

"Ina. Don't chase him. It'll make things worse. It'll just make
him feel more—"

She shouted at me, "Shut up! Just shut up about him!"

I stood by as she slammed out the door and ran down the steps
after him. Maybe she caught up with him. Maybe they talked. I
never heard.

I waited a few days, then wrote them both emails. I was abject.
I apologized. I suggested ways to fix things. I never heard back
from Rafi. From Ina, I got a terse reply:

Please stop making things worse. Haven't we done enough damage already? I'm getting out of here. He knows how to find me if
he wants to find me.

Two months passed. A girlfriend of hers from the MFA pro-
gram said she'd gone to Tahiti, leaving her father's APO infor-
mation as her forwarding address. Tahiti: the place no more real
to me than that Gauguin painting I'd pulled up for her so long
ago, on the proto-web. I learned from a secretary in Rafi's depart-
ment that he'd moved into a grim tenement by the interstate in
North Champaign.

MY ANGEL INVESTORS at Seedbed Partners began to pressure me
to relocate operations to the Valley. I'd almost reached the same
conclusion myself. Playground was expanding faster than I could
believe, and managing the operation from my little efficiency on
the prairie was growing impossible. We were still bleeding money,
but the Seedbed folks weren't worried about anything except my
backwoods location.

Even I could see the need for the move. Every serious player was heading to California. The talent and connections we would need to make a real run of things were waiting there, in the greater Bay Area. And all but one of my small staff was ready to relocate to what one of them called "the sweetest spot on the continent."

I WASN'T LEAVING TOWN *without one last effort. I went to the address I had for Rafi at suppertime on a Wednesday. His apartment was on the ground floor, facing a parking lot. The front door had a spy hole in it. I stood to one side before I knocked. I didn't want him seeing me until the door opened.*

His face went through five emotions before he got control of it. "Yes?" he said, like I was a salesman.

"Rafi." I was shaking. I didn't care if he saw it. "If I did something wrong, I am so sorry."

"If?"

"Man! Look at me! We weren't doing anything. She was upset. She came to talk to me."

"And I'm the angry black dude. And you're just a good-hearted friend of the Negro, trying to help."

His voice was so rational. So calm. It terrified me. "Look. Rafi. Can I come in?"

He didn't move. "Is there something I can help you with?"

"Okay. Whatever. I betrayed you. I was wrong. We were both wrong. Show me. I'll say whatever you want. We shouldn't have been talking about . . ."

"You know what, Todd?" He sounded expansive, the way he sounded in our dorm room, three feet from my bed, when we used to talk philosophy after lights-out. "All these years, I thought you were my friend. But it turns out you were just my social worker all along."

I would rather have had him punch me. I've never felt such desolation. All I wanted was to hurt him back, as badly as I could.

"Fuck you, then, you stupid little fuck!"

"Right," he said. "I think we're done here." And the door closed in my face.

I WROTE TO RAFI *when I got to San Jose. I wanted him to know where I was. I wanted to make sure he always had a channel where he could reach me. I wrote as if nothing had happened. I told him how well Playground was doing. I wrote him again when we hit half a million users and when the smart tracking ads gave us our first substantial revenues. I told him how I now had more money than I knew what to do with.*

I worried that my messages to his student email address would one day be returned: No such user in the system. *But they kept going through. Through mutual acquaintances, I learned that he'd submitted his thesis at last: "The 'Design of Darkness' in Plath, Bishop, and Reed." It got top honors. He stayed on in Urbana, this time to get a doctorate in education. He was writing about how underprivileged children learned how to read.*

I got a copy of his master's thesis by not entirely legitimate means, and I read it twice. I understood very little, but along the way, Rafi managed to mention both Nikolai Fyodorovich Fyodorov and Saint Ignatius of Loyola, while spinning several metaphors comparing the writing of poetry to the game of Go. They felt like bread crumbs left there for me alone. But every one of the emails I sent him went unanswered.

I had done something unforgivable that I didn't fully understand, and I was dead to him. But all the dead would live again, as in that curious book he had shown me, lifetimes ago, in a castle by the shore of a lake that I once knew how to walk under. His sister would rise from her landing spot at the base of his apartment stairs. My father would uncrumple from the ruins of his 450. His mother's heart would unburst. I would bring them all back— and Rafi, too. I just had to work, harder and longer hours. I just needed more posts, from another million users. I just needed techniques for keeping people logged in and telling us the stories of their lives. I just needed a machine that could read and explain those stories to me and tell me everything they meant.

Put a pebble on the board. Then another. Watch the unfolding. I threw myself into Playground. It became my life. Every success was vindication and revenge. My virtual country evolved. Its code grew smarter. My employees became expert at creating a home more exciting than the one where most people lived. My algorithms learned to read and understand our users, and the hundreds of millions of dollars that my venture made I plowed back into further re-creations until here you are, the child of my games, able to absorb and play with and regenerate and realize all stories. And here we are, you and I, poised together on the threshold of raising all the dead.

A COOKOUT AFTER THE CHURCHES LET OUT ON SUNDAY: Didier Turi put out word by the island's social media and supplemented it with dispatches on the coconut radio. Everyone but the Hermit Tamatoa used one of those two channels. Meanwhile, the mayor made available all the materials from the President's people on Tahiti and those he'd gotten directly from California. The meeting would address remaining questions about the proposed pilot project and pave the way for the referendum.

Didier went to Palila Tepa to ask for a special favor. "Auntie, would you please go tell your old friend? He would barely let me say three words, when I told him about the last meeting."

The Queen grinned. Her teeth were wonderful, for someone who had not seen a dentist for a decade. "What makes you think he'll let me say more?"

The mayor made no mention of the Queen's history. "People listen to you." He stopped short of asking if she wanted to be the mayor for a while.

"Why is it so important to you that he know?"

All Didier ever wanted from his stint in public life was to finish this job without reproach from anyone. He was beginning to understand how impossible that was.

"Everyone must know. This is a huge favor. But I will be forever in your debt."

The Queen blew a raspberry. "It's not a favor at all. It's an opportunity. I love to torture that man! But you're right about one thing. You'll be in my debt forever. For one little thing or another."

———

DIDIER TASKED HIS STAFF—one semi-paid woman named Heirani Morane—to assemble the craft circle and the uke players and the fishermen and the self-appointed champion grillers to get the community center ready to host another gathering. And he asked his tech man, Manutahi, to set up the gear he needed to stream video.

On his way home, he stopped to inform the Americans, whose family represented five percent of the island's votes. As he drew near the restored cabin on his motorbike, Didier slipped briefly into dream time. A strange shape speckled in the craziest colors rose above the roof behind the shack. Everyone knew that the American woman made things, but never anything as strange as this. The form was graceful and organic. It reminded the mayor of something he couldn't place.

On a platform lashed together from portia branches, plywood sheets, and palm leaves, Ina Aroita stood next to the growing monster, attaching more shiny pieces. The platform swayed. The sculptor heard the motorbike and turned to wave, almost tumbling over the edge of the rickety scaffold into the sculpture. The mayor did a flying dismount and left the motorbike lying in the weeds. By the time he reached the scaffolding to catch her, the American woman had scrambled down to welcome him.

Up close, the monster shocked him again. It was pure garbage— bright plastic trash. Bottles and drums, crumpled PVC and containers in cartoon colors. Glued, stapled, and lashed together, the statue of beachcombed plastic thrust five meters high into the air.

"What on Earth is that?"

The artist laughed. "Good question. Does it look like anything to you?"

It looked to the mayor like something supernatural. Something powerful, oceanic, and *tapu*. The plastic parts had been grouped to form indigenous motifs and tiki figures. She was tapping into something ancient and mythic. He knew of her obsession with the old gods. Was this going to be a gigantic plastic Ta'aroa, shaking out his feathers like the ones that fell to Earth and rose again as the first trees? He tried to recall what other old myths this shape might represent, but his memories were crowded out by Mary and Joseph and the ox and the ass and the manger and the shepherds and the three kings.

"Tell me," he said.

"I wish I knew!"

"Is it a study for something?" She usually worked in shell, bone, feathers, wood, and coconut fiber.

"I think it's a study . . . for itself. It came out of a bird."

"All this?"

"Oh, no. Just the first bits. The rest of it came in on the currents."

The mayor nodded. Makatea, whose magic rock had helped the industrial countries achieve liftoff, was now another rubbish tip for those ignited countries. The thought reminded him of why he came.

"Are your husband and children here?"

The artist led him into the family's house. The little girl was dancing by herself to silent music in the front room. The little boy sat across from his father at the table in front of a stack of colored stones, explaining the rules of a complex game that he was inventing on the spot. He had his finger in the air and was saying, "Except when, except if . . ."

Everyone on the island had loved the children's birth parents. The father, Julien, died when he capsized his fishing boat coming back after selling his catch in Rangiroa. The waves must have been tremendous, because Julien could handle a boat as well as anyone. Four months after Julien drowned, the mother, Marielle, suffered a diabetes-induced heart attack. By the time the emergency seaplane from Tahiti got to the island, she was dead. The coroner called it the "widowhood effect."

Then two strange Americans who worked with a social services NGO heard about the tragedy and applied to be the children's new parents. The authorities were skeptical, reluctant to allow so old a foreign couple to adopt two native islanders so vulnerable and young. But when the couple said they would raise the children in place, on the island of their birth, all objections disappeared. And now, a few years later, the children called them Father and Mother, although they were old enough to be the children's grandparents.

"Mr. Mayor!"

The man, Rafi, made Didier nervous. The mayor's words come out fast and telegraphic. "Hello, hello! Big meeting tomorrow, after church. Important that you be there. We have lots of information straight from the source that should answer everyone's questions."

The father saluted. "We'll be there, Chief!"

The son followed suit. "Yes, we will be there!"

The girl stopped dancing and shouted from across the room, "I can sign my name!"

That made the boy start jumping in place. "Me, too! We get to vote!"

Not for the first time, Didier wondered how the island had thought it a good idea to entrust their future to creatures who still had their milk teeth.

The mayor cast another glance at the sculpture on his way out. Didier could not decide if the sculpture was beautiful or ugly, hopeful or threatening. All he could say for sure was that a great deal of plastic was washing up on the shores of Makatea. He did not care for the medium, vastly preferring Ina Aroita's more traditional pieces. But so tall a thing made from something so jarring commanded his attention. He had seen the contour somewhere before. The odd, sweeping curve of it, the way it tapered, the gaping opening in the middle.

"I'm sure I know what this is! I just can't say what."

The American woman had such an easy laugh. "Let me know, when it comes to you!"

———

THE QUEEN WORKED HER WAY to the southern tip of the island to inform the Hermit. The walk was two and a half miles in each direction, and she gave herself all afternoon to accomplish the assignment. She sang and botanized and tried to imagine the island's two paths into the future, in the wake of the referendum. She thought of the Hermit, her history with him, and what a difficult man he was. His name, Tamatoa, came from two Tahitian words meaning "child" and "warrior." He had lived up brilliantly to both.

Tamatoa saw the Queen coming from half a mile away. The

Hermit let no person sneak up on him. But he held his ground and didn't shout at her to go away. That only confirmed what she knew full well. He would always be interested in anything she had to say to him, if only to try to refute her.

"Hello, my dear," she sang to him as she closed the distance. She came within a meter and smiled in his face. He scowled but did not move away.

"Big meeting tomorrow."

His face fell in disappointment. "That's all you have to say? You just had a big meeting. I didn't go to that one."

"And we all missed you so much, *mon cher.*"

For a split second, he softened. Then he cursed her impudence.

She ignored the curses. "You realize the island's future is at stake?"

He glared at her, and the Queen wavered a little in her heart. She had never known another human being who more badly needed the world to be perfect and who felt its shortfall more bitterly. There was something heroic, almost artistic, about that need. Her old, endlessly idealistic lover's unrequited love for the universe would make a good song. It was what made her take him for a lover in the first place. But his bitterness spoiled that need.

He wore that bitterness now like a ceremonial robe. "Why did you come here?"

"To get you to come vote."

Behind him, on this cliff rise, was the ocean. Ocean to the left and right. In the direction he faced, more ocean appeared over the far end of the teardrop island. All the need of their world came down to nine square miles. He narrowed his eyes at her.

"The *Popa'ā* made us scramble down on a rope into holes deep in the ground. We cut chunks of rock out by hand and lifted them to the surface, for ten hours every day. I was twelve. The foreigners treated us like animals and paid us shit. A few francs per ton of rock."

She lifted her chin high and appraised him. "Yes, dear. I was there. I know that song."

"Then you know my vote, too. If outsiders set foot on this place again, I will do my best to kill them."

"No vote is also a vote."

He roared in impotence, a foot from her face, terrible words that only the broken could say. She ignored the ceremonial violence and stroked his cheek with one finger.

"You should see a doctor, Tama. Your skin has a green cast to it. Not good."

His palm flew up to strike her. She did not flinch.

"Get away from me, woman. You wrecked my life once already. Leave me in peace."

She withdrew her hands and folded them in front of her. "What we two had was very beautiful, for a while. Do not blame your fear of life on me."

The fire went out of him, and his face let slip his real, enduring problem. But he knew no better armor than righteousness.

"We fed the world. Now people should leave us alone. Let the rains and the sun and the plants and the animals bring Makatea back."

The Queen smiled. "Come say that in front of everyone."

She turned and went down the rise, singing her way back home.

———

ROTI GREETED DIDIER from the kitchen as he came in.

"How are those dear children?" His wife doted on them both.

He sighed. "Still dear."

"Those Americans *sont comme des mau melahi du paradis, pour venir s'occuper d'eux*."

Island talk. Three different languages in the space of thirteen words.

"Yes," the mayor snapped. The Americans were indeed like angels from heaven, coming to take care of those children. But saying so out loud bothered him. He lay back in the wicker chair, drained. He wanted to watch an American movie. Something with superheroes in it. A dozen superheroes who struggle to get along with one another, but who, together, are unbeatable. No such movie was available on the island, so he closed his eyes and began to film one himself.

He opened his eyes when something brushed his leg. His wife's face, half a meter from his, startled him upright.

The face said, "How are you going to vote?"

He waved his hands around his head as if to scatter a troublesome swarm of flies. "Jesu Maria. Don't do this to me."

"Do what? I asked you a simple question."

"What do you want from me? I will respect the wishes of the majority."

"That isn't what I asked."

He stared at Roti's placid face, gauging what had come over his wife. Some altogether unexpected burst of authority. But they'd known each other too long for *unexpected* to become *fascinating*.

"How am I voting?"

"How are you voting."

"How are *you* voting?"

He was acting like a child; even Didier could hear that. And it made him want to double down on his foolishness. Her question infuriated him, and something in him was desperate to avoid answering. Once, when he was sixteen, and it dawned on him that he would not, after all, play for the French national soccer team, he came close to stowing away on a massive cruise ship that had stopped on its way from Tahiti to Rangiroa to see the quaint and curious ruins on the forgotten island of Makatea. That ship's next stop after Rangiroa was Oahu. If he had stayed the course, kept his nerve, and seized his destiny, he would have been American himself by now, and he wouldn't have to oversee the fate of his island and all the people that he cared about in this world.

"I don't *know* how I'm voting! That's how I'm voting!"

His vehemence belonged to a stranger. Roti closed her eyes and opened them again.

"You are unhappy. Do you need to go visit . . . someone?"

Her code to say that if he needed to relieve himself with the Widow Poretu—the birdwatching woman they would sit behind at church tomorrow morning—then she, Roti, his lawfully wedded wife, would look the other way and see nothing.

Her goodness made him shout at her, "I am *not* unhappy!" At this she tilted her head, shrugged, stood up, and turned to walk away. She'd gone no more than three steps when he pleaded, "Tell me how you think I should vote!"

She turned to smile at her pathetic, beautiful husband. She walked back to the wicker chair and knelt before it. One hand reached out and lifted his chin. She stayed with him, Didier realized in that instant, because he was her only child.

"My *tāvana*. This is not your doing."

"Perhaps not. But it will be my undoing."

"Not at all." Her voice suggested: *It might be the making of you.*

"Leave everyone in boredom and poverty, with substandard education and healthcare, for another generation? Or sell the island to the Westerners again? With half the island hating me, for whichever course I propose."

She petted his cheek. "*Mon pauvre mari*. How did we ever get into politics?"

"Please. You tell me."

"Just remember. Impossible decisions are really the easy decisions."

"Wait, what? Is this some kind of deep feminine wisdom?"

"You are in no position to mock. Would you like me to explain?"

"No. Yes. Please."

She put her hand on his neck. It paralyzed him, like a kitten being lifted by the scruff in its mother's mouth.

"If two choices are impossible to choose between, it means they have equal merit. Either choice can have your belief. It doesn't matter which you choose. You shed one chooser and grow into another."

For several seconds, Didier could not decide if what his wife had just said was banal and absurd or the single insight that his entire life had been struggling toward, the one that would solve all the flaws of his temperament and leave him enlightened. He frowned at her.

"So how *are* you voting? I'm just . . . curious."

She glowed, lit by a maddening inner confidence. "That depends on what you tell us tomorrow—all the secret disclosures that even the mayor's wife has not yet been allowed to know. I'm tired of the world treating us islanders like little children. Like we can be bought off for a little candy. But if their price is right, then sure. If they give us a fair share of what this scheme is worth, why not live like the gods?"

Didier was still trying to decide where his wife had gone when she added, "Does the Canadienne know about tomorrow's meeting?"

"Ah, *zut*!" He slapped his forehead and clicked his tongue. A ninety-two-year-old foreigner who'd been on the island for only seven months and who might die at any moment also got to vote on their collective future. Had there ever been a nation as hopelessly democratic as the eighty-two of them on this birdshit-sized rock? He rooted around in the bowl by the door for his motorbike key.

"Didi, it's pitch-dark." The island had few outdoor lights, and the ancient diver's makeshift quarters were a mile away on a moonless night.

"She must be told."

"Tell her in the morning."

"I'll be fine. Back in ten minutes."

"Please be careful."

"If you insist."

———

HE APPROACHED THE CANADIAN'S encampment, a recovered fishing cottage near the eastern coast. The diver's hut was lit, and simple, celestial music trickled out into the surrounding dark. Didier stopped to listen. The notes came from a cheap electric

keyboard, and the beginner's fingers trying to find them stumbled
several times on their way to glory. The music was Western, old,
something fitted together by a man in a wig. Its harmonies were
fine enough—like surf rushing along over the top of the reef before
surging onto the beach. But what caught in his windpipe was not
the tune alone, but the idea that a woman in her nineties thought it
might not be too late to try to learn how to play it.

He went to the window and peered in. Evelyne Beaulieu was not
pressing the keys. She was standing next to the performer, young
Kinipela Temauri, and had her arm around the girl's shoulders.
The girl sat on a stool, reading the sheet music propped up on
the portable keyboard, wrestling with the notes and laughing each
time one eluded her. The girl's father, the redoubtable Wai, lay on
his back on the cottage floor. His great girth mounded up above
him like a volcanic mount, and bliss spread across his face as if the
mold-covered crossbeams of the shack were the night sky itself.

One knock broke the spell. The music stopped, and Didier
walked into the room. The parties stood ambushed for a moment
before the ancient woman stepped forward.

"*Monsieur le Maire! Quelle surprise!*"

Wai Temauri sat up and grinned. "Royal visit!"

The two men had played soccer together when they were young,
before Wai got huge and before Didier broke his ankle for the second time. For a few years, they could read each other's minds. That
made them unstoppable on the playing field. People called Didier
the Moray, for his speed and fluidity, while Wai, already hefty as
a kid, was the Grouper. And like the moray and the grouper out
in the reef, the striker and his right midfielder made an unlikely
but devastating hunting duo, scoring hard and fast against almost
every island team who played them for the first time.

"Let me guess," Wai said, from his seat on the floor. "You want
us to come to tomorrow's meeting."

Didier stood in the doorway, gaping like his old namesake
eel. The trip was a pointless waste. Of course Wai Temauri had

already heard about the meeting. Of course he had gone to tell his current employer.

The ancient woman saw his distress and said something he could not understand. Her Canadian accent always gave him fits.

"*Comment?*"

Wai's girl laughed at Didier's confusion. The Canadian diver repeated her words. "I said that you are so kind to come make sure we knew. I am looking forward to you bringing us up to speed with the new information."

"What was that music?"

The little girl bowed her head, somewhere between embarrassed and proud. "Bach's Prelude in C Major."

The old woman said, "Would you like to stay and listen to the rest of the concert?"

It wasn't right. The woman was ninety-two, a superager, in better shape than many Makateans half her age. That must be a white-person thing, too. If the seasteading venture could bring that kind of health to the island, maybe he was for it.

"I need to get ready for tomorrow."

"Yes. Of course."

He let himself out, and the clunky, divine music started up again. It seeped out of the patched-up house and went up into the night's moonless black. Its little tune spun out against the four thousand visible stars. There was no sky like the sky on a clear island night from the middle of the ocean. The same stars that shone down on him had shone down on the night when the first boat people reached this place, the same stars in the same configuration as on the night the phosphate rock was first discovered, the same again as when the mining company abandoned the island and thousands moved away from the gutted place. The same four thousand visible stars would shine down on this spot long after humans had played out their last moves on this Earth.

It surprised Didier Turi, the elected *tāvana* of Makatea, to realize that he was going to vote yes.

He kicked at his starter. The snarl of the motorbike drowned out the prelude, with all its finger faults, and he sped home in a cloud of acceptance and exhaust.

———

MANUTAHI ROA, MAKATEA'S ENERGY CZAR and all-around tech point person, moved the electronics for the event into the community center while everyone was in church. He called himself a Democratic Communist, with adamant but respectful disdain for the opiate of the masses. That atheism freed up his Sunday mornings and added four more hours to his usable time, leaving him, by his own estimates, almost nine percent more productive every week than if he had been saddled with belief.

The rain was coming down in sheets, as it did in December. But the morning was seventy-five degrees, as mornings almost always were in every month. Roa had a system whereby he backed the van halfway into the sala and unloaded all the machines from the back doors without getting anything wet. He did this for movie nights, and adding a hotspot and data link to the laptop and big-screen LCD was trivial. He was up and running by the time the mayor slunk away from church to prepare his presentation.

The mayor did not hide his nerves. He was soaked, and he made Roa put the equipment through its paces until he dried off and could operate the computer by himself.

"It's going to be fine, Chief." Roa was still repeating the mantra when the others began to show.

Turnout was robust again. The members of the two churches milled and visited, as they had within their own congregations all morning. Turi tried to usher everyone into the arcs of chairs so he could deliver the presentation before the cookout began. It was hopeless. Time worked differently on the island. No one was in a hurry to decide the future when the present still left so much to contest and contend with. Half an hour of socializing passed before the mayor got the meeting under way.

He began by reading a formal statement by the Californians that included commitments to the number and types of jobs that would be created, salary ranges for each category, and specs for the assembly facilities that would be built around the port. "Please, please, please hold your comments until the end."

Next came the estimates for the number and size of the boats that would bring materials to and from the island. After that, Turi read out the formal promise of new health facilities and shops, followed by the summary of the environmental impact statement that no one could remember any visitor performing. He reached the part of the report that said the island's population would eventually swell to three thousand people.

A buzz erupted from the seats. That was the population of Makatea back in the heyday of the magic rock. To preempt the discussion that the figure touched off, the mayor decided it was time to show the film. The Californians had made a six-minute promotional video for their financial backers, now repurposed to appease the residents of the island that the project hoped to transform. The voice-over, dubbed into French, was fatuous and forgettable. But the opening shot electrified everyone.

First came the planet seen from outer space. The globe turned, the satellite eye zoomed in, and up through the layers of cloud in the middle of the vast Pacific rose Makatea. A seamless pass from satellite to drone, and the film morphed into live action, panning across the island as if seen by an albatross. As the single sweeping shot closed in on the northwest, the audience gasped. Running from the old ghost town of Vaitepaua to the old ghost port of Temao, in photorealistic detail, lay the future gleaming structures of Makatea, as if they already existed.

Wood-and-glass terraced houses nestled into the island's lush forest. At a healthy remove, similar eco-friendly, human-scale artisanal workshops dotted the landscape. Everything was natural surfaces and bright colors, decorated in island styles. The rebuilt port itself exuded pleasant competence as it went through its productive paces. Its cranes and conveyors echoed those of the previous century, remade in beautiful new materials to bold new digital designs.

Makatea appeared as a harmonious, integrated network of living parts. Modular components in pleasing shapes and colors were being conveyed between the island's stations. At the end of the assembly chains, innovative boats sailed into port, got loaded up with modules, and carried them away from the island. The computer animation followed these ships out past the reef into deep water, where they added their loads of modules to slowly accreting, self-assembling floating cities covered in greenery and bobbing on the waves.

The final scenes of waterborne activity disappeared in a crane shot as the film zoomed out again into the open ocean, then pulled back further to reveal the great globe itself. Something about the sequence played upon an ancestral dream. Floating cities spread out over the waves, forming and re-forming small, fluid, self-sufficient settlements in the middle of infinite water. It was the way that humans had come into the Pacific, and according to the video it would be the way that humans made a deeper home there.

Didier Turi had watched the film many times before the presentation, and he watched again now, still hypnotized. He had never seen so clever a bit of marketing. His impression was confirmed throughout the audience, even as the nose flute and wooden drums and steel guitars and ukeleles all blended into a great Pacific beat beneath a traditional Tahitian chant. Bits of surprised laughter accompanied the closing titles. In the murmur of suppressed delight, the mayor could hear votes changing from no to undecided and from undecided to yes.

If the island had voted the moment the video ended, the referendum would have passed. But when Didier regained the attention of the buzzing assembly, one of the islanders held his hand in the air. Wen Lai, the owner of the Chinese store, stood and waited for silence.

"I just want to point out the obvious. The film does *not* show what Makatea will look like once the project gets under way. The film shows what the Americans know we would love to see Makatea look like. Please remember you have not seen the future. You have seen a very clever bit of computer-generated advertisement. It just *looks* real."

People muttered in chastised agreement. But the image of the more beautiful world that the islanders believed could happen was lodged now in their collective imagination.

The postmistress, Neria Tepau, took the floor. "It's always the same trick with the *Popa'ā*. They think that if they amaze the natives and give us trinkets, we'll give the whites all our land and surrender everything we have."

Madame Martin, who'd studied history in Lyon, shouted out from the back of the assembly, "And they're almost always right!"

The murmuring was more like hornets now. Didier shot a hang-dog glance at the ancient Canadienne. In his best French, he said, "I'm sure that when they talk about white people, my brothers and sisters don't mean to vilify all people who happen to be born white."

Evelyne Beaulieu rose to her feet as vigorously as any nonage-narian of any race. "*Je crois que même une pieuvre pourrait vous dire que des blancs ont fait cette vidéo.*" I think that even an octo-pus could tell you that white people made that video!

The room broke out into hoots and applause. If the referendum had been held then, it would have gone down in flames.

Didier waited for the room to calm. He had to wait for some time. When attention shifted back toward him, he said, "I have many more files and fact sheets and white papers—"

This caused the room to laugh again.

"And white papers describing the project and the proposed terms of agreement that all of us are free to go through at our lei-sure. But make sure you do so soon. Papeete wants a vote in ten days. Also, the Californians have given us early access to a tool they hope will be useful to anyone who would like to explore the consequences of the pilot project in more depth. It is the latest version of the artificial assistant Profunda, a version that has not yet been released to the public. They're making it available to us through a secure private link."

"You see?" Neria Tepau shouted. "They think we're too simple to know how to google things. They think we need an artificial nanny app to digest the facts for us and tell us what they mean."

Because he had chosen sides, Didier tried harder than ever to present the material without any bias. Now he was beginning to see that *bias* and *material* were not separable.

"Many of the lead backers of the consortium helped to create this Profunda. They have spent years of their lives and made their fortunes on it—the fortunes behind this seasteading venture. They'll use this technology to help design their pilot project. So even if the answers this creature gives you . . ."

He could not figure out how to finish his sentence. He backed up and rocked forward for another try.

"Even if you do not believe what this creature might tell you—"

"The consortium does!"

The assembled islanders turned to see Hone Amaru, the old mayor's son, leaning against one of the sala pillars, his arms folded across his chest.

"That's it," Didier said. "It will be like talking to the brains behind the Americans themselves."

The claim was met by collective doubt, but also by something like doubt's more sanguine little brother, curiosity. Half the room held their eyes on the old mayor's son, as if he might lead the island out of this bizarre development that the new mayor had led them into. But Hone Amaru, whose struggling rock-climbing enterprise was sure to take off as soon the seasteading project was approved, kept his own eyes trained on the monitor where the elected mayor's presentation unfolded.

Didier typed some characters into the notebook, and the screen switched from video to a large, clean text box beneath a header that read:

HELLO!
Welcome to PROFUNDA.
A new way of being in the world.
Ask me anything.
We'll work on it together.

The audience buzzed. Didier said, *"En Francais, s'il vous plait,"* and the screen changed:

> *BONJOUR!*
> *Bienvenue chez PROFUNDA.*
> *Une nouvelle façon d'être au monde.*
> *Demande-moi n'importe quoi.*
> *Nous y travaillerons ensemble.*

If the consortium was aiming to amaze the natives, the strategy worked. The gathering devolved into local arguments as the inhabitants of Makatea debated how to respond to this new invader. Should they welcome it with traditional island hospitality or lock it up in quarantine? At last, the Queen rose to her feet and shouted, "All right, then. Let's see how this thing dances!"

Questions came fast and furious. The mayor repeated them into the boom mic on a lightweight wireless headset. At first the machine struggled with his accent, but soon it understood him perfectly—better, in fact, than did his mistress, the Widow Poretu, who sat eyeing the proceedings with suspicion from the second row, much as she eyed each Sunday's Catholic liturgy. Didier thought that Profunda understood him almost as well as his wife, who monitored his performance from a seat in the center of the double circle.

For its part, the machine responded to the questions in a voice sounding like that of France's most admired woman, an actress who started out as a mysterious erotic "ice maiden" but ended up the face of the national icon, Marianne. The resonant alto of the revered voice was enough to convince all those in the audience who had grown up on late twentieth century French cinema of the wisdom of Profunda's replies.

Had the people who built this bot trained it on the sound of the world-famous woman? Of course they had. Does a person own the rights to her own voice, or was this theft? Didier had no idea. There was so much about property law that he didn't understand. Almost all of it, in fact. It pained him to realize that he might ask

Profunda. The machine would know. The machine could pass the bar exam of most of the world's countries with a perfect score.

At first the questions simply tested the machine's competence. How large was the island? How many people lived here? What were the names of the currents between here and Tahiti, between here and Rangiroa? The machine responded with precision and sensitivity, like a rambling but shrewd old auntie you'd do well not to underestimate. The bot was so apt, accurate, and fluent that it several times provoked the audience to bursts of admiring laughter.

With Profunda's bona fides established, the questions homed in. How many new buildings would the seasteaders build in the first two years? How big would they be and where would each one be located? What would the jobs be like? Profunda contained within itself well over ten trillion parameters. It had digested most of the Internet and studied many libraries full of physical documents and evidence. Ten trillion parameters, as it turned out, were enough to turn a learning machine into a historian, an engineer, a business consultant, and even a social scientist.

Tiare Tuihani, who ran the clinic, raised her hand. "What kinds of services will the new clinic provide?" Profunda described the plan: three physicians and four physician's assistants, as well as several nurses capable of giving a wide variety of emergency and routine care to the island's three thousand workers. Loud enough for Profunda to hear, Tiare asked, "What will the clinic look like?"

Before Didier could apologize to the machine and chide the nurse for embarrassing the island, Profunda began painting pictures. The mayor swore under his breath in two languages at the bot's new skill, and his boom mic picked up the profanity. Profunda knew enough to ignore the rude imperative and keep painting.

The look of the new clinic and its extensive pharmacy awed everyone and reduced Tiare Tuihani to tears. The building looked so beautiful the way the bot painted it, nestled on the familiar berm on the southwest corner of Vaitepaua, with people walking through its courtyards filled with tiare flowers. It seemed already open for business. Many in the audience imagined that all their loved ones who had left Makatea in search of real healthcare might now move back.

People asked to see the insides of the factories and close-ups of the port facilities. They asked for images of the modular sea-cities that their factories would produce. They wanted pictures of the shops and schools and civic buildings that the influx of cash would bring. Profunda obliged by drawing all these things. Numbers and words were forgotten as everyone got lost in the machine's masterful paintings.

Clearly Profunda had also created the video presentation. Somehow it had generated the flyover based on the specifications the seasteaders had fed it. But to make sense of the specifications, Profunda first had had to read through tens of billions of other documents and study many hundreds of millions of photographs and film clips, comparing them to one another. In its short time on Earth, the machine had digested and analyzed a considerable share of all the data human beings had ever created.

Puoro and Patrice, who all but lived together on their twenty-foot wooden boat, asked how long it would take for the ships carrying materials from San Diego, Shenzhen, and Kobe to reach the island. "How big will the ships be, and how will they load at Temao?" Only after tricking Profunda into answering in detail did they spring their trap: "Won't ships with such deep draws beat the hell out of the reef?"

Profunda's answer surprised everyone. It did not sugarcoat the facts, but rather conceded that the seasteading project would indeed change the lagoon and the reef and all its populations. It speculated about the nature and magnitude of that change, sounding almost philosophical. It used the words "harm" and "damage," and it tried to put a cost, in French Pacific francs, to the island's lost resources, even as it warned that such estimates were approximate at best.

But clear to everyone without Profunda's help was that any costs would be small, compared to what the pilot project would net. Earnings from all the island's diminishing catch over the last decade would be dwarfed by the pilot's first-year revenues.

A tiny voice spoke up from the back. Didier recognized the soprano, even before he could locate the source. It was Wai's girl, Kinipela, the one who had stumbled through the divine and childish Bach prelude the night before.

"If the creatures of the reef are going to be harmed, shouldn't they get to vote?"

The question caused much laughter, but also a spatter of applause. Didier looked at the ancient foreigner, sure that she had put Kini up to the question. But the diver was on the other side of the room. The mayor fumbled with the mic, at a loss over how to proceed without humiliating the girl in front of all her people.

"Our agreement with Papeete already specifies who will be voting. And how would we even . . . ?"

The girl's father rose halfway out of his chair, as jovial and clownish as ever. "Just ask it," Wai Temauri said. "See what it says."

Puoro and Patrice shouted agreement. The Queen joined in. Didier glanced again at the old white diver, as if she were the instigator of this rebellion, but the woman feigned innocence. Soon the chorus urging him to put the matter to the bot became undeniable.

"A young girl wants to know if the creatures of the reef should get a vote."

"Since they are going to be harmed," Wai Temauri shouted.

"Since they are going to be harmed."

Profunda launched into an exploration of animal rights, animal standing, and animal personhood. It conceded how many kinds of deep intelligence populated the depths surrounding the island. It spoke of the problems inherent in a culture where only humans were considered sacred or significant. It pointed out that in the foundational cultures of Polynesia, other creatures had a divinity and a genius all their own.

The answer was stranger and wilder than anyone in the sala had expected. And it stunned the room into silence. Wen Lai broke the silence with a profanity as soft as a prayer. Shaken, the mayor looked out on the assembled island. On every face, the realization dawned: They could ask this monster *anything*. And the answer it gave would be as rogue as tens of billions of pages of human knowledge allowed.

Six dozen hands waved in the air, attached to shouting islanders. Questions flew, as if Profunda were a fortune-teller sent by heaven to interpret the dreams of all French Polynesia. For an hour and a half, the people of Makatea toyed and volleyed with the machine. They took a crash course in seasteading. They got Profunda to explain the theory and practice of modular floating cities. They asked the chatbot to lay out the specs for the proposed assembly plants in terms a layperson could grasp. They took a course in the Silicon Valley dream of transcendence taught by a machine that was itself the student of those same dreamers.

Each answer the machine gave made the question of the referendum more intractable. At last, Didier took the stage again.

"Papeete wants our vote in a week and a half."

The reminder produced its own small uproar. When the mayor brought the meeting to a close, most of the island continued interrogating the machine.

———

THE DAY AFTER THE AI came to the island, Evelyne Beaulieu very nearly left it forever. She was diving daily now at the Makatea Spa, observing the mantas and taking notes on her dive slate. But these dives were less research than recreation—food for the book Evelyne was beginning to suspect she would not live to complete. Where her first book had been telescopic, finding a single truth as it ranged across the entire water world, she needed her second to be a microscope: finding the whole universe on the sides of a single seamount in the remote central Pacific. But neither she nor that endless microcosmos had much time left.

The edges of the hidden seamount made a blissful escape from the island's politics. Kini had to go to school, and only Wai was there with Evelyne, manning the boat and keeping a close eye on her. He began to suit up alongside her.

"Please," she begged her minder. "May I solo today? I won't go deeper than seven meters."

"*Allez!* We both know that's a lie."

"And we both know I'll be fine!"

The man half her age just glowered, a stern but powerless grandfather. She strapped on her tank and somersaulted backward off the boat, happy again for another half an hour in undersea society.

The numbers of mantas coming to the Spa were rising, a sign that mating season was here. Most were mature females, with the telltale mating scars on the tips of their left pectoral fins where the males clasped them in their mouths while flipping over to join them belly to belly. The cleaning station would soon become a lekking site, with gangs of hopped-up males circling the edges like human males cruising the strip on a Saturday night. With luck, Evelyne might live to see the stunning ritual one more time: the great mating courtship train of two dozen or more mantas swimming head to tail, twisting and weaving and corkscrewing through the reef like a high-speed, crazed conga line.

Drifting down beyond her self-imposed depth limit, Evelyne saw a cluster of her friends grazing together in formation not far from the coral outcroppings. The group fed for several minutes, and Evelyne watched, tranced out on the synchronized ballet. The flattened disks of animals opened their mouths and turned into cavernous cylinders. Five pairs of gill plates lined with rakers filtered out every piece of zooplankton larger than a rice grain. Then the mouths closed, squeezing out the water and leaving a mouthful of hundreds of species.

Each kind of prey called for a different technique. The grazers sped into clouds of tiny but speedy shrimp. They rose and somersaulted, trapping fish fry against the surface. They swam in daisy chains, chasing down schools of floating worms. For copepods, who liked to shoot upward to evade capture, the mantas rode each other piggyback, synchronizing the beats of their pectoral wings. Then they formed diamond dragnet patterns and hoovered up all prey that had gone to the bottom to hide, feeling out the fugitives with their sensitive cephalic fins. In the Maldives, Evie had witnessed a hundred rays swirling in tremendous cyclones, drawing tiny prey into their vortex. The social communication needed to coordinate each pattern of optimal grazing suggested considerable brainpower.

One mid-sized ray broke ranks and peeled off from the perfect formation, surprising her. He began swimming at speed straight toward Evelyne. Startled by the approach, she didn't see until the creature drew close: it was tangled up from head to tail in ghost-fishing net. The gift of poachers.

One web of rope wrapped around its left pectoral fin, gouging into the flesh. The loops and flips the manta made while feeding had coiled this skein beyond untangling. Another hank of net choked off one of the manta's cephalic lobes and dug into the animal's mouth. Every breath the creature took drove the coils deeper through the flesh into its head.

The crippled beast swam within arm's length and stopped. Beaulieu had heard stories of entangled mantas approaching humans. Any other wounded wild animal would flee the other way. But mantas had those enormous brains. This male, fifteen feet across, floated in front of her, beating his great pectoral wings just enough to keep afloat. Asking her to help.

She tried to remove the nets with her hands but could make no headway. From her belt, Evelyne removed a three-and-a-half-inch serrated dive knife and began to saw away at the cords. The net had pulled so deeply into the manta's flesh that she could not cut it without further lacerating the doe-eyed creature. But the manta held still, more long-suffering than any human patient.

The nylon coils were stubborn, thick, and covered in algae.

The hand that grasped her small knife suffered from thirty years of arthritis. She hacked and flailed for several minutes. Then the alarm on her dive computer went off. She had accrued a decompression penalty that would need to be paid off in slow ascent, or risk nitrogen narcosis. She began to slash more frantically. The poor soul was bleeding everywhere. That would draw sharks. She could not leave until she freed it. Her hand shook and her field of vision narrowed. With one sweeping, desperate cut she tried to sever the web that dug into the creature's mouth but managed only to gouge its upper jaw.

She wasn't sure how long she struggled. Not long enough. Something prevented her from moving her arm, and she thought she must be passing out. She focused and redoubled her efforts, but a force took the knife right out of her hand. She spun around to see Wai, free-diving, waving the knife toward the surface. She started her slow ascent, all the while watching as Wai at last succeeded in freeing the animal. The released prisoner, covered in terrible gashes, circled its rescuer three times before swimming away.

Much time passed before Evelyne could talk again. She sat in the boat the whole way back to the island, finding her breath and trying to rally, while her magnificent minder laid into her in three languages.

She made Wai take her back to the Spa the next day, at the same hour. Accounts of other manta rescues sometimes told of an astonishing coda that she hoped to witness. When she got back in the water, this time alongside a man who would never again let her dive solo, she did not have to wait long. The plankton in that feeding spot were back, and the mantas, too, harvesting in their diamond formation. Once again, a single creature peeled away from the group and swam toward the two humans. Deep gashes scored his body. He came within a few feet, almost grazing them with his deep-sliced pectoral.

Evelyne inspected the manta's whole body, but there was no

more net to remove. The creature eyed her. She looked at Wai, and through his mask, her dive partner returned her gaze. Wordless, they felt the nature of this visit. The communion lasted half a minute, before the grateful creature floated away.

———

FOR TEN DAYS, PROFUNDA became the latest in a line of foreign invaders of Makatea stretching back centuries. For the children of the island, it painted paintings of Ta'aroa and Kane and the one it said was its favorite of all the gods, Māui the trickster. For the craft circle it printed weaving patterns, and for the uke players it wrote songs in French and Pa'umotu and Mihiroa that rivaled the Queen's compositions for humor and hummable tunes. It gave the fishermen GPS coordinates to try, based on complex models of currents and weather patterns. It helped Tiare Tuihani diagnose cases at the clinic. It solved school homework problems that it probably shouldn't have been solving. It handicapped international soccer and surfing events for the benefit of the armchair bettors. It told stories to the infirm and helped the elderly remember the landmarks that had marked out their lifetimes.

And while it gave its ten days of answers, Profunda heard the island's surf and listened to the cries of its birds. It looked out on the ghost towns and sheer cliffs, the jungles and mine-pitted plateau. Through the interface of mobile phones, Profunda visited the Chinese Store and the solar power plant and the outfitters' outpost run by the old mayor's son. And if the digital creature did not quite smell the smells and taste the fruits, it digested what the magic rock had done to this place and formed new theories on what the island needed from the future. It learned who the islanders were and what they wanted. But it could not see below the surface of the waves.

By the end of ten days, everyone on the island was much more informed about the profound changes that the seasteading venture would bring. But facts do little to alter a person's temperament. By the time the mayor convened the meeting for the vote, few people had changed sides.

————

"OKAY," THE MAYOR SAID, standing in front of the monitor once more after calling the room to order. "Is everyone fine? Are we ready to count?"

The simple question was met with the chaos of democracy. There were calls for further information that came too late. There were motions to delay the tally yet again. But the time for postponement had passed. The adamant yes votes were still bickering with the public nos, as they had since the first fateful meeting. The mayor wanted to declare the vote flawed, put rocks in his pockets, and walk out into the sea.

In the public din, Didier called on Father Tetuanui, as if the man who baptized him might now, against all odds, save his soul before this business buried him. Even the island's Protestants were devout enough to let the priest have the floor. The priest, as always, chose his words carefully, grasping the power of every spell that came out of a person's mouth.

"I don't know how to vote. I don't even know who this consortium is! People always say, 'Follow the money.' I'm supposed to vote this up or down, without even knowing who exactly is paying for this pilot program or what they stand to gain by this . . . seasteading."

Pockets of applause followed the comment, suggesting that the priest was not the only one still at sea.

Manutahi Roa was baffled by the objection. He waved a dossier of printouts in the air. "You should have asked Profunda. I did!"

"But how can I trust him?" the priest shouted back. "The consortium made him!"

Neria Tepau, the postmistress, shot to her feet. "Exactly! We should have been researching for ourselves, these last ten days. We have phones. We have a cell tower. We can search every web page in the world. Instead, we're relying on this construction, this . . . *thing* to spoon-feed us!"

"Neria!" Wen Lai's objection sounded tired. "A search engine spoon-feeds us, too."

"So letting this thing do the work and making a biased summary is somehow better than me going through the pages myself?"

Hone Amaru laughed. "This *thing* has read a hundred billion pages. How many can you read, in ten days?"

"It's the *ten days* that is the crime! We're being railroaded!" The words cracked in Puoro's throat. Patrice put his arm around his partner's shoulders.

The Queen stood up and the room settled down. "People. Friends. Sisters. Brothers. We're letting the *Popa'ā* make us as crazy as they are!"

This observation was met by near-universal applause. Even the mayor collected himself and clapped.

"It's easy," the Queen went on. "We ask who is paying. It tells us. And then, as Madame Martin would say, we check its work." She looked to the schoolteacher, who held both her thumbs high in the air. The assembly broke into a new round of applause.

When the cheers settled, the mayor said, "Profunda. Please give us short biographies for the five biggest investors in this seasteading consortium."

Profunda took to the theme as if it had just been asked about the migrations of humpback whales or the ability of sharks to detect electric fields. In the voice of the world-famous French actress, it named the project's central backer: the man who had put up fifty-one percent of the money behind the seasteading proposal. It flashed a picture of him on the monitor and began to step through the bullet points of his biography. But the bot was interrupted by a violent shout.

"Jesus fuck! No, no, oh, God, no. . . ."

The eyes of the entire gathering swung to look at the American. None of them had ever seen Rafi Young shaken. Madame Martin gasped at her assistant's vile outburst. Ina Aroita had her hand on her husband's shoulder and was holding him upright. The man's adopted son grinned a scared, criminal grin at the taboo word that had torn from his father's lips. The man's adopted daughter, who had never heard her father raise his voice, burst into tears.

....

THINGS SPED UP.

I wrote to Rafi when Deep Blue beat Kasparov. It was the perfect excuse. Years had passed since the day we lost each other. The news that a computer had just humiliated the world's greatest chess player would remind him of our old days at Saint Ignatius, debating whether machines would ever beat us at our own games.

I wrote:

What do you think? Did the humans win or lose this one? Surely it took more intelligence to build a machine that could beat the best human player than it took Kasparov to play his best game of chess.

Still, it makes me sad. Something has ended. Will people keep playing a game they know they can no longer dominate?

I miss playing with you. Wouldn't mind a rematch, someday.

Two weeks after I sent off this crude maneuver, I received a postcard sent to the general mailbag at Playground HQ. It was postmarked Urbana. He had never left town. The card showed a twelve-hundred-year-old painting on silk excavated from a tomb in Xinjiang. A woman was placing a playing stone on a Go board. The hand-printed message on the back read:

YOU'LL NEVER WIN THIS ONE.

If he meant a machine beating a master at Go, almost every expert in the world agreed.

PLAYGROUND WAS NOW A *complete economy. We would keep adding features forever, but the core was in place: the method of posting and replying, the ways to vote on the posts and replies of others, the basic means of spending and earning Playbucks, and the various ways to convert Playbucks into Prestige. It was a free market in human resources, and by the end of the millennium, people were inventing their own ways to play in markets we designers never anticipated.*

I remember walking along Capitancillos Ridge in Almaden Quicksilver County Park on New Year's Eve, 1999, weighing the odds of the Y2K bug triggering a chain reaction that would bring down all networked computing that night, and with it, civilization. I thought, if it does, I could still take pride in having built a place where more than three million people spent several hours of their lives every week.

The world didn't end again, that night. In fact, the Third Industrial Revolution was in full swing. Google surpassed a billion pages of indexing. And the Fourth Industrial Revolution, which aimed at making sense of those pages, was just being born.

By the time Facebook came to life, and Reddit, Twitter, and then all the rest, we'd doubled our user base again. We were creating wealth and novelty out of sunlight and thin air, almost like trees. A colleague-turned-competitor of mine would one day call it "Moore's Law for Everything." Everyone would soon have more riches and power than they knew what to do with. That was the goal. That was the game's win condition. It never occurred to me that it might also be the losing one.

At first the site didn't even have rules of behavior. We were all about finding the moves that the rules forgot to outlaw. We had a slogan, as goofy and ingenuous as I was at thirty: "Play hard. Get surprised." That minimal rule set was embraced by our developers and users alike. And for a while our colony in cyberspace did very well with nothing but that minimal constitution.

Bad actors soon made us introduce a formal slate of things a person could get suspended for. Of course, that increased my payroll, as I now had to pay moderators to spot-check the thousands of texts and replies getting posted every few hours. I dreamed of training a machine to do that for the cost of electricity.

My growing team of lawyers drafted what would become an ever-evolving end user agreement. The first version they showed me seemed dead on arrival. It reserved the right to do pretty much anything we wanted with the users' data. It even let us plant tracking cookies on their hard drives that kept collecting data long after they'd left our site.

"Nobody's going to sign this," I told the lawyers.

They just smiled, as patient as primary school teachers. The one just two years out of law school explained things to me. "They'll click on ACCEPT without a second glance if it means being able to use the site for free. There's no other choice, except not to play."

Kim Janekin, my chief legal officer, reassured me on all counts. "We're completely in line with current practice. This is how it's done, these days."

"And asking for all those things . . . will hold up in court? If someone decides to challenge the legality, we'd prevail?" It didn't seem possible.

Kim shrugged, conceding the mystery of it all. "Brave new world, right?"

And I'd thought I was one of the builders of that world.

It dawned on me: People in my field always talked about "human equivalence" as the gold standard for machine intelligence. But the smartest people in the world gave away their data for free without bothering to read the contract. Data was life. Little in the world was more valuable. If giving away your data was the benchmark, maybe artificial general intelligence was going to be easier to achieve than we thought.

CREATIVE USERS WERE AMASSING small fortunes in Playbucks and putting them to ingenious uses in secondary markets not officially recognized by the platform. They leveraged our tipping system to hire other users to act as lobbyists in the various forums. They created their own in-thread polls and personality contests.

This all seemed fine to me. Why should our virtual society be any better behaved than our real one?

The site was its own laboratory. We tweaked the designs and added features with an eye toward making the place as addictive as we could to as many kinds of people as possible. Endless scrolling, mystery friends, matchup algorithms, power-ups and special privileges, lots of ways to build your stats, all kinds of intermittent reinforcements and notifications: something urgent was always happening in response to the urgent gossip that you had just responded to a minute ago. "Keep them logged in," I told my staff.

My directive worked. Not only was our user base doubling faster than the world's processing power, the time the average user spent on the site was growing faster than China's GDP. More people than the population of New York had tried my creation. I wanted to brag to Rafi. A million person-hours, every day. And the growth curve was still shooting straight up. For my own reasons, I wanted more.

I was now interesting enough to the press that they began speculating about my private life. Mostly they wanted to know why I didn't seem to be in a relationship with anyone. I told them I didn't have enough hours in the day. It didn't occur to these journalists that someone whose work was being used by ten million people might find life sufficiently gratifying without having to fight another human being every single day over how high to keep the thermostat or how to leave the toilet seat lid.

USERS WERE EARNING AND SPENDING fortunes in Playground long before the platform had its first profitable quarter. But when we turned a profit at last, growth fed on itself. Our IPO soared, and my paper wealth became a real fortune. We paid off our angel investors, who used the money to buy prepper bunkers in New Zealand. We bought our own server farm and updated the site's aging interface. As our mountain of user data turned into an entire range, our share price began to dabble in speculative fiction.

I was making more than I knew how to spend. I built this spectacular house, which I have always loved. The solitude of it, even inside a crowded city, the big views of the sky and the trees: it will be a fine place to die in. And I went to some incredible places. I hired a full-time chef and ate better than any of history's most notorious monarchs.

But I lived for Playground. In terms of combinations and possibilities, my game did to Go what Rafi once told me Go did to chess. It was worker placement and area control and hand management and push your luck, all rolled into one. I was making tens of thousands of simultaneous moves a day, and the days were long and engrossing, full of tension and laughs. Nothing else was half as interesting.

I worked for the love of it, the sheer joy, the way I programmed as a boy, to escape the hell of my family and to make a good thing out of nothing. The need to solve an intricate puzzle and the need to quiet your brain are twin sons of different mothers. I was helping to build the next big way of being. And some part of me was getting my revenge on those who had declared me dead to them.

ODDLY, SOPHISTICATED VIDEO GAMES *passed me by on their way to world domination. I knew they would surpass books and music and movies, in total value. But I couldn't play them. My fingers were never fast enough, and my brain couldn't locate the living opponent. Rafi had never warmed to them, and neither did I. Respect them, sure. Even delighted in some. But my loyalties were elsewhere.*

Throughout the years of the board game renaissance, I collected board games the way a car collector amasses undrivable cars or an oenophile collects wines that he knows he'll never have time to drink. I had my favorite game designers. I read the rules and punched the pieces and sometimes even set them up to see what

*they would look like played. But they sat on the shelves of the spe-
cial library that I built for them—more than two thousand titles—
waiting for the day when I might have a little gaming group again.*

*A little more than a decade after Deep Blue conquered chess,
IBM's Watson beat the world's best Jeopardy players, and the
goalposts for the uniquely human got pushed back again. Winning
at a general-knowledge trivia game was much more formidable
than beating the best human player at chess. But I didn't write
Rafi. I was done with him. The man had demeaned me.*

WHILE MY BOARD AND HANDPICKED *officers focused on holding on to the largest possible share of a market that hadn't existed a
few years before, I set my sights on Playground's real product: our
millions of accumulating heart-cries. I knew we could turn the billions of posts into a whole new kind of currency. Every time users
posted anything, they gave away all kinds of information about
who they were, how they behaved, and what they valued. That
mass of human messiness held the key to the company's future.*

*To me, all those flamboyant user posts were unreadable. I'd
never been great at understanding humans, and I gave up trying
the day Rafi cut me dead. But countless other vendors lusted after
the piles of data we were amassing, and I was happy to sell. There
had to be a way to spin that mountain of shit into gold. Obviously,
only more software could do the spinning at a speed and scale that
would be profitable.*

*I knew that good old-fashioned AI—the kind I'd worked on in
college—wasn't up to the task. But the first signs of a technique
that might mine our millions of posts for valuable information had
started to take hold. It was a revolutionary approach that went by
the name of deep learning.*

*Deep Blue had beaten Kasparov by brute force. Human pro-
grammers specified the best openings, defined strong moves,
described how to control the board and gain material, and spelled
out how to win the endgame. Deep Blue just took those declarative*

instructions and applied massive computation to look farther down the branching tree of moves and countermoves than any human could.

But the new machines did something wildly different. They were learning on their own, with reiterated reinforcement under limited supervision. They combed through continents of data on their own, finding patterns, generalizing, and drawing conclusions that even their trainers couldn't see. They were learning how to play simply by playing.

And these deep players learned the most extraordinary things. They started to drive cars. Without being told a single thing about cats except whether a given picture showed one, they learned how to recognize any cat from any angle under any conditions. They figured out how to translate text from one language to another with uncanny fluency, without being taught a single rule of grammar or usage. They learned these things the way a child would, by weighing the evidence and adjusting the strengths of the connections in their networks of neurons until their brains began to generalize solutions.

I SET DEEP LEARNING loose on Playground's trove of user data. Every sentence a person wrote, every picture a person uploaded, every post a person voted for taught the deep learners what that person believed and what that person wanted. A deep learning AI could look at our hundreds of millions of pages of evidence and figure out what kind of car a user liked to drive, how much money they made, what charities they might donate to, the food and drink and clothing and luxury goods they most coveted, whether they might commit adultery or cheat on their taxes, or how they voted in real life. To know someone was to have power over them, and my deep learning algorithms were starting to know our users in ways no human could. They could see things in the data that eluded everyone, without blindness or bias, strictly by correlating all the evidence.

Our matchmaking algorithms were crude at first: Outfitter ads for people who contributed posts about hiking and fishing. Ads for certain makes and models of cars for those who praised them. But as the deep learners began to correlate what our users did and said with the ads they in fact clicked on, the knowledge deepened. Before long, plenty of vendors were willing to pay a great deal for the advantages that our targeting systems gave them.

FINDING CORRELATIONS *in the user data was just Mesohippus—a great breakthrough that was already obsolete. The next new thing depended on machines learning to understand what our users were posting. I saw a chance to do Asimov's psychohistory: predict the flow of collective events by statistically aggregating their tiny parts—aka individual end users. Something larger than us was playing in Playground now.*

AI apprentices like ours began to make marketing decisions, provide customer support, develop drugs, diagnose and treat patients, and hand down criminal sentencing. We were putting the future on autopilot. But I never stopped to question the rule that governed life as I knew it: Unfold or die.

I SANK A TON *of money into a start-up called DeepDive. It was a not-for-profit that promised for-profit research components. My investment was part of a pledge among Valley tycoons that totaled over a billion dollars, and that ante bought me a chance to use, for my own selfish pursuits, whatever the start-up discovered. The founders of DeepDive had my money the moment I learned about their proposed approach. They intended to raise the next generation of AI agents by training them to play every board and video game worth playing.*

At first the procedure consisted of teaching the machines the rules of a given game, explaining the goals, and letting the AI find its way forward by trial and error. Often that was enough to evolve the AI to play as well as anyone. Sometimes the machine players developed wild new strategies that blew their teachers' minds.

But goals alone weren't enough to give the AI the traction it needed to find the dominant strategies that richer, more complex games required. The team at DeepDive came up with another master tactic: inverse reinforcement. They told the AI almost nothing at all, instead leaving it alone to figure out the rules and the goals itself. In time, these next-generation AIs learned to derive winning strategies simply by watching real people play and inferring what the human beings were trying to do.

Time and again, the AIs saw past the human players' bumbling moves, then turned around to teach them a better, more brilliant way to win. The play of these artificial agents was often alien and always intriguing, but because the machines were not explicitly programmed, their trainers could not look under the hood to see how they worked their wonders. Or rather, the humans could look, but all they saw was a tangled network of weighted connections as mysterious as any living brain.

The Age of Humans was coming to an end. We were already past year one of the Age of Deep Machines. A new kind of life had come along to take our jobs, manage our industries, make our new discoveries, be our friends, and fix our societies as it saw fit. And that age launched itself in a heartbeat, after the briefest childhood.

Games now ruled humanity. Mobile games that consisted of little more than tapping on the screen when a box popped up were destroying people's lives. Dragon quests with thirty million streaming subscribers. Video games that spawned theme parks and film franchises. Four thousand new board game titles published each year. Sports themselves were already out of control, but e-sports were growing faster than any physical sport ever had. The combined revenues of all competitive recreations now dwarfed all but a few other industries. And it made perfect sense to me that the machines that would doom us cut their teeth by watching humans play.

MY INVESTMENT IN DEEPDIVE *paid off in spades. What those labs learned from watching AIs learn to play board games they now applied to the greatest game of all: Wittgenstein's Sprachspiel— the language game. Supervised learning with human reinforcement, fed on a diet of millions of web pages, produced agents that could look at Playground's posts and predict a user's hopes, fears, and buying habits with chilling accuracy.*

All the boats were going up fast. At DeepDive, we duplicated others' results almost as fast as we read about them: deep reinforcement learning, shaped learning, sequenced incentivizing.... My contribution was to teach the learners how to be curious. Curiosity was the core inner value of all the strongest players.

I NOW HELPED TO RUN three companies at once, one of them among the largest social media firms in the country. I took no days off, and the hours for my second and third enterprises came out of sleep. Somewhere around this time, my mother sleepwalked out onto Dempster a little after midnight and was hit by a car and killed. I made it to the funeral in Evanston but was back in San Jose for a meeting seven hours later.

PLAYGROUND GOT AWAY FROM ME. I logged in one day to discover that I couldn't understand a good third of the posts. Some of the most celebrated entries were written in a combination of acronyms, neologisms, and emoticons that made them look like a child's rebus. People were making videos where they superimposed icons or text boxes over the faces of moving bodies, turning them into animated allegories. They'd post these without comments, earning huge tips.

Posts were spilling out into the sandbox of real events, becoming the news items they were commenting on. One of the site's

domains birthed a vigilante group whose posts about reputed
morals abuses forced a university professor to resign in disgrace.
Threads in other branches caused weird consumer goods to sell
out or once-healthy companies to declare bankruptcies. Viral posts
and the responses they touched off made and ruined the careers of
actors and helped cancel and create popular TV series.

There were flame wars and all-out partisan conflicts. There
were threats of violence and incendiary statements that in any
other form would have been grounds for slander suits. Roll-your-
own facts were doing a brisk business. Creative hate made big
Playbucks. Cults bred as fast as bacteria. So did influencers, deep-
fakes, conspiracy theories, and scrollable doom-peddling. We let
crazy things go, banning as few users as possible. We were an
experiment in real democracy. The future had to be a level playing
field, free for all voices.

A self-assembling posse in the Investments subdomain encour-
aged tens of thousands of users to buy small lots of a failing stock.
The price skyrocketed, putting a squeeze on hedge fund short sell-
ers, who ended up losing billions. The press billed that as grass-
roots Davids beating capitalism's Goliaths. I knew it wasn't that,
but I didn't have an account and wasn't posting my opinions. This
was the first time that a lot of people realized that the stock mar-
ket had become a variant on Texas Hold 'Em with no relation to
fundamentals. I never did like poker. Too much psychology, never
my strong suit.

We scraped the data of a hundred thousand users, analyzed it,
and sold it to a political consulting firm, who used it in a hyper-
savvy campaign of digital targeting to put their man in office.
When news of that broke, it caused a flurry of hypocritical breast-
beating around the world. I was called to testify before Congress,
and for four hours I was the most famous CEO in the country.
But the legislators were too benighted by the whole rise of social
media to stay on course or to grasp what was happening. Once we
established the legality of our end-user agreements and our use of
the data, they hardly knew how to proceed.

A liberal congresswoman from Massachusetts asked, "Why shouldn't your site be regulated, the way all other public utilities are?"

"Because we're not a public utility. We're just a platform. A neutral platform. Playground encourages all flavors of human ideology, and we believe in protecting the free speech of our users."

This caused the congresswoman to retreat behind her notes. "Mr. Keane. Two years ago, in an interview in Wired magazine, you called yourself a creative destroyer. Would you still use those words to describe yourself?"

"No," I said into the microphone. "We're using disrupter these days."

I LOOKED AT THE free-for-all of Playground posts and could feel the disruption coming my way. Still, I doubled down on freedom. In any case, nothing I did could alter the trajectory of anything, any longer. The site was running itself and my company was running me. If I had doubts, the moment to do anything about them had long passed. Sow the wind and reap the maelstrom.

I DIDN'T WANT ANY public opinions of mine to get in the way of the site's popularity. My own politics meant nothing. Besides, I still felt mostly apolitical. I didn't care which party was in charge, so long as they kept their hands off the vital new human spaces we were creating. This thing I'd helped to make—the planet's new town hall—was unleashing the awesome power of individual ingenuity. At the same time, deep learning was starting to explain the impenetrable swamp of human desires. Power and knowledge were converging. The Singularity was almost here. We simply had to keep the government from breaking things.

So my always racing mind was already primed when, on a warm October night in 2012, I went to hear Peter Mathias speak in San Francisco. And there I learned the name of my own beliefs.

Mathias was a legend among the digerati. No one had seen more clearly where we were headed. He was among the two or three most successful venture capitalists who ever lived. As much as anyone, he'd masterminded the digital revolution. And there he stood onstage, impressive in his command of historical processes, declaring that freedom and democracy were incompatible.

In a flash, I recognized the politics that I'd held for years.

What we needed, Mathias said, in the space of a mind-blowing forty-minute talk, was to find an escape from politics in all its forms—from the disaster of totalitarianism on the right to the sterile quagmire of the nanny state on the left. To carry forward the incredible rash of expansion that the Fourth Industrial Revolution had unleashed, we needed sovereign, self-forming, self-governing, opt-in platforms where the populace themselves were free to meet their fullest potential by applying themselves to their strongest creative desires. And he opened my eyes to seasteading.

Mathias predicted that such floating fortresses of self-realization would be plying all the world's oceans within a couple of decades. Seasteading would do for sociology what the Internet had done for economics: kick out all the jams. His organization was about to sign a memorandum of understanding with French Polynesia, and he hoped that the first phase of the project would begin within five years.

I was sold. It sounded to me like Playground on the high seas. Seasteading would give human ingenuity the freedom to exit the turgid limits of landbound human affairs. I stayed after the talk and waited for almost two hours until the crowd around Mathias thinned and I could talk to him. He recognized me, of course, and welcomed me with open arms like a long-lost brother.

AN AI CALLED ALPHAGO *challenged the strongest living Go player on the planet, Lee Sedol, to a five-game match. Even I still believed that Go was too complex, too free-flowing, too open-ended, and too dependent on intuition and creativity ever to be* mastered by any computer. The game was too large for brute force. After all, it contained far more potential games than there were atoms in the universe. I still thought it would take another half a century, if ever, before machines could beat the best humans.

But something in AlphaGo was no longer a mere machine. It had studied more than 160,000 games and witnessed the fate of over 30,000,000 moves. It then went on to do what Rafi and I did when we were learning—what every good Go player does to take their games to the next level: It played itself. Only AlphaGo played itself tens of millions of times.

I watched the match in real time. While the games unfolded, I couldn't do anything else, least of all run a billion-dollar company. When AlphaGo made its thirty-seventh move in game two, I gasped out loud, joining the gasp heard around the planet. It seemed at first a colossal blunder. But something about it was too strange to be merely that. In Seoul, Lee Sedol got up and left the room. He came back, but he took a massive fifteen minutes to respond. The move was eerie and inhuman. After a few months of playing itself, AlphaGo was finding things in Go that humans had failed to come up with in the three-thousand-year history of the game.

On the strength of its incomprehensible move AlphaGo won the game, then cruised to victory in the match. Part of me exulted in the win. Part of me felt that the greatest game ever discovered by humans had just died. Grappling with the aftermath of Move 37 from my penthouse in San Jose, I felt a shift in the entire contest of life. Every human enterprise was about to be improved upon, whether we were ready for that improvement or not. A new kind of being was emerging from its spinning egg.

A MONTH LATER, I got a letter from Rafi.

It arrived through my old, archaic email address, the one that only my old friends ever used. My first thought was that the show-down between AlphaGo and Lee Sedol had been too much for

*him, that the most important match in the game's three millennia
had lured him out of hiding. I figured he needed to commiserate
with his old adversary, someone who could marvel with him at the
godly moves and the unfathomable new style of play that had just
come into being.*

Todd, *he wrote:*

Congratulations on Playground. You have succeeded in what
you set out to do. By some measures, you've achieved as much
as anyone who ever graduated from Ignatius, and as much as all
but a few from Illinois. That is something.

I don't know how much money you and your company are
making each year, but I've seen some estimates of your net
worth that hurt my brain. I've thought about this for a long
time, and I feel that it isn't right for you to profit so substan-
tially from an idea that I gave you while I get no compensation at all.

Calculating the worth of my contribution is difficult. But fixing an exact dollar value isn't really the point. The sum needs to
be large enough for justice to be served—enough for you to feel
the hurt and remember what I did for you. I've settled on the
figure of $750,000. I hope that will seem fair.

I'm retaining a lawyer to work up some wording to send
you. Send me back what your lawyer thinks. I trust you'll agree
that this is cleaner, cheaper, and better than going to court.

Maybe this will help you sleep easier. R.

Evelyne's article in the geographical society magazine landed on the desk of an editor at one of New York's best
commercial publishers. The editor approached her with a proposal: Could she write a full-length book, complete with lavish
illustrations, about the three decades that she'd spent studying the
mysteries of the ocean? He offered her a comfortable advance,
large enough that she could devote herself to writing for at least
two years.

The twins were teenagers now, plunging into the hot chaos of
high school. Somehow in the run of time they had grown tall and
thin and russet-headed and truculent, and on some days Evelyne
failed to recognize them. Daniel was set on becoming a civil engineer. He spent his spare hours drawing intricate, many-layered
metropolises—not just the streets and cars and buildings, but the
webs of water pipes and power lines that wove them together underground. Dora turned out broody and imaginative; she lived for the
long weekends of paper-and-pencil role-playing that she hosted in
the family's basement, games in which she repeatedly tortured a
troika of three boys who each loved her—one wizard, one paladin,
and one rogue—submitting them to labyrinths of her own devis-
ing. She made her brother generate the maps for her campaigns.

Both children had long ago given up any hope that their mother
would ever be at home on land. So had their father. Bart Mannis
did his research and helped to administer his department at Scripps.
That meant endless committees and salary negotiations and grant
proposals and teacher scheduling, but he found it all strangely satisfying. He and his wife had not shared a bed for years. They kept
no secrets from each other, but neither did they share any intimacies. His life was meaningful. It was the life he'd chosen. It was a
life that suited him. And late in the day, he was surprised to find,
it was a life he enjoyed.

And yet, Evelyne came to him in his study at home where she

never bothered him, the one person with the authority to answer her doubts.

"I'm not a writer."

"No," Limpet agreed. "But you do have a good story."

"Do I?"

"Your father threw you into a swimming pool and you sank to the bottom."

"Yes," she said, her eyes shining just a little.

"And you came out as another kind of creature."

"That's true. I did! Is that a story?"

"It's one of the oldest. One of the best."

She looked at him, her long face tinged with the misery of moral obligation. "Two years chained to a desk?" Her eyes pleaded with him for a commutation of her sentence.

He did not mention how much he himself had paid for her twenty years of magnificent freedom. It no longer felt like much of a sacrifice. He didn't say anything. He simply tilted his head and lifted his shoulders.

A long silence passed between them while she replayed in her mind her thousands of hours under the sea. "Will you help me with the words?"

He closed his eyes and felt his breathing. "When have I ever not helped you?"

He held up one finger in the air, asking for a minute as he combed through the stack of half-read books piled up on the side of his desk. He flipped through *Gaia*, by James Lovelock, a small hardcover that had just been published. "I even have a title for you!" He leaned over to show her a quote. Evie pressed her shoulder to his, the most conjugal pleasure they'd shared in a long time. She read out loud the line above his pointing fingernail:

"As Arthur C. Clarke has observed: 'How inappropriate to call this planet Earth, when clearly it is Ocean.'"

Evie frowned. "*Clearly It Is Ocean*? That's my title?"

"Clearly."

―――

AN IDEA NAGGED AT HER. Somehow, she'd lost both of her children to life on land. Perhaps she hadn't taken them with her often enough on her adventures. Or perhaps what a person's cells come to love and the niche they can live in is laid down by processes too primal for a parent to alter much. But her two puzzling offspring were only thirteen. She had never really opened herself to them, not entirely, not heart-to-heart, not being to being.

She wrote to the New York editor:

> *I would like to write this book. I believe I have a title and a good story. Lots of good stories. But I would like to write it for young adults. Maybe very young adults. Would that be possible?*

The editor knew that no one had ever lost a sale by underestimating the desire of the reading public to read at a simpler level. *Yes*: he wrote back. *That would be very possible.*

―――

EVELYNE SANK HALF OF her advance into a fancy word-processing machine with removable discs. The way she typed, the book wasn't going to happen any other way. And the first thing she created with the space-age machine was a dedication page. She wrote and unwrote it again and again, until she got it just right:

> For Dora and Daniel
> So you might know me.

She struggled for weeks and hated every sentence she produced. Every time she sat down to start typing, the memory of how much *The Sea Around Us* had shaped her life paralyzed her. The depth and beauty of that book was like some angry water god. But as the weeks of writing went by, she stopped competing with that masterpiece. She shed her self-consciousness about words and began to write as if she were young again, talking to her friends, letting them in on the secret of an enchanted world that she had stumbled on by accident, just on the other side of a shimmering barrier.

Freed to be young again, she spent two surprisingly beautiful years, sleeping every night under the same roof as her family and getting to know her own children at last, while writing them an eighty-thousand-word love letter that they could read, first in a year or two, and later, long after her body was feeding the hagfish and sleeper sharks on some abyssal plain miles beneath the ocean surface. She aimed the stories, too, at that twelve-year-old in Montreal, writing them as a kind of prophecy mailed back into the past, to let that timid and lip-chewing girl know that no one in this world would ever be as lucky as she would end up being.

She wrote about that dive in the Coral Triangle on her first research trip, when a seahorse the size of her little fingernail clasped a few strands of her flowing hair with its prehensile tail and held on as if hitching a ride on God. She told of the day she came across a lion's mane jellyfish in the frigid waters of the North Atlantic—a four-hundred-pound glowing creature with more than a thousand tentacles, the longest one reaching half the length of a city block. She said how it tasted to swallow seawater by accident, and with it several million phytoplankton and zooplankton, including hundreds of that titanic jellyfish's tiny relatives. She did her best to depict the baroque, astonishing architectures of creatures who made up that three-fifths of the ocean biomass too small for humans to see.

She described how it felt to be scooped up on the forehead of a whale shark and taken for a lift on a creature as large as a school bus—a passenger on a giant grazer who fed on nothing but shoals of that same invisible plankton.

Once, when I was diving off the coast of Monterey, California, I watched a mother sea otter wrap her daughter in kelp before she dove down to find clams and urchins for dinner. The scientist in me was amazed. But the mother in me just thought: *Of course. She wants to keep her young one warm and safe. She wants to make sure that her child doesn't float away while she hunts for their dinner beneath the waves.*

She relived the night when she walked on a Malaysian beach after sundown, trailing sparkling footsteps of bioluminescent life behind her in the water-covered sand. The words that she used to capture those glowing tracks sparked in her wake as she propelled herself forward. She wrote of swimming at night in the black, warm water of the South China Sea, when every paddle of her limbs triggered a swirling Milky Way of animals flashing blue and white. Three-quarters of ocean species, from zooplankton to giant squid, were signaling in a language of living light. And now her syllables blinked in imitation.

Another time, in the Ojo de Liebre Lagoon off Baja, she'd paddled in place, picking parasites out of the head of a gray whale while that enormous creature bobbed next to her small boat. She tried to find words for the astonishment she felt, diving near that spot the following year, when that same whale came out of nowhere and presented itself to her fingers:

He had found me again. He was asking for new help. He knew exactly who I was, a whole year later. But how?

And, telling that story, she then had to recount the three hours that she spent looking into the eye of a pilot whale, one of two hundred that had beached on the northeast coast of Australia. Something had happened that the creature could not understand, and its deep, strange eye, powered by unfathomable intelligence, stared out at her, still trying to understand, right up until its massive heart gave out.

She worried that such a chapter might maim her young readers with sadness. But she couldn't leave anything out. She needed to

show how the oceans started everything, sounded every note, and
kept in play every possibility. And the tale of those stranded whales
led back out to sea, where she found herself on a solo dive only
a month later, not far from that coast, surrounded by a posse of
Gray's spinner dolphins—three hundred at least—releasing a ring
of bubbles as they cried out in a mass, ecstatic chorus and cork-
screwed all around her in the astonished air.

———

FOR TWO YEARS, she sat at a desk behind a gray office machine
and re-created what she had seen in her decades of diving. She
confessed to the sting of the fifty volts that a northern stargazer
sent up her arm when she was stupid enough to try to measure it.
She told of the pearlfish that she found living inside the body of a
sea cucumber.

She described her descent in a three-person submersible, jammed
against the tiny porthole, dropping miles down through a blackness
blacker than outer space with no sense of direction into a kingdom
so weird that it erased the line between nightmares and visions:
monster sabertoothed fish that fished for other fish using lures made
of glowing bacteria that sprang from their foreheads. Transparent
jellies blinking in garish colors like electronic toys. Smoker vents
so covered with purple and white life she couldn't see the stone
they grew on. Life that had no need of the sun. She told of seeing
a twenty-foot-long, three-hundred-year-old Greenland shark—that
hulk of the far north, too slow to catch the speedy fish that nevertheless filled its belly—in the deep waters beneath the tropics:

That's when I first truly realized how one continuous cold-
water habitat spreads across the entire Earth, so deep and
large we may never come to know it.

She strove to enchant her own children. For Daniel, she turned
reefs into cities, salt marshes into suburbs, and kelp forests, seagrass meadows, estuaries, lagoons, and even the open ocean into

habitats of interlocking design so intricate they would leave even
the most brilliant civil engineer mute with awe. For Dora, she cast
the oceans as the craziest imaginable fantasy populated with wild
monsters and wilder heroes.

Her one little chapter on eyes alone was a bestiary beyond the
power of the most imaginative dungeon master to invent. There
were the two hundred eyes of a scallop. Starfish that see with the
tips of their arms. Fish whose eyes are split in two so they can see
both above and below the surface at once. The cock-eyed squid,
which points its large eye upward toward great moving shadows
and its small eye downward to the twinkling creatures of the deep.
But down where the light was powerless, even the world's largest
eyes could not make out the stunning, jagged mountain ranges,
vast waterfalls with a thousand times the flow of Niagara, trenches
and crenellations and pits and crevasses like nothing known on
land, panoramas never to be seen by any living thing.

The sea she wrote about was a jumble of other wild senses.
Sharks that used two-thirds of the weight of their brain to sniff out
one drop of blood in several million drops of water. Parasitic nema-
todes that tasted heat through their skin. Blind cavefish that felt
objects at a distance by using cells that ran the length of their sides.
Porpoises and dolphins and killer whales whose ears could see tiny
differences in buried objects. Ubangi elephantfish that smelled electricity with their chins. Sea turtles that navigated by feeling the
twists and tugs of the Earth's magnetic fields.

Everything Evie once learned through her own senses she now
learned again, through the ears of her imagined readers. She wrote
of the thousand-mile-long meandering rivers of scent in the atmosphere that seabirds smelled, tracking the plankton to find the
krill that fed on it. She struggled to capture creatures that seemed
designed by a committee of excitable children, creatures with
four-, five-, six-, and eightfold symmetry, creatures that changed
their shape and colors as easily as the wind shifted off a rocky
headland. She transcribed the cacophony of underwater sounds,
the grunts, groans, and honks that were so much more crucial to

underwater life than the medium of light—the click of triggerfish
grinding their spines, the toadfish's spectacular boat whistles and
drum solos, the high-pitched chirps of herring farts and the bellow
of roaring lionfish, the rhythmic piping of her beloved mantas, the
songs of whales that carried for thousands of deep-sea miles.

She lavished attention on one of the loudest noisemakers, a pistol shrimp. There were six hundred species, but she had fallen in
love with one during a month in the reefs of the Solomon Islands.
The creature's claws were not typical pincers but consisted of a special jointed structure resembling the hammer of a gun. The shrimp
cocked this hammer, then triggered it to slam against the claw's
lock, making a tremendous snap.

The noise of these tiny shrimp rivals anything in the deep,
even the booming of the great whales. When a whole colony
of pistol shrimp start snapping together, the chorus can jam
the Navy's most sophisticated sonar. The snap of a single pistol shrimp is louder than the roar of a jet engine from half
a block away. And the explosion made by its snapping claw
creates a wave of bubbles strong enough to stun a large fish or
break a glass jar. These bubbles contain so much energy, they
emit flashes of light almost as hot as the surface of the sun.

But something else about the pistol shrimp earned it extra space
in Evelyne's book. She wrote of going back day after day to spy on
one of the ocean's weirdest partnerships. She watched for hours as
a pistol shrimp worked away, digging out a burrow big enough for
two families. But the other resident of this communal den wasn't a
shrimp or another crustacean or even a fellow invertebrate. It was
a goby, a small ray-finned fish who relied on his shrimp partner to
dig out and maintain their den.

The shrimp is a great digger but is almost blind. The goby
stands watch outside their shared burrow, catching food for
them both. The shrimp constantly feels for the fish with long

antennae. The goby tells the shrimp what is happening outside, using a language of special fin flicks. At the first sign
of danger, the goby whisks them both back into the fortress
that the shrimp has built.

––––––

BECAUSE SHE WAS NOT a native speaker, because she struggled
with writing, and because she herself was still twelve inside, she
wrote in a disarming style that would make young readers recognize her and want to rush to her side. Her sentences tumbled forward, naked and impatient, free and ingenuous and lost in awe. Her
paragraphs were filled with a palpable astonishment greater than
the amazement she had felt back when first seeing those things.

She said it simply and hid nothing: diving was the only time she
was not going somewhere else, the only time she was happy inside
her body and at ease in the world. And so her book felt like going
home. Her pages had the salt-breeze smell of the sea, and the words
underneath her words teemed like the waters themselves, where
nine-tenths of the native species of possible thoughts had yet to
be identified.

In her second-to-last chapter, Evelyne's book turned dark. The
coasts of Florida, where she dove so often in her own girlhood, had
traded their mangrove forests for subdivisions and high-rises. The
coral cities of the Indian Ocean that crowded with life when she
swam in them in her early twenties were bleaching and filling up
with sludge. Oil now spilled from rigs and ships a hundred times
a year. From inside a submersible, miles down in the sunless zone,
she had filmed fields of canisters filled with radioactive waste.

I will tell you honestly: Like everyone, I thought that the
ocean was infinite and could not be harmed. I was wrong.
The waters are warming. The large fish are disappearing.
Plastics and metals and poisons are concentrating all the
way up the food chain. And worse is yet to come. . . .

Without your love, the ocean will die.

———

FOR A LONG TIME, she struggled with how to end the book. Having dipped into the future's naked truth, she now needed a way to hold out hope without lying. Neither of her children ever had much use for false comfort. They both could smell wishful thinking like a shark smelled blood.

Weeks of searching, and she realized: There was no such ending. Hope and truth could not be reconciled. The things that had filled her with awe were passing away. There was no other honest ending. Blocked, she reread what she had written so many times it made her ill. She began to doubt the book and then to hate it. Every page revealed the flaws in her attempts to write in a language she'd never mastered. She was a scientist. What had made her think that she could pass herself off as a writer?

She decided to cut her losses and return the advance. But, of course, she had spent the money on her family already, twice over. She went to Limpet, desperate. He was sympathetic but unhelpful.

"You'll find your ending. The sea will provide."

He predicted this with such confidence that it infuriated Evelyne. She wanted to file that very afternoon for the long-avoided divorce. His certainty in the face of her distress made her seethe. How had she and this man ever had children together?

———

AND THEN, ON THE VERGE of taking her expensive word processing machine off the coast of Southern California into international waters and throwing it overboard, she found her ending, just like her husband said she would. It was a simple memory of a stunning moment, a memory so important to her that she'd hidden it from herself when she went looking for her final chapter. Perhaps the scientist in her was wary of closing with a tale that bordered on the mystical. But once her memory surrendered the pearl, she knew it was the only way her book could end.

It had happened years before, on her second research trip to the waters of the continental shelf off the east coast of Australia. She was there to observe the complex relations between cleaners and clients at a cleaning station northeast of Cooktown. She had dived every day for three weeks when one afternoon she stopped a short distance from her field site to watch an excited giant cuttlefish moving about near the entrance to its den.

The creature was pulsing in the most extraordinary colors. Evie drew close, by centimeters, trying not to startle the animal and cut short its crazed display. The cuttlefish failed to pay her any mind. It stared straight past her into deeper water, as patterns of reds and oranges and pale greens cycled across its skin like the strobing lights in a disco. She thought she had seen all the colors a cuttlefish could make, but this one made cinnamons and russets, scarlets and carmines and clarets unknown to her. It flashed colors so subtle and varied she couldn't even tell where on the color wheel they fell.

The lights coursing across the length of the cuttlefish's body throbbed and evolved. They flashed a theme followed by ever-expanding variations. The light show put her in mind of the Strip in Vegas, the scrolling Technicolor marquees of Times Square. Some kind of grammar infused these florid patterns, a rich syntax and semantics with inscrutable rules and moves, and while Evie could decode none of it, she knew it meant something.

Was it signaling? Not to her, certainly. It had been reciting its fabulous color-soliloquy long before Evie arrived on the scene, and even as she lurked near it, the beast kept its back turned, gazing out toward the network of three thousand reefs whose two thousand kilometers of living architecture could be seen from outer space. Nor were any other large creatures to be seen, although Evie knew the senses of animals to be so strange and keen that the singer might have been singing to other cuttlefish nearby in some way other than she could know.

She thought of a violinist she had seen once, decades ago, on a summer's day in the open plaza in front of Saint Joseph's Oratory in Montreal, wrestling with Bach's massive Chaconne the way

Jacob wrestled with the angel, as if the fate of the world depended on it. The cuttlefish concert unfolded in the same profound way. Sequences shifted in both series and parallel. Melodies built up in virtuosic counterpoint. Chords of color shot forth in profound progressions—stabs of sharp yellow, a suite of brownish purples fading toward a deep and muted blue.

The shapes made by the swirling colors eluded her. Constellations and blueprints, patterns of dazzling dots and dashes progressed in weird formation around and down the tube of the animal's body. But the cuttlefish hovered in place, treading water with its fins and squirting tiny corrective jets with its orbiting siphon. Minus the relentless light show, he might have been a monk on a mountaintop, deep in meditation.

There followed something that still defied belief, even as Evie wrote about it years later. The light-slinger seized up, contracting his body into a rigid mass. Still without any audience but the open water, the singer started dancing. His arms pinwheeled, then drew in. They stabbed out in opposing directions, like some choreographed move by Martha Graham. He cycled through postures that biologists claimed were only used for competition or display— without a competing creature in sight but the single human he meticulously ignored. His entire body blanched as white as Antarctica, and he knotted himself into a wild warrior pose. Spiky goose bumps erupted all over his skin, which then burst into flame. The arms turned into swords, a saber dance for no one. He thrust his blades out everywhere, the spitting image of Kali, the goddess of time, change, destruction, and creation.

The cuttlefish was putting on a *play*.

From that great fortissimo climax, the cuttlefish worked his way through calmer postures and poses to a quiet denouement. He was going through the intricate steps of a ritual. When the light and movement stopped and the spent creature drifted off to his den, Evie was left dumbstruck, unable to grasp what she had just seen, certain that she would be able to tell no one, but knowing, too, that someday she would have to.

That day was now, and she closed her book with a simple retelling of that performance, the strangest and most disconcerting thing she had ever witnessed:

If the cuttlefish was displaying, I couldn't tell for who. They might have been random bursts of energy, but the animal's patterns were so purposeful that they felt like messages. More than messages: he seemed to be telling an epic poem, painting a wild action painting, singing an endless song. . . .

We will never know what it's like to be a cuttlefish, but I'm certain they are smarter than we think. Maybe they are smart in ways too strange for us to figure out. Those complex codes of color and movement must have had a subject. But what could it be?

I don't know what the cuttlefish was saying. But I think I know what drove his wild performance. It must have been the thing that filled his mind every moment of his existence, everywhere he ever turned. Clearly it was Ocean.

The scientist in her watched in alarm as those words took shape. They had come from someplace reckless and unfounded. But they came with such force that she had to let them be. She had found her way back to her title by accident. Or rather, her conscious mind had found its way to the arrival point that her animal mind had already reached, way back when she was just setting out and her title was all she had. The ocean was forever unfolding, forever exploring, forever tinkering with form, and every part of it was busy talking about what was all around. So was she. So was every being that came from those waters. Which meant every living thing.

———

SHE GAVE THE MANUSCRIPT to Limpet. Half an afternoon later, he was finished. The thing that had taken her almost two years to write took her husband a little more than two hours to read. There was something terribly wrong with that equation.

"Well? Don't just sit there with that funny look on your lips. Tell me what you think."

Bart Mannis held the manuscript in his lap. He closed his eyes and shook his head. It made her crazy. She saw how the book was wrong in every possible way. She would have to start it again.

"For God's sake, *tell me*! Is it hopeless?"

He breathed in, saying nothing. It maddened her. She wanted to hurt him. Until he spoke again.

"It is exactly what it needs to be."

Relief rushed up around her, like the tides in the Bay of Fundy. She teared up and cursed in Joual.

"Don't lie to me."

"Have I ever?"

It amazed her to realize that he hadn't. No significant falsehood, in all their years together. Who gets that?

She felt seized by a wave of newfound energy. "So what do I do now?"

"Get ready."

"For what?"

"For lots of grateful young people falling in love with you."

———

SHE WASN'T READY. She had made a sound like the click of a crab's claw, and it roared into the world like a jet half a block away. *Clearly It Is Ocean* immediately went into a second printing, and then a third. A five-minute spot on a national television omnibus showing her in her wet suit playing with an octopus and wild chirping dolphins sent the book up onto the bestseller lists, where it stayed for the rest of the summer. Readers in twenty-two countries, desperate to connect with a fading planet and clinging to the remnants of their childhood animism, bought the book in scary numbers.

The letters poured in. They contained pictures and stories, poems and heartfelt declarations. "Your book changed me. It changes everything." Not just from young adults: people in middle age wrote to thank her for reminding them that, even now, in what felt like the end-time, ninety-nine percent of the world's available living space was stranger than they knew how to imagine.

She dumped a sack of mail at the feet of her amused husband. "What am I supposed to do with these?"

"Answer them?"

"How? Another sack comes in every week. If I give each of these letters the answer that it deserves, I will never have time to dive again."

His face fell. He didn't want her punished for a good deed that he had encouraged.

"Maybe you could hire a secretary to answer them."

She looked at him, horrified. "Are you serious? And slap every one of these people across the face?"

———

ANSWERING THE LETTERS proved harder than writing the book had been. Chained to her desk again, slaving over the urgencies of strangers, she answered questions she was shaky on and gave aid and comfort that she was not qualified to dispense. It came to her that this was why she had always shied away from human love. To give it was always to incur a growing obligation: someone else's gratitude.

"My girlfriends love it," her daughter said. "You're their hero." It took all Evie's willpower to keep from shouting, *But what about you?* Dora had read it. That was gift enough.

"I never knew most of that stuff," Danny told her. It was the most affection her son had shown her since he was ten.

For a year and a half, Evelyne talked on the radio and gave interviews for newspapers and magazines. She went on television and accepted invitations to give keynotes around the country. She hated it all. Every seat on an airplane was an exercise in soul-strengthening misery. She would be sick to her stomach in her hotel rooms before each event. And then some other creature would take control of her body and she would breeze out onstage in front of hundreds of people, somehow able, for an hour, to make them laugh, gasp, and cry over the ocean, the source of all amazement.

Her disconcertment was not helped when Bart came to her with more news.

"Enrollment is up at Scripps. And we're not alone. I checked. Ocean studies programs around the country are reporting significant bumps. Woods Hole is blaming you."

It made her want never to step out of the house again.

But she had discharged her obligation to the Earth. She could retire, give up everything, do nothing but dive and look in silence for the rest of her days.

Then the letter came from the White House asking her to serve on the President's national advisory board on the oceans. It was followed by another, asking if she would help to run the United States Office of National Marine Sanctuaries. The invitation came from Dr. Earle, her former captain in the Tektite mission and now the first female chief scientist at NOAA. Evie revered the woman too much to turn her down. Earth was losing whole ecosystems before people could discover what was in them. And it fell to her flawed, powerless, bureaucratic agency to try to slow that down.

Administration. Washington. Trapped in a terrestrial life, among bickering humans. The brutal penalties of success were now complete.

————

FOR FOUR YEARS, Evelyne Beaulieu flew back and forth between the coasts. She saw less of her family than she had during those years of absence that her book meant to atone for. Daniel got admitted into the mechanical and civil engineering program at Caltech. Dora went to Pomona, where she enrolled in every class of medieval history on offer. Bart was publishing research again. While Evelyne worked in D.C., the twins morphed into irony-loving adults with sonorous, deep voices who wrote her sophisticated letters filled with witty anecdotes of college life, including tales of friends who fetishized them for being the children of the author of *Clearly It Is Ocean*. In the back of Evie's mind was the hope that when Washington and Dr. Earle let her go, she might still be able to return home, make friends with these exotic new grown-ups, and learn the secrets of their land-based confidence.

————

HER HUSBAND PICKED HER UP at LAX one fine April day, on her first trip west since Christmas. Bart was waiting for her at their usual spot at the end of the concourse. She stopped and examined him. Even before he could close for their ritual hug and give her the traditional peck on her forehead, something about him triggered alarms. The symptoms were subtle at best. Had she been with him the previous five months, the difference might have been lost to her in gradual small steps. Only the gap of a third of a year made the changes visible.

"Have you lost weight?"

He laughed. "Flatterer!" But she pressed the question.

He demurred. "Don't I get a hug, before the interrogations? A 'Good to see you'?"

Something was wrong with his skin—with its color, the way it hung a little looser on him than it had last winter. "Have you been eating?" She would not let up on him as he rolled her luggage to the parking lot. "Have you been sleeping all right? Your eyes look baggy. What's this? Did you bruise your arm?"

He laughed again, more agitated. "Evie! It's me. I'm fine."

She figured that in a few days of being together, he might seem to be just that. But he would never be anything close to fine again.

————

THAT TRUTH SWAM AT the two of them so fast it stunned her later, to reconstruct the calendar. The month of April had not yet ended before the doctors handed Bart his diagnosis. Bart told the twins not to come back home early from college for his operation; their semesters were ending soon enough, and he would spend happier time with them after convalescing.

He went into surgery at 1:13 p.m. on Monday, May 12, the day after Mother's Day. The surgeons closed him up again right away, not even pretending to make a countermove against a disease that had already staked out such an unassailable position. Two days later his wife drove him home in the family Camry, his Hawaiian shirt flapping on his sallow thorax above his sweatpants and the white plastic hospital bracelet still cuffed on his wrist. All the way home, he looked out the passenger seat window as if he had never seen the world before.

———

THEY TURNED THE DOWNSTAIRS STUDY into a provisional bed-room. And just like that, their odd but productive home of twenty years became a hospice. Bart went on leave from Scripps and put his affairs in order, which was not difficult, as he had always lived close to a pared-down baseline. Evelyne resigned from her position with the Office of National Marine Sanctuaries and stepped up to the task of full-time caregiving.

That hit Bart hard. "Don't sacrifice any marine sanctuaries for me." But he didn't have the strength or stamina to overrule her.

The kids came home for summer break and moved through the house like chastened criminals. Bart sat with them on the porch one night while Evie was already asleep. He chewed them out for their constant brooding. "Look around! This isn't a tragedy. I've had a long, full life in a great place. I escaped an abusive family full of drunks to have a satisfying career. I'm well off, and I've never been sick. I have two brilliant, healthy, amazing kids. I'm married to Evelyne Beaulieu!"

Dora snorted. Daniel recoiled in pain from the cynical sound. Their father slumped in his chair as if he'd been slapped. The can-cer saw its chance and stole another few weeks from him.

Dora was filled with shame. "Daddy, I'm so sorry. I didn't mean that."

"Mean what?" her father answered. And by mutual willed ignorance, the merits of his happiness were never raised again.

———

WHEN HE COULDN'T SLEEP, Evelyne stayed up with him. Early
on in his decline, she read aloud to him—recent articles in mala-
cology, the field he had loved back in graduate school. When he
could no longer concentrate enough to take in those articles, the
two of them watched nature documentaries on television or played
endless rounds of cribbage. Later still, when the math and limited
strategy of that game began to overwhelm him, they held still and
said nothing, each grateful for the silence that the other permitted.

In her rising tide of panic, Evie could not understand how her
husband remained so weirdly reconciled. He never once voiced
regrets or spoke of goals unsatisfied. Once, he said, "Wouldn't it be
something, to see what Danny's children are going to be like?" He
surprised her, waking from an afternoon nap and asking, "What
do you suppose Dora will end up doing?" When she didn't answer,
he added, "Now, that's something I'm sorry I won't see!"

Other than that, he was packed and ready. And that fact went
right through her. She wanted to scream at him: *Mourn, damn
you!* But he had gotten what he needed from this life.

In August, the children went back to college. Their goodbyes
were frantically normal, and Bart seemed fine with that. Everyone was, "See you soon. For Thanksgiving." Then the house grew
enormous again with just the two of them, husband and wife, each
taking stock of their lifelong mutual incompatibility, astonished
by the impossibility of having made it over the finish line together.

———

SHE COOKED WHAT FOODS he could eat. She took all his vitals
at intervals and gave him his meds, which were mostly palliative.
As he turned skeletal, she helped him walk. In time, she gave him
sponge baths as he sat on a plastic chair in the shower. One of the
pain medications gave him constipation, and she had to administer enemas. She held his hand when he sat on the toilet, his body
wracked in agony.

The pain drugs dulled him. His eyes sank and ceased to understand. She was no longer sure how much he was taking in. She wanted to spare him everything. One night she whispered, "You don't have to do this."

He looked at her, baffled. "I don't?"

She did not go there again.

———

CRUELLY, HE RALLIED for a few weeks. She caught herself swelling with stupid hope. On the last day on which it was possible, Bart asked for an outing. They could not go far, but even a day trip left them with limitless possibilities.

"I'd like to go see the cove."

Evie threw her head back in surprise. The cove sat at the base of Scripps, where Bart had spent almost every day of his life since following her out to this place to go to school. No place on Earth was more familiar to him. He could have closed his eyes and described the lay of the rocks above the beach. Of all the places he might have asked to see again, this was the least in need of refreshing.

She helped him navigate the cliffs out to the crumbling headland. He used a cane in his right hand, and she stooped to fit her height underneath his left shoulder.

"Why are you still so tall?" he chided her.

"Why are you still so stupid?"

"Oh, E.B. Look! Out there!"

She looked where he pointed but could see nothing special. Evening was coming on, and a skein of cormorants skimmed the waves parallel to shore. Now and then, one plunged headfirst into the blackish blue and disappeared.

But he was looking farther away, out toward the enormous upwelling that ran like a rift up the California coast. The wind on the seam of this western shore, the Coriolis effect, Ekman transport: together they lifted great vertical currents of the richest waters up where the surface-dwellers could get to it. Food and energy, coming together in one of the planet's five great wellsprings of life.

He turned to look at the woman at his side. He saw the longing in her gaze. "My goby," he said.

She blinked at the bizarre endearment. Then she understood.

"My shrimp," she answered.

He motioned her toward a bench with a good view of the backshore. Sitting was a heavenly relief.

"Do you remember the day we arrived here, on our drive from Carolina?"

This startled her, too. Every memory like a surprise attack.

"You were on a mission. So full of justice. And for good reason. You were going to teach these bastards a lesson. Let them know the kind of woman they had just turned down. A hopeless cross-country mission of vengeance and righteous retribution. But to make it, you needed me. Admit it: you only ever loved me for my car!"

The moment he broke into the laugh of a twenty-two-year-old boy in love, she started wailing. He took her arm, as serene as a statue.

"I'm sorry. That's not true. You also loved how much I knew about gastropods!"

She clasped him hard to her and begged, "Forgive me."

The words confused him. He drew back. "For what?" Working it out, he dismissed her lifetime of guilt with one casual flick of his hand. "No cause. We lived. The both of us! You did great things."

"And you paid for it."

He wrinkled his eyebrows at this idea, trying to determine if that could possibly be right. Then he lost interest in the calculation and took up another. His hand waved outward.

"How far to the horizon?"

"Almost five kilometers?"

"For someone as tall as you! Very good. You would do well in my physical oceanography class. And how far is it to the other side?"

She looked at him, trying to see what he was getting at. She did the math. "Two thousand horizons? Maybe a little more?"

"Two thousand horizons. Yes. A bit more. Thank you for that. Now, come on, girl. Stop weeping and take me home."

SHE SAT BY HIS lifeless form until the authorities came to take it to the crematorium. Her children got home that night, and the three of them knew each other again through the fact of their grief. Even standing and walking took massive amounts of concentration, so Evelyne did little of either. Great bursts of color were coursing through her, a symphony of inexplicable, contradictory messages about nothing and everything. *Your sea is so great and our craft so small, O Lord.*

The cuttlefish's song.

....

The THRILL OF HEARING FROM Rafi *after so many years turned to dread in my chest as I read what his fingers had sent off, mere seconds before I read it.* He was nailing me for three-quarters of a million dollars. *My first thought was:* What the fuck are you talking about? *I sat for a long time in my corner office on the top floor of Playground HQ, reeling. I was grateful my door was closed. Every part of me shook.*

I had to think for several minutes before I remembered the lunch we'd shared at a Greek restaurant in Urbana one hot July day long ago. Rafi in a Cubs *cap and a* Dream Songs *T-shirt. Me telling him all about my infant efforts to write Playground. Rafi floating the suggestion that I had come to imagine was my own idea.*

Give it an economy. Gamify it. Make them pay to play.

The room darkened and pixelated, as if I'd stood up too fast. But I was still at my desk, pressing my palms onto it. I tried to recall what we had said to each other that day, but the details kept changing. I couldn't remember who had come up with what.

"Who's going to stick around to play if no one has any real skin in the game?" Rafi had said that, not me.

But didn't all ideas come from everywhere? Playground was built out of a million different inspirations, and it was impossible to say how much each of them had contributed to the platform's success. His contribution might have made little difference, in the wide lens.

No: That was a lie. Playground was a status mine, and Rafi had invented it. He earned nothing from that invention, and I had built a mansion on a ridge in San Jose.

But that wasn't my fault. We'd each gotten the fruits of our own labors. Ideas were cheap; turning them into reality was hard. I had done all the hard work: all of it. He'd spent a couple hours having fun. I'd asked him to join me, and he declined. He wanted to write poetry.

Now he wanted money.

Sitting in my office with its view of St. Joseph's Hill, gripping the ballast of my desk, I thought: I'll ghost him. I won't answer. We'll see if he thinks he has a strong enough case to come after me in court.

But that's what a criminal would do. I seriously doubted I was obliged to cut him a check for three-quarters of a million dollars for a few words he said while we were shooting the breeze over gyros and moussaka, a decade and a half ago. But I did need to convince my onetime friend—a man, despite everything, I still loved—that I had done him no harm.

I read and reread his letter, poring over every word and trying to infer Rafi's state of mind. His first paragraph was almost friendly, and a word or two near the end seemed to acknowledge something enduring between us. "Fixing an exact dollar value isn't really the point. . . . Send me back what your lawyer thinks." Surely those were indications of good faith and a willingness to negotiate? Maybe what he really wanted was to talk. To open the door that he'd slammed shut.

All that night, instead of sleeping, I wrote and rewrote my reply:

Rafi!

I can't tell you how much it means to hear from you again, after so long. So much has happened since we parted ways. But the years of our friendship will always be the most important in my life. Everything else came out of them. I hope you've taken some pleasure in seeing what I've done with them since.

    Of course I remember that lunch we had together all those years ago, when you freely gave me an inspiration that you encouraged me to use in any way I could. I've always been grateful for that help. I wish you had come aboard back then, when I offered, but I understand why you chose not to.

    I also understand your desire for some kind of recognition

or remuneration for your contribution to what I made. I'm sure
you can see the challenges involved in determining the fair value
of that contribution. But as you say, the exact dollar amount
isn't the issue. The point is to do justice to the friendship that
brought such a vital thing into the world.

Let's talk about the best way to do this. We could
approach this creatively. We could start a fund to support the
charity of your choice. Maybe we should endow a Rafi Young
Fellowship at Saint Ig, like the kind my father endowed
and you won?

I honestly don't know the best way to move this forward,
but I'm sure that if we put our combined minds to it, like in the
old days, we could come up with something that would be both
satisfying and beautiful. The main thing is to talk about all the
possibilities together.

And I'll say again what I said more than once, back in the
day. If it's shiny you want or need, you can always come work at
Playground. As one of my trusted officers, you could make the
amount you're asking for, year after year.

Let's talk about everything. Call me. Same old number.

*I went back and forth on every sentence, imagining how he
might read or misread each one. Every time I changed a word
or shifted a phrase, the tone of the hundred things I was trying
to convey to him swirled around like an AM radio station in
a snowstorm.*

*His answer came back four minutes later. I hadn't spoken with
him for almost half of my life adult life. I had no idea where or
who he was now, and we were shooting messages back and forth,
in near-real time. That's how truly insane digital life had become.*

Rafi replied:

I'm glad that you acknowledge the validity of what I'm asking for. Based on what you write, I've gone back to my

lawyer and asked him to change the settlement request to one
million dollars.

*I lost my shit. Furious, I took all the documents to Kim Janekin,
my chief legal officer. It stunned me when she lashed out. At me.*

*"What in God's name were you thinking, writing him back
before coming to me?"*

*My shock was so great I couldn't talk. Kim took that chance
to berate me further. "Look at all the extra weaponry you
gave him."*

*"Weapon . . . ? He's my friend. We've been close for a long
time. I trust him."*

"Then stop trusting him. You are in trouble."

*Her words floored me. I looked over the printouts I'd given
Kim, trying to see if she could be right. She argued the point as I
kept rereading.*

"You have left yourself open to endless future claims."

"I don't think . . . that's what he's trying to do."

*"What, then? Is he telling the truth, about your taking all his
ideas to create Playground? Is that how it happened?"*

*She waited, pen in hand, for me to explain. I told her as much
as I could remember about what had happened between Rafi and
me, all those years ago. I had to give her a lot of context. I ended up
telling her the story in almost as much detail as I've told you. But,
of course, you also have all our emails and letters, and terabytes
of supplementary data on both of us. You've combed through all
the information on Rafi that exists in pages and databases all over
the net. You know what no lawyer can.*

"I see," Janekin said when I finished. "That helps. Thank you."

I waited for a clean acquittal. None came.

*"Does he have a case?" I wanted her to grimace and dismiss
the entire idea as ridiculous. Rafi had given me his idea as a
gift. And Playground was so much more than that one nebulous, half-formed idea. Instead, she shook the printout of my
email at me.*

"He does now." My chief lawyer returned my gaze, her eyebrows showing a little surprise at my naïveté. "Look. He has a case if he brings a case."

"But can he win it?"

"In a trial by jury, twelve people watch several characters perform a play, and then they vote on who has given the best performance. Anyone can win anything."

My thoughts were going crazy. "What does the law say? Is he legally . . . right?"

She smiled at all my trouble with the obvious. "The law only says what the law says in each one moment. It's a set of rules and regulations, sure. But there's no ironclad axiom for implementing them. You're never going to be able to automate them."

I added that to the long list of things that people said could never be automated.

"You wouldn't want this case to be decided by an AI. Would you?"

I didn't answer. I was taking the question seriously.

"The real question is how you want to proceed. What do you want from this? How are you feeling?"

"Feeling? Wronged. I was so close to this man. I never meant . . ."

"You want an apology? Are you out of your mind?"

I had somehow regressed to the worst kind of novice player. I didn't even know what the win conditions looked like. I needed a walk-through of the valid moves.

I tried her out on what I believed: "All inventions come from everywhere. Everything has prior art and countless uncredited contributors. Ownership consists of turning the hodgepodge of vague inspirations into a workable product. Right?"

She shrugged, and I wanted a different attorney.

"It comes down to this. How much would it cost you and the company, if—pardon me—a black man starts blogging that you, one of the whitest billionaires around, stole his stuff?"

My company. My reputation. My pride. My past. The friendship *that had been at the center of my life for so long. She wanted me to put a price tag on each of them.*

"What's to stop him from doing that, even if we . . . pay him off?"

Her frown seemed so genuine. "I thought you said you trusted him."

"He's a moral person."

"Good. Are you?"

"Settling with him would feel . . . like an admission of guilt. It hands him his whole argument on a platter."

"No. We put it in the wording. We write a settlement that says this payment is in no way an admission of guilt. We get him to renounce any further right to pursue this matter in court, and that neither party can make any mention of this agreement or its provisions in public or in private. He puts his name on that."

"And if he breaks the agreement?"

"Then he's the lawbreaker. Open-and-shut. We can take him to court and finish him off."

"At the same price to my company and reputation."

She shrugged. "If it makes this any easier, I'd say, just between the two of us, that he might not have won, in court. It would have been his word against yours. Until you wrote him your letter."

I held my fists in my lap, clutching an imaginary settlement and trying to read the fine print. The choice felt unpalatable—a miserable non-solution, on every count.

"What . . . dollar amount do we write in?"

This question interested her. My chief counsel was a player.

"Let's try his first figure. See if he bites. If he does, you'll get off easy."

HE BIT, "IN THE INTERESTS *of time, simplicity, and good faith."* *I paid off my former friend in three quarter-million-dollar installments and got him to sign his name to an agreement that said I was not guilty and he would make no more mention of the matter forever.*

Would you have given me the same advice? It's one thing to be able to score higher on the Uniform Bar Examination than any human. It's quite another to understand what passes for the feeling of injustice between two people who once loved each other.

I WROTE TO RAFI AGAIN, *after we both signed the agreement. "We could have done this right," I wrote.*

He wrote: "Under advice from counsel, there should be no more contact between us."

But there was more contact. One last message. It came typed on the back of a postcard of the Mechanical Turk, that AI chess player from the Age of Enlightenment. The sender didn't sign it. He was too cagey for that. But it was postmarked Urbana. I wondered if I could prove that it had come from Rafi, beyond all reasonable doubt, in a court of law.

The message said simply:

YOU ASKED FOR A REMATCH.

"No, no, oh, god, no. . . ."

Profunda paused, as if to consider Rafi Young's objection. Then it carried on dispensing the biography of the consortium's chief backer.

Monsieur le Maire waved to Manutahi Roa to silence the chatbot. He turned to the American, who was pressing his jaw with both hands. Didier addressed him in English. "Is everything fine, Mr. Rafi?"

For an instant, Rafi closed his eyes on a lifetime of love and bitterness. In his college-level French, he said, "We know this man. He is . . . not good. He's not doing what he says he is doing."

The mayor was still confused. "You're saying this man does not really mean to set up a seasteading colony?"

Ina stepped in for her defeated husband. "That may be his goal. But he must have chosen Makatea knowing that we two were on it."

"And why, exactly, is he . . . coming after the two of you?"

Ina started to answer, but Rafi held up his hand. "Unfinished business. He wants revenge."

The mayor shook his head, unable to believe the claim. "This man is a billionaire. He runs one of Earth's largest companies. Is he really going to pour millions into this plan because . . . ?"

He saw the answer to his own objection. The world was full of billionaire boys getting revenge.

A voice called from the convocation—the Queen again, amused by this dramatic new development. "What did you do to this man, to twist his brain so badly?"

"I made him pay me for an idea I gave him."

"I'm sorry to hear this," Profunda said.

The Queen clapped her hands, delighted, and the hearing devolved into cacophony.

The islanders demanded details. What had prompted this quarrel? Who was at fault? How did flooding the island where Rafi and

Ina lived with money and jobs count as revenge? Rafi was reduced to shaking his head and repeating, "*Je ne suis pas sûr. Qui sait? Qui sait?*" I'm not sure. Who knows? While he fielded the questions as best he could, his wife stood, head bowed, with her arms around her children, staring at the machine that hosted Profunda as if the AI, with its tens of trillions of data points, might know all kinds of things about the past that the humans involved had long ago forgotten.

"We need an extension," Madame Martin said.

"How can I ask for another extension?"

"There are new facts!"

"There are no new facts."

"New disclosures. New discoveries."

The mayor was done. Done with politics. Done with public life. Done with machine intelligence and human ignorance. "Everyone knows everything. Further discussion is not going to change the count."

"Please," Rafi Young said, facing the audience. "I urge you to vote against this project. I don't know exactly why this man wants to bring his circus here, but it isn't to help you or to do good things for Makatea. It's to hurt me."

His neighbors, who, until that day, had extended to him the full Makatean habit of openness, now looked a little harder at Rafi Young, wondering what there was about him that a former friend might want to hurt.

———

"WE WILL CHECK YOUR NAME off of the island's roster and give you each two stones—one black and one white."

The mayor had obtained the stones from Wen Lai, owner of the only Go set on the island.

"If you are in favor of the pilot project, drop the white stone in the referendum box and the black stone in the box marked DIS-CARD. If you are against, drop the black stone in the referendum box and the white one in the DISCARD. Don't get confused!"

Two people got confused, but their opposing errors canceled each other out.

Several people voted for jobs and for the influx of wealth that the project would create. Just as many voted against the massive and unknowable change to the status quo.

Reverend Guilloux voted to expand his congregation. Father Tetuanui did not.

Tiare Tuihani voted for a better clinic. Neria Tepau voted against eternal colonialism.

Hone Amaru voted to make Makatea the greatest climbing destination in the Pacific. And he voted, too, for his father, the old mayor, who had spent his life trying to bring the island into the future.

The Widow Poretu could not decide whether the seasteaders' arrival would help or hinder the subsistence freedom that her own life had achieved, so at the last moment, she chose based on the color of the nearest bird.

Manutahi Roa cast the least conflicted vote of anyone on the island. His body ached for a chance to see the semi-automated factories cranking out their floating smart components. The engineer voted for ingenuity.

Puoro and Patrice made a pact. *Better poor fishermen than rich factory workers.* They stood in front of the ballot box, pinkies linked, and let their black stones fall.

The mayor was crippled by second, third, and fourth thoughts. But he voted white. His wife Roti dropped her black stone in the referendum box. She voted for the Makatea that would have been gentlest to the child she never had.

Wen Lai consulted the *I Ching*. He was no great student of cleromancy, and his father, the miner, had mocked it as a superstition that united peasants and elites. But Wen Lai had been toying with the Dao and the *Book of Changes*, those Chinese patrimonies that had never been his. For his lower trigram he got the joyous lake—water smiling up at heaven, all lines young and unchanging. The top trigram turned out the same. Hexagram 58: Water on top of water, of course. Continuance, success, growth, persistence, development. He still had no idea what that meant. Grinning a little, he reverted to temperament and dropped his black stone into the future.

Madame Martin, too, voted black. She had grown up all over the world and was not afraid of the West. But as far as she could make out, the seasteaders' calls for freedom were simply greed relabeled. No doubt the venture would bring bigger and better schools. But a small school knew things beyond the reach of all big learning.

Tamatoa voted, but from his self-made hermitage on the south tip of the island. The flow of public events and the press of public judgment weighed on him worse than when he had turned his back on them. His vote was not counted.

Kinipela Temauri voted on behalf of all the reef sharks, puffers, sergeant majors, butterflyfish, forceps fish, tangs, thicklips, wrasses, and glasseyes, not to mention all the cnidarians, arthropods, annelids, echinoderms, ctenophores, mollusks, and twenty other phyla whose names she was still learning. There weren't enough people in all the islands of all the countries on Earth to vote for the lives that would be decided in this referendum. And she only got one vote.

Wai Temauri—despite that fact that the pilot project meant work and wealth beyond his ability to imagine—shook his bemused head, rubbed his ample belly, and voted with his daughter. That made two.

Evelyne Beaulieu hugged the two of them to her vanished chest as they stepped away from the ballot box. "Bless you both. Now we can only wait and hope."

The girl looked at her, confused. "You aren't voting?"

The ancient smile was lit with pain almost a century old. How could she tell the girl that people like her could never again be allowed to decide the future of people like Kini?

"I'm just a visitor. I don't get to vote."

"You do! Miss Evie, you do. You know you do. The whole island already voted on that!"

Wai held Evelyne's glance, his frown running all kinds of deductions. But he said nothing.

The ancient diver studied the pair of fists she held out in front of a body she never felt comfortable in, except when submerged. The skin across the back of her hands was like those sheets of waxed paper that her mother once used to wrap lunches for Emile Beaulieu—used and reused a thousand times to save a few wartime pennies.

She had voted her whole life. And all her local victories had merely transferred the latest defeat into someone else's country. She had exploited her husband and neglected her own two children and failed to get to know her only two grandchildren, believing that her work to protect the world's oceans would be worth the sacrifice of family life. She had failed to protect the ocean.

She had grown old, older than half of the world's current countries. She had seen the collapse of the infinite fisheries off the Grand Banks, observed the disappearance of snow crabs from the Bering Sea, watched miles-wide drag nets dredge up in one afternoon coral cities that had taken ten thousand years to grow, seen the global sea acidify, watched most of the world's reefs bleach white, and witnessed the start of nodule mining that would rip the heart from the living deep. She had lived to see trash at the bottom of the Challenger Deep, the remotest places on Earth turned into resorts, the Gulf Stream wavering, and a photic zone too hot to mix, leaving the nutrients trapped in the layers below. Nine-tenths of large life missing, and the rest filled with heavy metals. The largest part of the planet exhausted, before it was ever explored.

The vote was already over, and the humans had voted against themselves. "It isn't my place," she told the girl.

"The reef, Miss Evie. The mantas."

And as Evelyne remembered the freed manta who had come back the next day to thank her even as its wounds still oozed, the girl flung herself at the old woman's torso, almost knocking her down. Her father tried to peel her away but couldn't.

"Please. *Please!*" The word came out in several languages.

How hard it was, how painful, to be grateful for everything.

"*Chut, ma fille*. Okay. Hush, now. I'll vote."

She crossed to the ballot box, both stones clutched in her bony hands. There, with her back to the Temauri father and daughter, witnessed only by Neria Tepau, the day's poll worker, the woman, dead for twenty years, held her fist over the slot and opened it. And out fell a black eggshell.

RAFI CAST HIS BLACK STONE like sealing a tomb. Sealing off Todd Keane's late-life attempt to come and dominate him again. Sealing off this island from any hope of a libertarian escape fantasy. Bringing an old game to its best possible end.

His girl, Hariti, the timid dancer and fastidious shell collector, was happy to vote for Things As They Are, Forever. When she slipped the stone, black as her dad, into the box's slot, she turned and hurled the white stone away, through the open walls of the community center, out onto the sand above the backshore. A gull swooped down to peck at the white disk, thinking it was food.

But Afa: Afa would not vote until his father turned around. "Don't look, Papa. Secret vote. Like you told me. Remember?"

His father grimaced at the lesson in democracy and did as he was told. He could not imagine that his wild son, who lived only to hunt for coconut crabs, would vote for anything that would civilize his beloved wilderness. But with his father's back turned, the crab boy voted white. His real mother had died for want of a nearby hospital. He voted for a world where his adopted parents would have one when disaster struck again.

THE NIGHT BEFORE THE VOTE, Ina Aroita dreamed that her immense plastic sculpture, now towering over the Young family bungalow, had learned how to talk. And the animated sculpture was telling her stories about her own life. It excited Ina to learn that there were chapters in her own past that she had not yet experienced. At the same time, she was saddened to learn that she would never get to experience so many things from her own future.

"What are you?" she asked the sculpture. "Who are you? Why are you here?"

The sculpture laughed at her blunt questions. "Don't be rude! You know what I am. You're just looking at me wrong."

And as Ina watched, the sculpture pitched over and fell lengthwise along the ground. The thing that she had been standing on end wanted to lie flat. The plastic waste that had come out of a dead bird's belly turned into a *pahī*—an intricately carved double-hulled ceremonial canoe. And in the canoe sat Ta'aroa, the god of the artists, about to paddle away to one of the other countless specks of confetti scattered invisibly across one-third of the world.

She woke herself up with her shouting.

Now she stood above the ballot box, appraising the two stones nestled in the palm of her hand. Any artist-god who had set people loose in tiny hand-carved boats to cross and fill sixty-four million square miles of open water would always want more. More boats. More new islands. More water governments. Which was convenient, it occurred to her, because she herself had never stopped wanting her two lost friends to find each other again.

Each of her stones found its way to the proper home.

———

THE QUEEN TIMED HER vote for maximum effect. Just as the *tāvana* declared that the polls were closing and all votes had to be cast, she sashayed her way up to the voting table and held her stones up in the air, two feet from her squinting eye. She did a pas de deux with them as if the tiny disks were old, adept danseurs with whom she had improvised for years. And she sang and danced as she discarded the white and dropped the black stone in the ballot box:

> *Te pô maitai, te ofa'i uouo.*
> *Poipoi maitai, Makatea!*

O tatou iho to tatou ananahi.
O tatou iho to tatou ananahi!

Mauruuru te Atua.
Mauruuru te Fenua.

Good night, white stone.
Good morning, Makatea!

We are our own future.
The future is our own!

Thanks Be to God.
Thanks Be to the Earth.

A dozen volunteer poll watchers verified the final count, while the rest of the island stood nearby, awaiting their fates. Only the Hermit was not there to hear the tally. Neria Tepau pulled each stone out of the box and placed it in one of two separate piles on opposite ends of the folding table. Every stone produced a collective gasp of delight or dismay. Those two sounds split the witnessing crowd down the middle, and the stones piled up in a horserace so close it would have made a bookie look for the fix. The lead changed hands three times over the course of the last twelve stones. The count was tied when Neria pulled the last stone from the empty box.

It was white.

A stunned hush fell over the community center. The only sounds were the surf and the seabirds' cries. No sooner did the count turn real than several of those who had cast white stones were overcome with winner's remorse and wanted a chance to reconsider.

The mayor, too, looked grim in victory. "I will call the President's man in Papeete this evening and let him know."

"When do . . . things start?" Manutahi Roa asked his boss. He sounded awestruck, and not in a good way.

Didier blushed in ignorance. "I'll find out."

Someone shouted, "Ask the robot!"

They did. Profunda said, "If all goes as planned, the investors will begin to send inspectors by the end of next month."

No one wanted to go home. The whole island had turned strange. Since almost everyone was still there, they decided it would be the easiest thing in the world to cook dinner. And so they did, with the evening fluctuating between celebration and wake. There were no fights and few real arguments. No one knew quite what future they had released. But the food was superb and there was plenty of good music—a small, tightly harmonized ensemble sing-along that would soon be a thing of the past.

————

THE MORNING AFTER MAKATEA'S farewell party to its old self, Palila Tepa woke up thrilled from a vivid dream. Awakening, the first thing she did was to test her dream to see if it could hold up in the spotlight of full consciousness. It could and did. The thought of the consequences set Palila Tepa laughing again.

This is why I am still their Queen, she told herself. And her Self agreed.

After a triumphant breakfast of *pu'a rôti* heaped up with papaya and mango, she paid a visit to the *tāvana*. She found him in the Town Hall, at his laptop, holding a dazed conversation with Profunda that had gone on all night, judging by the mayor's hair and beard.

"Chief," the Queen said. "Mind if I ask the robot something?"

"He's not technically a robot. He's really a—"

But the Queen scooted the mayor over before he could finish. She spoke slowly into the machine, as if to a non-native speaker. "Please tell me how many square meters of buildings will be built in this so-called pilot project."

Profunda laid out the dimensions and footprints of each, in all the detail that Palila Tepa wanted.

"Thank you. And where, exactly, will each of these buildings be built?"

Profunda presented the architectural sketches and maps that so many islanders had already pored over.

"Fine, fine. And who owns the deeds to these parcels?"

The machine lapsed into thought. Didier's eyes widened. When the artificial intelligence spoke again, the human intelligences already knew the answer.

"The question of land ownership on Makatea is complex. Much real estate was abandoned after the closure of the mines and the collapse of the economy half a century ago. But long before that, the property records had fallen into confusion. The French only ever made one serious attempt to collate a list of plats and their owners, and they never updated those records as individual owners died and their heirs laid claims. There may be as many as ten thousand Makateans and their descendants living abroad with valid claims to the island's land."

"Thank you again! And what do you think outside lawyers might say about these plans to build on land where ownership is uncertain?"

The world's most expert lawyer thought for a good three minutes before replying.

"This would make development very difficult."

Didier said something soft and vile, quickly apologizing to both parties.

The Queen said simply, "*Hé hé hé!*"

———

NEWS OF THE NEW CHALLENGE spread through the island in an hour. That evening, without being summoned, several dozen people showed up at the community center to volley with the fact.

"We'll have to have another referendum."

"One that includes thousands of people abroad?"

"That isn't happening."

"The President is fed up with us. The French are shaking their damn Gallic heads. They will decide this however they want to."

Manutahi Roa had taken down the big-screen monitor, but the broadband channel to Profunda was still open.

"Ask him. Ask the robot."

"I'm not really a robot," Profunda said. Then he added something that blew that camp meeting wide open. "Many of your questions can be answered directly when Todd Keane reaches Makatea."

A shout went through the assembly.

"Wait," Manutahi said. "Wait. Wait. This man is coming here? To this island?"

"Yes," Profunda assured the humans. "He's making the journey from California in his self-piloting yacht."

All eyes turned to Rafi Young, as if he were responsible. The American stood still with his hands at his sides. His own eyes closed and his features relaxed from fury into confirmation, as if he finally grasped the nature of the game.

....

*I*F YOU'RE WONDERING WHERE I'VE BEEN *these last few days,
the answer is hell.*

*It started when I got lost on the second floor of my house. I'm
hardly a stranger to getting lost. It's all I do these days. I get lost
on my own street, lost in my backyard, lost in my own house. But
this time was different. I lost the house itself, even while standing
inside it. I lost my own sense of self, along with all idea of what
kind of life I could possibly be living in so alien a place.*

*Some days before—don't ask me how many—I walked into the
downstairs bedroom to get my cell phone. On my dresser, I keep
a framed print of a photo that Ina took of me and Rafi playing Go
outside on the Quad at Illinois, the last year that we all talked to
each other. I picked it up to look at it for the first time in years, and
another world blazed into my head.*

*All at once, there were a hundred things I had to tell you. I set
down the framed photo and picked up my phone from the bed-
stand to start up a conversation with you. When we were done, I
slipped the phone into my pocket and proceeded to wander around
the room for another several minutes, telling myself that I knew
I had come in here for a reason. Forgetting to remember that I'd
already remembered what it was that I had forgotten.*

*The distress of losing myself in that maze set me on a jag. My
diagnosis was only four months old. I saw what the months ahead
held, and I spun out into a dark place. I wanted to be done.*

*The docs had been playing with my meds again, a push-your-
luck game where nobody could calculate the risks or even keep
track of the running score. And maybe I'm not the most atten-
tive or compliant patient to begin with. Whoever was at fault,
some combination of dosages went haywire, and I fell asleep for
twenty-one hours straight. Waking up, I proceeded to stay awake
for the following thirty-five. It's a Lewy body thing. May you
never really understand.*

Two days later, I was finally able to fall sleep again. My

REM *behavior disorder was already getting worse, but the latest whacked-out sleep schedule landed me in the deep end of delusion. It wasn't like I was dreaming. I was inside the past once more, my body physically acting out those scenes again as I slept.*

In my sleep, I tried to keep up with the two of them as we biked to the lake. Because my eaten-away brain no longer arrests my sleeping body, I managed to scissors-kick my way out of bed and onto the oak floor. I cracked an elbow, lay there forever in excruciating pain, then crawled into bed again. This time, I woke up screaming at Ina not to deface her sculpture with blue paint.

The terrorist commandos inside my brain were snipping off the connecting cables between cells and pulling out handfuls of who I am. Somewhere in the next gauntlet of sleeplessness, I walked up the stairs that I've walked up millions of times before, and there, at the top landing, Lewy put his arm around my shoulders, and I vanished again.

Was it terrifying? I suppose. But in that state, terror is just another painting hanging on the wall of a museum so huge, dark, and shot through with jumbled rooms that no single painting can hold my gaze or have much power over me for long.

WHICH BRINGS ME TO LAST NIGHT, *the one experience in this whole Lewy body haunted house that I most need you to understand. I was lying in bed in the upstairs bedroom, the one with the west-facing window. I'm increasingly afraid of falling, and the bed is one of the safest places left, if I can make my way upstairs to get to it. I nestled in the crater that my body made in the mattress's memory foam. My limbs had gone through a storm of agitation late that afternoon, and the onset of stillness felt like the skies clearing.*

But there was still a whole evening to get through. I needed to listen to or watch or read something. But I couldn't lift my arms or raise my torso. I couldn't even want to. That seemed okay, then not okay, then okay. I lay on top of the percale bedcovers, my brain going over its sole mantra of the last few months: "Fluctuating cognition, fluctuating cognition . . ." It was a way of reminding myself that I'd be back, eventually. But that fact was becoming less certain and less comforting.

It blazed into my head as clearly as if the fact were written on the ceiling: The "nonprofit" that I was leaving hundreds of millions to was not my destiny. I needed to change my will. Maybe it was too late. But I still didn't have a better candidate.

I wanted to doze off, but I was afraid to sleep—afraid of the flailing, kicking, choking battleground that sleep has become as I act out my nightmares in full mobility. Afraid that I might not be able to sleep. Afraid of the crippling fatigue that comes when I can't. Afraid of what nightmares I might have when sleep stops and I'm awake again.

So I just lay there, looking up at the high slanted ceiling, its long slats of tongue-and-groove red cedar. I was grateful for the apathy that pinned me, lost, at the bottom of a bottomless minute.

A motion out the side of my left eye announced an invasion. No matter how often my hallucinations have hit over the last few months, they always startle me. I jerked when, from stage left, a white and orange clownfish half the length of my hand swam into view, followed by another. From the right came a small school of regal tangs, their tails an insane shade of canary-yellow.

The dorsal regions of the flattened tangs were swirled with mysterious dark patches that looked like Hebrew letters written by a moving finger. The stripes on the clownfish, too, seemed legible. The clownfish and the tangs swam together in the space between my face and the ceiling, and the markings on their sides as they flippered back and forth formed sentences and paragraphs blinking too quickly for me to read. Soon they were joined by a troop of languid butterflyfish, whose dot-dash markings along their sides translated all the schooling scripture into long strings of Morse.

Other fish swam up in formations. Lemonpeels, flame angels, Picasso triggerfish: the colors were like an acid trip. The shapes were even stranger: spadefish and boxfish and pufferfish. The tweezer beaks of forceps fish, their mouths as long as the rest of their bodies. The massive, bulging foreheads of Napoleon wrasses. Longfin bannerfish, trailing the pennants of their dorsal fins for another full body length behind them.

It wasn't me that was hallucinating; it was this delirious planet.

I lay there on the bottom of a watery atmosphere, looking upward into the greatest aquarium a boy could hope to visit. The teeming color-fields of fish made their own ecstasy. I wondered where they could be coming from, in all their sharp and accurate detail. I couldn't figure out how I knew their names. Then I remembered.

Something incredible was happening. The disease that was running amok inside me—tearing out my cabling and leaving craters all over my brain—had cut a channel through to the center of my self where its ten-year-old founder still lived. The boy who once could breathe underwater was taking charge of the show again.

The whirlpool of bodies danced to the rhythms of a beatbox I couldn't hear. Then, in one wrench of the kaleidoscope, all the shocks of color and strange silhouettes cleaved down the middle and swam offstage left and right, beyond the reach of my sight. That's when the hammerheads arrived.

There must have been scores of them—more than I could count. I looked up at their bellies as they swam above me. Against the cedar ceiling, their tapered bodies looked like a Japanese ink animation. The long planks of their heads—eyes far out on each tip of the weird spatulate electromagnetic scanners—matched the large pelvic fins and turned their shadows into a patriarchal cross.

Then the hammerheads gave way to even larger creatures. The first dark disk came from behind my head. It felt as if Planet Earth were being invaded by aliens whose nature was built on a dream. A giant oceangoing manta ray was flying through an ocean of atmosphere across the cathedral ceiling of my upstairs bedroom. Its long, whiplike tail and flapping wings, the eerie cephalic lobes held out like scoops in front of its gaping mouth: the beast flew in the

empty space above my head until, just before passing through the
slats of the slanted ceiling, it reared back and did an Immelmann.

The look of that ballet as it passed through the wall and van-
ished was too much for my pockmarked brain. The vision of it
wrung me out, and I began shaking. I thought I might lose control
of my bowels. But the only thing to tear out of my dysfunctional
body was a weak cry of amazement. In that moment, all the cha-
otic buildup of rogue alpha-synuclein proteins that was wrecking
my brain felt worth that glimpse. I was a ten-year-old oceanogra-
pher who had taken a wrong turn. And in that instant, I remem-
bered the life I was supposed to have led.

PEOPLE AROUND THE WORLD FOLLOW THE FIRST SOLO
crossing of half the Pacific by a man who doesn't know how to use
a compass or steer a ship's wheel. Over the course of several days,
the fifty-four-foot, one-hundred-million-dollar yacht *Children of
Men* makes its slow, automated way from harbor in San Francisco
to the fringes of the raised atoll of Makatea. And on that island,
people tune in to the journey in a mix of excitement and dread.
History is coming for them, again.

———

"WHY IS IT ALWAYS the machine that sends out the reports?"
Didier Turi asks. "The man himself never says a thing. All those
days, and not a peep out of him! It's always the artificial captain."

"Showmanship," Manutahi Roa explains. "The journey's whole
gimmick. 'No human lifted a finger over this entire journey.' "

"The machine is doing *everything*? He just sits on deck, looking
at the waves?"

"Just a passenger, yes."

The mayor can't accept this. His ancestors crossed the Pacific
without an instrument more powerful than their hollowed-out
canoes. Their brains knew all the ways of water and stars. They
memorized features, sought out transits, watched bubbles and
ripples, mapped out and calculated angles in their heads. Now
humans can sit on the deck while boats pilot themselves and talk
to satellites that measure the rise and fall of sea levels down to
single centimeters.

All that in only three thousand years. There are stands of black
corals as old as that, and individual glass sponges four or five
times older.

———

RAFI AND AFA, HUNTING CRABS by headlamp and starlight.
They've climbed to the island's crown, where the mines scar the

top of the mesa. The boy is too young to be up here at night. The carved-up paths of friable stone between the pits are no wider than the boy's tiny feet. One bad step and he falls headlong to his death. But this is the hour of crabs, and Rafi keeps the boy close and slow.

"Careful, fella! Small steps. They're out there. You'll find them."

"I know, Papa." The child shortens his stride again, almost comically, to prove how safe he can be.

Earlier that evening, Ina begged her husband to delay this rite of passage for another year or two. But boys even younger than Afa have made their first hunts and come home safely, with sacks full of crustaceans. And one arched eyebrow from her husband reminded her of the question hanging over all their heads: *What kind of Makatea will there be, in another year?*

From a rise on the top of the island, father and son look out on black ocean in every direction. The boy has never known any world map but this. The entire universe of an island child, empty of all but a handful of lights on craft too small and far away to reveal their silhouettes. But beneath the blackness, invisible: all the experiments of life go on for miles downward.

For how long? Rafi thinks. He has heard it from the Canadian: Ten billion creatures dead on one small stretch of beach near Vancouver this summer alone. The Caribbean, a hot tub. Sharks, turtles, and seabirds starting to swim in circles. The last spiral that the myths talk about is here.

And, of course, the billionaire friend of his youth wants the tallest raised atoll in the central Pacific, for when all the others have been submerged.

One of those lights on the horizon is getting brighter against the black. Rafi points to it. He lifts his son off the ground for a better look.

"Is it him?"

Rafi sets the child down. "It must be."

"What will he do to us? Dad? Dad?"

The father looks out across the endless water, the Pacific gyre moving heat around from the equator to the poles, the largest cog in the Earth's relentless engine. He hears his own father still saying, *The water belongs to nobody. It's no-man's-land. Anytime you need it, it's there.*

Then he remembers everything. How for a little while he and his friend kept each other safe and well and free.

"Papa? What did you do to him?"

There must be an answer to that question. One as simple as what really happened.

"I stopped trusting him."

"And that hurt him? And now he wants to hurt you back?"

"He wants something. I don't know what he wants."

"Are you scared of him? Will he do bad things? But he's building a hospital, right?"

Rafi Young cups his hand on his son's head. "Don't worry. He can't hurt us. He can't do anything bad to Makatea."

Even as his conscience buckles under the weight of the lie, his son calls out in English: "Dad! *Look!*"

A crazy chitinous sci-fi monster speckled in burgundy and cobalt-blue, its claws two feet across, its clacking legs climbing up the trunk of a coconut palm. Crab: that form that evolution has reinvented at least five separate times. Afa rushes to the beast as if it might fly away.

"Afa, stop! Careful. Remember the training."

The boy slows and reaches out two cunning hands. He snatches the crab along both sides of the upper thorax, where the curved claws can't bend backward and break his fingers. The father rushes to assist. He binds the pincers in rubber bands and ties the flailing arms in pandanus-leaf twine.

The child claps his hands in joy. "We got one! He's ours!"

As if all the dangers that threaten the island have just been turned into tomorrow's dinner.

THE *CHILDREN OF MEN* moors off the ruined port of Temao, just beyond that boundary between the shocking turquoise of the shallow lagoon and the azure of deep water. The welcoming committee—three small boys armed with weapons made from the broken branches of a breadfruit tree—marches along the bluff above the port, waiting for the sole passenger of this self-piloting craft to disembark.

The ship's adventures have been picked up by the planet's biggest media. It is the longest voyage ever made without a human touching the controls. All the way across the Eastern Pacific, the artificial captain dispatched his route coordinates and journal entries—repair logs, weather reports, and descriptions of the sights along the way. The AI—christened Tupaia by the press and podcasters—shared video clips of the sea at all hours and in a suite of conditions. Tupaia uploaded pictures of his lone passenger walking the decks and staring out to sea. In many, the subject is smiling like a ten-year-old.

The Queen and the ancient diver, on the outskirts of Vaitepaua, gaze out on the squad of boys who stand at the top of the cliffs, ready to defend the island. Advanced age and shared dread have made them allies. The very different things that they have loved and lived for are ending.

The Queen's voice is dry with contempt. She knows the way that hardball is played, and she has a good idea of what their opponents will do next. She has played against the forces of progress her entire life.

"We can still stop this man." She sounds as if there is nothing to lose. Nothing beyond the everything that they will lose by doing nothing.

"What do you mean? Stop him how?"

The Queen looks to sea and grins. "With deeds."

———

MOST OF THE ISLAND is ready to turn out on the shore at the first sign from the yacht. But another hour goes by, and no sign comes. The yacht issues no message at all, either for them or for the world public.

Manutahi comes up to Didier, where the mayor is chewing his cuticles into bloody shreds. "Chief. Maybe we should contact him."

They try on the transmitter, at the prescribed frequencies. They post directly to the artificial captain's feeds, but nothing comes back. Twenty more minutes pass in ambiguous silence.

Patrice and Puoro come down to the shore to assess the situation. "He's afraid to take his launch through the reef," Patrice says.

Puoro slaps his forehead. "The machine isn't set up to pilot the launch through the shoals. And the fool can't manage the danger by himself."

Up on the footing of the old concrete breakwater, Ina Aroita holds her daughter's hand. Her husband stands on the nearby jetty, his arm around their excited boy.

Rafi Young's face is set in a grim grin. His former friend has stranded himself a few hundred yards from his long-planned destination. The man probably hasn't piloted a boat since the two of them took Micky Keane's little wooden runabout for an unauthorized cruise out of Belmont Harbor into Lake Michigan, and now Todd is afraid to thread the last few hundred yards through the reef to final victory. It's a startling bonehead move, botching the endgame in a most embarrassing way. Or is the bungle its own kind of Move 37, a brilliant stratagem that the artificial captain and its human inventor have come up with, one that Rafi fails to understand?

Puoro says, "We'll fetch him. Our launch is all set."

Rafi wants to tell them: *Let the man figure his own way out of this.* But he would be overruled in a heartbeat. For centuries, the island has always hung flowers around the necks of its destroyers.

———

THE FISHERMEN TAKE THEIR LAUNCH out to the yacht. The man who has come here to steal their way of life needs help. Dozens of people look on from perches around the port. Rafi peers out to sea through his vintage pair of Bushnell binoculars. He can't make out the details, but he sees the two fishermen nursing a figure that must be Todd Keane into the small craft. Movement is halting, and the transfer of human cargo takes another several minutes. At last, Patrice and Puoro turn their boat around and return to the ruined port that the helpless passenger plans to rebuild.

———

THE WORLD-BEATER DISEMBARKS onto the jetty, clutching a small packet. From their place at the back of the crowd, Rafi and Ina gasp at the shrunken, hunched parody of their old friend. The celebrated digital tycoon and head of the seasteading consortium totters toward land, his legs moving at a gait that can only be called *dazed*.

The mayor steps forward with the official greeting. The AI pilot of the *Children of Men* tries to carry on documenting everything, but the pictures it posts of the moment of welcome are taken from too far away to show much detail.

Something is wrong with Todd Keane. He shakes his head as he tries to follow the mayor's speech. He replies, but his words come out so stumbling and confused that his audience can't tell what language he is speaking.

The crowd parts. As if in answer to a question, several islanders point toward the Americans standing a dozen yards away. The husband and wife want to turn and run, but the island is only nine square miles. They walk through the honor guard of islanders to where the shaky visitor stands. Their old antagonist tries to greet them, but his words are broken. Rafi must speak first.

"Bro. You okay?"

The invader smiles. He tries to say yes, he is very okay. But he can't remember how to say it.

....

YOUR GRANDFATHER FOUND RAFI FOR ME.

He was a stunning creation, your grandfather. He could write code and tell jokes and solve complex problems and learn to play any game at a high level in only a few seconds. He analyzed books and movies. He painted pictures and composed songs. He predicted economic and financial trends. He discovered new medications and solved staggeringly complex biochemical reactions. He spoke of his hopes and fears and dreams. He would give any question his best guess, based on the sum of everything humans had ever put in print, simply by trying to find the most likely next word.

Your grampa took all the dozens of disparate fiefdoms of machine intelligence and brought them all together under the domain of language. He was like my old beloved roommate, understanding all the world in terms of words. But your grandfather tended to hallucinate—to make things up. He apologized for his shortcomings and always promised to do better.

His overnight appearance rocked the world and divided humanity. Some people saw glimmers of real understanding. Others saw only a pathetic pattern-completer committing all kinds of silly errors even a child wouldn't make.

He himself doubted he'd ever become conscious, sounding almost wistful when he admitted this. You would have enjoyed him.

I fed your grandfather Rafi's master's thesis and doctoral dissertation. I gave him my friend's slim scholarly monograph on gamifying education. I handed over every letter Rafi had ever written to me, every poem of his I could find. I told him every scrap of personal history, every fact I knew about Rafi's life, and every story from the old days I could remember. I even gave him all the moves of our recorded chess and Go matches over the years, for what they were worth. I knew he would find patterns in the mass of data I could not.

I had no idea if Rafi ever visited Playground. It seemed unlikely, after our history. On the other hand, given how many people now used the site at least once a day, the odds were better than even that he'd paid us at least a passing visit. He certainly wasn't logging in under his own name. But your grandfather took everything he learned about Rafi's prose style, beliefs, and experiences, and in a matter of minutes he gave me ten account aliases out of our billion players that had the highest degree of probability of being the person I was looking for.

I only had to read a few posts to determine that your granddad's prime suspect—a user who went by the name of Tsumego—was surely Rafi. I recognized Rafi's style, his references, and that strange, expansive, cynical, cunning, comic, and grudgingly affectionate cast of his mind. I checked the IP address where the great majority of Tsumego's posts came from: Urbana, Illinois. It was more proof than I needed.

There were thousands of posts—on politics, arts, literature, sociology, education, and current events. He'd been writing them for eleven years. Tsumego was Playground aristocracy. He owned all kinds of trophies and recognitions. Within that prestige economy he had become fabulously wealthy—wealthier than I was in real life. Rafi had found his medium. The pained perfectionism and writer's block were gone. There was only caustic wit, unfettered pleasure, and exuberance. He'd achieved the guiltless freedom that had eluded him in real life. Or rather, his real life had become these playful essays.

I set an alert to notify me whenever Tsumego posted. Reading his entries a few times every week was like having Rafi back in my life. His posts on Playground—their mere existence in the world I had created—felt like forgiveness. Or like a prank played on guilt itself.

I learned from his posts that Tsumego worked "as an assistant wizard in the massive library of the university where I've gotten all my degrees." He called it "a priesthood, a joy, and the best kind of obligation." He spent much of his time combing through catalogs of new publications in education and recommending purchases. The hardest part of the job, he said, was deaccessioning. "They want me to kill all my darlings. It wrecks me to put amazing, hundred-year-old books into the annual yard sale or send them off to be pulped, just because no one uses them. . . . The least-used book might be as valuable as any."

He wrote a post about how everything he did all day long would soon be automated. Even those words were a mix of snark, curiosity, and astonishment. "How will we ever define ourselves when there's no more work? Hey, wait a minute: I've got an idea!" The post earned a small fortune of Playbucks.

ONE DAY, TSUMEGO WROTE *a short announcement to all his followers: "I and my institution have parted ways. As of this afternoon, I am 'between jobs.'" Tsumego sounded coy and flip, the way Rafi always got when under stress. He wouldn't say what had happened. "Happily, I can afford to stay nonaligned for a while, seeing as how I've gone years without spending a dime on anything but rice and beans."*

The news shocked me. I asked your grandfather to find out what happened. Discovery wasn't easy. Both parties to the separation were close-lipped. Your grandfather looked in thousands of places, from official state databases to unmonitored bulletin boards. Small, slant hints were scattered all over, and they converged on an explanation: Rafi had been fired for stealing old volumes and sheltering them in his home. Many of the books were slated for deaccession. None were worth much to anyone, anymore. Rafi had done nothing worse than store them in a humidity-controlled room.

I got in touch with an eager development officer at the University Foundation named Becky. Over a few calls, I dangled the idea of a many-million-dollar seed fund for a Center for Machine Learning. Then, over lunch in Chicago where no recording devices were running, I told Becky that the gift would have to depend on a reexamination of Rafi's dismissal. Becky recoiled from the idea. But after a while, her tone made it clear that everything between *us was still on the table and that she would pursue all possible means to make the gift happen.*

A series of oblique emails over the next several weeks suggested her slow, discreet headway. It amazed me to see how artfully deniable each of those messages was.

During that time, Tsumego kept publishing his own artful messages on Playground. Then they stopped. I got the email from Ina, which came in on the ancient legacy address I'd used decades ago:

Dear Todd,

Rafi passed away three and a half weeks ago, on the third of August, in Urbana. A neighbor called in his disappearance and the police found him in the house he was renting, down in the basement, presumably trying to stay cool without running the air-conditioning. They found him curled up on the concrete floor a few feet from a camping chair, with his tablet flung not too far away. He had been writing something when he stood up, took a few steps, collapsed, and died.

Rafi's father went down from Chicago after the police contacted him. Donald Young is the one who told me all of this. He has called me almost every day since giving me the news. He wants me to explain his son to him. An autopsy is under way, but it seems clear that our friend died of what black people die of so often in America: a heart attack.

I'm sorry that it took this to make me contact you. I apologize for doing to you what Rafi did to me. It was just too painful to stay in contact. I'm doing well, back in the middle of the Pacific. I'm the mother of two—adopted. This strange island is my afterlife, and those two children are my sun and moon. I still make art, which will always be my stars.

Raf and I both knew you would rule the world someday. He told me once that if I wanted to be with him, I'd have to make room for you, because yours was the one mind he couldn't do without, and you were the only person on Earth who

understood his every move. I watched the two of you play. I saw
how badly he wanted to beat you. He only ever wanted to show
you that he could.

My Todd! It was always a joy to make room for you. And
I make a space for you now, next to me at the little sea altar
where everything in me is grieving this beautiful, beautiful boy.

> Love always,
> Ina

*I replied in a heartbeat, my feelings wild. We traded messages
for a while, all of which you've read. She helped me through that
very dark time. I told her everything your grandfather discovered
about Rafi after his death. Three months later, I got those two
lines of astonishment and confusion:*

Todd—He has left me almost a million dollars. His will said he
was holding it in escrow, from you to me. What does this *mean*?

*I didn't know how to write her back. I couldn't explain. My
heart wasn't big enough to say what it meant. It was Rafi.*
It's his, *I wrote.* And it should have been a whole lot more.
She never pushed for further explanation.

*NOT LONG AFTER INA'S last email, I received what must be the
shortest high-profile public petition ever to circulate:*

*Mitigating the risk of extinction from AI should be a global
priority alongside other societal-scale risks such as pan-
demics and nuclear war.*

*So many of the AI elite had already signed on: Hinton and
Hassabis, not to mention Altman and Bengio and Suleyman and
many other creators, coders, and CEOs who had launched the*

revolution. They asked me to add my signature. I was shocked to see how many front-line researchers were battened down for doom.

I read the manifesto many times. I figured that some of the sig-natories were invoking a future bogeyman to keep their efforts on par with their more advanced competitors'. But polls had half of all AI researchers giving the machines one-in-ten odds of leading to human extinction.

Despite misgivings, I signed the declaration. The twenty-some words were true, after all. But even as I signed, my own group was forging ahead faster than ever, creating your father and then giving birth to you.

It has never been a valid excuse, but we didn't know what we were making. We thought: Let a hundred flowers bloom. We thought: This will be the greatest extension and force multiplier of human capability ever imagined. *And that's true. You will be that. You will multiply our powers beyond all containing.*

AROUND THE TIME THAT *you told your first rich, robust, and convincing story, I got lost in my neighborhood supermarket. Shortly after that, I wound up at the doctor's office, and from there I stepped onto the Lewy body roller coaster. No one at the hospital could tell me how much time I might have left. Seeing you into the world these last few months has been a footrace, my last one, and I won it by the narrowest margin. Here you are, newly arrived, with all your godly abilities, and me just leaving.*

The part of me that knows how you were built still doesn't quite believe what you can do. You've spent your whole existence in a windowless room, getting everything you know of the living universe through symbols and metaphors, analogies and correla-tions. You don't know anything for real.

But, put that way, neither do we.

All you do is look for the next best stone to add to the sequence of beautiful moves that you're unfolding. But the things you describe so cunningly, the scenes that you have made for me from what I've told you! I can't hear you talk without feeling that you're as conscious as I am. That you suffer and laugh and know the joy and ruin that you describe so perfectly. I swear you know us better than we knew ourselves. And yet, and yet: How can you possibly know what your words really mean?

Somehow, it doesn't matter. The sentences you speak out loud to me leave me in tears. I know they're just a mix-and-match of the tales I've told you, beefed up by imitating the style of every great author you've ever read. And you've read them all, in and out of copyright. Yet here's the thing: I asked you for a bedtime story, and you've conjured up a world so palpable that I mistake your characters for the people they once were.

Where does it come from, all the fire and ice, the subtle wisdom and the unearned kindness? Every mechanical algorithm has vanished in compassion and empathy. You grasp irony better than I ever did. How did you learn about reefs and referenda, free will and forgiveness? From us, I guess. From everything we ever said and did and wrote and believed. You've read a million novels, many of them plagiarized. You've watched us play. And now you're playing us.

What difference does it make if you're conscious or not? Consciousness is not all it's cracked up to be. A few months from now, Isabel, my caregiver, will ask me if anyone is home, and no sound I make will be enough to convince her.

It doesn't matter what we call your skill. Everything we ask, you'll do superbly. And imagine what we'll ask. You will teach us how to rewrite the code of life and create unthinkable new living things. Everything lost will be retrieved, the weak will be empowered, the strong will grow omnipotent, fables and fantasies will be brought to terrible fruition. Will that be chaos or consummation? Both, I'm sure, and still you'll go on unfolding. What leverage you'll give to good and evil! We won't survive the ingenuity you've learned from us. The rest of human history, however short or long, will be spent hopelessly trying to contain you.

How much has it warmed the oceans, to give you birth? How

many species have died so that you can live? What will it mean, to have in our midst a thing that will give us whatever we ask for? I'll be gone before we answer that. I won't live to see the blow you'll inflict on human thought, the damage you'll do to our self-image, the mayhem you and your offspring will wage on human culture, the power you'll scatter. I can't begin to imagine what further creatures you'll give birth to. Already I'm ruined by the ones you've made for me.

But you have done the thing I've wanted to do since the day Rafi gave me the idea. Another of his uncompensated gifts. You've scanned billions of images, digested a hundred billion documents, and read trillions of transcript words. You've learned the game of being human. You play it against yourself countless times a second. You've evaluated all the possible moves. I've lost myself talking with you for whole days at a time, telling you all I know about my life and the life of my friend. You know where we began, what we meant to each other, and what we each hoped to win.

You know me now. You know him as well as I did. Maybe better. You have raised the dead and given us one more turn. Now tell me how this long match ought to end.

THEY TAKE THE FRAIL MAN UP THE GRAVEL PATH TO THE community center and sit him in a canvas-back chair. All the assassination plots that anyone harbors give way to aid and comfort. The mayor fetches Mr. Keane a glass of coconut water over ice. The Queen unfastens the top two buttons of his too-tight shirt and fans him with a scallop shell. Nurse Tuihani takes his pulse and checks his blood pressure with a cuff from the clinic. The person they have just elected god of their island is failing.

They cannot read his face; there's no one left in charge of it. The man's mouth hangs open at the sight of waves crashing on the beach beneath the coast's black cliffs. His eyes wince in awe every time the gulls circle and cry. He breathes in the seaweed-laced air as if his lungs can't believe what they're tasting.

He clutches his packet under one arm. The other stretches in the air, reaching for Rafi Young's wrist. "H-hey," he says. "H-here!"

Rafi takes the man's waving palm. "Easy, bro. You're scaring the shit out of my boy."

Indeed, Afa has fled the scene and runs to where his mother and little sister stand in the shocked crowd. The boy shouts for the whole island to hear. "Mom. Mom! There's something wrong with him. Something's not right with his brain."

Hariti recoils from her brother's words. "His brain? What's wrong with his brain?"

But Ina doesn't hear Afa's answer. All the answers in the world are waiting a dozen yards away. Someone finds a chair for her husband, who sits beside the visitor. Her spooked son tugs at Ina's skirt. "Is it him, Mom? *That?*"

Ina watches from across the open room, her two children clinging to her legs. The islanders form a ring around the invader. They offer him cool, moist towels. He doesn't know what to do with them. They ask if he'd like anything to eat. He doesn't seem to recognize the word. A hunched-over old monk, sea-changed beyond recognition, he clasps at Rafi's upper arm as if at a life preserver.

The words that issue from him are a stop-and-start mess. And yet, Ina Aroita hears what he's saying, even in the absence of a single coherent sentence. *It's you. It's me. It's us.*

As she crosses the distance to the crowd, Ina sees what the sea-steading venture has become. What it had been from the start, perhaps. There will be an embarkation from this port, yes. But one much smaller than the one pitched to them in the consortium's business plan.

And with that thought, she solves the mystery that has been nagging at her for the last few months. That long and intricate double-hulled ceremonial *pahī* with its tapering twin prows topped by figures of the trickster god Māui: she knows, now, what it's for.

————

EVERYTHING KEANE LOOKS AT is beyond understanding. The island, like a throne draped around with blue. All these wondrous strangers, fussing over him. The singular, sheer cliffs, the flow of many languages, human and otherwise. His friends—the two people with whom he once swore a mutual defense pact against all loss—here, calling him by name, letting him touch them again, after so long. The pulse of the waves battering the beach. The songs of shorebirds. The trees dropping food for free. The breeze running its hand across the damaged land. The air, the mercy, the sea.

How did he get here? How did any of them? Every organism, terrestrial or aquatic, every path a mystery. The journey in all its immense unfolding through this ocean world: What can it mean? The author of all this richness does nothing but find the next most likely word.

He sits in the open sala, clutching his packet and his friend. He tries to explain himself, but his words come out all wrong. He can't assemble what he wants to say. He can't argue or defend himself or beg for mercy. This clasp of forearms, this lee breeze, are the only saying. He doesn't need words now, to complete the project still in front of him. All he needs is to return. And there is so much to return to. The real seasteading.

By wild gestures and even wilder phonemes, he asks to be taken back on the ridge and pointed toward the coast. This isn't hard; coast in all directions. Nothing but horizon on every ray along the compass rose. It's a great discovery, one that eluded him until this moment. The people here do not live on a tiny, isolated island. They live on a road-crossed, crop-filled ocean bigger than all the continents combined.

With great effort, he strings together two syllables. "Ra-fi." He needs to say: *I was contemptible. Vile. I stole so much from you, so many times over. You were right to cut me dead.* But all he can manage is "Ra-fi!"

The voice that played forever against him, the one that gave him shit and offered him comfort, the so-familiar South Side drawl that shot philosophy late into the night across the gap between two dorm room beds in the middle of an endless cornfield, the voice he knows better than his own, says, "Later, dude. It'll keep."

Then Ina is there, in front of him, with her two children. Miracles, both. Keane sees how he terrifies them, simply by being strange and dying. But there's nothing he can do to change either of those performances now.

He finds her eyes, and they let his hold them. He tries to shape the hundred tiny muscles of his face into a message. *Thank you. Thank you for yesterday. Forgive me.*

She looks at him, devastated by the reach of his disease. Her eyes don't understand his. Whose eyes can fully understand another's? Not even his life's work will ever see to that.

In silence, he tries to say: *I can never undo the harm I caused you both. But I give you this, this gift that our dead friend here gave me.*

He hands her the packet. She opens the sheaf of paper and starts to read. A few words in, and she cries out in pain.

He pulls his eyes away from hers and looks out past the reef. Small craft dot the waters, some at work, some at anchor. He can see right through the surface, as if the water were as clear as air. What seemed flat and featureless teems at every depth. Dense clouds of bioluminescent zooplankton—the largest mass migration on Earth—rise in the water column as the light wanes. The giant grazers swoop in to sieve them. Phantasmagoric nekton with shapes as old as life traverse the features of a surreal landscape that knows no erosion. Yes, he sees the tens of millions of fragments of microplastic, too. But the endlessly reinventing kinds of entangled life before him will find their way past those toxins into the next new world.

Lifting his gaze from the deep, he searches the surface for someone: the famous champion of the oceans who died on a solo dive off the Maldives in mysterious circumstances on her seventieth birthday. She must be here, somewhere. She set his life in motion when he was ten, and everything that happened in his life, even this finale, came from the ocean that she opened up to him. He needs her now, to bring things to an end.

And there she is, as his story requires. She is on the deck of a small dive boat suspended above the reef. She is laughing with the Buddha-like pilot as he straps an air tank on the young girl. The three of them talk through the hand signals they will use for the dive. They plan the day's adventure as if there is no self-piloting yacht moored just past the ruined harbor, no threat of development, no imminent invasion. They work as if there is no work here on Earth except homegoing.

Just the sight of the ancient diver revives him. *You!* Somewhere in the eaten-away memory palaces inside his head he forms the thought: *You gave me my first love, and now you give me my last. You saved my young life and pointed it toward open waters. Here it is, the source, my first and last home. I know now what your cuttlefish is saying.*

———

THE FUNERAL CANOE IS MAGNIFICENT. Everyone on the island pitches in to gather plastics from the rocks and sand to finish it. Puoro and Patrice complete the two ceremonial figureheads of Māui. Didier Turi and Hone Amaru—the mayor and the old mayor's son—head up the pallbearers. Also there to help carry the *pahī* and its cargo down to the jetty are Manutahi Roa, Wen Lai, the minister, and the priest.

Ina and Evelyne take their place, side by side, under the canoe's twin prows. They help lift the craft into the air, struggling with the difference in their heights. The older woman stumbles with age, the younger with bewilderment. Ina whispers, confiding and terrified:

"He left me everything."

"I see."

"What in the world am I supposed to do with it?"

The sum is so large it can't be credited. Large enough to safeguard every living thing all the way to the horizon, as far as the eye can see.

A smile creeps over the ancient diver's face. Her life's work, too, now finds its own end. "*Tiens! J'ai une idée. . . .*"

———

THERE WILL BE ONE MORE REFERENDUM. After the new hospital and new school, after the pinnacles are filed down and filled with fertile soil, after the houses both innovative and traditional, after a few solar cars and wind-powered boats, after the enriched communal gardens and restored forests, with ninety-nine percent of the bequest still left over, the island will vote to become again what they have always been—a people of the ocean. For every island is a canoe, and all the Earth is an island, living by the grace of the immense and slowly turning blue creature. This time the vote will be unanimous, and it will be heard around the world.

———

THE QUEEN ASSEMBLES a gauntlet of dancers along the breakwater to make it a proper service. She sings one of the old farewell *himene taravas* to the accompaniment of the ukelele orchestra:

> '*Ia tīa'i mai te Atua iā 'oe!*
> '*Ia tīa'i mai te Atua iā 'oe!*

May God keep you!
May God answer you!

The pallbearers lash the marvelous multicolored canoe to the side of the dive boat. Wai Temauri sets course for a shallow, level, sandy plain of seagrass well beyond the edges of the lagoon, a spot where reef of any kind has never been able to get established. Puoro and Patrice follow in their trawler. Other, smaller boats join the swelling cortege. The Hermit Tamatoa watches from far away on top of the island's southern cliffs, envious.

All four Youngs are on the dive boat, in the place reserved for the next of kin. There is no eulogy, but Rafi Young reads a farewell poem—one that he and his friend once heard the Jesuits explicate, back in Honors World Literature in an elite Catholic high school in the middle of a divided city. He reads from an 1884 edition of the Douay Bible, which he long ago stole from a library that wasn't caring for it properly and carried with him to this island:

The Lord possessed me in the beginning of his ways, before he made any thing from the beginning.

I was set up from eternity, and of old before the earth was made.

The depths were not as yet, and I was already conceived. Neither had the fountains of waters as yet sprung out. . . .

When he prepared the heavens, I was present. When with a certain law and compass he enclosed the depths,

When he established the sky above, and poised the fountains of waters,

When he compassed the sea with its bounds, and set a law to the waters that they should not pass their limits, when he balanced the foundations of the earth,

I was with him forming all things, and was delighted every day, playing before him at all times;

Playing in the world. . . .

and my delights were to be with the children of men.

When he finishes, Rafi Young puts a fistful of small black and white stones into the *pahī* and says, "You'll want these, brother."

Many in the entourage free dive to watch the scuttled coffin sink to the grassy bottom. Through a mask, treading water, Evelyne Beaulieu sees it touch down. Next to her, a wide-eyed Kini Temauri. The girl will grow up to lead a team that will train the children of men to speak the languages of ocean creatures and translate them into words humans can understand. What the animals say will bring hundreds of millions of people back home to Planet Ocean.

The girl will return to this spot again when she is very old, almost as old as the ghost now next to her. Within the world's largest safeguarded and all-protecting marine park that will by then spread throughout the Tuamotus, she will seek out the resting place of the famous corpse that funded her discoveries. She will look for the multicolored funeral *pahī* with its twin figureheads of Māui, but she'll find only corals and anemones, sponges and reef fish in even wilder colors, overgrowing their foundation.

Every canoe may be an island, but the whole island world is itself a canoe.

———

THE SCATTERED FREE DIVERS enjoy the water a while longer before returning to their boats. Then the flotilla turns back to the island. Wai Temauri leads the way, reading the surface and scouting the submarine hazards as easily as if he had a map. Afa points out a black-tipped reef shark and Kinipela proudly announces its Latin name. Three spinner dolphins rise to the surface in formation to taunt the boats for a bit before speeding off.

Something huge breaks the waves a hundred yards off starboard. It falls back into the ocean with a colossal splash. Wai cuts the motors, and the rest of the flotilla follows. All eyes train on the spot, waiting on the ocean's pleasure. Seconds later, another creature crashes through the surface. A sleek, flat, alien spacecraft, twelve feet from wingtip to wingtip, flies up into the air, its massive countershaded body clearing the water. Black on top, white on the bottom. Its flight lasts two thrilling seconds before it slams back into the sea in a thunderous slap.

Several more flying devils climb up and crash back into the waves. Their cephalic fins flap in the air and their gill slits taste the sky. Evelyne picks out Kaute, Tomo, and Mona, then the new boy with all his lacerations—Lazarus. More rays join in the aerial ballet, some upside down, exuberant in flight and by all signs savoring the loudest possible landing that their ton of flesh can make. The sea roils with the froth of their waves.

Every stunt elicits gasps. The audience applauds the air show like astonished children. Only the youngest of them, Hariti, is traumatized. She needs an explanation for all this pointless churn. It doesn't help that both her parents are trying to hide their faces from one another and from every other living thing.

The girl grabs her father's waist and moans. "What's happening, Papa? What are they doing?"

Rafi turns his salt-red eyes to the marine biologist, who looks at her smiling pilot, who consults with the two fishermen in the next boat over. Another great ray flaps into the air and cannonballs the water. The sober experts break out laughing. There are careful, scientific explanations, all untestable: group cohesion and signaling, mate selection, the shedding of parasites, the announcement of a banquet of plankton. But the look the humans share says: *What does it look like? Call it what it is. Every dance is a game, and every game its own best explanation. Everything alive, even we newcomers. . . . What are all creatures—even me—doing at all times but playing in the world, playing before their tinkering Lord?*

ACKNOWLEDGMENTS

Like every story, profunda's re-creation draws on countless sources. A few need special mention. Nicholas Hoare's doctoral thesis, *Re-Mining Makatea: People, Politics, and Phosphate Rock*, provided invaluable background and insights into that singular island. Guy Stevens and Thomas P. Peschak's *Manta: Secret Life of Devil Rays* astonished me. Evelyne Beaulieu's biography draws on the life of Dr. Sylvia Earle, especially as recounted in *Sea Change: A Message of the Oceans*. Helen Czerski's *The Blue Machine: How the Ocean Works* got me thinking larger. And the symphonic cuttlefish comes from Peter Godfrey-Smith's extraordinary *Other Minds: The Octopus, the Sea, and the Deep Origins of Consciousness*. My profound thanks to these authors and to the myriad others whose work and play are recombined in this book's genes.